JUL 04 1995
P9-DUP-500

TAKING ADVANTAGE

He had the advantage of her, for the fall she had suffered had wiped all memory of the past away. All Elizabeth knew was what Christopher told her. They were husband and wife. They loved each other. She had to prove that love. She could not yield to the panic she felt in his arms.

"I want you, Christopher," she said. "I need you."

Christopher raised himself on his elbows and looked into her eyes, his own filled with such yearning that she caught her lower lip between her teeth. And then she closed her eyes as he caressed her.

All doubts fled. All foolish doubts. This was the way it was, the way it should be. . . .

"Yes," she whispered to him without opening her eyes. "Yes, Christopher. . . ."

From Onyx—
Catherine Coulter's Captivating Historical Romances

Midsummer Magic

Their marriage was arranged, the surprise was their passion . . . When a Scottish beauty disguises herself as a homely country miss to escape marriage to a rakish earl, her clever plan goes astray. Chosen as his bride for that very reason, Frances is wedded, bedded, and soon deserted. But when she sheds her dowdy facade to become London's most ravishing leading lady, she arouses her wayward husband's ire—not to mention his desire. . . .

Calypso Magic

In the heat of the tropics, she surrendered to forbidden desire . . . Diana knew the rakish and hot-tempered Lyonel was a rogue, and she vowed that during her visit to London she would not be one of his playthings. But when she longs for her West Indies home, only Lyonel is there to escort her on the perilous journey home. And as they braved the raging fires of war-torn seas, passion's flames burned still more brightly within them, until Diana could no longer resist. . . .

Buy them at your local bookstore or use this convenient coupon for ordering.

NEW AMERICAN LIBRARY
P.O. Box 999 – Dept. #17109
Bergenfield, New Jersey 07621

Please send me ________ copies of MIDSUMMER MAGIC 0-451-40204-9 at $4.95 ($5.95 in Canada) and ________ copies of CALYPSO MAGIC 0-451-40087-9 at $4.95 ($5.95 in Canada) plus $1.00 postage and handling per order. I enclose ☐ check ☐ money order (no C.O.D.'s. or cash).

Name____

Address______________________________________

City ________________ State ____________ Zip Code ____________

Allow a minimum of 4-6 weeks for delivery.
This offer, prices and numbers are subject to change without notice.

DECEIVED

by

Mary Balogh

AN ONYX BOOK

ONYX
Published by the Penguin Group
Penguin Books USA Inc., 375 Hudson Street,
New York, New York 10014, U.S.A.
Penguin Books Ltd, 27 Wrights Lane,
London W8 5TZ, England
Penguin Books Australia Ltd, Ringwood,
Victoria, Australia
Penguin Books Canada Ltd, 10 Alcorn Avenue,
Toronto, Ontario, Canada M4V 3B2
Penguin Books (N.Z.) Ltd, 182–190 Wairau Road,
Auckland 10, New Zealand

Penguin Books Ltd, Registered Offices:
Harmondsworth, Middlesex, England

First published by Onyx, an imprint of New American Library,
a division of Penguin Books USA Inc.

First Printing, April, 1993
10 9 8 7 6 5 4 3 2 1

Copyright © Mary Balogh, 1993
All rights reserved

REGISTERED TRADEMARK—MARCA REGISTRADA

Printed in the United States of America

Without limiting the rights under copyright reserved above, no part of this publication may be reproduced, stored in or introduced into a retrieval system, or transmitted, in any form, or by any means (electronic, mechanical, photocopying, recording, or otherwise), without the prior written permission of both the copyright owner and the above publisher of this book.

BOOKS ARE AVAILABLE AT QUANTITY DISCOUNTS WHEN USED TO PROMOTE PRODUCTS OR SERVICES. FOR INFORMATION PLEASE WRITE TO PREMIUM MARKETING DIVISION, PENGUIN BOOKS USA INC., 375 HUDSON STREET, NEW YORK, NEW YORK 10014.

If you purchased this book without a cover you should be aware that this book is stolen property. It was reported as "unsold and destroyed" to the publisher and neither the author nor the publisher has received any payment for this "stripped book."

1

LONDON looked strange from the deck of the ship that was making its slow passage up the River Thames. Strange because it looked no different from the way it had always looked. One somehow expected that after almost seven years it would have changed, though the traveler who stood at the ship's rail, watching the banks of the river and the wharves and warehouses slide past and the city itself loom ahead, realized that the thought was somewhat foolish. Seven years, which had seemed more like seven decades to him, were a mere moment in time for a city like London.

''Sacré coeur!'' his companion said at his side, profound awe in his voice. ''It is a city to end cities, m'sieur.''

''Yes.'' The traveler squinted his eyes and gazed ahead to the dome of St. Paul's Cathedral. ''New York and Montreal really have nothing to compare with it, do they?''

Antoine Bouchard had grown up believing that Montreal must be the hub of the world. He had reacted to New York much as he was reacting now to London. He ought not to have been standing on deck as he was, his thick-set arms resting on the rail, his short sturdy legs splayed on the deck to keep his balance, though such a stance was no longer necessary now that they were in the smooth waters of the River Thames. Since he was a servant, he ought to have been below packing his master's trunks and preparing to leave the ship.

But then Antoine was not quite like any other servant. Indeed, he did not even call himself that. He had saved his present companion's life five years before when the latter had been a clerk with the Northwest Company of Canada trading furs far inland on the American continent and he had been a lowly voyageur or laborer with the company. He had sunk a knife into the belly of the native who had been about to do the same for the clerk. And since then he had attached himself to the man he had saved even when the latter left first the interior and then Montreal for New York. And now he was coming to England too as servant, valet, companion—it was impossible to define in quite what capacity he came.

"Sometime perhaps you will have a chance to explore the city, Antoine," the traveler said. "It is a marvel not to be missed. But not this time. Now we will merely pass through. We will stay here for one night and then purchase horses and a carriage and be on our way."

"To Pen'allow," Antoine said, pronouncing the word with such a heavy French accent that it sounded quite unfamiliar.

"Yes," his companion said. "To Penhallow. To Devonshire." To the reason for his return. He had sworn when he left England that he would never set foot on its shores again. He had gone below as soon as he had boarded the ship on the Thames, and he had not come on deck again until there was nothing to be seen all around but ocean.

"Good-bye, England," he had whispered to the eastern horizon. He had felt a little theatrical, though there had been no one close by to overhear him. But the pain of emptiness inside him had made the gesture necessary. "Good-bye . . ." But he had not completed her name. He had closed his eyes in a vain attempt to stem the flow of scalding tears. "I'll never come back." He had merely mouthed the words.

His lip curled now into a smile half of contempt and half of sympathy for the foolish, impressionable, cowardly boy he had been. And "boy" was an appropriate word even though he had been twenty-four years old at the time. There had been trouble, trouble that he could not have foreseen and that he had found himself quite unable to handle. Everything in his life had been spoiled and he had been able to see no way to unspoil it. He had spoken the truth but no one had believed him. And he had seen no way of proving that he did not lie.

And so he had fled. Turned tail and run. Left the field

to those who had proceeded to destroy even what little of his life he had left behind.

Well, he thought, he had not done badly for himself. Fate, in the form of the first ship to be sailing out of the Thames when he had needed one, had taken him to Montreal in Canada, where he had taken a gentleman's job with the prosperous fur trading company that had its headquarters there. Three years in the rugged interior had toughened him physically and given him back purpose in life. When he had almost lost his life, he had realized that it was after all precious to him. And his four years in New York, working his way up to partnership in another fur trading company, had toughened him mentally and given him a sense of his own worth.

The shy, uncertain, bewildered boy who had fled London almost seven years before no longer existed. His personality perhaps remained in the man who had taken his place. There was not much one could do to overcome a natural reticence of manner, an inability to make easy conversation with others or to speak from the heart to any but the closest of friends. And it was hard to teach oneself charm or even the art of smiling frequently when one was already past boyhood and had never learned either. Outwardly perhaps he had not changed. But inwardly . . . Oh, yes, he had changed. If all that had happened seven years ago were to happen now, he would not run. Not one inch. He would even take one step forward and he would force the truth on all those who had not believed him—on the whole world if necessary.

His jaw hardened. And now that he was back, he would find out the truth too. He would unravel the whole sordid mess even though the trail was cold by almost seven years. And then he would see her and throw the truth in her teeth. He would watch her as she realized all that she had thrown away through lack of trust and weakness of character. Yes, he would watch her. Her face had always been more expressive than that of anyone else he had ever known.

But not yet. First he wanted to go to Penhallow, his now since the death of his father as well as the fortune that came with it—at a time when he had been making his own fortune in America. Strange, he reflected, that he had never particularly thought that one day this would force him back to England. He wondered if all sons imagined that their fathers would live forever. His own had not even lived beyond the age of sixty.

Antoine leaned over the rail, absorbed with watching the ship come to anchor. His employer still stared off toward the city though he was not really seeing it. His hands rested lightly on the rail, not gripping it. They were long-fingered, beautiful hands, though the nails were now cut short and the palms were callused from hard work. Perhaps the strength of the hands added to the beauty they had always had.

He was a tall man, several inches taller than his small, sturdy servant, and slender. Though there was a breadth of shoulder now and a solidity of arm and thigh muscles that proclaimed him splendidly fit and strong. His lips were compressed into a thin line in his rather narrow face with its strong aquiline nose and high cheekbones. He had won the nickname Hawk in the early years of his fur trading, when he had been considerably thinner. And perhaps it was a suitable name. There was no weakness in his face, no sign at all of softness. Only strength and determination and perhaps even harshness. It was a weather-bronzed face beneath thick dark hair, which would doubtless be far too long for London fashions. The eyes that stared unseeingly at the dome and towers and roofs of London were a startling blue.

" 'Ow does one know where to go, m'sieur?" Antoine made a sweeping gesture toward the city with one arm. His voice sounded almost nervous.

"We take a hackney coach," his companion said, returning his attention to his surroundings. "To the Pulteney Hotel in Piccadilly. The best hotel in London. And then tomorrow—Devonshire."

"Mais oui," Antoine said. "Only the best for the Earl of Trevelyan. And only the best for 'is man." He chuckled.

"I think it would be better to postpone being the earl until after we have left London tomorrow," his companion said. "I don't want it to be generally known yet, Antoine, that I am back. Tonight I will be simply Mr. Christopher . . ."

"Bouchard?" Antoine suggested.

"Christopher Bouchard," the Earl of Trevelyan said, nodding in agreement.

Antoine grinned and went below to deal with the half-packed trunks strewn untidily about his master's cabin.

"They 'eard we were coming," Antoine said. "And so the celebrations, m'sieur. Non?" He looked at his employer with a grin, very white in his weathered face.

"Heaven forbid!" Christopher said. But he returned the grin. The mood in the London streets did seem rather more festive than he remembered its being on a normal day. And there did seem to be an unusual number of flags flying from almost every building, including the Pulteney.

"There is something unusual happening in London?" he asked the receptionist at the hotel after he had taken a suite of rooms for the night for himself and his servant.

The receptionist looked at him with blank incredulity. "You do not know, Mr. Bouchard?" he said. "You are French? An émigré perhaps? An exile?"

"French Canadian actually," Christopher said. "My man and I have arrived just today from New York."

The receptionist nodded as if the strange mystery of the newly arrived guest's ignorance was explained. "France has been invaded," he explained, "and Paris taken by the Allies. Wellington has come in from Spain in the south. Bonaparte has abdicated. The wars are over at long last, sir. The victory is ours. The news was brought from Paris yesterday."

The wars. They had affected both America and Canada, of course. But he had been almost unaware of them. He had forgotten. It was April 1814, and the wars were over. He had unconsciously chosen a good time to come home.

"The celebrations went on all last night," the receptionist said, "and will continue tonight, I do not doubt. Enjoy them, Mr. Bouchard. You have arrived in England at the perfect time."

And yet he had no wish to go outside the doors of the hotel to participate in any merrymaking, though the thought was attractive. No one knew how to make merry quite like the English. And yet he would not go out. He had found himself looking through the windows of the hackney on the journey from the river to the Pulteney, not at the buildings, but at the people. He had looked in something almost like dread for familiar faces. It was very unlikely that he would see any. He had lived most of his young life at Penhallow and only a year of it in London. And yet he found himself even now fearing that perhaps in the hotel he would meet someone he had known.

He was not ready for that. Not yet. It was not that he was afraid. He was certainly not. Just unready. The time would come. In the summer maybe. Or in the autumn. But not now.

He would have eaten dinner in his private suite, but he was no coward any longer. Unready as he was, he would not cower in his rooms out of fear of being seen and recognized. And so, though he would not go out to witness the early victory celebrations, he did go downstairs to the dining room. And he nodded amicably to the gentleman who occupied the table next to his, exchanged comments on the weather with him, and made no objection when the gentleman invited himself to take dinner at his table.

"Seth Wickenham," the gentleman said, extending a large hand before seating himself at Christopher's table. "Most people are out enjoying all the illuminations and basking in the glory of the victory. We might as well at least share a table in an empty dining room."

Christopher agreed and returned the handshake. And so he told of some of his adventures during the past seven years and in return learned some of the details of the allied victory and the decisive part the British had played in it, opening the back door into the Continent by taking first Portugal and then Spain from the French before penetrating into France itself. The new Duke of Wellington, it seemed, was the hero of the hour.

"A good time for a wedding too," Mr. Wickenham said when all the more important topics of conversation appeared to have been exhausted.

Christopher looked inquiringly at his companion for an explanation of this apparent non sequitur.

"Grand *ton* wedding tomorrow at St. George's," Mr. Wickenham said. "Hundreds of guests, so I have heard. Everyone who is anyone will be there. And half of the rest of Londoners will hang about in the square to gawk. The victory celebrations will just whet their appetites for more pomp."

"Yes, probably," Christopher agreed. "The bride and groom are of some importance?"

"Well, now"—Mr. Wickenham looked up, caught the eye of a waiter, and nodded to him to bring more wine—"Lord Poole is the groom. Baron, you know. He is one of the leading members of the Whig party, which puts him on the wrong side, so to speak, especially now that victory will boost the popularity of the Tories. But we need both sides in a free country like ours, don't we, sir? Or so I always say."

Christopher remembered Lord Poole as a rather dry old stick. Though he was not so old, either. He could be no more than forty now. His bride, whoever she was, must be marrying him for his title and fortune, poor woman.

"He is marrying Chicheley's daughter," Mr. Wickenham added.

"Who?" The air felt cold suddenly. Sounds seemed to come from far away. Christopher's table companion seemed to be at the end of a long tunnel.

"Chicheley," Mr. Wickenham said a little more distinctly. "The Duke of. Lady Elizabeth Ward."

Ward. Lady Elizabeth Ward. Christopher spread a hand over the top of his empty wineglass and shook his head. "No more, thank you," he said. "I must return to my room and have an early night if you will excuse me. It is not so easy to find one's land legs after weeks at sea."

Mr. Wickenham chuckled when Christopher stumbled as he got to his feet, though the stumble was neither feigned nor due to his inability to find his land legs.

"Good night," Christopher said abruptly. "Thank you for the company and conversation, sir."

"Mr. Wickenham returned the greeting and refilled his wineglass.

Christ! Oh, God. Christopher realized only when he was out on the street an indeterminate number of minutes later that he was wearing a cloak and a hat and carrying a cane. He could not remember returning to his room, but he must have done so. He did not know where he was going. He watched unseeingly as fireworks illuminated the sky from the direction of Hyde Park.

Elizabeth. He drew in a deep breath of the cool, rather smoky evening air and released it very slowly.

Elizabeth. She was nothing to him now. Not any longer. Nothing at all. Let her marry whom she chose. Even Poole. Especially Poole. She deserved him. By God, she deserved him. His knuckles tightened on the knob of his cane. He could not have devised a better fate for her if he had been given the choosing of it. Someone dull and respectable. Someone without humor.

Elizabeth. Christ!

He walked on, looking about him, trying to identify his surroundings. There was a strange novelty about knowing himself to be back on English soil. He tried to think about the victory that was so preoccupying the minds of his fellow countrymen. But how could he think of such trivialities?

Elizabeth, he thought, clamping his teeth together. And he felt sudden fury. And pain. And panic. Tomorrow morning. At St. George's, Hanover Square. Poole. She was going to marry Poole. Tomorrow.

Almost of their own volition his feet carried him back in the direction of the Pulteney. He walked faster as he drew close. He had had no idea that he had wandered so far. He was almost running by the time he arrived back at the hotel.

2

IT was her wedding day.

Lady Elizabeth Ward was standing alone in her dressing room. She had dismissed her maid, and everyone else but her father and her stepbrother had left for the church already. It was her wedding day. She stood before the full-length pier glass and gazed at her image. It did not feel like a wedding day. She did not look like a bride. Not really.

But then brides were supposed to be seventeen or eighteen years of age, not five and twenty, and they were supposed to be dressed in white with orange blossoms in their hair and adorning their dresses according to the new French fashion and bouquets of flowers in their hands. And they were supposed to be flushed and bright-eyed and nervous.

She was dressed in pale blue and had only a few flowers—not orange blossoms—in her hair, none in her hands. She hoped that Manley would not mind that she was not in white. But he knew that she was no girl, and white somehow seemed inappropriate. A large wedding at St. George's seemed inappropriate too. But both Manley and her father had been insistent about that, Manley because of his own political ambitions, and Papa because he wanted her to show the world quite publicly that the past was just that. The past.

And yes, he was right, Elizabeth thought, turning from the glass and wishing that she had decided to wear a bonnet rather than the girlish flowers. She had paid her dues to the past. Seven years of incarceration in the country in an exile that had been largely self-imposed. For the first few of those years she had scarcely wanted to live but had gone through the motions for the sake of others. For the rest of the years she had put herself back together again, taken charge of her own life, which she had never done even as a girl, made herself mistress of Richmond, her father's principal estate.

But she had grown restless. Life had more to offer than the part of it she was living, she had come to believe. She needed that life. All of it. She needed a man again. Marriage. But not as an emotional prop. All her life she had used men as her props—her father, her brother John, her stepbrother Martin . . . She brought the list to an abrupt stop. No, she no longer needed a man to help her to live. She needed a man with whom to share her life.

And so she had come back to London for the winter, much against the advice of Martin, who had lived in the country with her all those years, gently nursing her back to emotional health, giving her all the support and companionship she had needed. Dear Martin. She had been very selfish to keep him from his own life for so long. And yet he had never complained and had even tried to persuade her to change her mind when she had decided to return to town.

She had settled on Manley Hill, Lord Poole. He was almost twenty years her senior and was distinguished looking if not handsome. But far more important than either his age or his looks, he was a dedicated and ambitious politician—a Whig rather than a Tory, it was true, but then she could always respect sincerely held beliefs even when they differed from her own. As his wife she could be useful. She could work at his side to further his ambitions. She could lead a busy and a useful life.

She had chosen with her head and not her heart. She was no longer a young girl to believe that following the heart could bring eternal happiness. Happiness was fleeting at best. Contentment, a sense of purpose, a life of useful industry—they were far better goals for which to reach.

She may not feel like a bride, Elizabeth thought, looking back to the pier glass, and she may not look like one, but being a bride was not important. Being a wife was everything. She was going to make Manley a good wife.

And yet in spite of everything she felt a wave of nervousness, almost of panic. Almost as if she were about to burn all her bridges behind her. Almost as if she still hoped as she had hoped during those first empty years . . .

No, there was nothing to be hoped for. It was largely to put to rest the hopeless dream that she had come to London for the winter. It was finally to shatter the dream that she had deliberately set out to find herself a husband.

Well, she had found him. And she was satisfied. She lifted her chin and smiled determinedly at her image. And then she was looking beyond her own reflection to the opening door of her dressing room and the sight of her stepbrother standing in the doorway, dressed in all his wedding finery. Her smile held.

"Oh, you do look splendid, Martin," she said. "You look as if you should be the groom, not merely the bride's brother."

He laughed and propped one shoulder against the door frame as his arms crossed over his chest. "It is you who are supposed to be listening to compliments, Lizzie," he said. "You look lovely, as I fully expected. Nervous?"

"No, of course not," she said briskly. But she met his eyes and laughed. "Yes, of course I am. Christina was in tears when I sent her off to the church."

"Christina will get used to the idea," he said firmly. "You are quite sure it is only nervousness you feel, Lizzie, and not reluctance? It is not too late, you know. If you have changed your mind, I shall go and tell Poole so. We can go back to Kingston, you and I, and thumb our noses at any scandal that may ensue. What do you say?"

Elizabeth gave a mock shriek. "Oh, not now, Martin, please," she said. "Not when I am feeling at my most vulnerable. But you would do it too, would you not? Walk into St. George's with such an announcement, I mean. I know you have been troubled by my choice. I know you think I should wait for love and all that nonsense." She walked toward him and stretched out her hands to him. "But I know what I am doing. I am marrying into just the life that will give me a sense of purpose. I have no real doubts. I am just nervous. St. George's, Martin, and half the *ton* waiting for me there!"

Martin took her cold hands in warm ones and squeezed them. "Well," he said, "if you are sure, Lizzie. You know that all I want for you is happiness. I'll always be here for you, married or single. You know that, don't you?"

She leaned forward and kissed his cheek. "Yes, I know it," she said. "You have been like a real brother to me, Martin."

"Like a twin?" he said, reminding her of the old joke they had often shared. They looked rather alike, being of similar height and both having honey blond hair and gray eyes. They had been almost inseparable from the age of two, when the Duke of Chicheley had married Martin's mother, both of them recently widowed. Martin was three months older than Elizabeth.

"It is time you had a life of your own," she said. "You spent too many years at Kingston, Martin, just because I needed you. I will always remember that and always love you for it. But it is time for you to look about you for a wife."

His eyes smiled into hers. Martin's eyes always smiled, Elizabeth thought. When he was older he was going to have permanent laugh lines at their corners. He was also the most amiable and the least selfish person she had known. And it was not just partiality because he was her dearest friend and almost her brother. Everyone liked Martin.

"I am in no hurry to marry," he said.

"Of course." She clucked her tongue and laughed at him. "Twenty-five is shockingly old for a woman but mere boyhood for a man. So much for justice in this world."

"You will never be shockingly old, Lizzie," he said. "Especially not in my eyes."

"I wish John were here," Elizabeth said, suddenly remembering that the day would not be quite complete because her elder brother, a lieutenant-colonel with Wellington's cavalry, had not yet returned from Spain. "But I should not complain, should I? The best wedding gift I could possibly have received was the news of the end of the wars. Perhaps he will be home soon."

"We will hope so," Martin said. "We had better go downstairs, Lizzie. It does not do for a bride to be more than fashionably late for her own wedding, you know."

"And Papa will be getting impatient," she said. She drew a deep breath. "So this is it. Wish me well, Martin."

"It will be the happiest day of your life, Lizzie," he

said, kissing her on both cheeks before tucking her arm through his.

The happiest day of her life? She wished he had not said that. She was not marrying for happiness. And she had the uncomfortable feeling that she had heard those words before—*the happiest day of your life*. She felt cold suddenly and shivered as they descended the stairs. She did not want to think of the past. She was making a new beginning today. A decisive new start. She only wished she could leave her memories behind so that all could be new. But that, of course, was impossible.

Her father was standing at the foot of the stairs, leaning heavily on his cane and looking up at her with brooding affection. Several of the servants, who had no business being in the hall, were nevertheless there, also looking up at her, their faces beaming goodwill. A couple of the housemaids and one footman even broke into applause at her appearance. They had come to see her on her way to her wedding.

It was her wedding day, Elizabeth thought again. She smiled warmly.

A sizable crowd of the curious had gathered in Hanover Square to witness one of the free wonders that the capital sometimes offered in the springtime—a *ton* wedding. This particular wedding had perhaps even more than the usual attraction, it being one of the first of the year and the weather being sunny and warm and the mood of festivity strong on the whole city. Besides, the groom was a baron and the bride the daughter of a duke. And she had been involved in a very public scandal not so many years back. A few came to gaze at her for no other reason than that.

Some had been standing on the square in the sun and the breeze for an hour and more before the bride arrived. There had been ample entertainment to hold their attention as a seemingly endless stream of grand and fashionable carriages appeared, stopped outside the church, and deposited their gorgeously clad occupants, while the lookers-on craned their necks to discover their identities.

There was a buzz of heightened interest when the groom arrived with two other gentlemen and the female spectators could assure one another that yes, he was handsome and that yes, he looked nervous, poor soul. The men were perhaps more occupied with envying him the approaching wedding night—though they had not yet seen the bride.

There was a lull then of perhaps ten minutes after all the guests and the groom had arrived and before the bride put in her appearance. But no one seemed impatient to leave. This was the culmination of the morning's entertainment, this suspense preceding the first glimpse of the bride. Some would drift away after she had arrived rather than wait for the whole service within the church to be finished before the bells pealed out and the bride and groom could at last be seen together. But nobody drifted yet.

If only they had known it, the spectators were to be provided with far better entertainment than they had ever known on like occasions before and better than they were likely to know ever again. But they did not know it yet and waited with eager anticipation, craning their necks to stare off along the road by which the carriage would approach as if their very stares would bring it into sight.

And finally it came, an elegant dark blue carriage with the arms of the Duke of Chicheley emblazoned on the side panels, the wigged and stiff postilions in the duke's blue and gold livery, the white horses with plaited manes and golden plumes. The crowd buzzed and leaned forward. Some people even cheered.

A young man leapt out of the carriage first after the doors had been opened and reached up to help someone else out. He was the bride's brother, someone said. Stepbrother, someone else corrected, and soon all were agreed that the young man was indeed the bride's stepbrother, Mr. Martin Honywood, the bride's brother, Viscount Aston, being one of the heroes with Wellington in France. Mr. Honywood was looking quite splendid, dressed all in blue and silver and sparkling white. He was helping his stepfather out of the carriage. The old duke suffered from gout, the knowledgeable explained to those less so.

And then, the old duke safely on the pavement, one hand clutching his cane, the other the shoulder of one of the postilions, Mr. Honywood turned back to the carriage and extended his hand again. A buzz and an expectant hush swept over the crowd. The bride was being helped down all in a rustling cloud of pale blue silk.

"Ah!" several of the women said on a collective sigh of ecstasy. She was as pretty as a princess, her form slender and shapely beneath the silk, her flower-threaded hair the color of pale honey.

And yet almost at the same moment as she set one slippered foot on the pavement, all heads suddenly jerked away from their contemplation of her beauty. There was the discordant sound of galloping hooves, the totally unexpected sight of a dark horse carrying a dark-cloaked, dark-hatted rider, and the sudden shocking realization that the rider was masked, almost all of his face except his eyes and his mouth covered in black to match the rest of him. There were those who swore afterward that his eyes were red and flashing fire. There were those who swore that his teeth were pointed fangs. But for the moment everyone merely gawked. There was almost no sound.

And then the masked horseman galloped into the square and up to the church, taking his horse between it and the duke's carriage, and he leaned down from his saddle, gathered up the astonished bride with one arm, twisted her with incredible strength so that she sat sideways in front of him, and turned to gallop off back the way he had come.

It was only when the bride finally screamed that the spell was broken and pandemonium broke loose. But pandemonium came rather too late. The bride had gone. The guests and the groom waited in vain inside St. George's for the wedding service to begin.

3

It all happened so quickly and so totally unexpectedly that for a few moments Elizabeth did not comprehend what was happening at all. One moment she had her hand in Martin's and was stepping down onto the pavement outside the church, looking into his eyes for reassurance to counter the butterflies that were dancing in her stomach, and the next she was . . . Well, she did not at all know what she was doing next until she realized that she was on horseback, an arm tight about her waist, and that the horse she was sharing with the owner of that arm was galloping at dangerous speed away from the church and out of Hanover Square.

And then she turned her head and saw that her captor's face was almost completely covered with a black mask and that his lips were thin below it and his eyes glittering through it. It was then that she understood that she was being abducted. It was then that she screamed and flailed her arms at the man's face and chest.

"Be still, you fool," he commanded. "Would you commit suicide?"

But panic and terror had her in their clutches. She had no thought to spare for the greater danger that dislodging him or breaking free of his hold would bring. She fought in wild desperation for her freedom. This could not happen in the daylit streets of London, the part of her mind that was still rational told her. A masked man in the middle of London committing the crime of kidnapping? And getting away with it? Impossible!

She did not know how far from the square he galloped. Probably not far at all. She was not rational enough to note streets or landmarks. But suddenly there was a carriage, a plain carriage, as dark as the horse and rider, and a small fierce-looking man was holding the door open. She was being lowered from the horse's back and thrust inside. And the door was being locked from the outside. It was also shuttered on the outside. It began to move almost immediately.

The dimness of the interior and its emptiness were more frightening for the moment than riding with the masked stranger had been. Here no one could see her to know that she needed rescuing. Here the darkness and the walls were closing in on her so that she could not breathe. She turned and pounded her fists against the door through which she had been shoved. And then she pounded them against the front panel, calling to the coachman to stop.

She did not scream. She found it possible do so only when she was not thinking about it, as she had done when she had first realized her plight. She could not scream now though it seemed to be the only way to attract the attention of those people who must be walking or riding on whichever street they were bowling along.

But she could not scream. She sat down on the seat facing the horses and forced panic down with several deep and slow breaths. They were kidnapping her. Why? For money, of course. They would take her somewhere safe, probably outside the city limits, where her screams would be unlikely to attract attention, and they would apply to Papa for ransom. Or perhaps to Manley, though he was not yet her husband. Her stomach lurched at the thought. She should be beside him at the altar now at this very moment. She forced her mind to calmness again. It would all take a few hours. Overnight at the longest. By tomorrow she would be free.

It was amazing really, she thought, clasping her hands very tightly in her lap, forcing her breathing to remain slow and even, that this did not happen more often. *Ton* weddings were well publicized affairs, and the bride and groom were invariably of wealthy families. Any enterprising fortune hunter might make that fortune from kidnapping. She supposed that all the families who would arrange weddings at St. George's for the rest of the Season would be a great deal more careful. But she had been first and it had happened to her.

Thank goodness, she thought, and her hands began to tremble despite the strong hold she kept on them, and her breathing became erratic again—thank heaven that Christina had been sent on to the church early. Thank heaven she had been safe inside. If she was safe. Perhaps they had taken Christina first, before her. But no, she thought, closing her eyes and concentrating on not vomiting. No. They would not take two. Besides, if they had already taken Christina, there would have been a commotion outside the church when she arrived.

No, it was just her. They had taken only her, and Christina was safe. Elizabeth repeated the fact over and over in her head to calm herself. She must remain calm. She had already screamed and struggled and pounded against the door and the panel of the carriage. She would not give them the satisfaction of witnessing any other displays of panic or fear. She would be icily calm when next they opened the door.

But her nerves were put to severe testing over the next several hours. It was true they were taking her outside the city. She realized that before the first hour had passed. But how far? *How far?* Surely no more than a few miles if her father was to be communicated with that day and if an exchange of money and her person were to be made within the day. What would happen about the wedding? she wondered. Would the church and the vicar be available again the next day? Would all the guests come again? Would the wedding breakfast be irrevocably ruined?

How far were they taking her? She realized that in her present situation every minute must understandably feel like an hour, but even so those minutes or hours became interminable. Surely they must have traveled a sizable distance from London. She began to feel chilly. And hungry, though the thought of food made her feel bilious. And physically uncomfortable. She tried to keep her mind off her discomfort, but on what else could she latch it?

And then finally the carriage slowed and stopped. She clasped her hands in her lap and stared straight ahead, waiting for the door to open, not sure if her relief was stronger than her fear. But she would not show fear. She would die rather than do so.

She braced herself for a sight of that towering dark figure with his frightening mask. But it was the tough little coachman who opened the door finally. She turned her head to look at him disdainfully. But he did not signal her to descend as she expected him to do.

"We are at an inn, ma'mselle," he said in a French accent that was too thick to be feigned. "I shall bring you food and tea, but you must not scream, s'il vous plâit, or otherwise try to attract attention." He shrugged apologetically. "My master would not like it, ma'mselle, and 'e 'as a gun."

"I need to stretch my legs before I eat," she said icily.

"Ma'mselle." Again that apologetic shrug.

"I have needs more important than hunger," she hissed at him.

She saw comprehension dawning in his eyes and willed herself not to flush. He closed the door, presumably so that he might consult his master on whether she might be allowed to relieve that need. Elizabeth could feel fury building inside. How dare they subject her to this humiliation! And why were they stopping at an inn? How far were they taking her?

"Where are we going?" she demanded when the door opened again.

The little coachman shrugged. "You will be permitted to enter the inn, ma'mselle," he said. "I shall accompany you inside. But you will please remember the gun and that I 'ave a ruthless master. If you try to beg for 'elp, ma'mselle, someone else may get 'urt as well as you."

"Help me down." She stretched an imperious hand from the carriage. She had untwined the flowers from her hair some time before. Even so she felt quite inappropriately dressed for a country inn. She did not know the inn, she saw in a quick glance around when she was standing on the cobbles of the inn yard, or the road. She could not guess where they were. And there was no sign of the masked man or his gun, though his horse was being brushed down. Her stomach churned at the sight.

It was very tempting over the next five minutes or so to scream or to somehow try to attract attention to her plight. She might write a note, she thought when she was alone, and slip it to the innkeeper or a barmaid as she left. But she had neither paper nor pen and ink. Besides, the chances were strong that none of them could read. It seemed somehow bizarre to be inside a place as public as an English inn and be unable to draw anyone's attention to the fact that she was a captive, being taken somewhere against her will at gunpoint.

Bizarre but true.

The coachman had something over his arm, she half noticed when she joined him again in the taproom. She did not observe what it was until he handed it to her when she was inside the carriage again and he was about to leave to fetch her her food and her tea. It was a cloak. She reached for it with inner gratitude. The interior of the carriage was chilly since no sunlight was allowed to warm it.

And then she felt more chilly than she had felt throughout the hours of the journey. It was her own cloak, the one that had been packed on top of the trunk that was to accompany her on her wedding journey. That trunk had been in her dressing room when she had left for St. George's.

Elizabeth clutched the cloak in her hands and fought panic again. What was going on? Where was she being taken that was so far from London that they had to stop at an inn to eat? Where were they going that necessitated her trunk being brought with them? How soon was she to be ransomed? Or more to the point, and more frightening, how long was she to be held? And why?

She had calmed herself by the time the door opened again and the coachman set a large tray on the seat opposite her. She neither looked at him nor spoke to him. She sat looking quietly down at her hands until he had shut and locked the door again. A long time passed before she could persuade herself to eat or drink.

Christopher had forgotten just how far it was from London to Devonshire. Especially when one was forced to travel without stopping. It was bad enough to have to stop at an inn every few hours to allow Elizabeth to eat and to relieve herself. He certainly could not risk stopping long enough for her to sleep. And so after their evening stop Antoine handed her a pillow and two blankets and she was left to sleep inside the confined space of the carriage as best she could while they traveled on into the night. And on through the next day.

Apart from the one scream and the struggle outside the

church she did not once have the hysterics or prove to be a difficult prisoner. Indeed, if Antoine was to be believed and his own brief glimpses of her, she behaved with quiet dignity—even when it must have become obvious to her that this was no ordinary kidnapping for ransom.

She must have changed, he thought. The old Elizabeth would have panicked and had the vapors long ago. The old Elizabeth would have gone all to pieces. She did not look different. He had been too busy with his dangerous task in Hanover Square to observe her closely at the time, but nevertheless, he realized as he rode beside the carriage during all the hours that followed, he had seen and felt and even smelled a great deal more than he had realized at the time.

She was still as slender as a girl and still as shapely as that girl had been. Hauling her up onto his horse's back had been a far less difficult task than he had expected it to be. And her hair was still as soft and as honey blond as it had been—and her gray eyes as dark and as large. She had smelled of lavender, as she had always used to.

It was only after she was out of his arms and inside the carriage that he felt himself shaking with the realization that she was Elizabeth, that he had seen and touched her again, that he had put an effective stop to her wedding, that she was his, in his power, at his mercy.

He shook and felt cold despite the April sunshine. The night in London and the early morning had been incredibly busy while he and Antoine put into effect the hastily concocted plan, acquiring horses, a carriage, and suitable clothes, packing their own belongings, effecting the daring visit to the Duke of Chicheley's house to collect Elizabeth's trunk ready for the wedding journey—or so Antoine had said, posing as a servant of Lord Poole.

And now suddenly, before Christopher could at all reflect on the plan, it was accomplished. He had Elizabeth shut up inside the carriage, and he was taking her with all speed to Penhallow.

Christ, he thought as he rode beside the carriage, what had he done? What was he going to do with her once they reached Penhallow? And how would she react? With hysteria and tears and vapors when she saw who her captor was? With disgust and hatred? Certainly she was not going to fall into his arms or stay willingly with him. He was either going to have to keep her there a prisoner or else he was going to have to bring her back again on this long journey with nothing whatsoever accomplished.

And what did he want to accomplish anyway? He hated her, didn't he? Or if hatred was too strong a word, contempt surely was not. He despised her. He wanted only to force the truth on her face to face so that she would know finally that the fault for everything that had happened was hers. Though that was at least partly unfair. The fault for what had happened was someone else's. He had not yet discovered whose, but he intended to do so.

But he had not intended to go about it this way. How could he expect her to listen to him now when he had kidnapped her outside the church where she was to have been married and carried her a prisoner half across the country?

He had better let her know who her captor was before they reached Penhallow, he decided late on the afternoon of the second day when they were a mere few miles from home. He was reluctant to face her, but it was better to do it on the road than in his home. He rode forward to talk with Antoine, who was perched up on the box of the carriage guiding the horses, though he looked as tired as Christopher felt.

"Stop when we get to the other side of the crossroads ahead," he said. "I'll tie up the horse behind and travel the rest of the way inside the carriage." He tried to make his tone casual and matter-of fact.

Antoine tossed his head backward in the direction of the carriage. "Take your fists and your wits with you, m'sieur," he said. "That one is a sleeping volcano."

Christopher smiled a little grimly. A volcano? Elizabeth? More like a little clinging violet in all likelihood, he thought.

Fear came and went in waves as did anger and impatience and discomfort and tiredness. Mostly she wanted an end to the journey so that she might at least find out exactly where she was and why she had been brought there. Uncertainty, she found, bred fear. If she was to be ransomed, why was she being brought so far? If she was to be killed—sometimes there was blank terror at that possibility—why again was she being brought so far?

Strange, she thought several times during the day, her wedding and her wedding night should have been behind her by now. She should be Manley's wife: Lady Elizabeth Hill, Lady Poole. She wondered how he was feeling now. Was he worried for her safety? Was he searching for her? And what about her father? And Martin? Martin would be frantic. And he would be searching. He would leave no stone unturned in England to find out her whereabouts. There was comfort in the thought. Martin would find her.

And how was Christina reacting? Had she been told the truth? Or would they have invented some story to explain Elizabeth's failure to appear in the church and her failure to appear afterward? Christina, she thought, and she closed her eyes and swallowed several times. She would not cry. Nothing could make her cry. She never knew when the carriage was going to stop and the little French coachman appear at the door. She would not risk being seen with wet or red eyes. She would not give them that satisfaction.

Well, she thought wearily, she had spent long years growing up, learning to face herself and reality, learning to take charge of her own life, learning that she and no one else must decide its direction. Learning that if she did not come to depend upon herself, she could depend upon no one else. Except Martin, of course. She could always depend upon Martin, though even on him she would not lean any longer. It was not fair. She had learned through long years of suffering to be her own person. And now she was to be put to the test. She could not at the moment decide her own destiny, it was true. But she would not panic or grovel or plead.

She swallowed as the carriage slowed. It must be late afternoon again. A late tea? An early dinner? She waited for the door to open and the coachman to appear. She prepared her usual look of disdain.

But a few minutes later she felt rather as if a large fist had hit her hard low in her stomach and robbed her of breath. It was not the coachman who opened the door and came right inside the carriage to sit down opposite her and look at her silently from steady blue eyes. Nor was it the masked man who had snatched her up outside St. George's. Oh, yes, it was he certainly, but he no longer wore either the hat or the mask. Only his own long, thick dark hair.

"Christopher?" Her lips formed his name though she heard only a whisper of sound.

The carriage began to move again.

He had changed. His face, always narrow, always unsmiling, always a little frightening to her eighteen-year-old eyes now clearly showed the sharp angles of jaw and cheekbones and looked harsh and implacable. His aquiline nose looked more prominent than it had used to look. His fair skin was now darkly bronzed. His shoulders beneath his cloak, always almost thin, were now anything but. The slender, serious, sometimes morose boy had become a man.

She did not consciously notice the changes. She was too deep in shock. But part of her mind noticed them. And yet he was Christopher. Unmistakably Christopher. The man she had expected never to see again. The man whose name she had blocked from her mind on her wedding morning. Yesterday.

"You are surprised?" he asked her.

His deep voice was firmer than she remembered it.

She stared at him as if paralyzed. "What do you want with me?" she asked him at last. "Where are you taking me?"

"You must wait for your answers, Elizabeth," he said. "We are going to have a confrontation at long last. Think about that if you wish."

He said no more but merely stared at her, his eyes intent, his lips compressed. And she felt all the old fear robbing her of breath, though the fear then had been occasioned by the fact that she was eighteen years old and he had appeared splendidly handsome and mysterious to her and she had been afraid that she would never be able to pierce his reserve and touch his heart. She had been afraid that he felt nothing for her, a fear that events had confirmed all too painfully.

Now the fear was of his strength and his silence and his piercing blue eyes. And of the fact that she was his prisoner on her way with him she knew not where. And for a purpose she did not know.

But he had gone to Canada and had settled there. What was he doing back in England?

Fear mounted in the stretching silence so that she wanted to give in to panic, to beg him to let her go, not to hurt her. Under his steady scrutiny she felt herself reverting to the old Elizabeth almost as if he had her under some spell and seven years had rolled away.

But she was not the old Elizabeth. And she was not in his power even if she was his prisoner. Only her body was in his power. Even that was a terrifying thought. But he could not touch her. He could not touch the real Elizabeth. She must remember that. No matter what, she must remember that. He had destroyed her once so that she had not wanted to live. She had pieced herself back together again over long and painful years. She would not give him that power over her again.

"It takes two to have a confrontation," she said. "Perhaps you would like to think about that, Christopher. I have nothing whatsoever to say to you."

He continued to look at her for a while until he lowered his gaze to his hands and contemplated them, a brooding look in his eyes. And she realized something suddenly. He had sat down not quite opposite her, but in the corner farthest from the door he had entered, while she sat next to it. And he had closed the door quietly behind himself. It was not locked.

She would not be able to get away, of course. The coachman would stop the carriage and they would both be after her almost before she could touch the ground and regain her balance. The chances that there would be other people in sight to witness the fact that she was a captive were very slim. But it would be a gesture. A gesture that needed to be made. She had been his abject victim in the past. She might still be his victim, but she would never again be abject. Never.

She waited for a few moments to steady her breathing, to let her eyes rest on the handle so that she knew exactly how it would feel in her hand. And then she lunged at it, wrenched the door open, and flung herself out almost before Christopher's head could snap up, startled.

He cried out, as did the coachman, and he was out of the door after her long before Antoine could drag on the ribbons and pull horses and carriage to a noisy and ungainly halt.

But Elizabeth heard none of it. She landed in the fairly

soft dirt beside the hedgerow that bordered the road, bruising herself very little despite the fact that she was unable to keep her feet but sprawled full length on the ground. But her head landed with a dull thud on the squat and solid milestone that happened to be planted deep in the soil at just that spot.

4

TO many Britons with their love of formal and classical elegance, Penhallow would not have appeared beautiful at all. The house was built in wild countryside very near the coast of Devonshire. It looked much as it had looked for several centuries, like a medieval manor that was not quite a castle. Low round towers, a square gatehouse with narrow slit windows and a rounded arch leading through to the courtyard, gray stone walls liberally covered with ivy: it was not one of the showpieces of England.

Outside the walls little attempt had been made to create formal splendor, to force nature to conform to man's idea of symmetry and beauty. There was a small rose arbor to the west of the house, sheltered from the harsh elements by trees, and before the house there were rock gardens, which were a riot of color during the summer. Vegetable and flower gardens stretched to the east of the house.

The manor was built only a mile from the sea as the crow flies, but the wooded valley in which it was situated meandered eastward with the stream at its center for almost three miles before curving south toward the sea and ending in marshy land that cut through the cliffs to either side. A climb up through the woods to the back of the house would bring one up onto a windswept plateau of coarse grass and sheep droppings and a mile farther on to the edge of cliffs that dropped sheer to the ocean below, or when the tide was out to a wide stretch of golden sands. There was a precipitous path leading from the cliff top to the beach.

To lovers of solitude and wild beauty there was no place quite like Penhallow.

Such a person was Lady Nancy Atwell. She had lived

alone at the house, apart from servants, since the death of her father the year before. She had friends in the village and the surrounding countryside, but she never shunned solitude. She liked it better than company, she often thought. She could be herself at Penhallow. She could be free. She had left it once, seven years before when she had been twenty to journey to London for a belated come-out Season, and she had loved the bustle and excitement and everything else that had happened.

Everything else except for one thing. And that one thing had sent her scurrying home in haste and had kept her there ever since. She was not sorry, though she was very sorry for the incident that had sent her running. She was not sorry that she now lived at Penhallow, that it was her home, that it was her life. She was happy there.

She had spent a late April afternoon walking along the beach. She had even removed her shoes and stockings and carried them in one hand so that she could walk along at the edge of the water and feel her toes sink into the spongy sand and feel them also turn almost numb with cold.

She thought of her brother as she trudged up the cliff path, her shoes back in place but her hair loose and in wild tangles about her face and down over her shoulders. She very rarely wore her hair up except when she was visiting or expecting visitors.

She wondered if he knew yet about Papa's death. She had written to him immediately, but she knew from experience that letters could take up to a year to reach him in America. Sometimes two years passed before she had a reply to something she had written.

She wondered if he would come home. He had once said that he would never come back, but never is a long time. And people can change in seven years. Christopher must have changed. It sounded as if he was becoming very successful in what seemed to be a rugged and competitive business. He had had as solitary an upbringing as she. Papa had not sent him away to school. He had been nineteen when he finally went to university—a quiet, serious, dreamy boy who had not learned how to cope with life beyond the boundaries of Penhallow. Events had proved that.

He must have changed, she thought, pausing on the

cliff top to catch her breath and gazing at the western horizon and the sunset that was turning it orange and sending a golden band of light across the water. The wind blew her dark hair out behind her, creating further tangles. She shook her head, enjoying the sensation.

She must not expect him, she thought. At least not yet. It was very early in the year. She would hope for a letter, but she would not expect him. Then she would not be disappointed when he did not come. But she hoped as she turned for home and her hair was blown forward over her face that he would come. They had been very close as children, having had only each other for company. Their father had been a recluse, spending most of his days in the library among his beloved books.

She had missed Christopher, especially since the death of Papa. She wanted him to come home. But she would not expect him. She would hope for a letter. There had been a long one the year before, but of course he had not known about Papa when he had written that.

Nancy ran down the wooded hill toward the valley and the house. It was dusk already, but summer was coming and the evenings were getting longer. There was a great deal to look forward to.

She felt sandy, she thought as she entered the tiled hall. And she must look a great deal worse than sandy. But there was no one there to see her since she did not feel it necessary to keep a servant standing in the hall all day long. Besides, her servants were used to the sight of her. It must be almost dinnertime, though. She would run upstairs to change her dress and wash her hands and feet and pull a comb through her hair.

But before she could pass through the arch that would bring her to the staircase, she stopped and stood very still. Horses? It was hard to tell for sure since horses and carriages no longer came into the courtyard, but she was sure she had heard correctly. Everything was always so quiet about Penhallow that the slightest sound could be detected, especially at this time of day.

Nancy frowned. Who would be calling at this strange hour? But she had no time to play guessing games with herself or to wonder if she really had heard horses. The heavy oak doors crashed open suddenly and a small heavyset man rushed inside. Her hand crept up to her throat, though she stood her ground and made no attempt to duck out of sight. She was reminded, not for the first time, of the lonely location of Penhallow.

"Sacré coeur!" the man exclaimed, looking wildly about him and apparently not seeing her standing in the archway. "Where is everybody? Give some 'elp 'ere, s'il vous plait."

Two servants, one of them the butler, appeared at a run from the direction of the back stairs and Nancy stepped forward. But she stopped again as another man strode in through the open doors, a tall man wearing a long dark cloak and no hat. He was carrying the slight and motionless form of a woman.

"Christopher!" Nancy cried and she rushed forward again.

He looked at her, his face harsh and pale. "Nance," he said, "I need a room and a bed. And warm water and cloths. She is badly hurt, I believe. And a doctor. Hemmings"—he turned toward the butler—"send for a doctor. Tell him it is extremely urgent."

"What happened?" Nancy's eyes widened. She had no time to feel either surprise or joy. She had no time to look for changes in her brother.

"She jumped out of the carriage and hit her head," he said grimly, striding past her in the direction of the stairs. "Antoine, see to the horses."

Jumped out of the carriage? But Nancy had no chance to react to the strange words. She had glanced down at the woman's unconscious face as her brother strode past, and she felt that she had walked straight into a nightmare. Elizabeth!

"Elizabeth?" she said, her hand back at her throat. But Christopher was already on the stairs and her servants and his were all scurrying into action. She hurried after her brother. "Take her to the green bedchamber. I always have the bed kept aired for visitors in that room."

He rounded the pillar at the top of the stairs and strode along the upper hallway toward the room she had named. Nancy rushed ahead of him to open the door and turn back the blankets and top sheet. He set Elizabeth down with care, straightened her clothes, removed her slippers, and covered her with the bedclothes.

"I think she might die," he said, his voice harsh. "She

has not recovered consciousness since it happened. That was seven or eight miles back."

"Christopher," Nancy said, looking from the unconscious woman's face to the back of his head, "what are you doing back in England—and with Elizabeth?"

He turned to look at her and she was struck immediately with the change in him. He was a man now, a man who looked as if he were normally much in command of his life. His pallor suggested that perhaps this occasion was an exception.

"Picking up where I left off, it seems," he said. "Getting myself into one hell of a mess, Nance. I could not leave well enough alone. I kidnapped her."

"Kidnapped?" There was horror in her voice.

He turned back to the bed and leaned over Elizabeth to pick up one of her hands and chafe it. "Cold and limp," he murmured. "I was passing through London and happened to hear that she was to marry Lord Poole the next day. Can you believe the coincidence? I could not leave it at that. I could not leave her alone. I snatched her up from outside the church."

Nancy breathed through her mouth. She had thought it was all over. She had prayed that it was all over—both for him and for herself. Almost seven years had passed. It had begun to seem like ancient history. Yet now Elizabeth was lying unconscious on a bed at Penhallow. Christopher had kidnapped her, snatched her from her own wedding.

"What were you planning to do with her?" she asked.

But he merely shook his head and did not answer. "She is cold," he said, his voice toneless. "I think she might die."

It was Nancy's turn to be unable to find an answer. All she could think of was the unreality of the moment. Christopher was home after almost seven years. She was actually looking at his back and the side of his face. And Elizabeth was there. She hated Elizabeth. She was almost overwhelmed with hatred suddenly. Elizabeth had driven Christopher away in the first place, and now she had spoiled his homecoming. Completely ruined it if she died. Christopher would be a murderer. He was already a kidnapper.

"Where is that confounded doctor?" he asked with sudden viciousness, glancing over his shoulder.

Mrs. Clavell, the housekeeper, entered the room at that moment with a bowl of steaming water and cloths and towels, and a flannel nightgown over her arm. She clucked her tongue at the sight of Elizabeth's inert form, acknowledged her master's return home only with the demand that he leave the room or at least step aside while she put the poor lady comfortable, and turned her attention to the bed and its occupant.

He bargained with God for her life during the long hours of the night. *Spare her,* he prayed silently, his face harsh as he gazed down at her, *and I'll take her back to London as soon as she is able to travel and let her marry Poole without a word of protest and never try to see her again.*

Spare her, he prayed later in the night, *and I'll make no effort to uncover the truth of seven years ago. I'll leave things as they are and let the shame of something I did not do weigh on my shoulders for the rest of my life as it has for seven years. I'll forget about my plan to prove to her that she has been wrong about me all this time.*

Spare her, he prayed as the night progressed and there was no change in her. *Don't let her die. I'll stay at Penhallow for the rest of my days. I'll even go back to America if you will only let her live.*

He had sent Mrs. Clavell to bed even though she had offered to sit up through the night and call her master if there were any change. And Nancy had gone to bed long after midnight when she saw that he was not going to do so.

"After all," she had said, "one of us has to be up and fresh in the morning."

He had stayed, sometimes sitting beside the bed, sometimes touching her hand, more often on his feet pacing in front of the bed or standing at the window, looking out into darkness.

He had despised and hated her for seven years, despised her meekness and her weakness, her lack of trust, her dependence on her family. Yet all the time, he discovered now, he had not let her go. Hatred and contempt had been no good to him at all. He should have forgotten about her, put her out of his life. He should have forgotten his dream of clearing his name. To whom did it matter any longer except to him? And he knew he was innocent; he did not need to prove it to himself.

Now he had killed her. Or hurt her very badly. The doctor did not seem to feel that the egg of a lump on the side of her head threatened her life, though he himself was not yet convinced. Her other bruises were superficial, but even so they were bruises he had caused. He had ruined her wedding day and the chance for happiness she had chosen for herself, or that her family had chosen for her. She was nothing to him any longer—or should be nothing. What she chose to do with her life should not have concerned him at all.

Let her live, he prayed once more. No bargaining this time. Just the simple silent plea to a God who seemed not to be listening.

When the sky grayed with the first suggestion of dawn, he crossed to the window and stared out over the rock gardens to the wooded valley and the hills rising at the other side of the stream. It seemed strange to be back home. Back home without that sense of homecoming he had anticipated for so long. He had not even noticed the approach to the house the evening before.

There was a groan from the bed behind him and he turned sharply and walked across the room to stand beside the bed, his hands clasped behind him. She lay with her eyes still closed, but her head was moving slightly from side to side.

Let her live, he prayed fiercely and silently.

The bed was comfortable and the room was warm. She could feel the softness of a mattress at her back and the thickness of a feather pillow beneath her head. The warmth was dancing pink beyond her eyelids. There must be a fire burning in the room. She opened her eyes.

Yes. It was a coal fire, the black coals glowing red, the flames dancing cozily beneath the smoke, which was curling up into the chimney. There was a candle burning on the table beside her. And faint light was coming through the window. It must be almost morning.

But she could not for the moment remember where she

was. The room was high-ceilinged and square, she could see. The bed hangings were green brocade and shimmered in the light of the candle. The canopy over her head was green too, the brocade pleated and drawn into a sort of rosette at the peak. There was someone standing at the window. She could not see who it was.

She turned her head to look and pain hit her. She heard herself groan and closed her eyes again. Her head felt rather as if someone had pounded it with a hammer. She must have had some injury. It felt far worse than a mere headache. She tested the rest of her body, moving gingerly a limb at a time. Her right knee was hurting as if she had bumped or cut it. Her right elbow felt the same way. Her ribs were sore.

She must have fallen, she thought, and someone had been considerate enough to bring her to bed and undress her. She was wearing a warm flannel nightgown. It was comfortable, but she did not think she usually wore flannel.

She opened her eyes and saw the fire again and the light reflecting off the green canopy of the bed. And then she swiveled her eyes so that she would not have to turn her head too sharply to see the man at the window. But he had moved. He was standing silently at her bedside looking down at her. At least she thought he was looking down. The candle made only shadows of his face and the faint light from the window behind him made it quite invisible.

He was a tall man with broad shoulders and slim waist and hips. His dark hair needed cutting—but perhaps not. Actually it looked good as it was. As did he. He looked extremely attractive, in fact, she thought, even though she could not see his face. But he was standing unnaturally still. He did not move or bend toward her or say anything to her.

She was an intruder. She had inconvenienced him by having the accident outside his house and he had had no choice but to take her in. How embarrassing!

"Where am I?" she asked him.

There was a pause. And then a deep, attractive man's voice replied. "You are at Penhallow," he said. "We were not far from here when you had the accident."

"Accident?" she said.

"You fell out of the carriage," he said. "You bumped your head on a milestone."

"That explains the pain," she said, closing her eyes for a moment. But she opened them and looked at his shadowed face again. "Who are you?"

He looked down at her in silence for so long that she thought he was not going to answer. Then he walked around to the other side of the bed so that she could see his face clearly. It was a harsh hawkish face, rather narrow, with a prominent nose and thin lips and intense eyes. Blue? She could not see their color clearly. It was a face that looked as if it rarely smiled. It was a face that looked as if it had suffered. A wonderfully attractive face, she thought, full of character, even if it was not strictly speaking handsome.

"Christopher Atwell," he said. "Earl of Trevelyan."

Christopher. It was a name that did not seem quite to suit him. It was a cheerful name and he looked like an unhappy man. Or perhaps he was just worried. Worried about her. She had had an accident. She must have been unconscious. Perhaps he had been worried that she would not regain consciousness. Why would he be worried about her?

She felt sudden panic though she lay very still and brought herself under control with deep and even breaths. She licked dry lips.

"Who am I?" she asked him, blurting the unthinkable question, hearing it almost as if the words had come from someone else's mouth.

The silence was even longer this time as he gazed down at her, his face quite devoid of expression. Except that she could see a pulse beating in his temple.

"Elizabeth," he said at last. She watched his jaw tensing. "Elizabeth Atwell. Countess of Trevelyan. My wife."

The abduction of the bride from her own wedding caused a sensation in London. Most of the *ton* had been present inside the church when Martin Honywood walked down the aisle and talked quietly with the groom before both of them disappeared, presumably to confer with the vicar. A buzzing had started then among the congregation—the bride was already a full fifteen minutes late.

The buzzing had become an excited murmuring when Martin himself finally made the announcement.

Soon Hanover Square was filled with people, the members of the *ton* in all their wedding splendor on one side, the humbler spectators on the other. All gazed about them as if they expected to catch a glimpse of the masked stranger disappearing with Lady Elizabeth Ward. All those who had witnessed the abduction loudly clamored to be heard with their versions of what exactly had happened. Unfortunately for them, their only listeners were those who had seen as much as they. The wedding guests would not deign to recognize their presence.

As soon as the abduction had happened, Martin, it seemed, had jumped back inside the duke's carriage and roared for it to follow the horseman, but by the time the carriage had been turned and the horses set in motion, all trace of his stepsister and her abductor was lost. There must have been a carriage waiting just beyond the square, all agreed. And so Martin had been obliged to return, direct that the duke be helped back into the carriage, and undertake the unpleasant task of going inside the church to make the announcement.

At first it was assumed that the kidnapper had had the simple motive of drawing a handsome ransom. The wedding guests returned reluctantly to their homes and waited for news. The Duke of Chicheley would doubtless pay whatever sum was demanded. Everyone knew that he was as rich as Croesus and that he would not hesitate to spend the last penny of his fortune on his only daughter. Had not events already proved that? And yet all waited in eager anticipation to know exactly what the ransom demand would be.

The principals in the matter behaved predictably. The duke raged and roared. But raging and roaring would do no good whatsoever until he had the kidnapper in his own power. He swore that he would not hand over a single pound to such vermin, but everyone knew that when it came to the point he would part with considerably more than a single pound.

Christina cried bitterly and inconsolably. But no one took a great deal of notice of her. No one, that was, except those who were paid well to do so.

Manley Hill, Lord Poole, was beside himself with fury.

He had overlooked everything that had happened in the past and chosen Lady Elizabeth as his wife, he explained to Martin, and now this! Did the woman have a gift for placing herself in the middle of scandals?

She was hardly responsible for either of the two scandals in which she had been embroiled, Martin pointed out. But Lord Poole had been humiliated in front of the whole *ton*, and so his chagrin was perhaps understandable. He could not afford to be the subject of ridicule. As it was he was a Whig in a capital city that was going mad for a military victory that the Tory government appeared to have won for them. Yet he had hoped not so long before that his party would be swept to victory on a wave of public reaction against the war. He was an ambitious man. He might have expected to win respect from his marriage into a prominent Tory family, not lose it in such a manner.

"Whoever he is," he said irritably to Martin, "he had better not think he can apply to me for ransom. Elizabeth is not my wife yet, and perhaps never will be now. Perhaps she went willingly. How are we to know that it was not all staged, that he is not her lover? Eh?"

Martin felt sometimes that he was the only one who grieved. The wedding guests and the populace of London were enjoying the sensation, which for the moment had displaced even the victory celebrations in their minds. His stepfather thought only of the affront to his person and position. Christina thought only of her own comfort. Lord Poole thought only of his dignity.

Only Martin thought of Elizabeth, or so it seemed to him. He blamed himself for having agreed to bring her back to London the autumn before when they had lived so peacefully and contentedly in the country for several years. He should have persuaded her to stay there, though it had been becoming increasingly difficult to persuade Elizabeth against doing anything she had set her mind to. He blamed himself for not having held her hand more firmly as he helped her down from the carriage outside the church and for not guessing the intent of the horseman who had galloped into the square, taking them all so much by surprise. He could have bundled her back inside the carriage. But he had not been able to think fast enough.

And now she was alone with that masked man, perhaps in discomfort, perhaps having to suffer indignities. She would be frightened. And perhaps a whole night would pass before the ransom note was delivered and an exchange of money could be made for her freedom.

Martin waited in impatience and frustration for the note to arrive. He paced the hall of the duke's house on Grosvenor Square, his usually good-humored face so tight with fury and his eyes so wild with anxiety that the servants watched him nervously and gave him as wide a berth as they could.

The night came and yet no ransom note, no message from the abductor came with it.

5

SHE must have slept again. The room was light. But he was still there, she saw at a glance, standing at the window with his back to the room. Christopher Atwell, Earl of Trevelyan. Her husband.

She closed her eyes again and accepted the fact as an everyday reality. She relaxed and tried to trick herself into remembering. Of course he was her husband. Christopher. They . . . But the trick would not work. There was nothing there at all beyond the bare facts he had given her—his name and his title and his relationship to her. She was lying in a bedchamber at Penhallow. Her home. Their home. Where was Penhallow? What did the rest of the house look like? Who else lived there?

She could feel panic rising like nausea in her nostrils as she let her mind slide toward the greatest blank of all. Perhaps if she did not try too hard or allow herself to become too anxious it would all come back to her. Who was she? Elizabeth Atwell, he had told her. The name sounded quite unfamiliar. Was it really her name? Had she lived with it all her life? Or since her marriage at least?

There was nothing. A frightening nothing.

"Christopher," she said, and he turned sharply from the window and strode to the side of the bed. He looked even more handsome than he had looked in the candlelight earlier that morning. His skin was dark as if he spent much of his time out of doors. And his eyes were blue—her first impression had been correct. Wonderfully knee-weakeningly blue.

"Is that what I call you?" she asked. "Or do I call you 'my lord' or 'Trevelyan'?"

"Christopher," he said.

He looked very tense. This must be as dreadful for him, she thought, as it was for her.

"I am so sorry," she said, biting on her lower lip. "I can remember nothing. You are a stranger to me, and I am a stranger to myself. I will panic if I do not keep a tight hold on myself."

He sat down on the side of the bed and took both her hands in a strong clasp. His hands were warm and very reassuring.

"The memory will come back," he said. "Just relax and don't worry about it. You are alive and not badly hurt apart from the lump on your head. That is all that matters at the moment. How are you feeling?"

"Sore all over," she said, "and rather as if someone must have been trying to hammer me into the ground like a nail. What happened?"

"You fell out of the carriage," he said. "The door had not been shut securely and you leaned against it."

"You were with me?" she asked.

"Yes." His eyes looked haunted for a moment. "I thought you were dead."

She let her eyes roam over his thick dark hair, over his face and his broad shoulders. She tightened her hold slightly on his hands. But there was no sense of familiarity at all. She sighed.

"How long have we been married?" she asked.

"Seven years," he said.

Seven years. All wiped out by one bump on the head. Seven years!

"Was it a love match?" She wished she had not asked the question after it was spoken. She was afraid that perhaps it had not been.

"Yes," he said.

"And is it still?" She searched his eyes. "Do we still love each other?"

He nodded and raised one of her hands to his lips. It felt good there. Very good. She smiled at him, but she sobered quickly.

"Oh, Christopher," she said. "There must be so much familiarity between us, so many things that we usually say to each other and do together. I don't remember any of them. I am forced to treat you as a stranger. It will be very distressing for you."

"No." He shook his head and held her eyes with his. "I will treat it as a fantasy. A romantic fantasy. I will make you fall in love with me all over again."

"I don't think that will be difficult," she said. "You are so very handsome. Do I usually flatter you like that?" She smiled again.

"I think I am going to enjoy this," he said. And his eyes smiled back into hers for a brief moment.

"I must have taken one look at you seven years ago and fallen in love with you," she said. "Did I? Was it a whirlwind courtship?"

"Yes," he said.

"And did you take one look at me and fall in love?" she asked. But the deliberately lighthearted talk would no longer hold the terror at bay. Her smile faded and she felt as if she might faint. Her head was throbbing painfully. "Christopher, what do I look like?"

Terror was an ice-cold and a clawing thing, like an army of demons while she waited for him to bring a looking glass from an adjoining room. She did not know whom she would see in the glass. Would she recognize the face? And then would she remember everything?

It was a heart-shaped face, quite unremarkable, though not ugly, she saw with some relief. It was totally devoid of color. It was more colorless than her hair, which was honey blond and rather untidily spread on the pillow about her. Her eyes were large and dark gray and framed by long lashes, darker than her hair.

He took the looking glass from her hand after a while and set it down beside the bed. "You are the most beautiful woman I have known," he said.

Her head felt as if it must burst at any moment. It was perhaps, she thought, everyone's nightmare that one might one day look in a mirror and see a stranger looking back. For most people fortunately that fear never became more than a nightmare. For her it had become reality.

"Christopher,"—her eyes closed and she reached blindly for the comfort of his hands again—"what am I going to do? Oh, what am I going to do?"

And then she felt his chest against her own and his hands sliding beneath her until his arms encircled her. He raised her to a sitting position and held her close against him, her head turned on his shoulder.

"You are going to relax and let your body heal," he said. "And you are going to get to know yourself and me again. And Penhallow. When your memory returns, we will both be happy, but we will both look back on these days as an almost pleasant interlude, when we had a chance to get to know each other all over again."

She was in pain and her head hurt, and she felt dizzy with the shift in position. But there was warmth too and enormous comfort, both from his strong masculine body and from his words, murmured against one of her ears. She was where she belonged, she thought, and the thought brought enormous relief.

"I do love you," she said, rubbing her cheek against the cloth of his coat. "I can feel it, Christopher. It is a memory of feeling even though there are no facts to go with it. But it is something, is it not?"

"It is something," he agreed. "We will have to provide the facts in the coming days."

She lifted her head and winced. She did not know if he meant what she thought he meant by those words. His eyes were very steady on hers. And even more gloriously blue from this close than they had appeared a few minutes before. But of course he must have meant that. He was her husband. Her husband of seven years.

"Is this my room?" she asked him.

He shook his head. "We had you brought here so that you could be quiet for a few days," he said. "Your room is also mine."

"Is it?" She felt herself flushing and laughed a little uncertainly. "It must seem very funny to you that such a fact can make me blush after seven years."

He spread one hand behind her head, careful to avoid the lump. "Rather arousing actually," he said. And he kissed her mouth, his own closed and light and warm.

And wonderful.

"Hungry?" he asked her, laying her carefully back down against her pillows again.

"I could eat a bear," she said, breathless from the light kiss of a husband of seven years. "Do I usually eat them?"

"For breakfast every morning," he said. "I have never been able to break you of the habit."

She laughed and winced. "Christopher," she said,

"where is Penhallow? And who else lives here? Oh, I have a million and one questions to ask. And there are daggers twisting through my head."

"No more questions for now," he said. "I am going to leave you for a while so that you can rest. And when breakfast is ready, I will have Nancy bring it up to you."

"Nancy?" she asked.

"My sister," he said. "Your sister-in-law."

"Oh," she said. And she could feel terror waiting to invade her mind again. "Christopher?" She stretched out a hand to him. "Come back soon. I love you. I do love you, don't I?"

He took her hand, kissed the palm, set it carefully back down on the bed, and left the room.

She did love him, Elizabeth thought. She did. It was the one memory of which she was certain. Though it was not exactly a memory, perhaps. A feeling. But a feeling too powerful to have attached itself to a mere stranger, however handsome and attractive he might be. It could only be a remembered feeling.

She loved him. She clung desperately to that one certainty in her life.

Nancy took a breakfast tray up to Elizabeth half an hour later, though she did so with the greatest reluctance and with the uneasy feeling that she was acting as an accomplice to a wicked crime. They were jailers, she told her brother angrily. They were holding Elizabeth captive in both body and mind.

He looked harsh and implacable. "I don't want you telling her anything to contradict what I have said, Nance," he said. "That will only confuse her. She is bewildered and frightened enough as it is."

"So I am to lie for you," she said quietly.

He said nothing.

"This is not at all the homecoming I imagined," she said.

His expression softened and he reached out to touch a hand to her hair, which she was wearing loose as usual. "Your letter said that Papa's death was not a hard one?" he said.

She shook her head. "It was all over in two days," she said. "He was in a coma for most of that time. I wanted so much for you to be here, Christopher. I have longed every day since to see you ride into the valley."

"I am here now," he said.

She raised troubled eyes to his and went into his outheld arms. "Christopher," she said, "oh, Christopher."

"It will be all right," he said. "You will see. You will take her tray up, Nance? I told her you would. And you will say nothing to confuse her?"

"I will take her tray up," she said, turning to walk from the room without answering his other question. But he knew, and she knew, that she would say nothing to spoil his little game. Though it was hardly a little game either.

He would be found out, she thought as she ascended the stairs with the tray. If he kept Elizabeth at Penhallow, sooner or later someone was going to trace her there. And then they would come and all hell would break loose.

Her safe haven would be a haven no longer. There would be nowhere else to run. Who would come? she wondered. The Duke of Chicheley? John? She did not want John to come. She had spent seven years trying not even to think of him. But surely he would be in Spain or France with the armies. She did not know. Perhaps he was even—She tried not to complete the sentence in her mind. Some men always came back safely from war.

Martin, then. Yes, Martin would be the one to come. He had always been exceedingly fond of Elizabeth. Nancy had even thought at one time that he was in love with his stepsister, but perhaps not. Anyway, he would be the one to come, she thought with dull certainty. Her haven would be lost indeed. And there was nowhere else to run.

Elizabeth was very pale. Even her lips were colorless. And yet she looked quite as beautiful as she had ever looked. Nancy hated her.

"Nancy?" Elizabeth said.

Nancy smiled and set down the tray. "Yes," she said. "I know you don't recognize me, Elizabeth. Don't worry about it. Your memory will return. Are you hungry?"

"Yes," Elizabeth said, though she just swallowed and stared down at the tray when Nancy placed it across her lap. "You cannot imagine the terror of remembering nothing. Of not knowing people one should know or places one should know. Of looking inward and finding only a blank where the memories and the sense of self should be."

"It will all come back," Nancy said, seating herself carefully on the edge of the bed, careful not to tip the tray and not to jar Elizabeth's aching head. "Just give it time."

Elizabeth smiled at her gratefully and picked up a slice of toast. Nancy sat and watched her as she ate and talked on unthreatening topics like the weather and the quality of the food and coffee. She suggested a bath when Elizabeth finally leaned back against the pillows, her food half eaten.

"Oh, I would love one," Elizabeth said. "I feel so dirty and untidy. Is this my nightgown? It seems very large."

Nancy laughed. "We put it on you, thinking it would be more comfortable with your bruises," she said. "I shall fetch one of your own while you bathe." She got to her feet and took the tray, smiling cheerfully as she left the room.

She felt like a jailer again as she walked down the stairs. And the trouble was that she had found Elizabeth rather likable—as she had on their first acquaintance, before the woman destroyed Christopher and sent him in flight even across the ocean. She did not want to like Elizabeth. She did not want to have anything to do with her.

Or any other member of her family.

6

AFTER two and then three days had passed and brought with them no demand for ransom, it became obvious that the exchange of Elizabeth for money was not the primary motive of the kidnappers.

The Duke of Chicheley was beside himself with impotent rage, for there seemed to be no way of tracking the man or men who had abducted his daughter. He hired some Bow Street Runners and raged at their failure to turn up the kidnappers within the first day.

Lord Poole was in a taking. Sympathetic as everyone appeared to be to his plight, he could not shake from his mind the impression that he was being laughed at.

"It was damned poor timing," he grumbled to Martin when the latter called on him at his town house on Berkeley Square. "Why could they not have taken her the day before? And why right outside the church? You may depend upon it, Honywood, that they wanted to embarrass me. And what better way to do it?"

Lord Poole made no effort to find Elizabeth even though he seemed to feel that he was responsible for her disappearance. He left that to her family. Meanwhile he pondered ways of restoring his self-esteem. And ways of promoting his own flagging political interests.

Martin had been able to settle to nothing since watching helplessly as a masked man had ridden off with his stepsister. He paced endlessly at home. He called on Lord Poole frequently on the chance that perhaps a message had been sent there rather than to Grosvenor Square. Several times he felt on the edge of panic. For if three days had passed and there had been no word, perhaps she was dead. Or perhaps she was a victim of those traders in beautiful white females to the East. He forced that particular thought from him as blessedly unlikely—Elizabeth was twenty-five years old.

Only one thought consoled Martin during those dreadful days. If she came back—*when* she came back—she was going to be suffering from her long ordeal. One could only imagine the indignities to which she might have been subjected. The chances were strong that she would no longer wish to marry Poole or that he would no longer be willing to marry her. That at least was a pleasing prospect.

She would be his again, Martin thought. His to comfort. He would take her back home to Kingston Park and live there quietly with her until she relaxed and grew contented once more. Perhaps she would never grow restless again after this. Perhaps this time she would have learned once and for all that the world beyond Kingston had nothing but pain and heartache and indignity to offer her. Perhaps this time she would be content to stay for the rest of her life.

But first of all she had to be found. She had to be returned. And that fact would set him to pacing again and to feeling close to panic again.

At the end of the third day he went alone into the library and sat down behind the oak desk. Merely waiting was accomplishing nothing, he realized. And in all likelihood the Bow Street Runners would come up with no news more satisfying than that Elizabeth had disappeared off the face of the earth. They would not have a motive for finding her stronger than money. Martin had a stronger motive. He loved her.

Panicking would not find her, he told himself. And waiting patiently for her kidnappers to communicate with him was likely to make him an old man. If she was to be found, then he was going to have to do it himself. And yet it seemed a formidable task. Perhaps an impossible one.

What questions could he ask himself? Who had taken her? A masked man. There was nothing to be gained from that fact. There was no clue as to the man's identity. Where had she been taken? It was impossible to know. Somewhere inside the city, perhaps, or somewhere outside. There was no lead there. Why had she been taken? It was impossible to know.

And yet Martin's mind paused on the question. If there was one area in which guesses—educated guesses—might help him, this was the one. Why had she been taken? What were the possible motives? He listed them in his mind. Money. And yet after three days there had been no word from her abductor, no demand for ransom. It might yet come, of course, but it was no longer safe to assume that that had been the reason for the kidnapping.

What else, then? Embarrassment for Poole? Martin dismissed the idea without any great consideration. Poole had already been embarrassed by the news from Paris and its effect on the British people.

Love? Was someone so in love with Elizabeth that he would forceably prevent her marriage to someone else? It was a possibility. She was a beautiful woman and she had had several suitors since her return to London. But was anyone that deeply in love with her, that desperate? Impossible. Martin would have known. He had gone everywhere with his stepsister since their return from the country, and she told him everything. She had no secrets from him. No, there was no one.

Revenge? But revenge against whom? Poole he had already ruled out. The duke? The duke undoubtedly had enemies, but any who would get back at him in such a way? It seemed very unlikely. Against himself, then? But Martin had no enemies. If revenge were the motive, it had to be against Elizabeth herself. But everyone loved Elizabeth. No one hated her enough to kidnap her. She had been in London for only a few months. Before that she had been at Kingston for more than six years, alone with him most of the time, and before that . . .

Martin stared fixedly ahead of him for a long time. But no, it was impossible. Atwell had gone to Canada, telling Elizabeth before he went that he would never return. Besides, the man was a coward. He had gone running at the first hint of trouble. He had not even waited for the full storm to break over his head. Perhaps he did not even know that there had been a storm.

No, it could not be Atwell. And yet, he thought as his mind was preparing to move on to another possibility, the Earl of Trevelyan had died a year or so ago, had he not? That meant that Atwell was now the earl and owner of Penhallow and his father's fortune. Would he have come back for that? But if he had returned, would he not have stayed as far away from Elizabeth as it was possible to be?

No, Atwell was incapable of displaying the sort of courage the masked man had shown in abducting Elizabeth. He could have hired someone to do it for him, of course. Perhaps he had been waiting in the carriage that had undoubtedly been in readiness just beyond the square.

Martin sat at the desk for a while longer, trying to think of other possible motives for the crime. But there was nothing. His mind drew a blank. And so it returned eventually to the only possibility he had been able to think of, unlikely as it was to be true.

At least, he thought, it should be fairly easy to test out the theory. If the kidnapper was Atwell, then he must have come to London either from Devonshire or from Canada. If he had come from the latter, then he must have arrived recently. It was early in the year for ships from North America. Besides, if he had been in London for more than a couple of days at the longest, then someone would have seen him and spread the word. Even an old scandal has the power to arouse a certain degree of gossip.

What he would do first, Martin decided, was send to find out what ships had come to London from Canada or America during the past week or two and what passengers they had been carrying. If that line of inquiry yielded nothing, then he would send someone to Devonshire to find out if Atwell, or Trevelyan as he now was, was in residence or had been until recently. The chances were, of course, that if he really was the kidnapper, he would have Elizabeth confined at Penhallow.

For a few moments Martin was on the verge of calling out his carriage and setting off for Devonshire himself without delay. But if his theory proved incorrect he would be wasting precious time by chasing false theories. He must have patience. Late in the day as it was—it was almost dinnertime—he summoned Macklin, his most trusted servant, and sent him to make some inquiries at the docks and wharves of the Thames.

Martin felt better than he had felt for days and ate a hearty dinner. But he said nothing to the duke about his theory. If he was wrong, then he would merely make himself look foolish by explaining it. If he was right, then he wanted to be the one to discover Elizabeth and bring her back. He wanted her to owe her freedom to him. And so he hugged to himself the knowledge that perhaps, just perhaps, he was on the trail at last.

And yet the very excitement of the possibility bred its own anxiety. He missed her and he cursed the fact that always he had to vie for her attention, that he could no longer rely on the fact that they would always belong together as they had belonged when they were growing up. And the secret that only he knew and that no one else would ever know gnawed at him until he felt the familiar despairing fury.

It was spoiling his excitement, his hope that soon he would have her home again—not just home on Grosvenor Square, but home at Kingston, where she belonged. Where they belonged together. The fury was spoiling things, as it always did.

But there was no point in staying at the house every moment of the day and night as he had done for the past three days, he thought. The chance that a ransom note would be delivered now seemed very slim. Waiting for one could only bring frustration. He was free then to go out, and perhaps by morning Macklin would have some news for him.

Martin looked in at the opera for a while, not to listen to the music or the singing, but to eye the dancers. But there was no one new, and he had lost interest in the only one he considered worth watching when he had discovered six weeks before—the night Elizabeth and Poole had announced their betrothal—that she dissolved too easily into tears.

He took himself off to the brothel to which he always returned, although he was constantly sampling new ones in the hope of finding one even better.

"Lisa," he said to Madame Cartier, who always greeted her girls' customers personally.

"She is busy, Mr. Honywood," she said apologetically. "Will you wait? Or would you like to try Madeline? She is new and is proving very satisfactory. She is also blond, which is what you like, I know."

Martin was always willing to try someone new. "Whips?" he asked.

"Anything," Madame Cartier said, smiling graciously and leading the way upstairs and along the upper hallway, which was always surprisingly quiet. The rooms in which her girls conducted their business had been constructed with thick walls that let out almost no sound. "Madeline is very adaptable. You will tell her whether you wish her to scream or endure in silence. She is quite capable of both."

One reason Martin liked this particular brothel more than any other of its type was that here the customer was permitted to use the whips as well as have them used by the girls. Other establishments were too protective of their girls.

Martin opened the door indicated by Madame Cartier, stepped inside the dim room beyond, and closed the door behind him. The girl was kneeling up on the bed facing him. She was naked. Long blond hair covered her shoulders and draped over her heavy breasts. She smiled at him.

She was not unlike Elizabeth, Martin saw. Except that she was a slut and a whore. The fury he had felt at home earlier returned with greater intensity. He was instantly aroused. He turned to the row of hooks to the left of the door on which hung an assortment of whips and other flagellation devices. He selected a thin whip, the type he most favored, the type that would curl about the body. He would punish the slut with it, and then he would hand it to her and strip off his own clothes so that she could punish him.

His arousal became more painful. If she was good enough, the whipping would be sufficient and he would not have to soil himself with contact with her body. But rarely was it good enough. Usually he found himself grabbing the whip and hurling it aside and completing his own punishment inside the whore's body. And so he would punish her in advance for her probable failure.

"Stay where you are," he told the smiling girl, wrapping one end of the whip about his right hand and walking slowly toward the bed. "Scream if you will, but no one will rush to your rescue. You deserve what you are about to get, don't you?"

"Yes, sir," she said, still smiling, and reaching up one hand to move all her hair forward over her shoulders before resting both palms on the bed in front of her and dropping her head forward. "I'm a bad girl, sir."

Martin looked down at her exposed back. At least she had the grace to admit her evil. But there were red marks already on her back to show that there had been other customers, that repentance and punishment were merely ways by which she plied her trade. And to think that such a slut could dare to inhabit the same world as Elizabeth.

He bared his teeth and raised the whip.

Once the danger of Elizabeth's abduction was in the past and the crisis of her unconsciousness over, Christopher began to ask himself why he had got into such a mess. Why had he kidnapped her in the first place? If the accident had not happened, what would he have done with her? He really did not know the answers to his own questions. And what was he to do with her now? End the fantasy? Live it out until she regained her memory? What if it never came back?

"I want to leave this room," she told him two days after she had regained consciousness. She was out of bed, wearing one of her own robes over her nightgown, her hair loose down her back. She was standing at the window and had turned to look over her shoulder when he opened the door. She was smiling. "But I am afraid to. I would instantly get lost. Is it not absurd?" The slight breathlessness in her voice told him that she was a little frightened. But she was putting a good face on her terror.

"Are you well enough?" he asked.

"I still have a slight headache," she said, "though the lump has almost gone. All the other bruises are not troublesome. I am restless. Show me the house, Christopher? Perhaps something will spark a memory. This is a rather lovely valley. What is beyond the hilltops?"

He crossed the room to stand beside her. The top of her head, he noticed with an unexpected rush of familiarity, reached his chin. If she tipped her head sideways, it would nestle comfortably against his shoulder. He could remember that as a fact.

"Coarse bare grass," he said, "and some gorse bushes. A few stray sheep. We are very close to the sea here."

"We are?" She looked at him in amazement. "But I

might have guessed it. I have been watching seagulls flying overhead. Oh, Christopher, what is it like?''

''High cliffs and golden sand,'' he said. ''It is windy and wild and wonderful.''

''Take me to see it,'' she said, looking up at him sideways from beneath her lashes. It was another characteristic expression of hers that he had forgotten. ''Not today, but perhaps tomorrow or the next day. Will you? And will you show me the house today? Please? Am I being a nuisance?''

''A nuisance?'' He set an arm about her shoulders and drew her against his side. And sure enough, she turned her cheek and nestled it against his shoulder. He swallowed. It would be so easy to forget, so easy to be enticed by an old dream. ''How could you be a nuisance?'' Before he could stop himself he fell into an old pattern of behavior. He rubbed his cheek lightly against her hair and then turned his head to kiss her cheek. Soft and warm.

''I'll get dressed, then,'' she said eagerly. ''I'll ring for Doris. Will you return in half an hour?'' She flushed and laughed. ''Maybe I do not usually send you away while I dress, do I? But forgive me. I feel shy.''

She lifted her face for his kiss, and he set his lips against hers and lingered there rather longer than was good for him.

''What do you want to see?'' he asked her half an hour later when he found her ready and waiting for him in her room. She looked delicate and beautiful in a sprigged muslin dress—part of the trousseau she had bought for her honeymoon with Poole.

''Everything,'' she said. ''But is the house too large for me to see everything at once?''

''I'll show you the larger apartments,'' he said. ''Just as if you were a traveler and wanted to see only the more magnificent parts of the house.''

''Very well,'' she said gaily, linking her arm through his. ''I am a visitor to these parts and a stranger to this house. You must give me the grand tour.''

He took her down the great staircase inside one of the towers, its broad stone stairs twisting downward, lit by the mullioned windows high in the tower.

''Sixteenth century,'' he told her. ''A little later than

the hall and some other parts of the house. Doubtless this stairway replaced a very steep and winding one."

"It is magnificent," she said. "Like a castle. *Is* this a castle?"

"Not really," he said. "More of a manor house. But of course the medieval occupants had to be ready to defend themselves."

They passed through the stone archway at the foot of the stairs into the great hall with its tiled floor, its huge fireplace, its high oak-timbered ceiling and whitewashed walls hung with armor and weapons of various kinds.

"Oh," she said, relinquishing her hold of his arm and turning about, looking first up to the ceiling and then at the walls. "This is where we live, Christopher? And I have forgotten it? Is this where your ancestors used to eat?"

"And live and sleep probably," he said. "The medieval hall served all functions. The great table is now in the state dining room—not the one we use every day. And there are never state occasions here. But it is impressive to have state apartments."

"Don't we ever entertain?" she asked him.

"Not on a large scale," he said. "This is a rather remote corner of Devonshire, remember."

She pulled a face. "No," she said. "That is one thing I cannot do. Remember?" And she laughed again. He could see that she was trying to make light of her affliction.

He took her into the great salon, never used in his father's time, though he and Nancy had always thought that it would make a wonderful ballroom. But there had never been balls at Penhallow during their lifetime. The room was sparsely furnished, but the huge Dutch tapestries covering the walls, all of them depicting scenes from mythology, gave the room a wonderful magnificence. Elizabeth stood in the middle of the room and looked about her in awe.

"You see?" she said at last, when she realized that he was looking at her, not the tapestries, "I am suitably impressed as a visitor, am I not? It is all glorious and all totally unfamiliar." Her smile slipped for a moment and she looked suddenly lost and a little frightened.

He hurried toward her.

"Christopher." She reached out her hands to his, and they were cold when he took them. "How can I have forgotten everything?"

"Try not to worry about it." He squeezed her hands.

"And yet," she said, looking at him earnestly, "that is not quite true, you know. I remember some things."

He felt suddenly as if his heart might beat its way right through his chest.

"London," she said. "I can picture it in my mind: St. Paul's Cathedral, Westminster Abbey, the river, Bond Street." She looked at him for several moments with a slight frown on her face. Then she shook her head. "But no people. Nothing personal."

"It will come, Elizabeth," he said soothingly.

"I remember the war too," she said, frowning again. "Napoleon Bonaparte. Our men in Spain. The war is over, is it not? He has been defeated. Where did I hear that?"

"It is true," he said. "Everything will come back gradually. Just give it time."

"Yes." She smiled and took him by surprise by slipping her hands from his and clasping them about his neck. She studied his face from arm's length away. "You are the most familiar thing in my world, Christopher," she said. "It feels right to be with you. I know that I love you. That is one comfort at least. It would be dreadful, would it not, if I shrank from you in fear."

His hands could still almost meet about her waist, he discovered, setting them there. And he could still drown in her eyes if he gazed into them for too long a time.

"I think," she said, "that I love you very dearly. Do I tell you that often enough? Perhaps after seven years of marriage I take too much for granted and forget to tell you."

"It always bears repeating," he said.

She stared at him for a while. "Well?" she said. "Are you not going to return the compliment?"

It was unavoidable. But strangely he did not even want to avoid the moment. Perhaps it was even true. But of course it could not be that. Except, he thought, that hatred and love were very similar emotions, only the negative and the positive separating them. But both deep, passionate, all-consuming emotions.

"I love you," he told her, his voice little more than a whisper.

"Did I force it from you?" Her smile was a little uncertain. "I am sorry. I should not have done so."

His arms wrapped themselves about her waist and he held her to him fiercely. "I love you," he said, and he drew back his head, looked down into her face, and kissed her.

He was in deep waters, he thought, drawing back his head after what had been far too lingering a kiss. Hellish deep waters. And yet he had foreseen it all even before telling her that she was his wife. But he had told her anyway. And he was not sure that he would do differently if he had that minute to live through again.

"Christopher," she said, lowering one arm to twist the top button of his waistcoat, "I feel better. Hardly any aches and pains; almost no headache; no dizziness."

"Good," he said, but he knew exactly where her words were leading.

"I think my life should return to normal," she said, and her eyes slid from the button up his chest and over his chin to lock on his. She flushed deeply. "I think I should return to our room tonight."

He drew a deep breath. "Perhaps we should give it a little longer," he said. "Your ribs were badly bruised, the doctor said. Besides, it might be difficult for you to sleep beside a stranger."

"I am trying to face the possibility that my memory will not return," she said. "The lump has almost disappeared from my head, but there is no memory except those useless details about London and the wars. I want to try to live as normally as I can, Christopher. If nothing else, I want to begin a whole new set of memories. Don't you want me back?"

For answer he drew her to him again and set his cheek against hers. "I want you back," he said. And he abandoned himself to the words he was speaking. It seemed almost as if his normal sensible self had been possessed by a madman. But the possession was not undesirable. Quite the contrary. The temptation to give in to it was overwhelming—as it had been from the moment when Wickenham had told him about her wedding.

"I'll have Doris move my things back into our room, then," she said.

God help him, but he found her words arousing. And he would allow it to happen too. Of course he would. Why else had he brought her to Penhallow? Why else had he told her that she was his wife? And why else had he told her that they shared a bedchamber?

He nodded and kissed her lightly once more. "This is enough exploring for one day," he said. "You must be getting tired. I'll take you to the drawing room for tea. Nancy should be back from her visit to the village by now."

"Tea sounds good," she said, taking his arm and allowing him to lead her from the room.

After tea Elizabeth left the drawing room before the other two. She wanted to summon Doris, she said, to move her things back to her regular dressing room. And she wanted to rest for a while. She was going to come to the dining room for dinner.

"Provided you will come to escort me," she said, smiling at Christopher as she got to her feet. "Otherwise I might be wandering around lost and hungry all evening."

But she would not allow him to take her back to the green bedchamber from the drawing room.

"I can remember the way," she said. "I have been looking about me very carefully all afternoon."

Nancy and Christopher were left alone.

"Whose suggestion was it?" Nancy asked him after the door had closed, her voice tense as it so often was these days. "Yours?"

"No," he said. "She wants life to return to normal. She has a great deal of courage, Nance. She has changed."

She laughed shortly. "To normal," she said scornfully. "So you are going to carry the deception to its bitter end, Christopher. What has happened to you? Have you been so embittered by the events of the past? I hoped you had put it all behind you."

"I would rather not talk about it," he said, his face shuttered and harsh. "It is my concern, not yours."

"Except that I have to lie for you," she said. "But

that is not the point. The point is, Christopher, that she is not your wife."

"She might have been," he said. "I did not acquiesce in anything that happened after I had left, Nance. And I would not have acquiesced if I had been consulted. What if I do not accept the way things turned out?"

"You have no choice in the matter," she said. "She is not your wife."

He looked at her, his eyes hostile.

"She will be in your room tonight believing that she is," Nancy continued. "If she were making a free choice, Christopher, I would say nothing though it would still be wrong and I would still disapprove. But she is not making a free choice. To do that she would have to be in possession of all the facts. And then she would not be directing Doris to move her things into your room, would she?"

"She was not in possession of all the facts seven years ago," he said. "She was not free to choose that time either. But she did choose. And Chicheley was there to make sure she chose the way he wanted her to choose. Don't talk to me of freedom, Nance. There is no such thing."

Nancy got to her feet. "I am going upstairs," she said. "There is a book I want to finish before dinner. And I can see there is no point in pursuing this conversation. Your mind is made up and your heart is hardened against decency. I have hated her too, Christopher, but I can see that I have never hated her as much as you do now."

He stared broodingly after her as she left the room.

7

ELIZABETH stood in the middle of Christopher's bedchamber—no, theirs—and looked about her almost fearfully. It was a large room, surely twice the size of the green bedchamber, and high. The ceiling was coved and painted blue and gold. Inside the large gilded circle in the center was a painting of two nymphs, all in shades of blue, silver, and white. The walls were covered with Brussels tapestries, which must be very old though their colors were fresh and bright. The high canopy of the bed reached up into the cove of the ceiling.

It was a magnificent room. But the curtains at the windows and the bed hangings were dark wine in color and heavy. So were the two chairs, arranged on either side of the fireplace. Too dark and too heavy for the room. They gave it a thoroughly masculine look. It was a man's room, not a married couple's.

Elizabeth wondered if she had ever suggested to Christopher that they change the furnishings. Perhaps they had argued over it? Perhaps he liked tradition and she liked light and beauty. Did they argue? she wondered. But they must do so if they had been together for so long. Surely they did not see eye to eye on every issue. Wouldn't their lives be dull if they did?

The bed was unusually wide. Another heirloom? Her cheeks grew hot as she looked at it and waited for him to come. Yet how foolish she was being. They had occupied that bed together for years. They had coupled there innumerable times.

Elizabeth gripped the fluted bedpost at the foot of the bed, set her forehead against it, and closed her eyes. Perhaps if she concentrated very hard there would be something. Some memory connected with this room that would spark all the other memories. The feel of the bedpost, perhaps. Yes, perhaps something as seemingly insignificant as that. She ran her hand down its smooth polished curves without opening her eyes. Or a memory of lovemaking. She pictured herself on the bed with him. She felt herself there. She felt him touch her. but it was only anticipation that she could feel, not memory.

And then a door opened and he came into the room. Presumably that door led into his dressing room—he wore only a nightshirt. She tried to feel familiarity with the moment. He had come through that door a thousand times before.

"Do you realize," she said, smiling to hide her embarrassment and shyness, "that you could have told me any story when I woke up without a memory? That if I were not your wife at all, you could have persuaded me that I was?"

He said nothing, but merely came to a stop a short distance from her and looked at her with expressionless eyes.

"I should not have said that," she said, closing the distance between them and touching him lightly on the chest. "Forgive me? I know that this is as difficult for you, Christopher, as it is for me. Oh dear, I feel as nervous as if this were my wedding night again."

He touched one of her cheeks with light fingertips.

"*Was* I nervous?" she asked him.

"Yes," he said. "Very. And so was I. We were both virgins."

"Were we?" She laughed softly. That is lovely, Christopher. I am glad there has only ever been each other."

His eyes looked deeply into hers. Yet she could not read his expression. Uncertainty, perhaps?

"Was it good?" she asked. "Our wedding night?"

He swallowed. "Yes and no," he said. "I was awkward and fumbling and I hurt you. But you held me afterward and kissed me and called me every love word ever invented when I showed my distress."

She set her face against his chest and breathed in the musky scent of him. "No," she said. "You are making that up, aren't you? About being upset?"

"I had hurt you," he said, "when I had been trying to love you. I wanted to be perfect for you. But it was better the next time."

She raised her head and looked into his eyes. "The same night?" she asked.

"The same night," he said. "I never told you that I was a virgin. I thought it shameful and unmanly, I suppose, at the age of twenty-four. You must have thought I was merely clumsy or insensitive."

"But you were sorry and in distress," she said. "I must have known."

"No." His eyes were almost hard suddenly. "You did not know."

She set the backs of her fingers against his cheek. "But it has been beautiful ever since, hasn't it?" she said. "It must have been. I feel that I love you so very much and you told me this afternoon that you love me. You do, don't you?"

"I do," he said.

"Make love to me, then," she said, her eyes dropping to his mouth, her voice suddenly breathless. "I am only sorry, Christopher, that I do not know what I usually do. I do not know how to please you."

He set his arms right about her then and hugged her to him. "You please me just by being," he said against her hair. His arms tightened. "Elizabeth, this does not seem fair. Making love to you when you do not know me, that is. Perhaps you would prefer to wait. I can be content just to hold you if it is what you wish."

"But I do know you," she said, clasping her arms about his neck and looking earnestly into his eyes. Let him not be reluctant, she prayed swiftly and silently. If he did not want her now, perhaps he never would as long as her memory was gone. And perhaps her courage would fail her entirely if it did not happen now. "I know you with my heart, Christopher. That may sound absurd, but I know that I have loved you for a long, long time. And I know that I will always love you. I want everything to be back to normal or as near normal as it can be. Your arms about me feel so right. *You* feel so right."

He looked into her eyes for a long moment. And she could see indecision there again, the indecision of a man who wanted to make love to a woman who could see him only as a stranger. But he was not a stranger. He was her husband. She lost her fear suddenly. He was her husband.

She smiled at him. "I want to know what my loss of memory has deprived me of," she whispered.

It had deprived her of the feel of his mouth open over hers, warm and moist, faintly wine-tasting, of his breath warm on her cheek, and his hand cupping the back of her head, his fingers pushing up beneath her hair. And of his tongue, outlining her lips so lightly that sensation sizzled through her before it explored its slow and exquisite way deep into her mouth.

And loss of memory had deprived her of the feel of his hands exploring her body with light, feathering touches, beginning to arouse it for love.

"Oh, Christopher," she said when his mouth moved down over her chin to her throat, "how very beautiful it is. May I touch you too? I don't know what I am supposed to do." There was anguish in her voice as well as longing.

He lifted his head and kissed her eyes and her mouth again. "Touch me," he said, and she could see in his face and hear in his voice that he wanted her, that all indecision had gone. "Do whatever seems right and good. There are no taboos between us."

And so she touched him, feeling the powerful muscles of his shoulders and arms, the firm muscles of his chest and flat stomach. He must work hard, she thought, not spend all his time about the house with her as he had in the past few days. She must ask him how he usually spent his days.

But the thought and the intent barely touched her conscious mind. She pulsed with longing for him and made no resistance when he raised her nightgown up her body and off over her head, or when he lifted her into his arms and laid her on the bed. She watched him as he stripped away his nightshirt, and raised her arms to him.

"You are beautiful," she said, her eyes roaming over the splendid proportions of his body.

"And you," he said, lowering himself on top of her, twining his hands in her hair, laying his mouth against hers. "You are lovelier than you were as a bride, Elizabeth. You were only a girl then. You are a woman now."

She was frightened then, suddenly and unaccountably. Frightened of his weight and of his nakedness against her own. Frightened of the intensity in his eyes and the demand of his mouth. And convinced that her joke when he had entered the bedchamber must be true. She did not know this man. Or this place. Or this act.

"No!" she cried, struggling against him in her panic. "No, no."

He rolled off her immediately and lay at her side, one arm beneath her neck, his breathing labored. He had turned suddenly pale. His eyes had gone blank again.

She bit her lower lip hard.

"Hush," he said, his voice gentle, at variance with the harsh discipline of his face. He pulled the blankets up over her breasts. "It's all right. I am not going to force you into anything you do not want. I'll hold you. Just relax. Sleep if you can."

She closed her eyes and buried her face against his shoulder. She could hear his heart thudding against his chest. "I am so frightened," she whispered.

"You need not be." His voice was calm and quiet against her ear. "I'll just hold you. Or I'll move to another room if you wish."

"No, not of that," she said. "Just of having to face life like this—perhaps forever. I don't even know who I am apart from your wife. I don't know anything of my own family or where I lived. Or even what my name was before I married you. I'm sorry. I'm so sorry. I thought I had these panics under control. They are so pointless really."

"Sh," he said, and he kissed her on the ear and on the temple, and circled her warmly with his arms.

She felt unutterably sad. They were husband and wife. They loved each other. Their marriage had a seven-year history. But she was going to ruin it all because of an accident and because she did not have the courage to deal with such a frightening situation. She turned her head and kissed his throat and his chin. And his mouth when he moved his head.

"Yes," she said. "I want you, Christopher. And I think I need you. Come inside me. Please come inside. Help me deal with the loneliness. And let me give you some pleasure."

The passion of their earlier embrace had gone. In its place was something infinitely more wonderful, she discovered when he rolled her over onto her back and covered her again. In its place was tenderness and gentleness and love. Marital love.

He pressed his knees between hers and slid her legs wide and positioned himself. And he raised himself on his elbows and looked into her eyes, his own filled with such yearning that she caught her lower lip between her teeth again. And then she closed her eyes as he came into her, slowly and deeply.

All doubts fled. All the foolish doubts. This was the way it was, the way it should be. The only way it could be. Her husband inside her, beginning to love her.

"Yes," she whispered to him without opening her eyes. "Yes, Christopher."

And then his weight came back onto her and his palms came flat against hers and spread her arms wide on the bed so that she was spread-eagled beneath him, and he began to work in her with steady, rhythmic strokes that had her body first humming with pleasure and then aching with longing and finally taut with need.

"Come," he said at last, his voice deep against her ear. "Come with me. All the way."

And she came, trusting him because he was her husband and they loved each other. She shuddered beneath him while his hands pressed down on hers and his seed sprang deep in her body. And she called out his name. And shivered into stillness and sleep beneath his weight.

She awoke only when hands were covering her with the blankets again and one arm was sliding about her shoulders.

"Mm," she said, giving in to the pleasure of lethargy and letting him settle her damp body against his. "Is it always this good?"

"It always seems better than the time before," he said.

"Ten years from now it will be quite unbearably sweet, then," she said and slid back into sleep.

It was quite early in the morning. Christopher could tell that by the quality of light penetrating the heavy velvet curtains at the window. But he wanted to get up. He wanted to start using some of the pent-up energy that had found little outlet during the long sea crossing and the days since his landing. He was not accustomed to idleness. He did not enjoy it.

And yet it was ironic that he should feel so full of energy on this of all mornings. He had not had a great deal of sleep. Or relaxation. He had worked hard during the lengthy periods of wakefulness. She did not come easily, he had discovered during the two encounters that had followed that first. She was quickly aroused but seemed a little uneasy about her response, or even ashamed of it. He had had to take her slowly each time, bringing her to the brink of release with patience and skill. He had not wanted to come alone. Not with her. It had never mattered with other women—and there had been many women in Canada and America. But with her it did matter. And so each time he had held himself back and coaxed her over the edge of passion with him. Each time when she had finally come, it had been with a shattering intensity.

It had been a delirious night of sex—with a woman who was not his wife. Although—no, she was not his wife.

And now he was vigorous with energy. And determined to get up and start learning about his inheritance and taking responsibility for it. Penhallow had been well run for years by stewards, the Archers, father and son. But Christopher was a businessman. He was accustomed to having firsthand knowledge of his business dealings and very often an active hand in their workings. He was used to managing his own affairs. The knowledge that Penhallow was now his filled him with exhilaration. And today, he thought, he was going to begin learning the workings of this new business.

His hand was stroking absently through the silky tangles of Elizabeth's hair, his fingertips massaging the back of her head. She was fast asleep on top of him, her body warm and relaxed, her legs spread on either side of his. He was still nestled warmly inside her from their last loving. He turned her slowly and carefully to set her on the bed beside him, disengaging his body from hers as he did so. He did not want to wake her. The only less than perfect parts of the night, he had found, had been her awakenings. Each time he had searched her eyes for awareness—and each time there had been none.

She woke now. Her eyes opened. But they were languorous and smiling—the eyes of a woman who had been loved well and thoroughly through the night. She sighed with contentment.

He leaned over her and kissed her mouth. "Go back to sleep," he murmured. "I am going to ride into the village to see Archer—my steward. I have been neglecting estate business for the past several days. I will be back for luncheon. This afternoon we'll go to the beach. Shall we?"

"Mm," she said. "Christopher? Was I all right? I mean, was I a disappointment to you? Different from usual? Not as good?"

He kissed her again. "Did I act like a man who was disappointed?" he asked. "You are merely fishing for compliments. You know very well how wonderful you were. Go back to sleep."

"Later," she said, closing her eyes and turning into the warmth of the pillow where his head had been, "you must tell me how we met, Christopher. But I am so very glad we did."

She was sleeping by the time he got out of bed and looked down at her again. The blankets covered her only to the waist. She was gloriously beautiful, her breasts generous but firm. She would surely cover herself with haste, he thought, if she knew just how unaccustomed his eyes were to the sight of her.

And his body to the feel of her.

He was more convinced than ever, gazing down at her before turning sharply away, that there was little to distinguish the emotions of love and hatred. He hated her this morning both because of what she had done to him in the past and because she had caused him to hate and despise himself for last night's happenings. And yet . . . it was a hatred that felt very like love.

Nancy was an early riser and had breakfasted with her brother, but she joined Elizabeth later in the breakfast room and sat down to drink a cup of coffee with her.

Elizabeth was radiant. If she had stood on the table and shouted out that she had spent the night in Christopher's bed, the truth could not have been more obvious than it was just from the look of her. Nancy felt uncomfortable.

"Nancy," Elizabeth said, leaning forward in her chair,

smiling, "I have noticed that you do everything in the house. You consult with Mrs. Clavell and you go down to the kitchen each morning to discuss the day's menu with the cook, don't you? Do you always do those things? Or do I? Or do we share?" She flushed suddenly and looked anxious.

"You have been sick," Nancy said. "I—"

Elizabeth covered her hand with her own. "I know," she said. "And you have been wonderful to me, Nancy. I don't want to give the impression that I am jealous or resent your taking charge. I don't. But what is the usual arrangement? I know that there can be friction when two women share the same house. Has there ever been friction between us? I do hope not. I like you very much. I hope I always have."

Nancy was feeling angry. She had always been mistress of Penhallow. For the past year since her father's death she had run the house singlehanded and had kept an eye on estate business too. How dare a stranger—a total stranger—come there and try to take over.

But Elizabeth was the victim of a deception to which she, Nancy, had consented, however reluctantly. And it was very hard to dislike her although Nancy had been very prepared to do just that.

"We are friends," she said, swallowing her anger, "and sisters. We seem not to have any rules about who runs the house. I had not thought of it until you mentioned it now. But everything has always worked smoothly and we have never yet had to resort to pulling out each other's hair." She was not good at lying. She could not think fast and she was not sure she had a good enough memory to remain consistent.

Anger rose in her again, but this time it was all directed against her brother. Elizabeth seemed to have matured into a sweet and kind and fair-minded woman. The sweetness had always been there, though it had used to be combined with a meek dependence on her family and a tendency to turn to them at every crisis.

"I must do something," Elizabeth said. "I think I like to keep busy. I do, don't I? I was not made for an idle life."

Nancy smiled. "Why don't you take a week off?" she said. "I know Christopher is concerned about you and wants to spend some time with you. Relax with him and get to feel familiar with your surroundings again. Just for a week. By that time your memory will probably have returned."

"I hope so," Elizabeth said. And the glow came back to her eyes. "I'll spend the week with Christopher, then, if you don't mind, Nancy. We are going to the beach this afternoon."

"You will love it," Nancy said. "You always have."

"Is there no one special in your life?" Elizabeth asked. "You are so beautiful, Nancy, and so kind. You must be lonely here with only Christopher and me. Or is there someone?"

"I have no interest in men," Nancy said briskly. "Or in marrying. I am happy as I am."

"I am sorry." Elizabeth grimaced. "I have touched a raw nerve. If I just had my memory, I would not have been so tactless. Forgive me?"

"There is nothing to forgive," Nancy said, getting to her feet. "There is no one. I spoke the truth. Would you like to stroll in the garden and maybe along the valley? The trees are lovely at this time of year—all fresh and new."

"Yes," Elizabeth said. "I need air and exercise. I'll go fetch a cloak."

She was feeling envious, Nancy thought incredulously. She had seen Christopher earlier and now Elizabeth and instead of feeling outrage at what they had so obviously been doing through the night, she was feeling—envy.

Sometimes, she thought, armor did not protect as well as it was supposed to do. She had a seven-year armor about herself, but it had been pierced by one look at the face of a woman who had just emerged from a night of passion. And a night of forbidden passion at that.

Her thoughts went back, as they rarely did, to that spring of her come-out. To all the magical excitement of it. And the unexpected success of it. She had been twenty years old, well past the accepted age for a come-out. Christopher had gone up to London after finishing university at Oxford and had persuaded their Aunt Hilda, their mother's sister, to sponsor Nancy for a Season. And so she had had what she had always dreamed of, though she had never expected it or asked it of her father.

Over the years she had persuaded herself that that Season had not been so wonderful after all. That the life had not really suited her. Penhallow was where she belonged, where she was happy. London had merely been a dizzying and pleasant interlude.

Oh, but it had been wonderful. And wonderful to see Christopher as dazzled and as excited as she. At her very first ball her card had filled up by the time the third set began. There had been gentlemen wanting to drive her in the park and walk with her there and escort her to the theater and the opera. There had been bouquets of flowers.

There had been John Ward, Elizabeth's elder brother. Captain John Ward, Viscount Aston. And then Martin Honywood.

And finally her flight back home to don the armor. And to convince herself and everyone else that this was where she wanted to be and that a life alone was what she wanted. And it was true. Anything else was out of the question. She had a circle of friends and acquaintances around Penhallow, but she was distrustful of social contact beyond that circle. And the gentlemen she knew had learned that they must not try to come too close either to her person or to her heart.

But sometimes she felt envy. Elizabeth was a victim of her own loss of memory and of Christopher's ruthlessness and should not be envied. But how wonderful it must be, Nancy thought somewhat wistfully as she hurried upstairs to get her own cloak, to be free—physically and mentally and emotionally free—to enjoy making love with a man. Perhaps if she could lose her own memory . . .

A thoroughly foolish and distasteful thought!

8

CHRISTOPHER took Elizabeth up the hill behind the house, walking slowly so as not to tire her, though she claimed to be feeling quite fit again. He turned her at the top and let her arm drop away from his so that he might encircle her waist with his arm and draw her against his side. They looked down at the house and the valley. "There is quite a contrast between here and there, don't you think?" he said. "That is part of the charm of Penhallow, I always think. It is rather like an oasis in the desert. Though I suppose that is a poor image when the sea is so close."

"I walked partway along the valley this morning with Nancy," she said. "But not too far. She was afraid I would tire."

"You get on well with Nancy?" he asked.

She turned her head sharply and looked up at him. "Yes," she said. "Am I not supposed to? Do we not normally agree?"

"Of course you do," he said.

"But it is strange." She frowned. "We are two women living in the same house, she by right of birth, me by right of marriage, and yet there is no definite arrangement about who is the real mistress of the house—or so she told me this morning. Everything works amicably. It does not sound quite possible. Has it been difficult, Christopher? Have we been like two cats with claws bared? Have you been caught in the middle?"

"Nothing like that," he said. "Are you jealous of her now that you cannot remember how it was, Elizabeth?"

"I am very fond of her," she said. "She has shown a great deal of patience with me. I would hate to think that normally things are not so good between us. But perhaps we can learn from this experience. Perhaps I can learn to value her as she deserves to be valued—if it turns out that I did not do so before, that is.''

''You think I am lying to you?'' he asked, hugging her tightly to his side.

''No,'' she said. ''But shielding me from the full truth, perhaps. Everything you and Nancy have told me has made our lives sound perfect—as if we have had wonderful, trouble-free relationships. You and I have a seven-year marriage still being lived in the happily ever after. It does not sound quite real. Oh, I believe it in the main. I believe we love each other and are happy together. I feel that that must be so. But there must have been troubles too. We would not be human otherwise. We would not have been able to grow. We would have remained children. Was I only eighteen when we married? Tell me about some of the troubles.''

He turned her again and they strolled over the coarse grass of the plateau toward the top of the cliffs. He did not speak for a while and she wondered if she had hurt or even angered him. He had tried so hard in the past week to quell her fears, to reassure her that all was well with her life even if she could not remember it.

''I told you about our wedding night,'' he said. ''That was not quite idyllic. The first few months of our marriage were not. We had both spent lonely, sheltered childhoods. Neither of us was quite ready for the responsibilities of marriage or the adjustments to an intimate relationship that marriage involved. They were not easy months.''

''Tell me about them,'' she said. ''Perhaps they were not easy, but surely they were of value. We must have grown beyond them to our present contentment.''

''You had always been closely protected by your family,'' he said. ''They all liked to live your life for you. From the best of motives perhaps. But you did not know how to cope alone. You used to turn to them sometimes instead of to me. And you were dismayed or sometimes defiant when I complained about it.''

''How insufferable I must have been,'' she said.

''I had known no other women but Nancy,'' he said. ''I was shy and bewildered and hid my inadequacies behind frowns and morose moods and attempts to appear very stern and masculine.''

She laughed. "How insufferable you must have been," she said.

"We would have been a disaster together," he said, "but for the fact that we loved each other. And were also a little afraid of each other. I was afraid that I would never learn to protect you and hold your trust as well as your family had always done. And I think you were afraid that you could never measure up to my expectations. I think you thought I was an experienced man of the world. I tried to make you believe that, foolish puppy that I was."

"Oh, Christopher," she said, "you can remember all the pain of having lived through those months. I cannot, and I think the story charming. Charming in the sense that we must have had strengths of character that were not apparent at the time. We grew up and learned to shape a successful marriage despite everything. We can be proud of that. And so we can be confident of overcoming any trouble to our marriage, including this one."

He drew her to a halt and looked down into her eyes. "This must be distressing to you," he said, "but it need not be a trouble. I think we are working through it rather well, don't you?"

She touched his face. "Are there other troubles that we were working through?" she asked. "That we will have to face again when I remember?"

He lowered his head and kissed her, drawing her tightly into his arms. There was something a little desperate about his embrace. "Nothing," he said. "We are together. That is the only fact of any importance. You might have died in that accident."

She felt a wave of panic suddenly. There was something after all. Some lack of ease. But he was right. They were together and she knew that they loved each other.

"And whatever it may be," she said, "we will work it out, Christopher. Again and again throughout our marriage. We will continue to grow together and deepen our commitment to each other."

"You have changed," he said. "Since I first knew you, that is. Thinking back on the way you were makes me realize that."

They came very quickly to the top of the cliffs, to the point at which the coarse grass and yellow gorse bushes gave way quite suddenly to a sheer drop and there was nothing before their feet but emptiness and the sea far below, blue and sparkling in the sunshine.

She drew in her breath sharply and let it out slowly again. "Ah," she said, "how can I have forgotten this? It is magnificent. It is creation at its wildest and most beautiful."

"It's home," he said, tightening his clasp on her waist as if he half expected her to take a step forward and disappear forever from his grasp.

"Perhaps that is the very reason why I cannot remember it," she said. "It is too close to me, too personal. Unlike London and the wars. I know of those but I cannot place myself in relation to either. Almost as if I were a disembodied spirit." She looked down at her feet. "I really do have substance, don't I?" She laughed.

"I would have to say a definite yes to that," he said, "if I think back to last night. There was nothing disembodied about you then."

"It was wonderful, wasn't it?" she said. "My only memory of our making love. As if it were the first and only time."

"We will have to pile up more such memories for you in the nights to come," he said.

"Mm. Yes, please," she said, laying her cheek against his shoulder and laughing softly. "I think there are some advantages to a memory loss, Christopher. Not many, it is true. But it is as well to be able to look on the bright side, I suppose. To me our marriage is an idyll. A honeymoon. You can remember all the troubles and you know that even now everything is not perfect between us but that there is something to be worked out when I remember. But for me there is only perfection—your gentleness and patience with me since I woke up with a headache like an erupting volcano. And last night. And now this afternoon. I am having the honeymoon that we seem not to have had when we were first married."

He turned his head and found her lips with his again. "Do you want to go down to the beach?"

"Is it possible?" she asked. "Do we hold our noses and jump?"

"There is a path," he said, laughing. She was totally distracted for a moment by the sight of his face lit up with amusement, of the laugh lines at the outer corners of his eyes, of his white and even teeth. It was only then that she realized he rarely smiled. "If you are good, I shall lead you down it."

"How good do you want me to be?" she asked.

But he merely smiled at her again, took her hand, and led her off to their right.

She felt frightened again suddenly—a feeling that she could not escape entirely, it seemed, a feeling that leapt at her every few hours whether she tried to keep it at bay or not. There was something between them. All was not as wonderful as it seemed. But she was not going to give in to fear or gloom. They would solve whatever the problem was. They had done it at the start of their marriage and they must have done it since. They would do it again. After all, was not that what life and relationships were all about?

In the meanwhile, since she had no choice in the matter anyway, she would accept her loss of memory and enjoy the unexpected honeymoon it had brought to their marriage. She did not know much about herself, but she knew enough to understand that life did not have unlimited happiness to offer even to the most fortunate of people. Happiness had to be seized when it was available and enjoyed to the full. Only so could one endure the miseries and hardships that were also one's lot in life.

She grasped his hand a little more tightly.

Christopher knew that he had complicated his life quite hopelessly. Whether she regained her memory or not, he had got himself into a mess. He could not keep her ignorant forever. Sooner or later he was going to have to tell her the whole truth. And at any moment she might remember it all for herself.

His life had been complicated in another way too. He had never intended to become involved with Elizabeth again. Oh, he had wanted to prove his innocence to her, yes, partly for pride's sake and partly to punish her, to show her what she had lost through her lack of trust. But he had been convinced that he hated her, that he wanted nothing more to do with her.

And yet now he was very involved with her again and not at all sure whether to try to extricate himself if it were possible to do so or to grasp the moment and enjoy what chance had offered him.

It seemed that he was doing the latter without ever having made a firm decision to do so. The temptation was too great—the temptation to forget the past as she had been forced to do and seize the pleasure of the present. There was a great deal of pleasure to be derived from Elizabeth's company, he was discovering.

For this afternoon at least he was going to live the fantasy—if he could. This evening he would decide how best to proceed.

"It is easy to stumble on these rocks," he said, turning to her when they reached the bottom of the steep path from the cliff top to the beach. And he swung her up into his arms and carried her over the shifting stones and pebbles down onto the sand of the beach, where he set her on her feet again.

"Was that an excuse?" she asked, and her eyes laughed up into his.

"An excuse?"

"To hold me in your arms," she said.

"I was merely being a gentleman," he said, making her an elegant bow. He knew that she was drawing answering smiles from him. He ought not to smile, he knew.

She laughed again. It was almost a giggle and he was reminded of the eighteen-year-old Elizabeth he had known—very often laughing when she was not worrying over something.

"Do we now walk sedately along the beach?" she asked. "Is that what we usually do?" But her eyes were dancing with merriment, and she caught up her cloak and dress suddenly so that she would not trip over them and turned without warning to run away from him. "I'll race you to the water's edge," she threw back over her shoulder.

The tide was out as far as it could go. Beyond the band of soft sand beneath the cliffs, the beach was flat and hard where the water covered it at full tide. He waited for her to reach the hard sand before taking off after her. And he watched her incredulously. This was Elizabeth as she had become? Carefree despite the great burden of her affliction? Had she gained so much strength of character over the years?

He let her stay ahead of him until they were close to the edge of the water and she was convinced she was going to win the race. She looked over her shoulder, her cheeks flushed from the wind and her exertions. She was laughing. And then with a few yards left to go, he scooped her up into his arms again and continued on until his boots bogged down in the spongy sand at the water's edge.

"You are not going to throw me in, are you?" she asked, clinging to his neck, laughing.

"You would make a lovely splash," he said. "And you did lose the race. I think I will."

"But you won't," she said.

"Why not?"

"For two reasons," she said. "You would be splashed too and I would make too cold and soggy an armful afterward."

"Maybe I would not want to get close enough to find out," he said.

"Oh, yes, you would," she said.

"Would I?"

"Yes." Her eyes were on his lips, and then she nuzzled her face against his neck, kissed him below his ear, and nipped his earlobe with her teeth.

He took a few steps back onto firmer sand and set her down on her feet. "You have convinced me," he said, kissing her firmly on the lips, darting his tongue into her mouth, and deciding regretfully that it was neither the time nor the place.

They each set an arm about the other's waist, she laid her head against his shoulder, and they strolled along the beach, keeping close to the edge of the water, talking nonsense or, more often, keeping to a companionable silence.

Almost as if it were all real, he thought. Almost as if the past could be wiped out with a single knock on the head. Almost as if he could forget too.

"Christopher," she asked finally, "why do we not have children?"

The slight breathlessness of her voice told him that the question had been in her mind for some time, that it was one that bothered her. He could think of no immediate answer to give. The question had taken him totally by surprise. *Because I have been in Canada and America for seven years and you have been in England?*

"Have there been any?" she asked. "Any stillbirths or miscarriages? Or deaths?"

"No," he said. "None."

"Ah," she said quietly. "I have hit a raw nerve again, haven't I? It is something that has saddened us? I have been unable to give you an heir or other children."

He closed his eyes tightly. "It doesn't matter, Elizabeth," he said. "I have you. You are all I need."

"You must have said that many times over the years," she said sadly. "And I must have been as hard to convince all those times as I am now. I cannot be all you need. And perhaps you cannot be all I need."

They had stopped walking and he had turned her into his arms. Their lighthearted mood had disappeared. "It is something we have never allowed to cloud our happiness," he said. "And we must not allow it to now. Anyway, it could still happen. You are still young."

He turned cold inside. It was something that had not even crossed his mind the night before. He had always felt it safe to assume that women knew how to take care of themselves and prevent conception. But Elizabeth would not know. And three times the night before he had filled her with his seed. He wanted to ask her where she was in her monthly cycle, but it was not a question he could ask under the circumstances. Besides, she would not know.

"Oh, Christopher," she said, gazing up into his eyes, "there is so much I do not know. There must be so many layers to our lives and to our relationship. So many complexities. And all I can see is the topmost layer—the icing but not the cake. But icing can taste too sweet and too sickly without the cake to go with it."

"These days have been too sweet?" he asked her.

"I don't know," she said. "Have they? But then a honeymoon is meant to be sweet. Can we start again, Christopher, if my memory never comes back? Or will we always be haunted by a past I cannot remember?"

"Let's take it one day at a time, shall we?" he suggested, tightening his arms about her. "One hour at a time? The past is gone whether it is remembered or not, Elizabeth, and the future is all ahead of us and may never come. But today is ours. And today we are together and love each other. Don't we?'' God help him, he thought, he was not consciously lying.

''Yes.'' She turned her head to set her cheek against his shoulder, and closed her eyes. ''Yes, we do. I have spoiled the afternoon, haven't I? We were so very carefree and foolish. Kiss me again.'' She raised her face to him and smiled.

''So that all the world can line up on top of the cliffs and watch us?'' he said. ''Shame on you.''

She looked up to the cliff top and laughed. ''The world must be busy doing other things,'' she said. ''You see? There is no one there. But as you wish—take me somewhere more private and kiss me.''

''There is a sizable cave beneath the cliffs,'' he said.

Her eyes widened. ''A smugglers' cave?'' she asked, and her eyes sparkled.

''With chests of forgotten treasure left behind?'' he said. ''Alas, no. Merely a lovers' cave.''

''Ah,'' she said. ''This sounds good.''

He turned to walk her up the beach, rather more briskly than they had been strolling. He and Nancy had used the cave countless times as children for games of smugglers and pirates and sometimes house and school. They had always felt shut off from the world when inside it, though the mouth was wide and only a large boulder several feet in front of it prevented it from being quite open to the beach.

''Oh,'' Elizabeth said, rounding the boulder and stopping at the entrance to the cave. ''Yes, a lovers' cave indeed. Do we come here often? Do we make love here?''

''Actually,'' he said, ''we never have. We have been too decorous, maybe, and too sensible. We will be horribly covered with sand if we make love here—and we have a perfectly serviceable bed only a mile away. Of course . . .''

''Of course,'' she said, smiling up at him and setting her hands on his shoulders, ''there is plenty of water at Penhallow with which to wash the sand away.''

''You completed my thought for me,'' he said, grinning at her and undoing the clasp of his cloak and spreading it on the soft dry sand of the cave floor.

This was Elizabeth, his mind told him, openly propositioning him, smiling at him enticingly, wanting him. Her eyes were growing dreamy with desire. She had changed so much, though whether the changes had come before or after the bump on the head he could not be sure.

He drew her into his arms, tossed her cloak aside, and laid her down on his, lifting her skirt to her waist as he did so. He knelt beside her and removed her shoes and stockings and her undergarments. He was going to make love to her again, he thought. For the fourth time in twenty-four hours. He was going to spill his seed in her again.

He closed his mind yet again to guilt and to fear of the very possible consequences.

"Didn't we come here to kiss?" she asked as he adjusted his own clothing and lifted himself over her. She positioned herself so that she cradled him between hips and thighs.

"Yes," he said, bringing his mouth to hers. "That too."

She sighed against his mouth and sucked inward on his tongue as he came into her body without more foreplay. He moved in her, marveling at the fact that she was wet and ready for him.

He could hear the calling of the gulls and the roar of the breakers as he loved her, heralding the fact that the tide was on the turn. He could smell the sea, and he could taste its saltiness on Elizabeth's lips. And sand, he discovered, even dry and soft sand, made a hard enough mattress and did not yield to the thrustings of his body. He had to cushion her with hands cupped beneath her buttocks. He could feel sand gritty against his knees and against the backs of his hands despite the cloak he had spread beneath them.

And yet it was all wonderfully erotic. The moist heat in which he was sheathed, the soft shapeliness of her body beneath his, her warm and searching mouth. He willed himself not to come too soon. But she was moving to his rhythm, and her legs had twined themselves about his, and her hands had found their way beneath his shirt and were raking at his back. And she was moaning.

"Yes," she was whispering into his mouth. "Yes. Oh, yes, yes. Please, yes."

She came without any coaxing on his part, exploding about him, clinging to him, crying out. He held her close, letting her enjoy her climax and relax into the lethargy that followed it before bringing his own pleasure to completion. She lay relaxed beneath him and held him with arms and legs while he did so.

"If that is your way of kissing," she said a long time later, after he had moved to her side, "I like it. And I can see why it needed more privacy than the water's edge."

She was smiling and totally at her ease with him despite the broad daylight and the fact that her clothes were either off altogether or bunched up above her waist. She was totally trusting, he thought, believing implicitly that they had been married and intimate together for seven years.

How could he put an end to it now that he had allowed it to start? How could he tell her the truth after they had lived for a night and a day as man and wife? After he had put her in danger four times of having to bear his child? More to the point, perhaps, how could he bear to end it now that he had started it?

"I suppose we should make ourselves respectable and see if we have enough energy left to climb up that path again," he said against her ear.

"Mm," she said, a sound that was more a purr than anything else. "Have we really never made love here before, Christopher? How slow we have been. It was wonderful. I don't want to leave yet. Is there any hurry?"

"No," he said, settling his cheek against the top of her head. No, there was no hurry. Soon enough reality was going to break in on their idyll. "No. We can stay here forever if you want."

"Mm," she said with a sigh of contentment.

They did not fall asleep, but they lay in a state of pleasant languor, her hand circling his chest lazily beneath his shirt, his own brushing over her hip and her buttock and the top of her leg.

"Christopher," she said at last, "let's always remember the magic of these days when I have regained my memory—do you notice how I so positively say *when* and not *if*? Whatever difficulties there have been or will be, let's remember that it can be like this between us. Shall we? I know we need everyday problems and difficulties to enable us to grow, but we also need times like this. Times to show us that nothing matters really except being together and loving each other. Life is so precious and love is so precious. Let's make a pact that we will always remember."

"Pact," he agreed, but her words chilled rather than warmed him.

She turned her face up to smile at him. "Kiss me again," she said, but the sparkle of mischief in her eyes told him that she was asking for more than a mere meeting of mouths.

His hand moved around her leg to her inner thigh and upward to the moist heat and the core of her femininity.

"If you insist," he said and watched her eyes grow dreamy with passion as his fingers began to work on her with the experience of years, preparing her for penetration again.

And his seed again.

9

MARTIN had not received any positive encouragement from his inquiries along the docks and wharves of the Thames. But then there was no positive discouragement either. Two ships had arrived from America within the past two weeks, none from Canada. The one ship had carried no passenger by the name of Christopher Atwell, and no Earl of Trevelyan either. The second ship had needed extensive repairs, and the crew had been disbanded until it was needed again. Even the captain had left his ship, apparently to visit his mother-in-law in Portsmouth.

Martin sent Macklin in search of Captain Jamie Rice in Portsmouth, and proceeded to wait with growing impatience for the return of his servant. The Bow Street Runners in the meantime had turned up nothing, as Martin had expected. They appeared to be involved in a long and pointless search for a carriage and horses no one had witnessed.

Finally Macklin returned.

"I thought perhaps you had taken ship to America to find Captain Rice there," Martin said coldly to his unfortunate servant. "I thought I might have to wait until next summer for my reply."

Finding a ship's captain in Portsmouth, Macklin reported, was rather like finding a needle in a haystack, especially when Captain Rice did not have a home of his own there and bore a different name from that of the lady he was visiting. And then when the house had finally been located, it was found to be empty, Captain Rice and his mother-in-law having left to visit another relative who lived in a fishing village fifteen miles away. And then the captain had not wanted to talk to Macklin, certainly not to divulge the passenger list of his last voyage.

Martin interrupted the rambling tale. "I assume that money eventually talked," he said. "And I sent you with a bundle. What was his answer?"

"There were a Mr. Christopher Atwell on board during his last crossing, sir," the servant said, "but no Earl of Trevelyan."

Martin's eyes gleamed with triumph. "One out of the two is quite good enough," he said, and he crossed his room to a small bureau, handed a roll of banknotes to the man, and sent him on his way before smiling with satisfaction and slamming one of his fists into the palm of the other hand.

"I knew it," he muttered to the empty room. With the passing of the days he had become more and more convinced that Atwell's—Trevelyan's—return could be the only explanation for Elizabeth's disappearance without trace. The fact that he had indeed returned just a day or two before the wedding was too much of a coincidence for there to be no connection between it and her kidnapping.

Martin had found her at last. He was in no doubt that Trevelyan would have taken her to Penhallow. It was said to be a lonely and remote place, more of a medieval castle than a civilized gentleman's home. That was where he would have taken her. Martin was so sure of the fact that he changed his earlier plan, which was to send someone down to Devonshire to discover if they were there. Precious days would be lost with that plan, he decided. He would go himself.

And yet it did not take many minutes for his early elation to fade. He had found her, yes, or he was almost convinced that he had found her. But she had been gone for almost two weeks. And all that time she had been with Trevelyan. The two of them had been alone together on a lonely estate.

Martin clenched his fists until his knuckles were white. What was the explanation? Was she being kept there against her will? If so, was she being molested? Or was she staying there from choice? She had come to hate Trevelyan over the years, but then hatred could be a more dangerous emotion than indifference. And she had been besotted with him once. What if she were staying there from choice? Martin almost preferred the mental image of her confined in a dungeon.

He was breathing in short gasps. If there was one man he had hated more than any other during his life it was Trevelyan. Atwell had been twenty-four years old when he had met Elizabeth for the first time, and he had thought within no time at all that he could lay claim to her love, that he could carry her off to live with him for a lifetime. And she—sweet impressionable Lizzie—had fallen for dark good looks and sweet words of love and had forgotten those who had loved her all her life.

Well, Martin thought, stretching out his fingers and flexing them, he had rescued her once. He would rescue her again—even if she was staying willingly at Penhallow. But he did not think that was the case. Elizabeth had done a great deal of growing up in seven years and was not nearly as impressionable as she had used to be. Even he, Martin, did not have as much influence over her as he had once had.

He and Macklin would be leaving for Devonshire at first light tomorrow, he decided.

Two weeks after her accident had robbed her of all personal memories, Elizabeth felt more than ever that icing could be too sweet without the cake to go with it. And a honeymoon could be too sweet when there was no courtship, no relationship, no wedding to precede it. The two weeks had been too sweet. She felt guilty and ungrateful for thinking so because undoubtedly the sweetness had been wonderful.

In many ways those days had been an idyll. She had nothing to do but gradually to relearn her surroundings and become reacquainted with those she loved. Christopher spent the mornings about the estate with his steward, but he devoted the rest of each day and all of the nights to her. They walked and rode and talked and laughed. And loved. Physically and every other way there was to love. They were deeply in love—she knew that she was not alone in her feelings. They were like young lovers, new to each other and new to the emotion.

It was wonderful. It was delirious. Though she tried very hard sometimes to remember, to trick or jolt her memory back, she also dreaded remembering. For they could not be in love in quite the way they were now, and she was afraid of what the reality might be. Perhaps their love had matured into something deeper and more lasting than that wild youthful passion they were experiencing now. Or perhaps it had cooled and become something mundane and dull. Perhaps they both felt their marriage to be empty with no children to give it depth.

She dreaded remembering. She wanted things to remain as they were now. Forever. And yet she was not quite happy even now and felt guilty for her unhappiness. Everything was too sweet, too perfect, too—oh, it was too much without challenge. Both Nancy and Christopher were protecting her as if she were a fragile doll or as if she were—a prisoner.

The thought made Elizabeth unhappy with guilt. How could she feel confined when they were both so good to her?

They both protested against her leaving the estate. Elizabeth wanted to go visiting with Nancy. She wanted to go to church with Christopher. It was true that she would not know friends and neighbors she was expected to know, she admitted when they voiced that objection, but people would understand when the facts were explained to them. She would have to get to know them again some time if her memory was not going to return.

But both of them urged her to give herself time, to give her memory a chance to return and save her from the distress and embarrassment of going out into a world that she no longer knew. And because she loved them both and trusted their love for her, she agreed. But unhappily. It was as if life had been suspended and she had lost the power to bring it into motion again.

And so she spent her days willing her memory to come back and dreading that it would do so. She loved Christopher so much, she thought sometimes when she looked at him, especially at night when she woke up and he slept beside her, his arm always about her shoulders. She loved him so much that it was almost painful. And she was afraid of what their marriage had been like before she lost her memory—an unreasonable fear since they were together now and clearly loved each other. But she could not quite shake anxiety from her mind.

It was the fear of the unknown. And the longing to

remember so that at least the fear could be faced. And the equally compelling longing never to know, never to have to face what might be an unpleasant reality.

Christopher was feeling irritable. He had wasted the whole of a gloriously sunny morning at the cottage of one of his tenants who had a grievance—admittedly a genuine grievance that would have to be looked into, as Christopher had agreed at the time—yet now when he and Elizabeth were both in their dressing rooms getting ready for a ride along the valley, clouds had closed in and rain was imminent. There was no point in trying to convince himself that they were not rain clouds.

He wondered for a moment if they should go anyway, since a ride along the valley last time had meant a ride to the beach and along under the cliffs to the cave and an afternoon of lovemaking. But even so it was a long ride. They would not even make it to the end of the valley. A few stray raindrops were already spitting their warning against the windowpanes. They would have to remain indoors. He would have to share her with Nancy unless they were blatant about their desire to be alone and retired to his bedchamber for the afternoon.

He had had a nasty row with Nancy before luncheon. She had pointed out to him that they could not continue to keep Elizabeth a prisoner at Penhallow for much longer without telling her quite bluntly that she was just that.

"She is restless and unhappy, Christopher," she had said. "She needs wider horizons. She needs other people and other activities."

"She is not unhappy," he had said harshly. "She loves being here." Even to his own ears he had sounded like a petulant schoolboy.

"Yes, God help her," she had said, her voice cold, "I believe she does. And she loves you too. But love does not necessarily bring happiness, Christopher."

He knew it. And he knew she was right. He had abandoned himself to an enjoyment of these days too and could no longer deny that his feelings for Elizabeth involved far more love than hate. Yet he too was not quite happy. How could he be with such a burden of guilt on his conscience? He had always a sense of waiting—waiting for something to happen, waiting to move on to the next scene of the drama. There was no possibility of totally relaxing into the wonder and magic that these days were undoubtedly bringing them both.

And of course Elizabeth was his prisoner. Why else would he have told no one outside the house about her? And why else would he have instructed his servants to say nothing in the village about her presence at Penhallow? Why would he not let her leave, even to go to church with him and Nancy? She was his prisoner as surely as if he had her locked in chains in a dungeon.

And now the afternoon with Elizabeth he had looked forward to was spoiled. It was, he supposed, the perfect opportunity to begin to put things right. The change in the weather was like the warning of the end of an idyll. He should make up his mind to end their liaison. To tell her the truth. To adjust his own mind to reality. The reality was that she had no part in his life or he in hers. The reality was that she had destroyed him in the past, that he had made something of his life despite her. The reality was that he hated her.

But for all the good sense of his thoughts he knew that he would not tell her. Not yet. The temptation to try to prolong the idyll would be just too strong when he saw her again.

There was a tap on the door of his dressing room even as he turned to it, and it opened before he reached it. Antoine Bouchard came right inside and closed the door behind his back.

"You 'ave a visitor, m'sieur," he said. "I was passing through the 'all when 'e arrived and said I would inform you."

"Blast!" Christopher said. "Who is it, Antoine? It will have to wait until tomorrow. I am otherwise engaged for this afternoon."

"Captain Jamie Rice," Antoine said.

Christopher frowned. "Captain Rice?" he said. "What the devil does he want?"

"Except," Antoine said dramatically, "that 'e is not the captain, m'sieur. This man I never see before."

"Ah," Christopher said. There was almost a feeling of relief. So someone had found him.

"I fear you 'ave been found out," Antoine said. "And

'e is 'oping to get you downstairs unsuspecting. It was a good thing I was there, eh, m'sieur?"

"Yes," Christopher said. "It looks that way. Where is this visitor, Antoine?"

"In the visitors' salon," the Frenchman said. "Only one servant came with 'im, m'sieur, but I do not trust the situation. I will come with you with a gun, non?"

"Good Lord, no," Christopher said. "I had better see who it is and what he wants." He walked purposefully from the room and down the stairs, still feeling that strange relief along with some apprehension. Something was finally happening. Anything was perhaps better than nothing, though he said a regrettable good-bye to his idyll as he crossed the hall and nodded to Hemmings to open the doors into the salon. Who would it be? he wondered. Chicheley? Poole? Or someone quite unconnected with his kidnapping of Elizabeth?

"Martin!" he said, stepping into the room and waiting for the doors to close behind him. Of course, he might have expected that of all people it would be Elizabeth's stepbrother who would come. He had been with her and the duke outside the church in Hanover Square, had he not?

Martin was standing with his back to the fireplace, his usually good-humored face looking decidedly grim. He took his hands from behind his back as the doors closed and pointed a dueling pistol directly at Christopher's heart. He held the gun with both hands.

"Where is she?" he asked.

"Elizabeth?" Christopher said. "Upstairs. You do not need the gun, Martin."

"Have her brought down," Martin said, not moving a muscle. "If you have harmed her in any way, Trevelyan, I am going to kill you."

Christopher nodded. "I can understand your feelings," he said, "but this can be settled amicably, Martin. I am not dangerous, though I believe my man might be. He is at the window with a far larger gun than yours. If I die, you will be very fast on my heels."

Martin took one jerky look over his shoulder toward the window that looked out on the courtyard, where Antoine was standing with a large hunting gun trained on the visitor.

"He spent years in the Canadian wilderness, where one shoots first and asks questions afterward," Christopher said, "and where one does not live long if one does not have a deadly accurate aim. Put it down, Martin, and let's talk. We used to be friends, didn't we? You were my only friend at the end, I remember."

Martin lowered the gun slowly, walked a few steps to set it down on a table, and then resumed his place before the fireplace. Christopher nodded to Antoine, who disappeared from the window.

"Upstairs?" Martin said. "Locked up? Tied up? How long did you intend to keep her here?" His face was grim and his hands trembled at his sides.

Christopher shrugged. "Originally I suppose the idea was to keep her as long as it took to convince her that she should not marry Poole," he said. "I thought you cared for her, Martin. Why the devil didn't you talk her out of such a ghastly marriage?"

"Poole is thoroughly respectable," Martin said. "He is a Whig, of course, but that does not make him a pariah. He is what Elizabeth chose and what she needs—someone respectable and ambitious and socially prominent. The past needs to be wiped out once and for all."

Christopher ignored the last sentence. "Deuce take it," he said, "Poole is the dullest dog one could find in London. She would not be happy with him for a fortnight."

Martin shrugged. "Is she locked up?" he asked. "I want to see her."

"I'll bring her down in a moment," Christopher said. "But I need to prepare you first."

Martin paled and his hands opened and closed convulsively at his sides. "You have not . . ." He took a step forward.

"No, I have not beaten her black and blue," Christopher said. "But she did fall—from the carriage when I was bringing her here. She is fully recovered from her bruises. But she has lost her memory."

Martin stared at him.

"Actually"—Christopher licked dry lips—"actually I could not be happier to see you, Martin. She knows nothing, you see, except what I have told her. But it is time she knew the truth. Perhaps seeing you will jolt her memory. If not, then you and I will have to start telling her what she has forgotten. But gradually, I think you will agree. We don't want to throw her into a state of shock on top of everything."

"What does she know?" Martin was standing very still.

Christopher drew a deep breath. "I have told her that she is my wife," he said. He looked very directly at Martin. "We have been living together as man and wife. Very contentedly, I might add."

He had calculated the number of steps Martin would have to take to reach the pistol and knew exactly how he would cut him off and make sure that it was never fired. He had also prepared himself for a frontal attack with fists. Or for a verbal blistering. What actually happened was that Martin continued to stand very still, his hands still opening and closing. He pursed his lips after a while.

"I see," he said unexpectedly.

"You know I was innocent, Martin," Christopher said.

"I believed so," Martin said. "Against all reason. I liked you, Trevelyan, and thought you incapable of hurting my sister in just that way."

"You believed so. Past tense," Christopher said quietly. "You changed your mind?"

"Why did you run?" Martin asked. "It made you look hellish guilty, you know. And then those other things came pouring out after you had gone. Did you think they would remain hidden? Some of it at least had to be true. There could not have been all that smoke without some fire. I wanted to believe you innocent. You were my friend. I like to be able to stand by my friends. And I admired you—I was only eighteen and you twenty-four. You were a type of hero to me. But in the end I was forced to admit that you had made a fool of me."

"Those other things?" Christopher raised his eyebrows.

"Yes," Martin said harshly. "It all came out—every filthy detail—after you had gone. These things tend to happen, you know. I was shocked, I must confess, though I liked to think myself worldly-wise. It almost killed her, Trevelyan."

"Well," Christopher said quietly, "perhaps I was in more danger from your pistol a few minutes ago than I realized. It seems that more happened after my departure than I know about. Someone must have hated me with a dreadful passion. But more of that later. Will you cooperate with me on this at least, Martin? You will not try to force the truth on Elizabeth too suddenly if she does not know you when I bring her down? We will discuss together what is to be revealed and when?"

"Bring her down," Martin said. "You don't have to beg me to do what is in her best interests, Trevelyan. I have always done what I thought to be best for her."

"Yes," Christopher said, extending his right hand, hoping that it would be taken, "I have to give you that, Martin. You have always loved Elizabeth more steadfastly than any of the rest of us. For that I must honor you and still think of you as a friend even if you no longer do the like for me. I assume you have cared for her during the past seven years too—while I fled."

Martin looked at his hand for a long moment before taking it in his own. "Who knows?" he said. "Perhaps you have reformed your character in the last seven years. I certainly hope so. I have missed your friendship. Now I want to see Elizabeth."

Christopher turned without another word and left the room.

Rain was beating against the window of Elizabeth's dressing room by the time the tap sounded at her door and Christopher came inside. It was actually more like a sitting room than a dressing room. She had already sat down in a comfortable chair with a book to await his arrival. She looked up and smiled, setting the book to one side.

"It is raining," she said, pulling a face before getting to her feet and raising her arms to set up about his shoulders as he crossed the room toward her. "Could anything be more disappointing? I was looking forward to an afternoon in the lovers' cave. Aren't I shameless?" She laughed.

He kissed her, wrapping his arms right about her and hugging her hard.

She leaned back in his arms and searched his eyes. "What is it?" she asked.

He set a hand at the back of her head and drew her

face against his neckcloth. She felt him swallow. "The real world has come to call," he said.

She kept her head where it was though his hand was exerting no great pressure. She felt breathless. So this was it, she thought. Something had changed. Something irrevocable. Nothing was going to be the same again. The idyll was over. The honeymoon was at an end.

"Your brother—your stepbrother—is waiting downstairs for you," he said.

She had never asked him about her family and had been half conscious of the fact that the omission had been deliberate. She had not wanted to know too much about her family and her past, about that whole bulk of her life that had been lived before she met Christopher. She had been unconsciously afraid that she would remember everything.

"My stepbrother," she said, her voice toneless.

"Martin," he said and paused. "Do you remember him?"

"No," she said.

Martin? Her stepbrother? No, she had no memory of him. She felt frightened again. She had not felt frightened for almost a week.

"Come down and meet him," he said softly.

She drew back her head and looked up at him. Into steady blue eyes. "I don't want to," she said. "I am afraid. Why am I afraid?" She laughed.

"Come and meet him," he said.

She drew away from him and brushed at the folds of her dress. His arm was waiting to take hers. She took a deep breath and linked her own through it.

"Martin," she said, "does he know?"

"Yes," he said.

"Has he come from far away?" she asked.

"London," he said.

He was as nervous as she was, she realized. Why? Was he afraid that she would remember everything? Or afraid that she would not? She felt dizzy suddenly and had to concentrate on her breathing. But she drew her arm from his when they reached the hallway. She could do this without having to cling to him.

She did not know the man who was standing before the fireplace in the salon. Of that she was sure. He was not very tall, perhaps no taller than she and there was a suggestion of stockiness about his build. His fair hair was wavy. He was good-looking though not startlingly handsome. He was about her own age, she guessed. She had been expecting an older man for some reason. He was elegantly dressed.

"Lizzie?" The name was spoken very quietly, but his hands reached out and he was striding across the room toward her.

Lizzie? She recoiled from the name. But she recovered herself and set her hands in his.

"Martin?" she said. "I am afraid I do not know you. I believe Christopher has explained. Is it a long time since I saw you last?"

"Just over two weeks ago," he said, "in London. Lizzie, it's me. I am here now. You are going to be quite safe. I won't let anyone harm you. I never have, have I?"

In London? Just over two weeks ago? She tried to draw her hands away from his without openly pulling on them. But he had them in a strong clasp.

"We were returning from London," Christopher said from behind her, "when you fell out of the carriage, Elizabeth. We were there with your family."

"You are safe now," Martin said.

She did not like him. Were they usually close? Or had she always disliked him? "I know," she said, an edge to her voice. "Christopher always keeps me safe. You are my stepbrother?"

"Your father married my mother two years after yours died in childbed," he said. "I am three months older than you, Lizzie. We grew up from the age of two as brother and sister. Or more like twins really. We even look a little alike. It has always been a bit of a joke—like married couples sometimes grow to resemble each other."

His manner was jovial and kindly. His face was open and good-humored. She felt guilty for being slightly repelled by him. She tried again to withdraw her hands from his and succeeded.

"Who is my father?" she asked.

"Chicheley," he said. "The Duke of Chicheley. Good Lord, Lizzie, surely everything cannot have been blanked from your memory, has it?"

"Everything, yes," she said. "Is he still alive? And your mother?"

"He is still alive," he said. "Mama died when we were sixteen. Don't you remember? You cried as if she were your own mother."

"Are there any more members of our family?" she asked.

"John," he said. "Your brother, Lizzie. He is five years older than us. He is a lieutenant-colonel with Wellington's cavalry. They have been fighting a war, but peace has been declared at last."

"Yes, I know," she said. "It seems that it is only the personal part of my memory that has gone. I remember less important things. John." She tried to picture a thirty-year-old brother, a cavalry officer, and failed.

She set her hands loosely over her face and shook her head. "Sometimes," she said, "I feel as if I am living in the middle of a nightmare. Why is everything so blank? Why is it that I recognize no one? It is all so terrifying."

It was Martin's arms that came around her even as she felt Christopher's hand against the small of her back. And it was Martin who hugged her and rocked her and murmured soothing words to her. She stiffened and jerked away and turned blindly toward her husband. He took her shoulders in firm hands and squeezed reassuringly.

"Enough for now," he said. "She is bewildered, Martin. Let's take matters a little at a time. I'll have you shown to a room where you can freshen up. And then we will have tea in the drawing room. You are probably ready for some refreshments. Nancy will join us there. You remember my sister?"

"Yes, indeed," Martin said. "How could one not remember Lady Nancy? Though it is many years since I last saw her."

"She will be pleased to see you again," Christopher said. He patted Elizabeth on the shoulders before releasing her in order to open the salon door and send a servant on his way to summon Mrs. Clavell. "Our housekeeper will take you to a room. I will come myself in half an hour's time to bring you back down to the drawing room."

Martin turned before leaving the room and kissed Elizabeth on the cheek. She forced herself to smile and not flinch.

"I don't like him," she said when the door had closed again and she was alone with her husband. "I feel threatened. I don't think I want to remember. Can we just send him on his way, Christopher?" She laughed. "That was a stupid and extremely unmannerly thing to say, wasn't it?"

He framed her face with his hands and gazed into her eyes. His face was expressionless and rather harsh. "You are very fond of him, Elizabeth," he said. "And so am I. He has always been a good friend to both of us. To everyone, in fact. Martin is that kind of person—always more concerned for other people's happiness than his own. Try not to flinch from him. It must hurt him when you do so."

She bit her lower lip. "I will try," she promised. "He does have a kind face. I just wish he would not call me Lizzie and talk about keeping me safe just as if you were not even here."

He lowered his head and kissed her warmly on the lips. She wrapped her arms about his neck and relaxed into the comfort of his embrace.

10

NANCY was playing the pianoforte in the music room. But she was not concentrating and kept having to go back to replay a phrase she had stumbled over. She had seen the carriage arrive. A strange carriage. And since no servant had come to call her, she must assume that the visitor was for Christopher.

He had been discovered. They had found him. And now he was going to be in the worst trouble of his life. This time he would not be able to plead innocence—not that the plea had done him any good the first time. No one had believed him except her. She was not even sure that Papa had believed him.

She wondered who had discovered him. Who had arrived? Some constables with a magistrate, perhaps, to haul him off to prison? The Duke of Chicheley? John? Her fingers stumbled over the keys. She hoped it was not John. Martin? She stopped playing altogether, pushed back the stool, and walked to the window.

Oh, please God, please dear God, let it not be Martin. But she knew it would be he just as she had known for days that he would come.

The door opened behind her but she did not turn.

"Here you are, Nance," her brother's voice said. It sounded strained. "I have been looking for you."

"Who is it?" she asked. "Who has come?"

There was a pause. "Martin Honywood," he said. "He tracked me down. I might have guessed he would. He was always fonder of Elizabeth than all the rest of them put together."

"Yes," she said. "Yes, I guessed it would be he. He must be dreadfully angry."

"He met me with a pistol," Christopher said, words that caused her to turn at last. His face was pale. "But once we got past that crisis, he was remarkably civil and understanding. But then he always was fair-minded. And he understood, of course, that Elizabeth has to be treated with care under the circumstances."

"Well," Nancy said, crossing the room to fold the sheet music and put it away, "it looks as if you are going to get off easily after all, Christopher. Unless the duke turns nasty when he knows what has happened to her, of course. They are leaving immediately?"

"Who?" He looked at her blankly.

"Elizabeth and her stepbrother," she said. "There is a good deal of daylight left. He cannot intend to spend a night under this roof, surely?"

"They are not leaving," he said. "That would do terrible things to Elizabeth. She has no memory of Martin or Chicheley or anyone. She is going to have to be told the truth very gradually. Martin and I have just spent some time talking about it and we are both agreed on that. He is being very decent about the whole thing."

Nancy sat down on the stool. She was not sure her legs would support her without shaking. "He cannot stay at this house," she said. "I will not have it, Christopher."

He raised his eyebrows.

She closed her eyes briefly. "I sometimes forget," she said, "that this house belongs to you. I am so used to being mistress here. So you are to tell Elizabeth tomorrow?"

"Over the next few days," he said. "We have planned it carefully. We are not going to rush her. I came to fetch you to tea, Nance. You will be civil?"

"I will be absent," she said firmly. "I want nothing to do with any member of that family."

"Nance," he said, his head to one side, "he could have come here with half an army and a warrant for my arrest. He is trying to be fair. And he is trying to do what is best for Elizabeth despite what he might feel about me."

Nancy got to her feet. This was it, then. She had known deep down that she could never find a haven that would be safe for life. She had known that sooner or later she was going to have to confront her nightmares. She had even known that this business with Elizabeth would bring it on.

"Very well, then," she said, taking her brother's offered arm, "I will be civil, Christopher. But don't expect any more."

Martin had been a boy when she saw him last, a good-looking, sunny-natured, charming boy whom everyone liked. He had changed very little, Nancy discovered when she entered the drawing room on Christopher's arm. He had gained a little weight, perhaps, and he was now a man rather than a boy. But he still looked good-natured. He rose to his feet, smiled, and reached out a hand to her.

Sometimes over the years she had wondered if she could have imagined everything that had happened. Now she found herself wondering again.

"Lady Nancy," he said, "how pleasant to see you again. Some ladies, I see, only improve with the years."

Christopher had left the room to fetch Elizabeth down for tea. Nancy pretended she had not noticed the offered hand and seated herself.

"I trust you had a pleasant journey, Mr. Honywood," she said. She talked determinedly about his journey and the weather until her brother reappeared with Elizabeth. But she gradually forgot about her own distress during the next hour in her interest in observing the other three occupants of the room.

Elizabeth sat close to Christopher, though she did not lean against him. She sat straight-backed and self-possessed and silent. She scarcely removed her gaze from Martin. But there was no recognition in her look and no fondness. If anything, Nancy thought, there was hostility there, though Elizabeth was too polite to show it openly.

Strange, Nancy thought. Those two had been more like twins than brother and sister—or stepbrother and stepsister, to be more accurate. Could Elizabeth see Martin differently now that memory had stripped away all preconceived ideas about his character? Or was that unfair? Perhaps what had happened, dreadful as it had been, had been uncharacteristic of Martin. He had, after all, been under considerable strain at that particular time.

But Nancy was glad that Elizabeth disliked Martin. And glad too that Martin knew it and was smiling all the harder to hide the fact that he was hurt.

"Why did you come?" Elizabeth blurted at last, looking directly at Martin and interrupting a rather labored conversation in which only the two men had been participating.

"To see you, Lizzie," Martin said gently. "Trevelyan sent to tell us about the accident and I left without delay. I was sick with worry about you."

"Why did my father not come too?" she asked.

"He suffers from gout and finds long journeys difficult," Martin said. "But he sent his love, Lizzie. I'll be staying for a while. Perhaps your memory will return in that time. But even if it does not you will have a chance to get to know me again before I take you back to London."

Elizabeth stiffened. "I am not going to London," she said. "I am going to stay at home with my husband. This is where I belong."

Martin smiled and changed the subject.

Nancy wanted Elizabeth gone. And Martin too. She wanted them on their way as soon as possible—preferably today or tomorrow. And yet perversely she found herself silently cheering Elizabeth's answer.

Elizabeth cuddled closer to Christopher beneath the blankets, burying her nose against his nightshirt below his chin. He had not unclothed them before coming to bed as he very often did and had made no move to make love to her. He just held her in his arms. It was what she most needed.

"Do I have to?" she asked him.

"Have to what?" he asked, his lips brushing her hair.

"Spend the morning with him," she said. "With Martin. Can you not take the morning off for once and be with us?"

She heard him inhale slowly. "Things cannot remain as they are, Elizabeth," he said. "You have not been totally happy, have you? I think we have to assume at this point that your memory may never come back. If that is so, then you must reach out and get to know your family again and your history. Only so will you be able to get to know yourself again. Martin is no threat to you, believe me. He has always been devoted to you."

"You want me to know everything, then?" she asked.

He kissed the top of her head before replying. She

heard him inhale again. "To be quite honest and quite selfish," he said, "no. These two weeks have been surprisingly good, Elizabeth. But it is not fair to you to keep you from the truth forever."

"These weeks have not been typical of our life together, then," she said and her words were not a question. She felt infinitely sad and tried to burrow even closer. "But you are right. You must go about your business as usual tomorrow and I shall go walking with Martin. Up onto the cliffs, perhaps. But not down onto the beach. The beach is ours. I'll not take him there."

He kissed the top of her head again.

She was aware that she was clinging to him. Surely by the age of twenty-five she must have learned to be less dependent on others than she had apparently been at the time of her marriage. She must have learned to depend upon her own strength. And yet it was so easy to give in to terror, to want to climb right inside him, to want to beg him to protect her, to shield her from reality. She knew reality was going to be painful. She had seen it in his eyes when Martin arrived. She could feel it now in his arms.

She took his hand in hers and lifted his arm away from her shoulders, setting it at his side.

"There must be a great deal to tell," she said. "Twenty-five years to explain to me. I have a feeling that you and Martin, and perhaps Nancy too, have decided on a plan—what to tell first, what to keep until last. Am I right?"

"Something like that," he said.

"What is to be kept until last is the most painful part," she said, her voice dull. She knew it as a certainty.

"Why do you think there is anything painful to tell?" he asked.

"I know," she said. "You have told me without saying so in words. Do you think that because I have forgotten everything about you except what I have learned in two weeks I do not know you? I do. There is something painful. And not in the past either. In the present. Or at least something that has continued to the present. I don't want to know, but I realize that I must. Is that why I lost my memory, do you think? Was my mind unable to cope with the pain?"

"Elizabeth—" he said.

"You must not be afraid that I will crumble," she said. "I will not."

He tightened his hand around hers.

"And I will not stop loving you," she said. She could hear that her voice was shaking. "Perhaps I was out of love with you when I fell from the carriage. But I don't care about that. I will not stop loving you again when I remember. I don't even care if you don't love me."

"Elizabeth—" he said.

"Make love to me," she said. "I need you very close tonight. Closer than close. And I don't care if I am being bolder than I normally am or bolder than a wife ought to be. I don't care about anything tonight except you and me. Make love to me. Please?"

He did not remove their nightclothes. He did not spend time preparing her with lips and tongue and hands. He turned her onto her back, raising their clothes as he did so, parted her legs with his own, and thrust deeply inside her. He said nothing, but pressed her into the mattress with his weight and moved in her for many minutes with a slow rhythm that only gradually increased in pace and depth.

There was almost no passion but in its stead an enormous comfort and sense of closeness. She was almost sorry when the familiar aches finally began and she knew that soon she was going to come and that then he would finish and it would be all over, that he would withdraw his body from inside hers and she would be alone again.

"Just you and me and here and now," he whispered, finding her mouth with his, and they sighed out the shared cresting of their pleasure.

Sleep came almost immediately.

Martin was happy enough to find that Christopher was leaving the breakfast room as he was entering it the next morning. He had no wish to waste energy on smiling and being polite and feigning friendship with a man he hated with a red-hot passion. They had gone up to bed together the night before, by God, Trevelyan and Lizzie. Martin would not easily forget the feeling of helplessness he had had as he had smiled and watched them go. He would not forget the bile that had risen to his mouth.

Trevelyan was going to spend the morning with his steward. Martin was to spend the time with Elizabeth, beginning the slow process of filling in the void in her memory. Trevelyan trusted him to follow the plan they had spoken of the day before. And the trouble was, Martin thought as he took his place at the table, he would have to move slowly indeed. Lizzie perhaps would not be able to stand the shock of having the truth forced upon her too quickly. Martin ground his teeth in impotent rage against Trevelyan who had brought about this coil.

His hope that perhaps Elizabeth's memory had returned during the night was dashed when she joined him in the breakfast room a few minutes later. She still did not know him. More than that, she felt uncomfortable with him. She merely bade him a good morning, made some remarks about the weather, and sat down, her eyes lowered to her plate.

It hurt badly. He wanted to take her by the hands as he had the previous day when Trevelyan had brought her downstairs. *It's me, Lizzie,* he wanted to say to her again.

He smiled. "You are still coming walking with me, Lizzie?" he asked.

"Yes," she said, looking up at him uncertainly. She hesitated. "Please have patience with me, Martin. I have been told that you are my stepbrother, that we have been together almost since birth, and that we have a close relationship and a deep affection for each other. But it is one thing to know something with one's head and another to feel it with one's heart. To me you are a stranger. I will have to learn to love you all over again."

Sensible, brave Lizzie. They were qualities she had learned during the pain of the past seven years, years when he had stayed with her, offering her all the comfort of his love. They were qualities that had not deserted her with her memory.

"I have all the patience in the world, Lizzie," he said. "That is one thing I have always had. All good things come to those who have the patience to wait for them."

"Thank you," she said. She glanced across the room to the window. "I am glad it is not raining today." She smiled, but it was a forced expression, he knew. It was not Lizzie's usual warm smile, the smile she kept just for him. He felt strangely like crying.

They strolled later up the hill behind the house and out of the wooded valley that had taken him so much by surprise the day before. The countryside had seemed bleak and bare, and then suddenly there was the valley and the stream and the house and gardens. She walked a little apart from him. He sensed that she did not want to take his arm so did not offer it.

"Shall we sit down?" he suggested when they reached the top, testing the grass with his hand to make sure that it was dry.

She nodded and they sat looking back down into the valley.

"I love it here," she said, her voice sounding almost defiant. "I am sure I was very happy to come home from London two weeks ago."

"We live in Norfolkshire," he said. "That is where you are from, Lizzie. From Kingston Park, a house and estate that would dwarf this." He nodded down at Penhallow. "We grew up there together and scarcely left it until we were eighteen. We were wonderfully happy there and did not long for the outside world at all. You resisted Papa's insistence finally that we go to London so that you could be presented at court and have a come-out Season."

She clasped her arms about her updrawn knees and rested her forehead against them while he talked for perhaps half an hour about their childhood and early youth. About those golden years that he ached to recapture if only it were possible. It hurt him deeply to know that she had forgotten them, almost as if they had been unimportant to her. Though he knew that was being unfair to her.

"Oh," she said with a sigh when he stopped talking at last. She looked up at him with weary eyes. "It is all like listening to stories about other people, Martin. I cannot believe that I was involved, that I was that happy girl you describe. I keep expecting there to be some spark of recognition, but there is nothing."

He moved closer to her and set an arm about her shoulders—and was alarmed at her almost violent reaction. She twisted away from him and pushed at his arm.

"Don't touch me!" she said, a look of terror and revulsion on her face. And then she stared at him with dismayed eyes and bit her lower lip. "I'm sorry. Oh, I'm so sorry, Martin. But you must remember that I cannot think of you as a brother. Only as a strange man. I cannot feel comfortable with any man's touch but my husband's."

"You remember him, then, Lizzie?" he asked, stung.

"No, of course not," she said.

"Who told you that he was your husband?" he asked. "Him? And you believed him? How do you know he was telling you the truth?"

She stared at him, her eyes wide. The color drained from her face. "He is my husband," she whispered. "I love him."

"How do you know," he said, "that he did not just take advantage of your loss of memory to ravish you? Why do you put more trust in him than in me? I am your brother, Lizzie. I have always stuck by you through thick and thin."

But she had scrambled to a crouching position. "Don't," she said. "Oh, please don't. He loves me. He is my husband."

"Lizzie." He reached out a hand to her. But she backed away from him, got to her feet, and began to flee down the hill toward the house, dodging trees as she ran.

Martin took a few steps after her but then stopped. He was not sorry, he thought, though it pained him almost beyond bearing to see her panic-stricken and to know the turmoil that must be in her mind. She had to know sooner or later, and sooner was better than later. Ultimately there was no way to save her from pain. And he would be there for her to comfort her against the pain, as he always had been. The greater the pain, the greater the comfort she would need. Poor Lizzie. Would she never learn that his love was a free gift to her, that he hated to have to hurt her so that she would accept it?

If only she could remember. She kept waiting for something to spark a memory, she had said. Was that how it would happen eventually, if it was going to happen at all? Something to spark a memory?

There was one thing that might do the trick—one spark that would surely work if anything could. And even if it did not jolt her memory, it was something she must know.

And soon. It was something she would not be able to ignore, something that would finally convince her.

Martin began to stride down the hill after the fast disappearing figure of his stepsister. He would send Macklin back to London without further delay, he decided, thankful now that he had thought it wise to bring a servant with him. In three days Macklin could be back again.

In three days. It seemed an eternity. She would be with Trevelyan for three more nights. Martin clenched his hands into fists as he walked.

Elizabeth took the stairs two at a time. Christopher was not in their bedchamber or in his dressing room, just as he had not been in either the morning room or the library downstairs. Of course, she had known that he would be nowhere in the house. He had gone for the morning and the morning was only half over. She left his dressing room and raced blindly along the upper hallway.

Nancy was in her private sitting room, sewing. Thank God she was in the first place Elizabeth had thought to look. Oh, thank God. And she was rising to her feet and setting her sewing aside, a look of surprise and concern on her face.

"Oh," Elizabeth said, "I did not knock. I am so sorry, Nancy."

"What is it?" Her sister-in-law's face was pale, her voice tense. "Your memory?"

"Nancy." Elizabeth realized how breathless she was only when she tried to speak. "I *am* married to Christopher, aren't I? He *is* my husband, isn't he?"

She watched Nancy close her eyes briefly. "Has anyone said anything to make you doubt?" Nancy asked. "Martin?"

"*Are* we married?" Elizabeth felt as if she had walked into a nightmare and could not force herself awake.

"You were married seven years ago," Nancy said quietly. "On the Duke of Chicheley's estate. At Kingston Park."

"Tell me about it." Elizabeth raised the back of her hand to her mouth and could both see and feel it trembling.

"I can't." Nancy sighed and sat down again and motioned her to do likewise, though Elizabeth continued to stand just inside the door. "I was not there. But it was a fairly small affair. I believe you and Christopher thought it was the most wonderful wedding there had ever been. I suppose all brides and grooms feel that way."

"Why weren't you there?" Elizabeth asked.

"I was there for your betrothal party," Nancy said, "and was supposed to stay while the banns were being read. You were both eager to marry as soon as possible. I—I got homesick and came back here a week before the wedding though both you and Christopher were upset about it."

"So we are married," Elizabeth said, almost afraid to let relief wash over her.

"What did Martin tell you just now?" Nancy picked up her sewing again.

"Only that I cannot know for sure whether anything that has been told me in the past two weeks is true," Elizabeth said. "He was upset, I think. And hurt. He tried to put his arm about me and I would not allow it. I told him he was a stranger to me."

Nancy bent her head over her work.

"It felt wrong," Elizabeth said. "I felt as if he was trying to—to seduce me. And I am horrified at my reaction. Christopher has told me that Martin is my brother and my close friend."

"Stepbrother," Nancy said.

"No blood relation." Elizabeth shivered. "Christopher says that he has always been devoted to me and that he has been a good friend to both of us. I must try to love him again, mustn't I, Nancy?"

Nancy executed three careful stitches before replying. "Perhaps a loss of memory enables one to look at the people in one's life with fresh eyes," she said. "Perhaps one can then see in them qualities or shortcomings that habit normally blinds one to. I don't know if you should try to force your feelings into any mold, Elizabeth. I really don't know. I don't know how to advise you."

Elizabeth was surprised and alarmed to see a tear plop onto the cloth over which Nancy had bent her head.

"I think," Elizabeth said, forcing her voice to steadiness, "that the sooner I know all there is to know, the better it will be for me and everyone else. This is putting a severe strain on you, Nancy, and I am sorry for it. But I'll not try to force anything else from you. I am sure you must be caught between your loyalty to Christopher and your sympathy for me. I will wait for Christopher and Martin to tell me between them. Martin has just been telling me numerous stories about our childhood—stories about two strangers."

Nancy looked up, her eyes bright with tears. "I am sorry, Elizabeth," she said. "I am so very sorry. And sorry that I ever disliked and even hated you. I think perhaps you were as much a victim as Christopher was. In fact, I am sure of it."

Elizabeth stood very still and drew a slow breath as her sister-in-law grimaced and closed her eyes very tightly and bit hard on her lower lip.

Elizabeth turned and left the room.

Nancy felt quite ill at her slip of the tongue. She had not meant to say anything despite her great disapproval of everything Christopher had done since his arrival in England. She had certainly not meant to bring that stricken look to Elizabeth's face.

Poor Elizabeth! She had paid dearly in the last two weeks for the weakness of character that had made Nancy so despise her in the past. She was no longer weak, only bewildered and frightened and doing an admirable job of holding herself together and coping with a situation that must be terrifying. And now matters were becoming even more difficult for her.

Damn Christopher, Nancy thought, dredging up one of the worst words in her vocabulary. Damn him. She had so longed for his return. And yet now she wished him in the farthest corner of the Canadian or American wilderness—whichever was most distant. He had made a disaster of his return. A total disaster.

She could no longer concentrate on her sewing or on anything else indoors. She must get outside into the fresh air. Her first instinct was to walk up over the headland and down the path to the beach. But that was no longer a safe haven. Martin had been outside with Elizabeth when she had come running home. Perhaps he had gone to the beach. The thought made Nancy feel even more ill.

She would go out to the kitchen gardens, she thought, to cut flowers. The dining room and the drawing room needed new arrangements. But she had not been there five minutes, bent to her task, when she became aware of a pair of Hessian boots at the corner of her vision. Christopher would not be back yet, she knew. And none of the servants ever wore Hessians. She straightened up.

"Good morning," Martin said.

She pushed her hair back over her shoulders. She had left it loose that morning the way she liked to wear it. She was forgetting that she no longer had Penhallow to herself.

He was smiling. But of course Martin always smiled. She felt a wave of hatred so intense that she wondered for a moment if it had contorted her face and he had noticed. But his smile did not falter.

"Good morning," she said.

"I thought," he said, "that ladies are supposed to decline in beauty once they have passed their twentieth year. You disprove the theory."

He had forgotten, she thought contemptuously, that he had said almost the same thing at tea the previous afternoon. She set down the scissors and the small bunch of flowers she had gathered on the square of canvas she had brought into the garden with her. She would pick them up or send someone for them later. She removed her gloves and dropped them too.

"Thank you," she said, stepping carefully over the flowers to the grassy verge on which he stood. "I must go inside to tidy up."

"Don't," he said. "Not yet. I was nervous about coming here, you know. Not just because I suspected that Trevelyan had Elizabeth here and did not know how I would be received. But also because I was afraid you would be here."

She brushed some flecks of soil from her dress. She doubted he had given her a thought before his arrival. "Afraid?" she said, raising her eyebrows and looking at him coolly.

He laughed. "I think I owe you an apology," he said. "A long overdue one."

"I would prefer that you did not offer it," she said.

"Good manners might dictate that I accept. And the last thing I ever want to do on this earth is forgive you."

"Ah," he said, "so it did upset you, what happened. And you do blame me. Well, perhaps you are right. Certainly I have always felt guilty about it. But I was eighteen, you know, with no experience of the world whatsoever."

"I was twenty," she said, "and matched you in experience, more is the pity. May we change the subject? Or better yet, may we close this conversation entirely?"

"You are bitter," he said. "And you are not prepared to consider forgiving me."

"You are a guest in my brother's house," she said. "I will be civil to you. I am going inside. I really do need to wash my hands and change my dress."

"You were so very lovely," he said. "I was infatuated."

"And comb my hair," she said.

"And jealous of John," he said.

For the first time her eyes blazed anger. "And of Christopher," she said. "Especially of Christopher."

He shrugged and gave her a rueful smile. "It felt rather like losing my right arm when Lizzie fancied herself in love with him." he said. "I was very young. I quickly got used to the idea that times were changing and that I had to change with them."

"*Fancied* herself," she said scornfully.

"I liked him," he said. "I was not really jealous. Envious, perhaps, of their happiness. And lonely. I thought she had made a good choice. I even continued to think so long after everyone else had turned against him. I liked him too well and was too concerned for her happiness to believe all the evidence that began to pile against him."

"One piece of evidence," she said, "and it was false. But yes, he did write to say that you had stuck by him until he sailed for Canada, that you were the only defender he had left. For that I thank you." She spoke grudgingly and was not even convinced that her thanks were justified. Understandably she supposed after what had happened she felt a deep distrust of Martin.

"But you will not forgive me for the other," he said. "I am truly sorry."

"I hope you mean it," she said. "Shall we leave it at that?"

She should have turned and hurried away at that point. Certainly she wanted to get away from him. But curiosity held her a little longer. And perhaps fascination with a man she did not understand at all.

"Why are you staying here like a family guest when you must hate Christopher with a passion?" she asked. "Why have you not taken Elizabeth away this morning while he is gone? Why did you not use the gun you brought with you?"

"It was not loaded," he said. "I cannot even shoot a rabbit, Lady Nancy. How could I shoot a man, even my sister's kidnapper—and seducer? Elizabeth has to be my main concern. Had she been told the truth as soon as she regained consciousness, of course, I would have taken her away yesterday even if he had tried to prevent me. I will use my fists, you see, even if I cannot bring myself to use a deadlier weapon. But she was not told the truth and so the damage must be undone slowly and gently."

"And yet," she said, "you hinted to her this morning that perhaps Christopher is not her husband after all."

"I did not mean to put doubts in her mind so soon," he said. "But eventually she must know that he is not. I am not sure that there is any totally gentle way of breaking that news considering the fact that he has been bedding her for two weeks."

She shot him a startled glance at his choice of words and flushed.

"Do you hate him?" she asked.

"I hate no one," he said. "I try very hard to see everyone's point of view, to understand even if I cannot always condone. I think perhaps he is genuinely sorry for what he did in the past and would like to atone for it. Unfortunately he has acted as impulsively now as he did when he ran away. And as disastrously. No, I don't hate him, Lady Nancy, but I do fear the effect that the repeated rapes of the past weeks will have on Elizabeth when she knows the truth."

She flinched. And she knew suddenly beyond a doubt that despite his words and his smiles he did hate Christopher. "She appears to have some strength of character," she said.

"Prolonged suffering in the past has made my sister a strong person," he said. "I think she can live through this too. And she will have my support."

"As always," Nancy said, turning finally and striding back toward the house.

"Yes," he said. "As always. I am sure you are as supportive of your brother, Lady Nancy. You have not been exactly contradicting his lies in the past two weeks, have you? And I am sure you will do all in your power to comfort him when I take Elizabeth away eventually."

It was true, she thought reluctantly, walking briskly ahead of him. She did not want him to catch up to her. She did not want to have to walk by his side. If he offered her his arm, she would die. Or at least she would cringe as Elizabeth had done earlier.

"Lady Nancy," he said when they reached the house and she hurried through the hall to the staircase arch. He was smiling when she looked back, though his eyes were sad. He was again the charming boy she had once known. "Can we not be friends? Won't you forgive me for a youthful indiscretion?"

Her eyes strayed downward to his hands—short-fingered hands with square clean fingernails. She felt an inward shudder. "I need to tidy up," she said. "Christopher will be home soon for luncheon."

"Ah," he said as she turned to the stairs.

11

MARTIN went back outside. He walked briskly down through the rock gardens to the stream and along the valley in the direction of the sea, until he was lost among the trees. Then his footsteps slowed.

Patience, self-control, he told himself, his hands alternately flexing and curling into tight fists. They were what he needed now more than anything else. He drew in deep breaths of salty sea air and released them slowly. But his usual methods of calming himself were not working. Perhaps it would be as well after all, he thought, to order out his carriage and force Elizabeth to leave with him. But she disliked and distrusted him. That fact more than any other had shaken him. She had never done either, even when she had fancied herself in love with Atwell the first time or even when she had planned her marriage to Poole.

What if her memory never returned? He could explain the truth to her, of course. But if he forced her away from that damned villain Trevelyan now, would she ever forgive him? Would she ever love him again? Perhaps he would lose her entirely and forever if he did not exercise patience now. He could not risk that happening.

But to have to stay beneath Trevelyan's roof and to be forced to act the part of courteous guest! It was almost too much. And to have to put up with the insolence and the contempt of that slut, his sister. And to know that the two of them had more influence over Elizabeth at the present than he did himself. He did not know if he would be able to bear it for three more days—until Macklin returned from London.

But bear it he would, of course. He would bear it for Elizabeth's sake. His consolation must be that when she finally knew the truth she would be destroyed even more effectively than she had been seven years before. He would be able to take her back to the peace of Kingston and keep her there for the rest of her life. Even if she did not recover her memory, she would come to depend on him after she knew the truth as she depended upon Trevelyan now.

There was a woman in the flower garden, Martin saw when he was making his way back toward the house. At first he thought she was Lady Nancy—she was picking up the blooms and the scissors and gloves Lady Nancy had left behind. But she was just a maid, with blond curls escaping from beneath her mobcap, her generous breasts accentuated by her bent position. Martin stopped.

He was smiling when she straightened up and turned toward him, startled. "I have been trying to decide," he said, "which makes the prettier picture, the flowers or you."

Her face relaxed into a smile. "And what did you decide, sir?" she asked pertly.

Ah, a flirt. "Which am I looking at?" he asked, widening his eyes, and watched her blush. "It is a lovely morning after yesterday's rain, is it not? Stroll with me a little way and show me this beautiful valley."

"It is beautiful, sir," she said, "but her ladyship is waiting for me to bring the flowers. I am to help her arrange them."

"Her ladyship will wait," he said, reaching out to take the flowers and scissors and gloves from her arms and laying them on the grass at their feet. "Come." He took her arm.

At first she was flustered. Then she was indignant. It was only when he increased his pace and she had to trot along at his side to keep up with him that she became alarmed. He stopped briefly when they were out of sight among the trees and smacked her several times sharply on the bottom.

"Quiet!" he ordered her. "Have you never taken a stroll with a gentleman, girl?"

"N-no, sir," she said, her eyes large with fear.

"You are a liar," he said. "Do you think I do not know that you are a slut?"

He took her a little farther into the trees before stopping at one with several low branches. He bent her forward over one of them, grasped her skirt, and threw it up over her head. He had to slap her bare buttocks hard several more times to quieten her cries to blubbering sobs. But he was not interested in giving her a prolonged beating since doubtless she lacked the experience to know how to beat him in return. He loosened his clothing quickly, rammed himself into her, and punished himself inside the body of a woman who resembled Elizabeth only superficially. He ignored her one scream and the subsequent loud moans. They were far enough from the house.

"Listen," he said when he was finished and had re-adjusted his clothing. He took her firmly by one arm and hauled her upright. She was sobbing uncontrollably. Her face was red and ugly. "You can bathe away the blood at the stream when I have gone. You must say nothing about this to anyone. Do you understand me? I suppose you value your job?" He waited for her to answer.

She could hardly get the word out. "Ye-e-es."

"And good jobs are hard to come by in these parts, especially when one is not given a character?"

"Ye-e-es."

"You will lose your job if your mistress finds out that you are a slut and a whore," Martin said. "Do you understand me?"

"Ye-e-es, s-sir."

"Very well, then." He hesitated for a moment, undecided about whether he would pay the girl. He took some coins from his pocket, dropped them down the front of her dress into her cleavage, and turned to walk away.

His terrible frustration had subsided for a while. The girl had offered a timely diversion. But the familiar self-hatred was taking the place of frustration. Self-hatred over the fact that he had given in to the compulsion to soil himself with a whore because he could not have Elizabeth. This particular whore had not even known how to punish him so that some of the guilt and hatred could be eased.

Christopher went directly upstairs when he arrived home. He had not been able to concentrate on any work all morning. He should not have left, he had been thinking the whole time. How did he know that he could trust

Martin not to tell Elizabeth the whole ghastly story? How did he know that Martin would not after all bundle her into his carriage and make off with her back to London as soon as his back was turned?

Would he go after her if that had happened? Would he feel justified in doing so?

She was not in her dressing room. Neither was she in their bedchamber. Panic grabbed at him—a totally unreasonable panic since he had looked in none of the daytime apartments. And she might still be out walking with Martin. He had returned somewhat earlier than usual.

He opened the door to his own dressing room and felt himself almost sag with relief. She was standing at the window, her head turning back over her shoulder. He closed the door, took a few steps forward, and held out his arms to her. She came the rest of the way and walked straight into them. Her face, which she rested against his neckcloth, was pale.

He could think of nothing to say to her. Guilt had been gnawing at him all morning as well as anxiety. He had got himself into a hell of a mess and perhaps had done her irreparable harm. He closed his arms about her and rocked her.

"Christopher," she said, "tell me about our wedding."

He held still. It was all beginning to come out, then, as he and Martin had planned. Soon she would know everything except those hardest of all events to tell. There would be only the seven-year gap in her history. But before they told her, he was going to persuade Martin that he had not been guilty. He was going to persuade him to tell her that, to tell her that he had fled merely because he was too young and inexperienced to cope with adversity. It was after all the simple truth. Together he and Martin would tell her the real truth, not what she had thought was the truth. They would set history straight.

"It was at Kingston," he said. "Kingston Park in Norfolkshire, your father's estate. In the chapel there. We would not have it in the village church or at St. George's in London as your father wanted. The chapel was too small, he said. But we wanted only our families and close friends present."

"Did we have a long betrothal?" she asked against his neckcloth.

"Only one month," he said. "We were in love and wanted to be married."

"And all our family was there?" she said.

"Yes."

"It must have been wonderful," she said, "to marry with all our family about us."

"It was." He rubbed his cheek against the top of her head. "It was wonderful beyond words, Elizabeth. We were in love, and it was our wedding day, and only the happily ever after was ahead of us."

She drew back her head and looked into his eyes. "Your father came?" she said. "And Nancy?"

"Yes." He gazed back at her. "No. Nancy went home just a week before the wedding. She was afraid that Penhallow would run away with no one to keep an eye on it, I suppose. She was homesick and insisted on coming home. I stormed at her and you pleaded with her, but nothing would keep her."

"Your story matches hers," she said. "Have you spoken with her since you came home?"

"No." His eyes searched hers.

"Martin reminded me," she said, "that I have only your word for it that I belong here, that I am your wife, that we love each other." She laughed suddenly. "I have only your word for it and Nancy's and Martin's that I am who you say I am. If my name were not Elizabeth Atwell, I would be none the wiser. What was my name before I married? It was not Honywood like Martin's, was it? He is my stepbrother."

"Ward," he said. "You were Lady Elizabeth Ward."

She was quiet for a moment, considering. "Another stranger," she said.

"Do you believe I am that too, Elizabeth?" he asked her quietly. "A stranger, I mean. Do you believe I was a stranger to you until two weeks ago?"

She looked at him with troubled eyes and said nothing for a while.

Tell her, a voice inside his head instructed him. It was the perfect time. She was doubtful anyway, and the whole question had been opened up conveniently. *Tell her.*

She shook her head slowly. "No," she said. "I knew

you and I loved you. If there is one thing I am certain of, it is that. Christopher, can't we send him away? He came out of concern for my health. Well, he has seen that my health is perfect except for the obvious. There is no further reason for him to stay. I am where I belong, and he can see that you are looking after me admirably. He can see that I am coping with the situation, or beginning to anyway. Can't we ask him to leave?"

"He is your brother, Elizabeth," he said. How he wished he could just do as she asked. How he wished that life were that simple.

"Stepbrother," she said. "No blood relation at all. He touched me."

Christopher frowned.

"He put his arm about me," she said, "and I panicked. He seemed like a stranger. I don't want anyone touching me but you. I don't want him touching me."

"Brothers put their arms about their sisters," he said. "I do with Nancy."

"But he is a stranger to me," she said.

"I was a stranger to you just over two weeks ago," he said. "You let me make love to you, Elizabeth."

She sighed deeply and set her face back against his neckcloth. "I can accept the one relationship but not the other," she said. "It does not make sense, I know. I only know that with you it feels right while with Martin it feels—I don't know. He made my flesh creep. Let's go down for luncheon, then, and I will keep practicing to be the affectionate sister. It is easy with Nancy, not so easy with Martin. But no one ever said that life was easy. I will even let him touch me if you say it is right and natural for him to do so."

Holding her to him, rocking her again, he wondered what would have happened if he had ignored the news that she was to marry Lord Poole the day after his arrival in London. And he wondered if he would do anything different if he could go back now and react all over again to what Seth Wickenham had told him at the Pulteney.

Somehow he doubted it.

"Yes, let's go down," he said. But he hugged her to him again when he should have let her go. "I wish I could shield you from the pain and bewilderment these days are bringing you, Elizabeth."

She looked up at him and smiled. "You are doing so to a very large degree," she said. "You cannot know, perhaps, how wonderfully safe I feel with you. That was why I was so shaken when Martin tried to put doubts in my mind."

She held up her face for his kiss. She did not know that every sexual encounter now, even one as seemingly innocent as a kiss, burned his guilt deeper on his soul. He met her mouth with his, opened it, licked into the warm cavity with his tongue, gave her all the comfort and reassurance for which she was so obviously seeking.

Christ, she was going to hate him. Yet he very much feared that he was going to find it impossible ever to hate her again.

Antoine Bouchard was finding England difficult to adjust to. He missed the wide open spaces of the American wilderness. The valley in which Penhallow was built was pleasant, of course. Everything was pretty but so very small and confining. The sea, now, was another matter. The sea fed Antoine's soul.

And so he was in the habit of getting away from the house as often as possible. He usually took a horse and rode along the valley to the sea and galloped along the open beach, in the opposite direction from that sometimes taken by his employer and the lady the two of them had kidnapped in London. Antoine sometimes wondered what would happen when that lady recovered her memory. She and Lord Trevelyan were very cozy at the moment, but when she knew how she had been tricked . . .

There was that new arrival, of course—the man who had pretended to be Captain Rice and had then greeted Lord Trevelyan in the visitors' salon with a pistol. Antoine did not entirely trust the man's smiling face. If it were he, Antoine, and someone had run off with his sister just as she was about to marry someone else and had then proceeded to live with her himself—if it were he, Antoine thought, there would be no smiles. Only a knife straight through the heart.

Either the smiling Englishman was stupid or he was sly. Antoine leaned rather toward the latter opinion.

His employer returned before luncheon from a morning of farm business, and Antoine came out to the stables to rub down his horse. The other servants of the house looked at him askance when he did such things, he knew. He was not a groom, the housekeeper had pointed out to him once. He was his lordship's valet, wasn't he? It seemed that in England one could be only one thing, never two or more. Antoine did not care. He carried shirts up to his employer when they were needed, and he rubbed down his horse when it had been out.

And he took horses from the stables for his own use and made the other grooms nervous. But they said nothing to him. He suspected that they were a little afraid of him. The thought made him chuckle. He took a horse after finishing with the earl's, and followed his usual path along the valley toward the sea. He would not be popular for missing luncheon and arriving back as hungry as a bear before it was teatime—that delicate English meal when one was supposed to nibble at delicacies that teased the palate rather than satisfying it.

Someone was among the trees, he saw as he rode. A woman. She was far back from the stream and she scrambled to hide behind a tree trunk as he approached. That was the fact that made him curious. If she had waved or even ignored him, he would have ridden on by. He turned his horse and guided it among the trees, dipping his head to avoid branches.

"Winnie?" he said when he drew closer. She was standing behind a tree, her back against the trunk, but she was unmistakably Lady Nancy's personal maid. She liked to flirt with him—and with the second footman and one of the grooms as well. And yet, the groom had told Antoine with a sigh, no one ever got anywhere with the girl. She was looking for a wedding ring, that one, Antoine guessed.

She did not answer him. Her silence set him to frowning and swinging down from the horse's bare back. He looped the reins over a tree branch and walked toward her.

"Go away!" she said when he came into her line of vision. Her voice was shaking. "Go away!"

"Winnie?" Her face was red and swollen. The hem of her dress was dark with wetness as if she had been wading in the stream. There was a smear of blood down the front of her skirt. "What 'appened?"

She averted her face and closed her eyes. Her hands were gripping the tree trunk behind her, her nails digging into the bark like talons. "Go away!" she said.

She had hurt herself and was ashamed of her tears. He reached out to touch her shoulder—and found himself fighting with a wild thing. Except that he was not fighting. He held up his hands palm out.

"Don't touch me!" she shrieked at him. "Don't touch me. Go away!"

He took a step back. "I'll not touch you," he said quietly. "What 'appened?"

"Nothing," she said. "Nothing at all. Go away."

It was not embarrassment or a minor accident. Antoine's eyes narrowed. He had not been born yesterday. He was twenty-seven years old.

"Who was 'e?" he asked. The groom? he wondered. "William?"

"No." She shook her head. "He was nobody. Nothing happened. I came out for a walk, that's all. I have a cold. Go away. Please go away."

The footman? But no, not the footman and not the groom. Antoine knew suddenly who it was. "The visitor from London, was it?" he asked. "Mr. Martin 'Onywood?"

She shook her head and began to cry against the back of her hand. It looked as if she had been doing a deal of crying. If Antoine had not known her before, he would not have guessed that she was pretty.

" 'e raped you?" he asked quietly.

"No, no," she said through her sobs. "Go away."

"You 'ave blood on your dress, Winnie," he said. "Don't tell me you 'ave fallen. Mon Dieu, it was that son of a bitch, non?"

She looked at him with red and miserable eyes over the top of her shaking hand.

"Come," he said, "let me 'old you. You need someone's arms, non? I will not 'urt you, ma petite. I 'ave six sisters. Come to me. I'll not frighten you by coming to you." He opened his arms to her.

She hesitated and then flung herself forward until his arms closed strongly about her. "I didn't come willing," she sobbed against his shoulder. "I told him I had to get back to my lady. He forced me to come, Mr. Bouchard. I didn't ask for it. I didn't, I swear. And then he—he—"

"I know," he said. "I'll 'old you for a while, Winnie.'E'll not touch you again. I kill the bastard for you."

She jerked back her head. "Oh, no, Mr. Bouchard," she said. "They'll hang you for sure."

"Then I follow 'im to 'ell and kill 'im again," he said. "I come with you to tell your mistress when you feel better."

Her eyes grew round. "Oh, no," she said. "No one must ever know. Please, Mr. Bouchard, you must not tell anyone. I would lose my position. My mum needs the money I send her."

"Lose your position because that pig raped you?" Antoine's frown was ferocious. "Did 'e tell you that? Threatened you, did 'e? It's nonsense."

Her look became frantic. "You don't understand," she said. "Maybe it's different in the wild land you come from, Mr. Bouchard. But here gentlemen are always right. And girls like me are always sluts once they have lost their m-maidenhood. That is what I will be called if anyone knows. Or whore. Please, Mr. Bouchard." Her hands clawed at the lapels of his coat.

"Sh, ma petite," he said, drawing her into his arms again, soothing her. "Sacré coeur, sometimes I forget that now I am in a civilized nation where maidens who are raped are sluts and 'ores. Civilization is a wonderful thing, n'est-ce pas? Your name will not be dragged to the dust because of me, 'ave no fear. But that son of a louse 'ad better grow eyes all about 'is 'ead. One of these days the knife of Antoine Bouchard is going to sheath itself in Mr. Martin 'Onywood's 'eart."

Winnie made no protest this time. She sniffed against his shoulder. "It hurt so much," she said. "I feel dirty all over, Mr. Bouchard. I don't believe I'll ever feel clean again."

"You are as white as snow, ma petite," he told her. "Come, I take you back to the 'ouse and smuggle you upstairs to your room. You send a message down that you have the bad 'eadache, non? They will send up something to 'elp you sleep. And tomorrow Antoine talk to you again and make sure you feel safe."

She nodded and he took his horse's reins in one hand and set the other arm protectively about her shoulders until they came in sight of the house. Antoine wished fervently that he had fired his rifle through the window of the visitors' salon the day before and blown the bastard's head off. Better still, he should have blown his balls off.

But, he thought, there was more satisfaction to be gained from taking the life of a man who deserved to die with the point of a knife. He knew that from experience, having killed men both ways.

Mr. Martin Honywood should perhaps be thankful that Winnie was not one of Antoine's six sisters. If she were, then Antoine's knife would be used to perform surgery before being plunged to the heart.

The following two days were almost anticlimactic in their quietness. It was as if all of them had taken fright on that first morning of Martin's visit and had decided that matters needed to be taken more slowly.

Martin set himself patiently to win Elizabeth's trust and affection. He no longer touched her or tried to force information on her, welcome or otherwise. He waited for her to ask questions, as she began to do, and make overtures of affection to him. She kissed him on the cheek each night.

Christopher was very quiet, always there to hold Elizabeth when she needed to be held, to reassure her when she needed reassuring, to love her when she needed loving.

Nancy kept quietly in the background, waiting for the inevitable explosion, helpless to do anything to prevent it.

Gradually the story of Elizabeth's past was filled in so that she came to feel familiar with the life of that other woman, Lady Elizabeth Ward. But it was still hard to grasp the fact that she was that girl, or had been once upon a time.

Perhaps she was half conscious of the fact that all the stories she was told—and there were many of them—ended abruptly seven years before with her wedding to

Christopher. Without fully realizing it she was developing a dread of hearing about those missing years. What was wrong? Something was. But she never asked the question, even in her conscious mind. Her mind skirted around it, ignored it, behaved as if the question were not shouting to be asked.

Martin and Christopher had a few private conversations together. Martin considered it important that Elizabeth be told the full truth. And soon. They must not delay indefinitely. There was no point in further delay. It was not fair to his sister. Christopher agreed in the main. But they could come to no agreement on what the truth was that she must be told. Martin, it seemed, had come eventually to believe in Christopher's guilt. Elizabeth should be told everything.

"She will surely forgive you," he said reassuringly. "After all, it was a long time ago, and she has grown up since then. Then she expected you to be perfect. Now she realizes that no one is. She will surely still love you even when you have fallen from your pedestal. I sincerely hope she does anyway. But you can never be at peace with yourself, Trevelyan, if you hide part of the truth. Better to make a clean breast of everything now. Besides, her memory may come back one day and she may take it hard if you have deceived her."

"But I want her to see things as they really were," Christopher insisted. "I want her to know that the only way I wronged her was in running away."

"Well," Martin said, "perhaps we can compromise. We will tell her what everyone believed, including me in the end, I must confess. And then you can tell her your story. She can decide for herself. She will doubtless decide in your favor. She loves you again, I can see, and I'm not sorry for it. And even if she cannot believe you, she will forgive you."

They shook hands on that. After all, Christopher thought, Martin was going out of his way to be fair and decent, ignoring the very real crimes that had been committed during the past two and a half weeks.

Christopher had made arrangements to spend all of the fourth full day of Martin's visit and the next day too with his steward. They would wait then, he and Martin decided, until the day after that. Then together they would talk with Elizabeth and tell her about the past seven years.

It felt a little like a death sentence to Christopher.

12

ELIZABETH was trying hard to like Martin, to feel comfortable with him. He was being very patient with her, she noticed, and he was always friendly with Christopher. She did not know why she could not like him when it seemed that she always had. And Christopher could not understand her aversion to Martin.

She tried hard to overcome it. When Martin asked her after luncheon on the first day Christopher was away if she would care for a walk, she smiled at him and suggested they go up onto the headland.

It was a cool and blustery day with heavy clouds hanging low though it was not raining. They were buffeted on top of the cliffs and looked down on a leaden and foam-flecked sea. It made Elizabeth shiver with more than cold.

"That is a path?" Martin asked, pointing to their right. "Shall we go down onto the beach? It will be more sheltered down there."

She felt herself stiffen unwillingly. The beach belonged to her and Christopher. "The path is too steep," She said. "I always prefer to stay up here."

"I would hold your hand," he said, smiling at her. "But never mind."

They strolled along the headland, away from the path.

"Lizzie," he said, "I think it is time you came home with me. Tomorrow perhaps or the next day."

"You mean to London?" she said. "I *am* home. And I don't want to leave here for a while, Martin. Certainly not without Christopher."

"Do you have any memories of this place?" he asked her. "The sea? The cliffs? The house? Anything?"

"I have told you," she said a little impatiently, "that I remember nothing."

"And yet," he said, "you have told me that you remember something of London. Why not of Penhallow, then? Is there not even a feeling of familiarity here?"

"No." She sighed. "Persistent questioning is not going to bring anything back, Martin."

"Have you ever thought," he said, "that perhaps it would not be familiar to you even if you had your memory? Have you considered the possibility that you were brought to Penhallow for the first time after you fell out of that carriage?"

She looked at him sharply. "Don't," she said. "You are frightening me." She laughed but she was feeling anything but amusement. "This is Christopher's home and I am his wife. Of course we have been living here. Where else?"

He shrugged. "Perhaps at Kingston," he said. "Perhaps you have been living there, Lizzie, with Papa and me."

"Don't do this to me, Martin," she said. "Why are you trying to confuse and frighten me? Why would we have been living at Kingston when we belong at Penhallow?"

"You alone," he said. "Perhaps Trevelyan has been at neither place. He did not inherit until his father died last year. Has he told you that? Have you asked him where he met that rather strange valet or groom or watchdog that he keeps for a servant?"

"Mr. Bouchard?" she said. "He was in London with a fur-trading ship and wanted to stay."

"And Trevelyan and he just happened to cross paths?" he said. "The man is French-Canadian, Lizzie. He is the type of man known as a voyageur. That is, his job is to man the fur-gathering canoes into the interior wilderness beyond Canada. It is not part of his job to sail on the trading ships. He would have done that only if someone he had met in the course of his job had persuaded him to leave it and take another—as a servant, perhaps."

"What are you saying?" Her voice and manner were determinedly calm as she stopped walking and turned to face him. "That Christopher and I have been living apart?"

He set his head to one side and regarded her with sad,

kindly eyes. "It is at least a possibility, Lizzie, is it not?" he said.

"But not a probability," she said. "It is not true." But she could feel her hands begin to tremble.

"Lizzie," he said, "let me hold you. Let me hold you tight. Let me take you home."

"I *am* home." Her chin came up and her eyes sparked. "But I wish you would go, Martin—to Kingston or London. I wish you would not stay just for my sake. I want to be alone with Christopher again. I was happy before you came. You have told me much about my past and I am grateful. But I don't think I want to hear any more. I don't think I need to hear any more. I am happier as I am."

"There is one thing you must know, Lizzie," he said.

"No."

"I am not going to tell you now," he said. "My servant should be back from London tonight. I sent him there a few days ago. He is bringing something that you must see—tomorrow morning."

"No," she said.

"Yes," he said. "You must."

She turned and began to walk back in the direction of the house.

"Lizzie." He hurried after her but did not attempt to touch her. "It breaks my heart to see you like this. You are afraid to know the whole truth, aren't you? You are afraid that it will make you unhappy. You were not unhappy, believe me. Quite the contrary. You were wonderfully happy."

"And still am," she said. She looked across at him, at his pale, concerned face. "Very well, Martin. I will look at what you have to show me tomorrow morning. But only if you will promise me one thing. Promise that you will leave Penhallow immediately after. I cannot beg Christopher to ask you to leave. He likes you and insists that I do too and he must, of course, be a courteous host. But I am asking. Promise me you will leave?"

"I promise," he said. "I will leave as soon as I have shown you what Macklin is bringing."

They walked back to the house side by side and in silence.

* * *

They had not made love and for the first time Elizabeth had not snuggled against him in bed and invited his arms to come about her. She was lying on her side facing away from him. She was breathing quietly. Christopher could not tell if she was asleep or not.

He should leave well enough alone, he thought. He should close his eyes and go to sleep. He had had a busy day and there was another to come. And then the day after that he and Martin were to fill in the final gaps in her story and she would know that he had no right to bring her to this house. Or this bed.

Then he was going to have to start fighting for her. Or forgetting her. He still had not decided which it would be.

He touched her lightly on the shoulder and felt it stiffen almost imperceptibly. So she was not asleep.

"Do you want to talk about it?" he asked.

He thought for a while that she was not going to answer, but then she rolled over onto her back and stared up at the high canopy over their heads.

"How long have we lived at Penhallow?" she asked, her voice toneless.

Ah, he thought, Martin had not waited after all. How much had he told her?

"Have we been here for seven years?" she asked.

"No," he said quietly.

"Had I been here at all before my accident?"

"No."

"Where were we?" she asked.

He lifted himself on one elbow and looked down at her. "How much has he told you?" he asked.

She continued to look straight upward. "Nothing really," she said. "Only suggestions of what might have been. Have we been together?"

Each question was like a knife stabbing into him. "No," he said.

Her eyes closed at last and they were both silent for a long time. "Why?" she asked at last.

"There were misunderstandings," he said. "A dreadful quarrel. You would have none of me and I ran away."

"To Canada," she said.

"Yes."

"And have just recently returned."

"Yes."

She laughed unexpectedly. "If I knew of all this happening to a stranger," she said, "I would be horrified. But it happened to me. There are details missing, aren't there? Many details. I don't want to know them. Not now, Christopher. Just tell me one thing." She breathed in slowly and exhaled raggedly. "Were we happy to be together again? In that carriage before I fell out, were we happy?"

He opened his mouth and drew breath, but he could not bring himself to answer.

She laughed again. "There is a whole story behind just that one incident, is there not?" she said. "How on earth did I come to fall out? Or was I pushed?"

She began to cry then. She continued to look upward and made no attempt to cover her face or to turn it away from him. He could see her tears in the dim light from the window.

"Elizabeth." He set the backs of two fingers against her cheek, expecting her to flinch away or to slap at his hand. Instead she grasped his wrist and brought his palm against her mouth and held it there.

"I don't want to know any more," she said between sobs. "I don't want to, Christopher." She turned her head to stare at him. "I hate him. Perhaps I shouldn't, but I do. He is evil and he is going to tear us apart."

He swallowed. "Nobody can tear us apart except ourselves," he said. "I have . . ."

But she surged over onto her side and pressed a hand over his mouth. "Don't," she said. "Don't say any more. Please don't." She withdrew her hand. "I won't stop loving you, Christopher. Don't expect it of me. I just won't."

It was not a gentle lovemaking. Before he plunged into her, making her cry out with mingled pain and desire, they were both somehow naked and their mouths and tongues had ravished each other, and their hands had stroked, pressed, explored, aroused pain and pleasure. He pressed her downward, pounding into her, only half feeling her fingernails drawing blood from his back, only half hearing her cries and his own. He lay spent on her after it was over, heedless of the fact that his full weight was on her.

That could well be the last time, his mind told him as rationality began to return. And his throat and chest ached with unshed tears as he lifted himself off her. He held her wordlessly, not sleeping, knowing that she did not sleep either, until perhaps an hour later when they made love again tenderly, slowly, and wordlessly.

There really was nothing to say.

Though they both knew that soon there would be a great deal to be said.

After riding to and from London at a punishing pace, Macklin was back at Penhallow early enough that Martin could have pressed matters and taken Elizabeth aside during the evening. But he wanted her to be quite alone when she saw what he had to show her. She would need to be alone. This was one thing at least that he was going to have to explain to her quite openly and clearly. There was to be no beating about the bush on this matter. No more hints. Only the final denouement.

Christopher had left already when Martin went down to breakfast the next morning. He would be gone all day again, then. It was a relief to know that he had not changed his plans. Martin breakfasted with Elizabeth and Nancy. The latter treated him with cold civility. As if he cared, Martin thought. Silly bitch—did she think he cared how she treated him?

Elizabeth was bright-eyed and slightly flushed. She knew that the crisis was coming that morning, Martin thought, and she believed that she would be rid of him once she had faced it. Poor Lizzie. She thought she would be glad to see the back of him. He ached for the suffering he was about to cause her. And he ached to have it over and out of the way so that he could begin to comfort her, so that he could take her away to safety again.

"I have promised to spend an hour with Martin, Nancy," Elizabeth said, rising from the table when they had all finished eating. "Do you mind?"

"No, of course not," Nancy said briskly. She smiled at Elizabeth and did not even look at Martin. "There are a few matters I need to attend to."

Elizabeth faced him when they had left the breakfast room. "You wish to walk outside?" she asked.

"No," he said. "I think a private room would be best."

He saw despair in her eyes when she nodded to him before turning to lead the way to the library. She knew it was the end of her little idyll, he thought, and his heart ached for her again.

"Your servant has returned?" she asked, turning to him as he closed the library doors behind him.

"Yes," he said.

"Well?" She had squared her shoulders and lifted her chin.

"It is a small something I have to show you," he said, drawing a package out of an inner pocket of his coat and slowly removing the silk wrapping.

She watched without moving. Her hands clasped in front of her were white-knuckled.

"It is a portrait," he said. "A miniature, Lizzie. And a very good likeness. We were all agreed on that when it was painted at Christmas time."

From across the distance between them she looked at the picture in his hands. Her face was expressionless, stony almost.

He took several steps toward her and turned the little framed miniature in his hands so that it was facing her.

She looked into his eyes for what seemed a long time before looking down. Only her eyes moved. Her lips trembled and she reached out one finger to touch the frame. "Christina," she said.

He held his breath. "You remember?" he said into the silence.

"No," she said, snatching her finger back as if it had been burned. "Is that her name? I don't know her. She has dark hair and blue eyes. She looks very like Christopher." Martin watched her rub one palm up and down over her hip and outer thigh, her fingers spread back. He heard her swallow. "She is his daughter, isn't she? And mine?"

"Yes," he said.

She continued to look at the picture for a long time, her hand still rubbing her side. And then she caught up her skirt and ran, fumbling and tearing at the knob of the door in her haste, fleeing along the corridor and through the archway into the great hall. Martin followed behind her but made no attempt to catch up to her. He stood in the archway and watched her jerk open the front doors without waiting for a servant to open them for her. She fled outside into the courtyard.

Martin looked down at the miniature of his six-year-old niece—his stepniece—and forced himself to stay where he was at least for the time being. She had remembered her daughter's name. Perhaps that was the crack in the armor that was needed to bring everything flooding back. But whether it was or not, she clearly needed to be alone for a while. Her reaction had been more violent even than he had hoped it would be.

It was a chilly morning and she was wearing only a thin dress. He turned toward the stairs. He would fetch a cloak from her room and go to meet her after a while.

Elizabeth ran all the way up the hill and along the mile of headland to the edge of the cliffs, the wind blowing in her face. She paused for a few moments to catch her breath and press a hand to her aching side and then ran to the top of the path and down it, heedless of its steepness or the dangerous drop to one side of it. She stumbled on the loose pebbles at the bottom of the path, scraping her knee painfully.

Christina. The sharp pain brought the name back and all the cause of her panicked flight. She had known the name of the child in the portrait, though it had seemed to be a picture of a stranger. But she had heard herself speak the name. Christina. And then she had known without any real doubt that she was their child, hers and Christopher's, and yet she was not at Penhallow with them. And he had never mentioned her. Even when she had asked him why they had never had children.

Elizabeth stood very still suddenly and pressed clenched fists to her mouth. Christina was suckling at her breast and she herself was crying. Constantly crying. The baby was always fretful. The child was not getting enough milk, the nurse said. They were trying to persuade her to hire a wet nurse. Who were? The nurse. Her father. The physician. Not Martin. Martin was soothing her, comforting her, telling her that she must stop crying, that she must put her grief behind her, that she must draw all her happiness from her daughter. He was telling her that if she could do that, then her milk would come back and Christina would be contented.

Elizabeth lowered her hands from her mouth and stepped onto the sand of the beach. The tide was half in, she saw. The air was cold. There were goose bumps on her arms. But she only saw them; she did not feel them. That had not been a real memory, had it? She had no memory. She remembered nothing. She was suddenly very frightened.

They had not wanted her to name her baby Christina. Papa had wanted Sarah—her mother's name. Someone else had suggested Elizabeth. Anything but Christina. It would not be fitting under the circumstances, they had said. Except Martin. Martin had understood. He had sat carefully on the side of her bed—the opposite side from where the newborn baby lay asleep—and had taken her hand in both of his and smiled his usual kindly smile.

"You must name her whatever you wish, Lizzie," he had said. "She is your daughter."

"They say she should not have a name like his," she had said, gripping one of his hands, trying to draw on his strength. "But she is his daughter, Martin. And I loved him." The inevitable tears flowed again.

"Yes," he had said gently. "And now you have me to love you instead, Lizzie. And to stand by you too. I'll speak up for you, never fear. You must call her what you wish."

"She is Christina," she had said and she had smiled at him through her tears.

"Yes," he had said. "Christina Ward. That is her name, Lizzie. I'll explain to Papa."

Not Christina Atwell? She had closed her eyes wearily. No, perhaps not. But she had a Christian name like his and she had his dark hair and his blue eyes, if they stayed blue. The new nurse Papa had hired for the baby had told her that most babies have blue eyes, but that they often change color with time. She did not want her baby's eyes to change color. Christina was all she had left of Christopher. All she had ever had of him.

Elizabeth was rubbing her arms with her hands when her mind returned to the present. God. Oh, dear God, what was happening? What had happened? She turned to walk with hurried steps along the beach as if she could outstrip the flashing memories—if they *were* memories.

Martin had stayed with her when Papa had returned to London. At Kingston. He had stayed at Kingston with her. She would have wanted to die if it had not been for Christina. Her baby had given her a reason for living. And not just for living. Her daughter had given her a reason for growing up. There had always been people to look after her, to make her decisions for her, to shield her from pain and problems. She had never had to be strong in herself. She had been taught that it was unfeminine to have a strong character.

But she had stopped crying so that Christina might have milk. And she had learned to smile and look happy so that her daughter might have a secure childhood. She had learned to do something useful with her life. She had spent far more time with her child than most mothers of her acquaintance did, and she had involved herself with the affairs of the neighborhood as the lady of the manor. She had been that since the death of her stepmother, she supposed, but she had never taken on the responsibilities the position entailed. Now she did.

And gradually, very gradually, she had come to feel that she wanted to live on her own account. She had come to feel that life was worth living despite everything.

Martin had stayed with her at Kingston although he had had no need to do so. The dreadful scandal had not touched him nearly. And London was surely where he ought to have been. He was a young man and must crave the social life and the pleasures young men look for. He had not been obliged to stay with her. But he had—throughout the years. And he had become again her very dearest friend, her emotional prop until she had learned through determined effort to rely more on her own strength and less on his. Then he had been her companion, her confidant.

Sometimes she had wondered why he did it. Why did he give up his own pleasure just because she needed him? He was not even her brother, only her stepbrother. Sometimes she even wondered if that fact were significant and wondered if it were possible for a man to marry his stepsister. Was it legally possible? But Martin's affection for her never seemed loverlike. And for that she was profoundly thankful.

She had needed a brother, not another lover.

Elizabeth walked along the beach, her head down, her arms wrapped about herself. She could no longer feel any doubt that the images running through her mind were real memories. She was remembering. And yet her memories were like the small and tantalizing glimpses of one's surroundings one sometimes has in a dense mist. Tiny patches of clearness in an otherwise blank world.

What had happened? Where had Christopher been? She knew the answer, of course. He had been in Canada. But why? Dear God, what had happened? And how had she come to be here with him now and without Christina?

She had reached the cave. The lovers' cave. But she felt no desire to go inside. She set her back against the large boulder before its mouth, leaned her head back, and closed her eyes.

Christopher did not know about Christina. She had only been suspecting when he left that she was with child, but she had not told him about her suspicions. She had wanted to be quite sure before sharing the wonder of it with him. And afterward they had persuaded her not to tell him—even Martin. Not that they had known where he had gone anyway at first. They had assumed he had gone back to Penhallow.

He had left. He had left her forever. He had gone to Canada.

Elizabeth pressed her body back against the rock as if by doing so she could prevent what was happening. And she desperately held her mind blank, opened her eyes to look up at the sky, across the blue of which clouds were scudding in the wind. She must hold her mind blank. Oh, God!

And then the floodgates opened.

The letter.

The half-naked woman he had been holding when she had gone with Martin to that house in response to the letter, disbelieving. And the woman's child. *His* child.

His protestations of innocence despite the fact that she had caught him red-handed. His constant attempts to explain, to lie his way out of the situation.

Her removal to her father's house and her refusal to

see him. Her father's enforcement of that refusal though she had always hoped that he would break his way in to see her.

His disappearance.

Those other stories. Terrible, incriminating stories, showing her a ruthless and cruel side to Christopher that she had never suspected.

The whore. The whore who had fallen and killed herself after being severely beaten by a customer. By Christopher.

The poor man who had been cheated out of his fortune—by Christopher—and had then taken his own life in despair.

The divorce Papa had demanded. Oh, God, the dreadfully public and scandalous divorce.

And the pain. The pain that went on and on until she had hoped that it would kill her.

And his continued absence. He had not come back to defend himself or to fight for her. Or to know that they were to have a child.

The divorce! Elizabeth staggered away from the rock and back along the beach, blindly hurrying toward safety and comfort. Toward something that did not exist. Panic set her to stumbling, gasping and sobbing.

She and Christopher were divorced!

She had to stop when she was halfway up the cliff path. All her breath was gone, there was a stabbing pain in her side again, and her legs felt like jelly. She looked upward. There was a man standing at the top of the path and she almost turned and ran back to the beach. But it was not him. It was Martin.

She dragged herself upward again, seeing at last the safety she had been running toward. Martin! He was walking slowly downward toward her.

And then she remembered Manley. Lord Poole. And St. George's. St. George's this time, Papa had insisted. She would do it right this time—and she had reluctantly agreed with him. She would do everything right this time. With the head and not the heart. She remembered the masked rider who had snatched her up outside the church. And the terror of the long journey in the darkened carriage. And Christopher getting into it with her eventually.

And her attempt to escape through the unlocked door.

"Martin." She could scarcely gasp out his name. But she did not have to walk the final few steps toward him. He came to her, wrapped a cloak about her, and caught her up in reassuringly warm and strong arms.

"It's all right, Lizzie," he murmured against her ear. "I have you safe now, love. No one is going to hurt you. Not ever again. I won't let it happen again."

"Martin," she said. "He kidnapped me and then he lied to me. He told me I was his w-w—"

"I have directed your maid to pack your trunk," he said, holding her tight. "I'll have you on your way home in no time at all, Lizzie. Don't worry about a thing. Leave everything to me. You know you can trust me, don't you?"

13

ELIZABETH was in a fever to be gone. Christopher would be away until late in the afternoon, she knew, and it was not even noon yet. Perhaps it was not even past the middle of the morning. But she was terrified that he would return unexpectedly and try to prevent her from leaving. She was, after all, his prisoner at Penhallow. She knew that now and understood fully why she had not been allowed to leave the estate. Perhaps he would try to stop her from leaving her prison even though Martin was with her.

And yet she did not rush down to the carriage immediately when Martin sent his servant to tell her that it was waiting at the door. She hesitated outside the door of Nancy's sitting room and then opened it without knocking. Nancy looked up, startled, from her escritoire, where she was writing a letter, and then stood up hurriedly.

"I am leaving," Elizabeth said. "Immediately. Tell him not to follow me, Nancy. If he does, I shall have him arrested and charged with kidnapping. My father will see that the charge sticks. He is very good at that."

"Elizabeth—" Nancy took one step toward her.

"And I might have you charged as his accomplice," Elizabeth added. "My memory loss certainly played into his hands, didn't it? Prisoner in body and mind. How delighted he must have been. And what a fool you have both taken me for."

"Elizabeth—"

"He took me away from the life I had made for myself at great pains and despite him," Elizabeth said. "I was about to marry a good man. And he took me away from my responsibilities. When he snatched me away outside that church, he left a six-year-old child inside who would not understand why her mother had abandoned her without a word. He has made that little girl suffer for almost three weeks.

"And you, Nancy—you might have helped me but did not. Did it mean nothing to you that I was helpless in body and did not even have a memory to help me fight him? Can you not imagine what it is to be a woman at the mercy of a man's whims? You must have known what has been happening between us for longer than two weeks. You would have to be blind not to have known. Yet you allowed it to happen, knowing that I believed myself to be his wife when I am not."

"Elizabeth," Nancy said, reaching out a hand toward her, "I am so sorry."

"Elizabeth laughed. "Strangely," she said, "those words mean nothing to me. Nothing at all."

She turned without another word and left the room. She hurried down the stairs in a frenzy again to be gone. Martin was waiting beside his carriage and handed her in. He jumped in after her, sat down on the seat across from her, and took both her hands in his. No one closed the door.

"Lizzie," he said, "I am sending you on alone for the first stage of the journey. Your maid is going with you. She is just waiting for me to finish speaking with you and then will join you. And Macklin will be riding beside the carriage. He is a good man."

She looked at him in some alarm.

"My coachman knows where to stop for the night," he said. "I'll be there by tomorrow morning. I'll hire a horse and come after you. I must stay and talk with Trevelyan first. I have to make it clear to him that he must on no account make any attempt to follow you or to communicate with you. I must make him aware of the consequences if he is foolhardy enough to try."

"Yes," she said, squeezing his hands tightly. "Stop him from coming after me, Martin. I am afraid of him. I am afraid of what he will do."

"Leave him to me," he said.

"But, Martin," she said, alarmed suddenly, "don't hurt him. Please don't."

"Hurt him?" He smiled ruefully. "You know me, Lizzie. I could not bring myself to offer anyone bodily harm unless he were directly threatening you. Then I would do something, I suppose. But I don't think he would do that. Now listen to me. I am going to take you to Kingston Park. You don't have to worry about a thing. I'll explain everything to Papa and Lord Poole. I'll see them when I go to London to fetch Christina. Then you will be able to relax and forget that you ever decided to try London again. We will be contented in the country again, the three of us, as we were before you grew restless. We *were* contented, weren't we?''

''Yes,'' she said, tears welling into her eyes. ''How foolish I was to want to leave, Martin. Yes, take me back there. And you will look after everything? How wonderful you are. How would I ever manage without you?''

''You don't have to,'' he said, smiling and leaning across the gap between them to kiss her cheek. ''Now, we will talk about it in more detail later. I can see you are anxious to be on your way. Take care, then, Lizzie. I'll see you tomorrow morning.'' He got to his feet, squeezed her hands before releasing them, and vaulted from the carriage. A minute later Doris had joined her, looking half frightened and half excited by this new adventure, and the carriage was on its way.

Elizabeth closed her eyes and leaned her head back against the cushions. She concentrated on controlling the panic that she supposed would be with her until Martin arrived at the inn the following morning. And perhaps even then, Christopher would come after her, she thought, and he would force her to go back. Except that this time she would have to be a real prisoner. This time he would have to lock her up. This time there would be no pretense of love or marriage.

She needed Martin, she thought. She needed his good sense and his quiet affection and his strength. She wished he had come with her. And she wished they were well away from Devonshire and back at Kingston again. She always felt safe there. And at peace. She should not have left. She knew that now. Martin had tried to persuade her to stay and had even been prepared to stay with her indefinitely. But she had insisted. What a fool she had been!

And yet, she thought suddenly, she did not want to go back. Oh, back to Kingston, perhaps. It would be good to be there again, to be home again. But she did not want to go back to the way she had been after Christopher left her the first time, or after she had left him—it was hard sometimes to know who had left whom more decisively. She did not want to go back to being that weeping, cringing poor creature. There was terror in the very thought.

And if he thought he could destroy her by all he had done to her in the past few weeks, she thought, then perhaps it was time he was taught a lesson. No, she would not crumble. She would not!

Elizabeth turned her thoughts deliberately to her daughter, whom she had last seen before the wedding when she had sent the child on her way to the church. Christina had been rather tearful. She did not like Manley and was afraid of losing her mother's love once this new marriage had been contracted. Poor Christina. She must have felt in these last weeks that all her worst fears had been realized.

Elizabeth felt a sudden ache of longing to see her child again. To see the daughter who had kept her sane six years before and perhaps throughout the years since.

Christopher came home somewhat earlier than he had the afternoon before. He had found himself quite unable to concentrate on work. He could not rid his mind of a strong sense of foreboding and an equally strong conviction that he should have stayed home for the day.

He did not really blame Martin for what had happened the day before, even though the two men had agreed that they would speak to her together about those years. She would inevitably have asked questions, of course, and Martin would have answered them. But he should have stayed with her himself to hear those questions and to contribute to the answers. Perhaps by now she had discovered more. Perhaps she knew that they were no longer married and had not been for more than six years. He spurred his horse on its way home.

Antoine was in the stables. He held the horse's head while Christopher dismounted. "Trouble," he said, jerking his head in the direction of the house.

Christopher eyed him warily.

"She's gone," Antoine said. "Left this morning. Captain Rice"—he spoke the name contemptuously—"is still 'ere. An evil one, that. One to be watched."

A leaden weight settled low in Christopher's stomach, but he showed no outward reaction. "Did she leave willingly?" he asked. "She was not forced, Antoine?"

"She was not forced," Antoine said. "But 'e sent 'er on 'er way. Don't trust 'im, m'sieur. I would trust the diable 'imself before I would trust 'im."

Christopher left his horse in his servant's care and turned his footsteps toward the house, his heart heavy. He had lost, then. He had lost his battle to prove his innocence to her even before he had started trying. There had not even been the chance to say good-bye. Just like the last time.

Martin was pacing the great hall when Christopher came through the doors. "Disaster, I'm afraid, Trevelyan," he said.

Christopher closed the doors behind his back.

"Her memory came flooding back," Martin said. "One minute I was talking with her in the house about nothing in particular, and the next she was rushing outside without even a cloak and ran all the way to the beach. By the time I caught up with her it had happened."

Christopher clasped his hands behind his back and said nothing.

"I wanted her to stay," Martin said. "I told her that you wanted a chance to explain about seven years ago, and I tried to convince her that you acted purely from impulse and a concern for her well-being when you snatched her away from her wedding. But there was no talking with her, I'm afraid, no reasoning with her."

Christopher nodded. *I won't stop loving you, Christopher. Don't expect it of me.* He could hear her speak those words just the night before, her voice urgent. But her memory had returned.

"She wouldn't stay," Martin said. "I would have had to force her, Trevelyan, and you know I would never do that. My concern for her had to come before my word to you. I hope you understand that."

"Yes," Christopher said. "I do. Why did you not go with her? Will she be safe alone?"

"I sent Macklin with her," Martin said. "I'll catch up with them tonight. I was tempted to go with her this morning, but it would have been the coward's way out, I'm afraid." He smiled, but it was an apologetic smile.

Christopher raised his eyebrows.

"I have to play the part of heavy-handed brother now," Martin said. "I must, Trevelyan. You must realize that."

Christopher did. He said nothing.

"But not just that," Martin said. "Honest friend as well, perhaps. The sort of friend who must have the courage sometimes to tell brutal truths. I would like to be able to assure you that once she calms down she will realize that you did it out of love and that she still loves you. I don't believe that will happen. I think it may take her as long to recover from this as it did for her to recover from what you did to her before."

Christopher felt turned to stone. Not a muscle of his body or face moved.

"I would like to encourage you to go after her," Martin said, "to try to explain. I don't believe it would accomplish anything. Much as I would like to give you the benefit of the doubt, I don't think you can hope to clear yourself of all those charges against you in the past. And there is no way of clearing yourself of guilt this time. If you will pardon me for calling a spade a spade, you are guilty of two of the worst offenses in our criminal code."

"Two?" Christopher said.

"Kidnapping and rape," Martin said. "With a bit of bodily harm thrown in. You are going to have to forget her, Trevelyan. There must be hundreds of women who would fall all over themselves for the chance to be your countess. You could have a happy life without Lizzie."

"I don't need you to offer comfort," Christopher said.

"Sorry." Martin flashed him a smile. "Habit, I suppose. I always feel sorry for people who are down even when I should consider them my enemies. I can't quite think of you as my enemy. I used to admire you. You were quite a hero to my eighteen-year-old self when you met and married Lizzie. And I thought of you as a friend too. I think I was almost as hurt as she was when you fell off your pedestal. Though I suppose that is a damn fool thing to say. No one could have been as hurt as she was. I thought she would lose her mind."

Christopher did not move.

"Now the heavy-handed brother part," Martin said, clearing his throat and looking down at the tiles rather than into Christopher's face. "I'll have to tell Chicheley everything. I won't hide the truth, Trevelyan, and I'll make no excuses for you. For Lizzie's sake I will tell the stark truth. You must know, then, that it would be dangerous for you to set foot in London for at least the next few years. I don't think he will pursue you here. If he considers it, I will try to deter him. Our family does not need any more public scandal. But he will go after you if you try to come close to her. You would be fortunate to escape a noose. You do understand this and why I must do it, I suppose?'' His eyes were anxious and troubled when he looked back into Christopher's.

''Yes,'' Christopher said, ''I understand.''

''Well.'' Martin drew a ragged breath. ''I suppose there is nothing left to say, is there? I'll be leaving immediately. I'm sorry, Trevelyan. I'm just sorry everything has turned out this way. I think you and I could have been really good friends. More important than that, I think Lizzie could have been happy with you if only you had been—oh, a little less impetuous, perhaps. Despite all the evidence, I can't believe that there is any real vice in you. Well. I am talking too much. Good-bye.''

''Good-bye, Martin,'' Christopher said. He stood to one side when he realized that Martin was not going upstairs but was all ready to leave the house. He must have sent his baggage on with his carriage. ''Take care of her, will you?''

''I'll always do that,'' Martin said. He hesitated when he neared the door and reached out a tentative right hand. Christopher took it and they clasped hands for a few moments before Martin continued on his way out into the courtyard.

Christopher turned toward the stairs and climbed them slowly. He rang the bell when he reached his dressing room and instructed Hemmings that he was not to be disturbed for the rest of the day—not by anyone or for any reason.

He stood staring sightlessly out of the window.

I won't stop loving you, Christopher. Don't expect it of me.

If you will pardon me for calling a spade a spade, you are guilty of two of the worst offenses in the criminal code.

Kidnapping and rape.

Despair, he remembered now from an earlier occasion, could hurt as keenly as an open knife wound.

Elizabeth did not sleep a great deal, but then she did not expect to. She probably would not even have lain down if Doris had not been sharing her room and sleeping on a truckle bed at the foot of her own bed. In all fairness, Elizabeth could not expect her maid to share her sleepless night.

Surprisingly she did sleep in fits and starts. But always the coldness and the emptiness of the bed woke her, and the absence of an arm about her shoulders. Through twenty-five years she had slept alone except for the three months her marriage had lasted and except for the past two and a half weeks. And yet the emptiness of her bed troubled her.

For most of the night she lay awake, either staring upward at the shadows cast by the light in the inn yard on the ceiling or with closed eyes as if willing sleep to come. She tried to think of Christina and the happy reunion there would be when Martin fetched her from London to Kingston. Her child had been the main focus of her life, her main source of happiness for the six years since her birth. She ached to see her again.

But thinking of Christina, of her thin, solemn little face with its trusting blue eyes always brought Elizabeth's thoughts back to Christopher. She thought of her very first meeting with him. She was in London at her first ball, eager and frightened. John on one side of her, splendidly handsome in his scarlet regimentals, Martin on the other, very youthful, very reassuring. He was smiling at her while John was eyeing the other ladies, a large number of whom were returning the compliment.

She could scarcely find the courage to raise her gaze from the floor, and it could not be said that gentlemen were flocking to sign her dance card, though of course there were acquaintances of Papa's and John's who had signed it out of a sense of duty and perhaps because they had been persuaded to do so. Martin had signed her card twice, John once.

And then she saw him. And jerked her eyes away again in confusion because he was looking directly back at her.

She stole another look less than a minute later to find that he was standing in exactly the same place and that he was still staring at her. This time when she looked away she was careful not to look back again.

But she was left with the impression of a tall and slender and darkly handsome man. She felt her heart beating faster and she wanted to turn and run because if he was still looking at her, he was seeing a timid, blushing, gauche girl.

And then he was standing before her with their hostess and was being presented to her and to John and Martin and he was signing her card—not for the next set, which had been reserved by one of John's fellow officers, but for the next after that.

Elizabeth turned onto her side and stared at the window. She wondered if the light in the inn yard below was kept burning all night and if guests in this particular room ever found it possible to sleep. And yet Doris's breathing suggested that she was deeply asleep.

He was not much of a conversationalist, and he did not smile as John did all the time when he danced, and he did not have the easy charm that Martin had even at the age of eighteen. But he watched her as they danced with eyes that were a pure blue, and he made her feel that she was the only woman in the room worth looking at. By the time they had finished dancing she was in love. As deeply and as irrevocably as only an eighteen-year-old can be.

She dreamed of him all night and sighed a little too because he had danced with her only the once and had said nothing about seeing her again. She had not known then that he would call the next afternoon to take her driving or that less than two months later they would be married.

Elizabeth's eyes shut though she still saw the imprint of the window against her closed eyelids. She had loved him totally. She had been young enough to believe in knights in shining armor and in happily ever afters.

Yet all she had had left of that love after three months of marriage was heartache, and eventually a child who resembled him to an almost uncanny degree. Christina. She thought of how her daughter's thin arms would twine about her neck when she came to Kingston and of how her mouth would pucker for a kiss.

At Kingston? Exile again? She would hide from the world all over again, nursing a broken heart, clinging to Christina for love and to Martin for support and strength and companionship? Would she? Was that what she really wanted? Was she capable of nothing better?

She lay determinedly still beneath the covers, wondering if morning would never come.

Morning did come eventually and with it Martin tapping on her door. Elizabeth flung herself into his arms.

Martin looked closely at her after they had exchanged greetings. "Lizzie." His voice was concerned. "You have not slept, have you? There are shadows beneath your eyes. I don't suppose you feel like breakfast either, do you? But don't worry. I'll have your maid bring up some laudanum and then we shall set out on our way and you can sleep with your head on my shoulder. I am with you now, and you need worry about nothing. Once we reach Kingston you will soon feel at peace again."

"I want to talk to you about that," she said. "And I am ravenous. I could not eat dinner last night. Can we talk over breakfast, Martin?"

"Of course," he said. "Whatever you wish, Lizzie. I am glad to see that you have not gone quite to pieces."

"Aren't you proud of me?" She forced herself to smile.

When they were sitting in the dining room over breakfast, Elizabeth found that she was not really hungry after all. But she forced herself to eat two slices of toast and to drink a cup of tea. This was not going to be a repeat of the past, she had decided during the night. He was not going to destroy her again.

"We are not going to Kingston," she told Martin. "We are going back to London."

He stared at her, amazed. "Lizzie," he said, "it is all arranged."

"With the coachman?" she said. "Then he must simply be told that the destination has been changed. I am not going to run away, Martin. I have done no wrong."

He was silent for a while, stirring his coffee, watching what he was doing. "Of course you have done no wrong," he said. "But you know enough about society, Lizzie, to know what the tabbies will do with your story. You have been gone for almost three weeks. Of course you were taken by force. But what does that prove—as far as society is concerned, that is? Some people were already murmuring before I left London that perhaps you had connived in your own abduction. Even those sensible enough not to believe that will remember that you have been almost three weeks alone with your kidnapper—or they will choose to believe that you have been alone with him. They will draw the inevitable conclusions."

"And be perfectly right," she said. She flushed but looked him directly in the eye. "But I am not going to run away, Martin. People may think what they will. How did Manley react?"

"You cannot think of marrying him now, Lizzie," he said, reaching across the table and taking one of her hands in his. "I know it is what you wanted, but it is out of the question now. If we go to Kingston—"

"We are not going to Kingston," she interrupted. "It would be grossly unfair to you, Martin, for me to drag you there again. You have devoted enough of your life to my troubles. And why will he not marry me? I was kidnapped from my own wedding. What happened to me after that was not done with my free consent. I shall explain to Manley. If he is anything of a man, he will want to resume our plans."

"Lizzie"—he squeezed her hand—"you are merely asking for further rejection. I am sorry about it, truly sorry, but that is the way life is. As for me making sacrifices for you, you know that is so much nonsense."

"No, it is not," she said. "You are twenty-five years old, Martin. It is time you started thinking about your own happiness and your own marriage. I'll not be guilty of holding you back from that any longer. I am curious to know whom you will choose. And I will be quite prepared to love her, you know. I will not be jealous even if you and I are almost twins. I'll be like you were. I can remember how determined you were right from the start to be Chr—" she drew a deep breath—"to be Christopher's friend. He let you down as surely as he did me, didn't he?"

"Lizzie," he said, "are you quite determined to do

this? Is there nothing I can say to convince you that you are just inviting further suffering by going back to London?''

''No,'' she said quietly. ''Besides, Martin, Christina is there and I cannot wait even one day longer than necessary to see her again. I am going back.''

''We will have to plan this carefully, then,'' he said. ''We cannot tell the truth, Lizzie.''

''Why not?'' she asked. ''Isn't the truth always the best in the end?''

He picked up his coffee cup with both hands and swilled the liquid about inside it. ''Not in this case,'' he said. ''We must not mention Trevelyan. And we have to explain your three-week absence.''

''I was kidnapped and held prisoner!'' she said.

''No.'' He shook his head, still watching his coffee. ''You were kidnapped and you fell out of the carriage trying to escape and knocked your head and lost your memory.''

''You see?'' she said. ''The truth. Though who will believe it, I don't know. It sounds highly improbable.'

''Your kidnapper had to make off in haste,'' he said, ''because there was another carriage approaching. So you were taken up by a perfectly respectable lady, who has given you shelter ever since. I found you, having been asking around about you until I was finally directed to the correct house. And the sight of me restored your memory. And the sight of Christina's portrait, of course.''

''I don't really see the point in the lies,'' Elizabeth said, frowning.

''They will prove that you have been living respectably during the time you have been missing,'' he said. ''And they will explain why there was no ransom note. It's the only way, Lizzie, if you insist on going back. Do you know what society would do to you if they knew you had been with Trevelyan again? And what they would do to Papa?''

The last idea stayed the protest that was on her lips. ''To Papa?'' she said. ''It would be a dreadful embarrassment to him, would it not? And to you, Martin. I sometimes forget that I cannot act from purely selfish motives.''

"You can forget about me," he said. "But it might be hard on Papa, Lizzie. And on Poole. He would be made to look a pretty fool, wouldn't he?"

"Yes," she said. "If it became known that it was Christopher who took me away, it would be easily believed that I went willingly. Oh, yes, that would be dreadful for Manley. I cannot do it, can I?"

"It is my story or Kingston, I'm afraid, Lizzie," he said. "You know which I favor, but I'll let you make up your own mind as I always do. Your freedom means a great deal to me."

She drew a deep breath. "Your story, then," she said. "But I am not sure how good I am at lying, Martin. We are going to have to decide on some details so that we both tell the same story. And what if someone decides to check the story and discovers that there is no lady who took me in?"

"We will work it out on the way," he said. "I'm sure I can come up with someone who will be willing to back our story. You are quite mad to choose this course, Lizzie."

"Yes." She smiled determinedly at him. "It's about time, is it not?"

14

NANCY did not see her brother until the morning following Elizabeth's departure. She had needed to talk with him and had twice stood outside the door of his dressing room during the evening, her hand raised to knock, despite Hemmings's warning that his lordship did not wish to be disturbed for the rest of the day. But both times she had walked away again without knocking.

He was not at breakfast. Nancy sat alone, picking at her food, wondering if he had eaten and gone out already or if he had missed breakfast as he had missed dinner the evening before. He was in the library, Hemmings told her when she asked. And so she went there finally and let herself in without knocking. The chances were that he would have either ignored a knock or called out to her to go away.

He looked up at her from behind the large oak desk, his face a stern mask. There was nothing spread on the desk before him, only a paper knife balanced on his palm. He held her eyes with his and set the knife down quietly.

"So, Nance," he said, "you can go about your business with a clear conscience again this morning. That mad episode in my life is at an end. I returned to England at just the wrong moment, it seems. A day later and she would have been married already and none of this would have happened. But no matter. We have summer at Penhallow to look forward to together."

"Christopher," she asked, "did Martin stay long enough to speak with you? I gather he did not leave with Elizabeth during the morning. What did he tell you?"

"That her memory came back," he said with a shrug. He picked up the knife again, balanced it on one finger, and twirled it slowly. "We knew all along that it might happen suddenly like that. I can only be thankful for her sake that it did happen, I suppose. I know it distressed her to have no sense of her own past or even of her own person. The trouble is now, of course, that she has a few more memories to add to all the ones that were lost—forcible abduction, deceit, imprisonment. Pleasant memories all, aren't they?''

''Christopher,'' Nancy said, taking a few steps toward the desk, ''she spoke to me before she left. She said something that I think you should know about.''

He laughed harshly. ''You were to tell me from her to go to hell?'' he said. ''No need to pass on the message, Nance. I am more than halfway there already. But no matter. The past cannot be changed, can it? I can only—''

''She said you had taken her away from someone,'' Nancy said. ''There was someone inside the church who would not understand why she had gone away without a word. She was upset at the thought.''

''Poole,'' he said. ''Goddammit, she loves him, then.''

''A child,'' she said, watching him, wondering if she could possibly have misunderstood Elizabeth. But the words had been almost free of ambiguity. ''A six-year-old child. A little girl. She would not understand where her mother had gone, Elizabeth said.''

He looked at her blankly, but he sat unnaturally still. The knife clattered unheeded to the desktop.

''I think the child must be your daughter, Christopher,'' Nancy said.

She watched his eyes close and his hand lower to clench around the knife.

''She is six years old,'' Nancy said. ''She must be yours.''

His eyes closed more tightly. But when she took a few hurried steps toward him, he lunged to his feet and turned sharply away to a window.

''Well, Nance,'' he said after a lengthy silence, ''it seems that we are a pair of villains, Elizabeth and I, quite worthy of each other. I have been guilty of kidnapping her during the past three weeks. She has been guilty of withholding a child from me for the past six years. Are they equal villainies, do you think? I think perhaps they are. Or perhaps hers is worse.''

"Christopher," Nancy said, but she could think of nothing else to say to him.

"A child," he said. "A daughter. Did she call her by name?"

"No."

He laughed softly. "I have a six-year-old daughter," he said, "and do not even know her name. Or what she looks like. I went away and she was carrying my child. I have known for a long, long time that I should never have gone. I should never have made it so easy for them. They kept my child. To her they are her family. She probably does not even know of my existence. Do you think she has been told I am dead, Nance? I think that is probably what they told her."

Nancy walked up behind him and set a hand lightly on one of his arms. She knew by the sound of his breathing that he was fighting tears.

"Well," he said at last, so quietly that she knew he was talking to himself more than to her, "they have had my wife for almost seven years and my daughter for six—Chicheley and Aston and even Martin. That is long enough. Too long. It is my turn again."

"Christopher"—Nancy tightened her grip on his arm—"what are you going to do? You are not going to do anything foolish, are you?"

"I'm going to London," he said, turning to her and speaking as calmly as if he were announcing that he was going to call upon his steward.

She held up both hands, palm out. "You can't," she said. "You know it is impossible, Christopher. The Duke of Chicheley will have you arrested. You know from experience that he will not hesitate to use his power against you. Who knows what will happen to you after that."

"A hanging," he said. "I don't think they will do it, though, Nance. I don't think they will want to admit publicly that it was Elizabeth's divorced husband who ran off with her and proceeded to live with her for three weeks. And Chicheley will not want to hang the father of his granddaughter. He has too much pride for that. A firing squad or a chopping block might be genteel enough for his tastes. But not a common hangman's noose."

Nancy felt as if she might faint. But she could not afford to be vaporish. She must make him see sense.

"You cannot take the chance, Christopher," she said. "Elizabeth said that she would press charges herself."

He laughed. "I wonder what the penalty is for kidnapping a man's child for six years," he said. "Nothing, I suppose, when the kidnappers are the mother and the very powerful grandfather. I'm going after her, Nance. You might as well save your breath and sit down before you fall down. I want to see my daughter. And I want to have a few words with my wife—with my ex-wife." Both his face and his voice were grim.

Nancy took his advice and sank into the chair behind the desk. "For weeks now," she said, "I have been waiting to wake up from this nightmare. But it has become too bizarre to be a dream. It can only be reality." She set her elbows on the desk and rested her face against her hands.

"Poor Nance," he said, setting a hand on her shoulder, "my nightmare has been almost seven years long. I was a newly married man, deliriously happy, poor fool, when I fell asleep. I have not woken up since. But I will. I had better go and set Antoine to packing. I'll leave at first light tomorrow."

Nancy took her hands away from her face and slammed them palm down on the desk. "Oh," she said, "you fool, Christopher. Do you think for one moment that they will let you see the child? But save my breath, you told me. Very well, then, I will say no more. I have to go upstairs to summon Winnie. One day is not long when one has to pack for perhaps several weeks in town."

"Nance?" he said as she got to her feet.

"Well, someone has to watch over you," she said, whirling on him, angry at last. "Someone has to come and visit you in jail. Someone has to be present at your execution who is not treating it as a morning's rare sport."

"It is the Season in London, Nance," he said. "And probably this one is busier and more frantic than any other with the victory to celebrate. Are you sure you want to leave Penhallow to get involved in all that?"

She quailed at the very thought. "I said nothing about wanting," she said. "But I will go, nevertheless. I fear you will get yourself into deep trouble. Perhaps I can help avert it. I don't know. Perhaps Elizabeth will forgive me more readily than she will forgive you. Perhaps the duke will listen to me. Perhaps Joh—perhaps John will listen. However it is, I have to be there. How could I stay here with my imagination running wild?"

He squeezed her shoulder. "You are a good sister, Nance," he said. "The best. I am sorry I have dragged you into all this."

She looked at him with a grimace that was her best attempt at a smile.

He gripped her shoulder harder suddenly. "God, Nance," he said almost in a whisper, "I have a daughter. I am a father."

She circled her arms about his waist and rested her forehead against his chest.

Antoine sensed that the other servants at Penhallow, who had tolerated him at first as something of an eccentric, had now become rather hostile toward him—especially one footman and one groom. He did not much care. On the other hand, it did not hurt him at all to know that he and the earl were to leave for London with only a day's notice.

Winnie had changed. She was no longer the sunny-natured and flirtatious girl who had played off three male servants—himself included—against one another so that she could keep her heart free for the young man who would eventually come along and capture it for life. She had lost a great deal of her prettiness and was losing some of her pleasant plumpness. Her eyes, which had been bright and frequently smiling, were now haunted and rarely looked directly at another person, especially if that person were a man.

And yet she met Antoine at least once each day. He had suggested it and she had accepted with gratitude. They made no secret of their meetings. The other servants naturally assumed, Antoine thought, that they were lovers. And yet they could all see that Winnie was not happy, that she was perhaps even frightened. And so they must assume that he was a rough and a jealous lover. They disliked him. It was natural enough. Antoine did not resent their hostility or the fact that he could not justify himself to them.

England and the English did not much interest him,

though he was looking forward to seeing more of London than he had seen on the day of his arrival from New York.

Winnie seemed to look upon him as some kind of big brother—though in fact they were of almost identical height. As an older brother, perhaps. She prattled to him about herself and her family and her upbringing. She had a younger brother to whom the earl had just offered a job as soon as the boy reached his sixteenth birthday the following month. Then Winnie would not be the only one responsible for supporting their mother.

And Antoine talked to her as he had talked to no one else since leaving Montreal. He told her about the hard labor and the adventure and danger of being a voyageur on the fur trading routes beyond Canada and about the ambition of all voyageurs to earn enough money to buy a small farm eventually back near Montreal and the St. Lawrence River. But the voyageurs were paid in Montreal on their return from their long, hard journeys inland and invariably went wild in spending everything on food and drink—mostly drink. Then they had no choice but to sign up for the inland voyages again.

"I agreed to stay with 'im," Antoine told Winnie, jerking his head in the direction of the house, "so that I would find a way to save some money. Though I like 'im too. 'E don't put on the airs and graces." He shrugged. "Some day I go back, Winnie, and I buy that farm of my dreams and I raise crops and children. Many children. My mother, she 'ave fourteen. Twelve living. Me? Maybe seven or eight. I do not want to wear out my wife, eh?"

Winnie laughed. She rarely laughed these days, and only ever when she was with him. And he was the only man she would touch now or allow to touch her. She always clung to his arm when they walked. Sometimes, if she had seen Martin Honywood that day or if she could not stop herself from remembering, she would burrow against him and draw comfort from his arms about her.

Once she even put her arms about his neck and smiled at him almost radiantly—because Martin had left Penhallow and was not coming back.

"I feel safe at last, Mr. Bouchard," she told him. "You cannot imagine what it has been like never to know when I was going to meet him on the stairs or pass him in a corridor. You cannot imagine the terror and the sick feeling in the stomach." But her smile soon faded. "Do you think I will ever feel clean again?" she asked him rather wistfully. "Do you suppose I will ever forget?"

She met him on the day following Martin's departure with troubled, anxious eyes. Lady Nancy was leaving for London the next morning and Winnie was to go too.

"To London, Mr. Bouchard," she said. "I can't go there. There are so many people there. And *he* is there, isn't he?"

"You come to London, Winnie," Antoine said, "and you lift your nose to 'im if you see 'im. Antoine will keep you safe, ma petite. And maybe 'e will 'ave a chance to sink 'is knife into the smiling Mr. 'Onywood. Right up to the 'ilt, non?"

"No," she said urgently. "You must never do such a thing for me, Mr. Bouchard. Please, you must not even think of it. You are going to London too?"

"Mais oui," he said. "The earl does not go nowhere without Antoine. What would I do 'ere without 'im?"

"Oh," she said. "Yes, of course I should have realized that you would be going too. I will feel safer in London than here then. Mr. Bouchard, am I a nuisance to you? I didn't used to be like this." Her eyes filled with tears. "But I only ever feel quite safe when I am with you. I will get over that in time, won't I? I will forget in time. You are not the only good man in the world, are you?"

Antoine chuckled and drew her arm through his. "We walk, non?" he said. "Soon we must be back to pack the trunks. Trunks and more trunks. Ah, these wealthy English. They 'ave more clothes than they 'ave days in which to wear them. 'Ow many times can you make a pebble bounce on the water today, eh? Twice it was yesterday, non? Shameful. Today it must be three times, or four."

"I cannot flick my wrist the way you do," she said, laughing and looking for one fleeting moment, Antoine thought, like the pretty little maid he had used to enjoy flirting with. The little maid whose spirit had been killed by a man whose body would be killed in return.

An eye for an eye, Antoine thought grimly. Or perhaps

an eye and a half for an eye in the true spirit of wilderness living. And in the true spirit of justice too.

Elizabeth knew she should call on her father first when she arrived home. But Martin could do that and explain the story they had agreed upon. She did not even spare a look or a smile for the footmen on duty in the hall. She raced up two flights of stairs, her skirts gathered above her ankles, and flung open the door of the nursery.

Christina was seated beside her nurse, a book open on their laps between them. The child gave a cry, flung the book aside, and hurled herself across the room and into her mother's arms.

There could be no greater joy in life, Elizabeth thought, her arms closing about the slight form of her daughter and lifting her from the floor, than to hold one's very own child. Her arms had been so empty. So very empty. She closed her eyes and found herself quite unable to control her sobs for a few moments.

"Mama!" Christina was crying too.

"Sweetheart." Elizabeth tightened her hold. "I am home to stay. Oh, how I have missed you."

The nurse was putting the book away and leaving the room quietly. Christina was crying loudly.

"Mama," she said through her sobs when Elizabeth had crossed the room with her and sat down on a low chair, her daughter hugged close on her lap. "Mama, I won't be bad again. I promise I won't be bad again. Don't leave me again, Mama."

"Bad?" Elizabeth kissed the child's cheek, smoothing back the soft dark curls from her thin face. "My angel? You are never bad."

"I cried on your happy day," Christina wailed, "and you went away. I won't do it again, Mama. I won't mind him being my papa as long as you don't leave me, Mama. Promise? Promise, Mama?"

Elizabeth rocked her, crooning to her. "I was taken away," she said, "and came back to you as soon as ever I could, Christina. I came up here to you even before seeing Grandpapa. I would never leave you, sweetheart, even if you cried a pailful of tears every day. And even if you really were bad. You are Mama's very own girl. How could I live without you?"

Christina cried a little more, but they were comfortable tears as she burrowed closer into the safety of her mother's arms. "Grandpapa said I was bad," she said after a while.

Elizabeth kissed her hot temple.

"And Uncle Martin told Nurse to keep me in the nursery where no one could hear me," Christina said.

"They were both worried because Mama was taken away and they did not know where I was," Elizabeth said. "But I am back now."

"Uncle John read me stories until I fell asleep yesterday," the child said.

"Uncle John is home?" Elizabeth kissed her and rocked her again until Christina's eyelids began to flutter. She was fast asleep within a few minutes.

This was happiness, Elizabeth thought. Just this. A home and quietness and safety and one's child asleep in one's arms. She looked down at Christina, at the narrow little face and the straight nose and the long-lashed eyes—eyes of intense blue that had looked up at her with such contentment just a few minutes before. And the dark hair in tumbled curls over the child's head and about her face.

So like. Oh, she was so very like. It was no wonder that a mere portrait had revealed her paternity. Part of Elizabeth's happiness—perhaps most of it—evaporated. Her arms were full with her child, and her heart was too. But sometimes one needed more than a child. Sometimes one needed the child's father too. Sometimes one needed a whole family—mother, father, and child, and the hope of more children.

Sometimes one longed for the impossible. And so the little happiness that one might have lived on disappeared too. It was the reason why she had come back to London last autumn in search of another husband. Manley. But Manley was not Christina's father.

Christopher was. Her heart ached on.

The nursery door opened and she looked up, happy for the distraction. She smiled in answer to the grin of the tall man standing in the doorway.

"John!" she mouthed.

He came across the room toward her and peered down at Christina. "Fast asleep," he whispered. "Here, I'll take her." And he stooped down, lifted the child into his arms, and carried her through to her bedchamber to set her down on the bed. Elizabeth drew back the blankets and tucked them about her.

"John," she said again when they had tiptoed back into the nursery. "You are home and safe."

"I might say the same of you," he said, drawing her into a hard hug. "I have been worried out of my mind."

She drew back her head and looked up at him. "There were so many casualties all the time," she said. "It seemed almost too much to hope for that you would come through unscathed." She ran a finger along a scar that followed the line of his jaw on the left side, almost from ear to chin.

"Someone tried to shave me with a bayonet instead of a razor," he said with a grin. "It was an experiment not to be repeated."

She shuddered. An inch lower and his throat would have been slit. He would not be standing there grinning at her.

"Martin has been telling the damnedest story to Papa and me," he said, "if you will pardon my language. I am going to have to clean it up now that I am back home, aren't I? All about escaping from carriages and banging heads on milestones and losing memories and villains making off into the sunset and benefactresses nursing you back to health and Martin on a white charger to your rescue with a portrait of Christina. All high drama and highly improbable. He was not telling the truth by any chance, was he?"

"Yes, he was," she said warily. "I did not know who I was for almost three weeks, John."

"Well"—his smile had disappeared and he looked at her searchingly—"one shudders to know what the real truth is. You must tell me one day when you are ready. But for the time being it will do. People will not believe it, of course, but how are they to refute it? Are you ready to carry it off, Elizabeth? Martin says you will not hear of going back to Kingston until everything has blown over and some other poor soul has stepped into the scandal arena."

"I can carry it off," she said. "I am not going to run to Kingston, John. Not this time."

"Good girl," he said, smiling affectionately at her. "I always knew you would be one hell of a woman once you grew up, Elizabeth. And damn it, I am going to have to relearn the English language before I murder your ears and have Papa ringing one of his famous peals over my head."

"I had better go down and see him," she said.

"Good Lord, yes," he said. "You must have far more courage than I suspected if you could come up to the nursery before reporting to headquarters, Elizabeth. I had better come with you and offer my sword in your support. But dash it, I am not wearing it."

"Come anyway," she said, linking her arm through his. "It is so good to see you safe and alive, John."

"And with all four limbs intact," he said. "You look as if you might not have slept in a week, Elizabeth."

She smiled at him.

He was just Christopher's height, she thought. She had noticed that seven years before, of course. In fact, she could distinctly remember having them stand back to back on one occasion so that she could prove the point.

She held her smile in place.

At first it seemed that Christopher and Nancy were not going to be able to acquire rooms at the Pulteney. The Prince Regent had invited numerous European rulers and dignitaries to London for a state visit in celebration of the victory over Napoleon Bonaparte. The Grand Duchess Catherine, sister of the Tsar of Russia, was in residence at the Pulteney, awaiting the arrival of her brother.

Not every common traveler was going to be allowed to share the hotel with the Grand Duchess, it appeared. But when it was known that the new arrivals were the Earl of Trevelyan and his sister, Lady Nancy Atwell, then a suite of rooms was discovered to be vacant and they were bowed into their new accommodations.

"Whew!" Nancy said when the doors closed behind them and they were alone together. She wandered to the window of their sitting room and gazed out on Piccadilly and Green Park beyond. "We can see the towers of Westminster Abbey from here, Christopher. And Buckingham House. What a splendid view.''

He came to stand at her side. ''London,'' he said. ''There is nothing quite like it, is there? I can say that even after traveling abroad and seeing other cities. There is something about the sight of London that grabs one about the heart and makes one proud to be English. Do you feel it too? Are you sorry to have left the peace of Penhallow for this, Nance?''

He looked at her curiously. But there was color in her cheeks and a glow in her eyes, reminding him of how she had reacted to her first visit to London and the very short Season she had had here. She had come to life during those weeks and loved every moment—or so he had thought. But she had been taken away to Kingston Park by his betrothal to Elizabeth and then kept there by their decision to marry as soon as the banns could be read. But even there she had appeared unhappy. Until she had come to him abruptly late one evening to tell him that she was homesick and could not bear to be away from Penhallow for even one more week so that she could attend his wedding. She had left the following morning.

He had raged against her and felt a personal affront at her desertion. But he had been too wrapped up in his own sense of euphoria to question her reason for going. And after that he had had little chance to do so. But he wondered now. Why would a twenty-year-old woman who was beautiful and who had been made much of suddenly decide to retreat to her father's remote country estate and declare her intention of spending the rest of her life there alone? Especially when she had apparently enjoyed her come-out so much.

Had something happened? he wondered, and was ashamed that he had not asked such an obvious question before.

''No,'' she said, her voice dreamy, ''I am not sorry to have come, Christopher, apart from the danger to you. I have always longed to see it again. Just once more.'' She turned to smile at him rather self-consciously. ''The scene of youthful frivolities.''

It was hard to believe that she was twenty-seven years old. She had the type of startling dark beauty that did not fade with the first blush of youth. Maturity seemed only to have added to her loveliness.

"Perhaps it will be the scene of more frivolities this spring," he said. "There is going to be a dizzying number of entertainments to choose among."

Her smile faded. "What are your plans?" she asked. "To try to see the child and then leave? They will never allow it."

He shook his head. "No. They would not. I might as well batter my head against a brick wall as call at Grosvenor Square. I'll have to go about it more patiently, Nance. How do you fancy another Season and a chance perhaps to mingle with such exalted personages as the Regent and the Tsar of Russia and the King of Prussia?"

Nancy raised her eyebrows.

"I plan to start paying calls," he said, "and leaving my card everywhere. It is a shame that Aunt Hilda went to live in Scotland, but I don't believe her absence will hamper us. I am after all the Earl of Trevelyan and possessor of a large estate and fortune, and you are the daughter and sister of an earl. And I am notorious, a fact that will make me quite irresistible if society is as it used to be. England has known precious few women who have been divorced for misdemeanors. But men? I will be a freak, a curiosity, Nance. We will be invited everywhere, I can guarantee."

"Oh, dear," she said. "Won't you hate being stared at, Christopher?"

"We will be invited everywhere she is invited," he said. "Sooner or later our paths are bound to cross. Society will adore it, Nance. They will be able to view us meeting again almost seven years after such a bitter ending to surely the shortest marriage in history."

Nancy came and took both his hands in hers. "Let's order tea and sit down to relax for a while," she said quietly. "I don't like it when your face tightens like this, Christopher, and when your voice hardens. We will be going to *ton* events again, then? I had not expected that. The very thought makes me feel as if I had run a mile uphill without stopping. I am going to have to go shopping. I have nothing to wear."

"We'll go together tomorrow morning," he said. "I

wonder if she will get wind of our arrival before coming face to face with me. I hope not. But she can't hide away forever, can she? Sooner or later Lady Elizabeth Ward is going to have some explaining to do."

15

THE Duke of Chicheley had surprised Elizabeth by supporting her decision to return to London. And as far as he was concerned her betrothal was still a fact. All that needed to be done was to arrange a new wedding date. All must be done openly and decisively. Only then could the *ton* be convinced that there was really no cause for scandal.

Elizabeth fell in with his plans though she was not at all sure that she really would be able to marry Lord Poole now. Certainly she would not be able to do so without telling him the truth of what had happened during those weeks of her absence. But she agreed to a meeting with her betrothed. She needed to get her life back to normal again. She had chosen Manley with great care as a man who could offer her the sort of life she needed. She still needed that life. There was a great deal of brooding she could do if she would allow it. But she would not.

Christopher was to be forgotten. That was more easily resolved than done, of course, but the best possible way to ensure that she did forget him eventually was to continue with the plans she had been making for her own future and Christina's. Christina needed a father.

Manley Hill, Lord Poole, was a distinguished looking man. A little taller than Elizabeth, his figure was beginning to thicken around the waist, but he still looked fit and quite youthful. His brown hair had receded a little from his forehead and was silvered at the temples. He looked rather uncomfortable when Elizabeth joined him in a salon after he had had a private interview with the duke. But his bow was deferential, and he reached for her hand and carried it to his lips.

"Elizabeth?" he said.

"Manley." She smiled ruefully. "I little thought when

I stepped from Papa's carriage outside St. George's more than three weeks ago that I would not set eyes on you until now. It was rather a unique wedding day, was it not?"

"It was a huge embarrassment," he said, "to be waiting at the front of the church with the whole *ton* in attendance for a bride who never came."

"I hope you felt more than embarrassment," she said, "when you knew what had happened."

"Of course," he said, making her another slight bow. "I have been frantic with worry about you, Elizabeth."

"Well," she said, "that is something at least."

If she had expected, and perhaps hoped, that he would sweep her into his arms as soon as she crossed the threshold of the room, then of course she was being grossly unrealistic, she told herself. Manley's feelings for her were not strongly emotional ones, just as hers for him were not. He had chosen her because she was a duke's daughter and wealthy and respectable despite the past scandal.

They were to have an amicable and civil relationship. That was what she had wanted and still wanted. It was foolish to be disappointed at the undemonstrative way he was greeting her return from a kidnapping.

"His grace thinks we should continue with our plans to wed," Lord Poole said. "I agree with him, Elizabeth. If we do not do so, there will be whispers that you jilted me by going off with that masked man, and that will do neither of our reputations any good. It will make me look like a fool and you like a—"

"—slut?" she said.

He frowned. "Hardly that," he said.

"I was taken away by force, Manley," she said. "But you are doubtless right that the whole situation must be smoothed over by our continuing with our plans."

"I think we had better plan a summer wedding, though," he said. "I cannot agree with his grace that we should marry now in haste before the foreign dignitaries arrive from the Continent. Everyone is too preoccupied with that event to be interested in a wedding."

It was perhaps a strange reason for postponing the event, but Elizabeth was relieved and thankful. If he had wanted to marry immediately, then she would have had to tell him without delay that there had been no kind lady to take her up after she banged her head and lost her memory, but only the kidnapper himself, who had turned out to be her divorced husband.

Now she could delay the telling. It must be done before their wedding, of course, but she was cowardly enough to welcome delay. And she could persuade herself that it was best to leave matters just as they were for the moment. Manley seemed to feel that it would be best for them all—himself included—if their betrothal went unbroken.

And so she said nothing about the identity of her kidnapper. And nothing about the two-week idyll she had enjoyed with him before she recovered her memory. She should have been enjoying a honeymoon with her new husband during those weeks but instead had honeymooned with her old husband.

"I like the idea of a summer wedding, Manley," she said. "It will give us both a chance to recover from the ordeal of the past few weeks. It is good to be back home again. I was overjoyed to see Christina yesterday, and am very delighted to see you today."

"That is settled, then," he said, taking one of her hands again and raising it to his lips. "It is important that we be seen together in public as soon as possible, Elizabeth. That will silence any gossiping tongues. Lady Drummond is giving a ball three evenings from tonight. Word has it that the Grand Duchess Catherine will be there. It would be the perfect occasion for us."

"Then we must go," she said. "Shall I order tea? You must tell me what has been happening in London since I went away and what you have been busy about."

"Some other time, Elizabeth," he said. "I have a meeting to attend. The poor Princess of Wales is being shabbily treated by that apology for a husband, the Regent, and my fellow Whigs and I are trying to decide what we can do about it."

"Oh," she said. She did not approve of the very vulgar princess. But then she did not greatly approve of her estranged husband, the Prince Regent, either. She thought they were a sorry couple to be at the very head of government. "I will not keep you, then. Thank you for calling."

"Yes, well," he said, "there were matters that had to be settled. I think everything will be smoothed over quite satisfactorily. You must not worry."

"No." She walked with him out into the hallway and saw him on his way. "I shall see you before the ball, then, Manley. You will come to dinner and escort me?"

"My pleasure," he said, bowing once more and taking his leave.

He had not asked any questions about the weeks of her absence, she thought, standing in the hallway after he had gone and staring absently at the front doors. And none about her health or well-being. Perhaps he was being tactful? Doubtless Papa had given him all the details of the story she and Martin had told him.

Anyway, she thought, she was glad he had not asked. She did not want to pile lie upon lie. He was going to have to know the full truth before their summer wedding. She was glad he was not demonstrative. She did not want him in love with her or even overly affectionate toward her. She wanted a mild friendship. A relationship of mutual respect and civility.

She had had enough of love. Too much. Altogether too much. She wondered what *he* was doing at that precise moment. Standing on the headland at Penhallow? Walking along the beach? Working with his steward? Thinking about her? She wondered if he had been laughing at her throughout the time when her memory was gone. Or had he loved her just a little during those weeks? Had he felt any remorse at all for what he had done to lose her in the first place? Or had he merely reveled in the fool he was making of her?

They were among the questions that teemed in her head almost constantly. But she was learning to be patient with herself. She must concentrate on replacing those questions with concerns of the present and future. Her betrothal with Manley was still on. They were to be married during the summer. They must decide exactly where and when. They must discuss whether to try to duplicate the wedding they had planned the first time or to have a smaller, more private ceremony. And there was Lady Drummond's ball to attend. It was an evening to be looked forward to, Elizabeth thought. She must decide what gown to wear.

She turned toward the stairs, her mind fully occupied with present concerns—except for that one corner of it that was picturing a certain cave on the beach at Penhallow with a cloak spread on the sand inside it and herself lying on it against a man's body and in his arms, warm and comfortable and smiling into his very blue eyes.

"You see?" Christopher said to Nancy when she joined him in their sitting room for breakfast two days after their arrival in London. "All those calls we have been making have had their reward already, Nance. This morning's delivery has brought no fewer than five invitations."

"Oh, what?" she asked, seating herself beside him at the table.

He had been interested to notice that the past two days had also brought back the Nancy of seven years ago. She was behaving more like an eager girl than a mature woman. He had teased her the day before on Bond Street that she had ordered more evening gowns and other clothes than she could hope to wear in two years of entertainments and that she had bought enough fans to raise a storm over London. She had merely laughed at him.

"A soirée, a literary evening, a private concert, and two balls," he said, picking up each invitation in turn and setting it down in front of her. "With which shall we open the campaign, Nance?"

"Oh, one of the balls, I think," she said.

"Lady Drummond's is tomorrow evening," he said, "and Lady Elgard's five evenings from now. Perhaps we had better choose Lady Elgard's. None of your gowns will be ready by tomorrow, will they?"

"Oh, but, Christopher," she said, leaning eagerly toward him, "Winnie heard from some of the servants here that the Grand Duchess may be going to Lady Drummond's ball tomorrow evening. And if I send to the modiste's and can succeed in sounding imperious enough, I do believe they could finish one of my gowns in time. The green, I hope."

"If the Grand Duchess is going to Lady Drummond's," he said, "or is even rumored to be going, then everyone will be there. Elizabeth too in all likelihood."

"Yes," Nancy said. "But what if she does not go, Christopher?"

"Then we will keep accepting every invitation in sight," he said. "We know she is in town. Mrs. Monkton could not resist dropping that tidbit of gossip when we called on her yesterday. I just hope Elizabeth has not heard we are here. If she has not, she will soon. Another reason for not waiting until the Elgard ball. I'll accept the invitation for the Drummond affair, then, Nance?"

She nodded.

Lady Drummond's ball was pronounced a great success before it was even half over, for the ballroom and the public salons were so filled with guests that movement was restricted. And the unpredictable and temperamental Grand Duchess did indeed put in an appearance even if she did leave early with a headache brought on by the heat and the crowds and the loudness of the music. The Drummond ball, however, could boast something in addition that no other London hostess would be able to match, even in June after the state visitors arrived.

A few days before, Lady Elizabeth Ward had returned to London with her stepbrother after an absence of three weeks following her spectacular abduction outside St. George's on the morning of her wedding. The story of those three weeks that she had brought back with her had been told and retold in the drawing rooms of London, and while no one believed such a bizarre tale for a single moment, one had to find it intriguing nonethless. After much speculation it was found—to the disappointment of some—that the lady arrived at the ball on the arm of her betrothed. It seemed that he had not after all been jilted.

But if their arrival added a pleasant spice to Lady Drummond's ball, another arrival ensured that it would be remembered as one of the foremost entertainments of the year. The other arrival was the Earl of Trevelyan, Lady Elizabeth's divorced husband, who had left England before the divorce, presumably forever.

When he arrived—late—with his sister, Lady Nancy Atwell, the guests waited almost with bated breath for the first encounter between the estranged couple. At least, they all assumed and hoped that it was the first encounter. They wondered if either of the two knew that the other was to be there. The presence of the Grand Duchess was almost overshadowed.

* * *

It was almost a relief to be at Lady Drummond's ball at last, Elizabeth found. She had not been much from home since her return to London and she had been dreading her first appearance in public. Not that she would show her fears to anyone, of course. She had smiled at her father's nod of approval when she appeared before dinner in a new ballgown of shimmering golden silk, and at Martin's compliments and John's wink. And she had greeted Lord Poole graciously and had conversed with everyone at dinner.

But inside she had quailed. She hated the thought of appearing before the *ton* for the first time since she had failed to appear before them at her wedding. She knew very well that she would be the focus of all attention when she arrived at Lady Drummond's. And she was, of course. Everyone in the receiving line had special words of sympathy or welcome home and sharpened glances that seemed to see right beyond her social smile to the truth. And when she stepped into the ballroom on Lord Poole's arm, there was an unmistakable buzz of conversation shifting to a different topic.

But it was almost a relief, anyway. At least she would no longer have to imagine what it was going to be like. And soon enough people would grow tired of looking at her and would return to looking at one another.

"It is not quite pleasant to be notorious, is it?" she said, smiling at Lord Poole.

"When you become a politician's wife, Elizabeth," he said, "you will grow used to being stared at. You have nothing to be ashamed of. You may keep your head high in such company."

If he only knew, she thought, looking determinedly about her, resisting the temptation to avoid meeting people's eyes. Martin and John had come along the receiving line and had also stepped into the ballroom.

"You see, Elizabeth?" John said. "You have your own private court. Three gentlemen to one lady. It is odds I do not much relish myself, especially when the lady is my sister. We must look about us, Martin, and see if we can arrange the situation more to our liking. Who is new this year? Anyone ravishingly lovely or fabulously wealthy? Or both, dare I hope?"

"No one," Martin said. "Just the usual crop. We had better stay close to Lizzie. This might be a difficult evening for her."

"Nonsense." John grinned down at her. "There are doubtless several dozen ladies in this room who would give a right arm to enjoy the attention Elizabeth is drawing at this moment. Of course the fact that she is the loveliest woman inside the loveliest gown in the room must help."

"Flatterer!" she said, laughing. "Is this what you have been learning on the battlefields of Spain and Portugal?"

"Of course," he said. "You cannot imagine what a dismal proportion of women to men there was, Elizabeth. A ready tongue became as important a weapon as a sword if one was not to be left quite womanless."

She wondered if he was deliberately making her laugh and setting her at her ease and guessed that he was. Manley was being stiff and dignified; Martin was looking rather tense. John was grinning and looking endearingly handsome in his scarlet-coated dress uniform. Without a doubt he was drawing many female eyes that would otherwise have been on her.

"You are dancing the opening set with Poole?" John asked. "Make the second one mine, then, Elizabeth. It is a waltz, I do believe. In the meantime I am going to stroll about to try to prove that there must be another lady here who is at least as lovely as you. If there is not, it is a crying shame, you know. Are you coming, Martin?"

"I'll stay with Lizzie," Martin said, stationing himself at her left so that she had a gentleman at each side to protect her.

Dear Martin, she thought. He was so worried that she would not have the strength to cope with the developments of the past few weeks. And he was so determined to be there at her side to lend his support and protection if she should need them. She knew that she must make a very special effort to prove to him that she could take command of her own life. Then perhaps he would start thinking of himself for a change. It was time he started looking about him, as John was doing, stopping in his promenade about the room to greet old acquaintances and shamelessly eyeing the ladies as he did so. Martin should be doing that too instead of worrying always about her.

The musicians were tuning their instruments and the first sets were forming. Elizabeth set her arm on Lord Poole's, smiled at him as he led her forward, and prepared to enjoy herself. It was good to be back in her own world again, she thought, her mind slipping unwillingly to a sandy, windblown beach. Oh, yes, it was.

"I feel like a young girl making her come-out again," Nancy murmured to Christopher as they climbed the wide staircase from the hall of Lady Drummond's town house and turned at the top toward the ballroom. They were late. There was no receiving line to pass along. "The orchestra is tuning up. It must be the second or third set already."

"Yes," Christopher said. It seemed as if word of his arrival had not spread all over town despite the fact that he had left his card at several homes during the past few days. The hall and stairway and the corridor outside the ballroom were crowded with people, several of whom gave him both first and second glances and then turned hurriedly to share the moment with friends and acquaintances.

He had been expecting to arouse attention. So had Nancy. That was why she was prattling at his side. He only hoped that the definite interest his presence was arousing was a sign that Elizabeth had indeed come. It seemed almost too much to hope that he would be fortunate first time. And yet, he thought, if she were there, it might take him a while to find her. Half of fashionable London must be inside Lady Drummond's home.

She was in the ballroom. He saw her almost immediately when he stood in the doorway with Nancy. How could one not see her? She drew the eyes like a magnet, her slender shapely figure shown to great advantage by her shimmering gown, her hair drawn back elegantly from her face and curled intricately on the crown of her head. His eyes found her and watched her just as they had done at his very first meeting with her. She was far more lovely now than she had been then.

Curious eyes were on both of them, he knew, and he was aware that people who had been outside the doors or even on the stairway were coming into the ballroom—all eager to enjoy the show, he did not doubt. She had not seen him yet. She was beginning to dance a waltz with her elder brother. Aston had come back safely from the wars, then. They were smiling at each other.

Christ, but it felt strange to see her again. The last time he had seen her she had been asleep in his bed, grumbling sleepily as he withdrew his arm from about her shoulders so that he could get up to spend the day with Archer. By the time he had come home she had gone. It was hard somehow to believe that she was that same woman.

"Nance." He looked down to find his sister pale and trembling at his side. "If I wait until the end of the set, she is going to refuse to exchange a single word with me. And she will be surrounded by her watchdogs. She is already with Aston, and Poole and Martin are in conversation close to the orchestra. Chicheley might be prowling somewhere on the premises too. Dance with me, and when we get close to them, we will change partners."

"Christopher!" she exclaimed as he took her by the arm and drew her toward the dancers. "No!"

"It is a waltz," he said, taking her hand in his and setting his other hand behind her waist. "Have you never danced it?"

"Yes," she said. "At the assemblies at home. Don't dance close to them, Christopher. Don't do it this way."

"Because everyone is watching?" he said. "All the better, Nance. She will not wish to make a scene, and neither will he."

"I can't dance with him," Nancy said, panic in her voice.

"With Aston?" he said. "Of course you can. He is not a stranger, Nance. You met him at Kingston and even in London before that. Smile and talk about the weather. You never used to lack for conversation."

He knew that he was pressing her into something she really did not want to do, but he had this one chance and he did not want to lose it. Aston was making Elizabeth laugh, he saw as he danced Nancy nearer to them. Incredibly, neither of them had yet seen him. And then one final twirl brought the two couples together and Lord Aston looked up, startled, expecting a collision, and found that Elizabeth had moved out of his arms while another young lady was taking her place.

"May we?" Christopher said, and he slipped an arm about Elizabeth's waist while her shocked eyes met his. He lowered his voice. "Don't make a scene. We are very much on display."

Her hand touched his shoulder and she was dancing with him, her eyes locked on his.

"How dare you," she said.

"I'll explain to you how I dare," he said. "But not within earshot of everyone who dances by us, Elizabeth, and not in view of anyone who has the skill to read our lips or our expressions. Somewhere private."

"You have to be joking or insane," she said. "Do you know what will happen to you with just one word from me?"

"Why have you not yet spoken that word?" he asked. "I understood from the message you left with Nancy that your father would have me arrested if I dared show my face in London. Martin said much the same thing. I showed my face here several days ago yet am still a free man. You did not even tell your father, did you?"

"Because I did not think you would dare follow me here," she said.

"Didn't you?" he said. "You don't know me very well, then, Elizabeth, do you? But then you never did."

"I want you to leave immediately," she said. "Now, even before the end of the set."

"I shall leave when I am ready to leave," he said. "That will be after you and I have had a private talk."

"You must be mad if you think I will talk privately with you," she said.

"Very well, then," he said, "we will talk publicly here. But I warn you, Elizabeth, that we are likely to be quarreling rather more vehemently than we are doing now. Are you sure you want that witnessed by such a large audience? It does not matter to me."

"I am here with my betrothed," she said, and there was a whiteness about her mouth that proclaimed her anger. "We will be marrying this summer. It would not be at all the thing for me to go off somewhere private with another gentleman."

"Especially when that gentleman is your ex-husband?" he said.

"And the man who abducted me from my own wedding and then used me most shamefully," she said.

"The readers of lips are doubtless rubbing their hands in glee," he said. "Your father is not the only one to have been kept in the dark, is he? I will wager that you have not told Poole who I was or how we spent those weeks. Or Aston either. Surely either one of them or both would have slapped a glove in my face at the very least by now. I think it is time for that private talk, don't you?"

She fixed her eyes on his waistcoat for a while and said nothing. "Everyone will see us go," she said. "Do you not realize what that will do to my reputation when it is already on shaky ground? Do you not understand what an ordeal this evening is to me even without this? It is my first appearance in public since—"

"Since your private idyll with me," he said. "No, don't give vent to your fury. Look, we are almost at the doors. There must be some private room in the house, surely. We will find it, Elizabeth."

"If you are planning to abduct me again," she said, her voice shaking slightly, "you will not find me such a docile prisoner. Not as long as I have my memory."

"I want to talk with you," he said, setting his hand at the small of her back when they reached the doors and guiding her through them. He looked about him grimly. If there was one private corner in this sad squeeze of a *ton* entertainment, it would be a minor miracle. "Downstairs. Perhaps there is a room there that has not been opened up for public use."

She did not resist the pressure of his hand.

16

"WHAT the devil?" John said. He looked at the woman in his arms and at Elizabeth and her partner already dancing away from them. He looked back at his new partner. "Nancy? It really is you, isn't it?"

"I am so sorry," she said. "This was not my idea." She wondered if she would be able to continue dancing or if she would suddenly give in to panic and run. His hand was warm against her back. She had not noticed the heat of Christopher's hand.

"That is Atwell with Elizabeth?" he asked. "Or Trevelyan. Did someone tell me that your father had passed away?"

"Last year," she said. She did not believe she had ever felt quite so humiliated. She had forgotten how his eyes seemed always to smile and how his mouth seemed to curve upward at the corners. She had forgotten the way his fair hair curled against his neck. There was a long scar along his jaw that had not been there before. She had never before seen him in uniform. She felt as if she might suffocate.

"He is back, then," he said. "Poor devil, he should not have gone in the first place. He should have stayed and brazened it out. This is going to give the tabbies enough to talk about to last a month. Did she know he was back? She has not said anything to me."

Nancy said nothing. And then his eyes returned to her and roamed over her face and her dark hair smoothed back from her face and dressed in ringlets at the back of her head, and down over her almost bare shoulders and the dark green silk gown that had been finished and delivered to the Pulteney only that afternoon.

"Nancy," he said, smiling at her, "I believe I told you once that I would never see anyone more lovely than you. Romantic nonsense, you might have thought. But now I know I was right. Where is your husband? Point him out to me so that I can challenge him to a duel."

"I am not married," she said.

"You are not?" He looked at her in some surprise. "Then you must have been beating suitors away with a club. I find the thought consoling. I thought perhaps it was just me. You were the first woman I ever offered for, you know. And the only one too. Though I did not exactly offer, did I? I asked you without ever thinking of speaking with your father first. For very pride's sake I was glad of that after you had said no and fled home the next day. Was I so very terrifying?"

He was smiling and his tone was light, but he was looking searchingly into her eyes.

"No." She shook her head. "I was just homesick as I said at the time."

"Well," he said, "I believe I even shed some tears over you, Nancy. You are in town for the Season? Was it the victory celebrations that drew you? The Prince of Wales is going to milk this victory for all it is worth, I do believe."

"Yes," she said, grasping at the explanation he had suggested, "that is why we came. We are at the Pulteney." She thought of all the tears she had shed—for days and weeks and even months. Secret tears, on the beach and far down the valley. She had not thought that she could ever reconcile her mind to having to live inside her soiled body for perhaps years and years. But she had had no choice beyond suicide. She had even considered that briefly.

He raised his gaze from her then and looked about the ballroom. "Where did they go?" he said more to himself than to her. "But she will be safe with your brother, of course. He always worshiped her, didn't he, even though it turned out that he had other interests and responsibilities too. I am just a little nervous when she is not in sight. She was kidnapped less than a month ago and disappeared for several weeks. Had you heard? I believe it is the latest *on dit.*"

"No," Nancy said, "I did not know."

"The music will be at an end soon," he said quietly,

returning his eyes to her. "You cannot wait to get away from me, can you, Nancy?"

She had not expected that he would sense her terror. His hands seemed to hold her prisoner even though they were just lightly in waltz position. His body heat and the smell of his cologne were making it difficult for her to breathe. She was fighting panic and had thought she was succeeding rather well. The panic had taken her a little by surprise. She had danced with other gentlemen and this had never happened. Not after the first year or so anyway. But it was happening now.

"You do not like men at all, do you?" he said.

Her eyes widened in shock as the implication of his words hit her. "Oh, no," she said, "it is not that. That is not it at all. I am not like that."

"I'm sorry," he said. "It really is none of my business why you have not married. After all, I am not married, am I, and I am only a few years older than you. Perhaps male pride sets us men sometimes to inventing satisfactory reasons for a lady's rejection. The music is ending at last. Doubtless we will meet again in the course of the next few weeks."

"Yes," she said. But his words, she knew, were a polite way of saying good-bye. If they saw each other at other entertainments, they would merely nod distantly to each other. She was safe.

She felt a sudden longing for Penhallow. She could remember falling as quickly and as deeply in love with John as Christopher had with Elizabeth.

"Thank you," she said when they had reached the edge of the dance floor. He hesitated, realizing that she had no one to return to, then bowed to her and made off across the room. There was no sign of either her brother or Elizabeth.

Martin had been feeling sorry that he had warned Trevelyan not to follow Elizabeth to London. At the time, of course, he had thought that he was taking her to Kingston. But when she had decided to go to London instead, Martin had seen that there might have been some advantage to be gained from Trevelyan's following her there.

His surprise, therefore, when he suddenly spotted Christopher in Lady Drummond's ballroom with his sister and actually taking Elizabeth from John was not altogether unpleasant. Something could surely be made of the situation. The easiest course would be to denounce Trevelyan and watch Elizabeth destroyed with him in the ensuing scandal. But she would never forgive him for doing that—nor would several other people.

No, Martin thought, watching the two of them disappear from the room after a few minutes, patience had always been one of his stronger points. He would wait and see how the situation could be manipulated to his own advantage. With a little patience he could rescue Elizabeth from all the men who flocked to her and cared not one damn about her deep down. And then he could keep her safe for the rest of her life.

"Was that who I thought it was?" he muttered, frowning, so that Lord Poole, who had been talking to someone on his other side, turned to look at him. "No, impossible."

"Who were you looking at?" Lord Poole asked, glancing about him.

"No, no," Martin said, shaking his head. "He took Lizzie out of the ballroom for some air. For one moment I thought it was Trevelyan. Foolish, eh? He has been in Canada for years."

"Trevelyan?" Lord Poole frowned. "She was dancing this set with Aston. She must have been feeling faint. It is devilish hot in here."

"But John is dancing with someone else," Martin said. "By Jove, do you see who it is?"

Lord Poole looked. "I've never seen the woman before," he said.

"Lady Nancy Atwell," Martin said, amazement in his voice. "Trevelyan's sister. Can I have been right, Poole? Would he dare?"

He had the satisfaction of seeing Lord Poole's jaw tense and his nostrils flare.

There were a few rooms downstairs that were not in use for the ball. Christopher guided Elizabeth to one of them and opened the door despite the dubious look cast on him by a footman, who did not like openly to object. It seemed like a small reception room. There was a branch of lit candles on the mantelpiece despite the fact that the room had been closed to public use.

Elizabeth crossed the room to the fireplace and stared down at the unlit coals for a while, collecting herself. Christopher closed the door behind them and stood with his back against it, his arms crossed over his chest. She turned eventually to look at him.

"Make it brief," she said. "I wish to return to the ballroom and my betrothed." It felt strange to be seeing him again with her memory intact. He looked different. It was hard to believe that for those weeks at Penhallow she had trusted him, believed that she knew him. Now he looked grim, unknowable.

"What is her name?" he asked.

It was the last thing she had expected him to say. But she did not misunderstand him or pretend to do so. She remembered what she had said to Nancy before she left Penhallow, and was still not sure whether she had spoken deliberately or whether it had been a slip of the tongue. Without consciously doing so had she wanted him to know? Had she always wanted him to know?

"Christina," she said.

"Christina." He regarded her silently for a few uncomfortable moments. "That must not have been a popular choice with dear Papa. He must have been thankful that it was not a son and could not therefore be called Christopher."

"She was my baby," she said. "I named her what I wanted."

"She was *our* baby," he said quietly.

"I'm sorry," she said, stung. "I could not consult you. You had taken yourself off to Canada and had made it clear that you were never coming back."

"You had left me, if you will remember," he said, "and had let me know in no uncertain terms that you were not prepared to see me again. Your father was admirably firm about enforcing that. Do you blame me for leaving? You would not have believed me even if I had found a way to talk with you again. There are only so many ways of protesting one's innocence."

"Innocence!" she said scornfully.

"Even if I had been guilty," he said, "the crime hardly merited the hysterical reaction it got, Elizabeth. Most of the respectable married men in this city have mistresses, and many of them have children too. If all adulterers were divorced, there would be scarcely any marriages left."

"You have shifted ground," she said. "Now you are trying to convince me that what you did was not so bad after all. I do not care about other men and their way of life, Christopher. I will not stand for such behavior in any man who is to be my husband. I would rather live with the stigma of being a divorced woman."

And yet she had thought she would die—she had wanted to die—when her father had insisted on the divorce. She had scarcely known what divorce was until he had explained it to her. And foolishly, until that time she had expected that someone would come along to wave a magic wand and make all well again with her marriage.

Christopher looked at her broodingly for a while. "It is rather ironic," he said, "that you married that rare phenomenon, a male virgin, and yet believed three months later that he had been conducting a long-term affair since his Oxford days and had fathered a year-old child."

"I *saw* you with her," she said. "Do you forget that?"

"Hardly," he said. "But you will not believe, will you, that the same malicious person—whoever he or she may be—who sent you to that house had also sent me. We were a couple of lambs to the slaughter, Elizabeth. A couple of foolish innocents."

She had so wanted to believe that at the time. But he had been in embrace with the woman, and she had been half naked. His coat had been almost off already. Besides, who would have done such a thing to them? It did not make sense. No one had hated them enough to try to break up their marriage. But oh, how she had wanted to be convinced. How she had wanted him to break through to her when Papa had guarded her far more carefully than she had expected him to do. Instead, Christopher had gone to Canada.

"Adultery," she said, "gaming, cheating, cruelty, murder. Did that same malicious person arrange all of those, Christopher?"

He stared at her with a totally unreadable expression. He had always been good at masking his feelings. Or it had always been his problem, perhaps. That was what he had used to say when they first married. He found it hard to relax and to smile and to speak from the heart. She would have to be patient with him, he had used to say, usually when she had been upset and bewildered at some imagined harshness of his. She had loved him to distraction; she had also been a little afraid of him.

"There have been hints," he said, "since I arrived back in England that that woman and child were not the only issues at play in our divorce. Perhaps I left too soon, Elizabeth. Perhaps I do not know the whole sordid story. Of what exactly was I guilty altogether? I would be interested to know."

"Did you think the rest of it would all remain hidden?" she said. She could feel the old pain and despised herself for allowing it still to hurt. But how she had loved him! And how those feelings had returned at Penhallow when she had not remembered just who and what he was. She could remember telling herself over and over again when she had begun to realize that there was something terribly wrong with their marriage that when she knew or when she remembered she would not stop loving him, no matter what. But how could one love someone so lacking in principle and conscience?

"Obviously it did not," he said. "You had better tell me just which of my villainies came to light, Elizabeth. Perhaps some of them remained hidden after all. Murder, did you say?"

"That dancer," she said.

"Ah, yes, that dancer," he said. His voice was harsh with sarcasm. "A delicious little redhead, I believe? I assume I was being unfaithful to my mistress by sleeping with her? But who can resist such spritely beauty? I killed her? That was rash of me. I smothered her with a pillow, if I remember correctly."

"She was beaten," she said, "until she fell and struck her head. You were the one who took her away from the opera house, the last person to be seen with her. Next morning her body was discovered."

"I see," he said. "Why was I not arrested before I could sail to Canada? Or did this happen the night before I left and I escaped in the nick of time?"

"Mr. Rhodes saw you leaving the opera house with

her," she said. "He was afraid to come forward until after you had gone. But then he told Martin. Martin tried to hush it up, but Papa found out anyway. I was glad you had gone when he told me about it, Christopher. And I was glad he had told me though Martin was very upset with him for doing so. Up until that time I was foolish enough to believe that perhaps I had done you an injustice. Or that perhaps I should have forgiven you."

"Rhodes," he said. "Well, it is as well to know the full truth before judging another person, isn't it? It must have been a comfort to know that you were being divorced from an unconscionable villain."

She said nothing. She was trying not to remember that this harsh, sneering man standing against the door at the other side of the room was the same man who had loved her and held her close and made her feel marvelously safe for all those nights at Penhallow—so very recently.

"And the gaming and the cheating?" he said. "Was I a gamer, Elizabeth? And a dishonest one at that?"

"Did you know that he shot himself after you had taken everything from him?" she asked. "You left him with nothing but despair. But of course you must have known. How could you live with yourself afterward?"

"Morrison?" he said, his eyes narrowing. "Are you talking about Edgar Morrison? When I was at Oxford? I have always felt dreadful guilt that I stood by and watched the poor devil being stripped of everything. He had very little to start with. Good Lord, Elizabeth, it was an experienced card sharp who did that to him. I was not even playing."

"There are those who said you were," she said. "And that you were the big winner."

"Well." He stood away from the door at last and clasped his hands behind him. "Someone worked very hard to blacken my name. You were fortunate to have a father powerful enough to free you from such a demon of a husband."

"Yes," she said. "I was."

He looked at her for what seemed long moments of silence. "I did not come here to talk of all this," he said at last. "It is somewhat pointless when you believe me guilty and I cannot prove my innocence—yet. I will do so, Elizabeth, though there is somewhat more to clear myself of than I believed. I brought you here to talk about Christina. She is six years old? Does she look like you?"

"No," she said.

"Like me, then?" He raised his eyebrows.

"She has dark hair and blue eyes," she said.

"A constant reminder to you," he said. "How unfortunate."

"She is a beautiful child," she said angrily. "And she is a person in her own right."

"And you called her Christina," he said. "A deliberate reminder. Why?"

"I like the name," she said.

"And it is very similar to mine," he said.

She said nothing.

"I want to see her," he said.

"No." She felt instant panic.

"Perhaps you misunderstood me," he said. "I was not asking. I want to see her, Elizabeth."

"What does she know of me?" he asked, his eyes narrowing again. "Does she know that her father is an adulterer and a murderer? Does she know that she has a half sister somewhere—my, er, mistress's child was a girl, wasn't she?"

"You are not my husband any longer," she said. "You have no right to see her. I will not allow it."

"And Papa will not allow it either, will he?" he said. "She is my daughter, Elizabeth. You must have known you were expecting her before I left. Did you?"

She said nothing.

"You kept me from all the joy of knowing that I had begotten a child in you," he said. "And all the anxiety of the birth. You kept her babyhood from me and her young childhood. My own child, Elizabeth. My only child, though perhaps you believe otherwise. I am not sure I can ever forgive you for such cruelty."

Somehow everything was topsy-turvy. She should be the angry one. She should be the one talking about the impossibility of forgiveness.

"What does she know of me?" he asked.

"That you are dead," she said. "I want her to go on believing that."

"I have been annoying enough to have myself resurrected," he said. "When can I see her?"

Panic was like a large ball in her stomach. Years ago she would have given in to it. She would have been begging, pleading, becoming hysterical. Now she concentrated on breathing slowly and evenly.

"You can't," she said. "It is best this way, Christopher. Best for her. Think of her feelings even if you cannot consider mine."

"How long," he asked, "do you think you can keep the truth from her, Elizabeth? Perhaps through her childhood when she can be confined to the schoolroom or to carefully supervised outings with you or a governess. Eventually she will know what happened and what villainies I was accused of. She will know that I came back when she was six years old. Is she also to know that I did not care enough for her to see her?"

"She has me," she said, "and Papa and Martin and John. She is about to have a new papa. I am to be married during the summer."

"She does not need a new papa," he said. "I am very glad now, Elizabeth, that I prevented your marrying in April. Perhaps you are free to choose a new husband. But you are not free to choose a new father for my daughter. I am her father."

She was afraid of him. He had changed in seven years. This man would even stand up against her father if he must, she suspected.

"Do you ever take her walking?" he asked. "In the parks?"

"Sometimes," she said. "Christopher, I'll not let—"

"Tomorrow afternoon," he said. "Hyde Park. Between three and four o'clock, before the fashionable hour brings out the crush. We can meet by accident, Elizabeth, and I can see my child." He held up a staying hand as she was about to speak. "Think carefully before you say no. My guess is that we are about to provide the *ton* with gossip and entertainment enough to fill in the time before the foreign visitors arrive and the victory celebrations start in earnest. Do you want them gossiping about my call at Grosvenor Square and the explosion that would follow upon such a call?"

"That is blackmail," she said coldly.

"I seem guilty of almost every other crime ever invented," he said. "Why not of that too? I merely want you to realize that I am not going to take no for an answer. A chance meeting in the park seems the best plan to me. Does it not to you?''

''And will that be the end of it?'' she asked. ''Will you be content to see her once, Christopher?''

He shook his head. ''I don't know,'' he said. ''I somehow doubt it.''

She looked at him in despair. ''Promise me one thing?'' she asked him. ''Promise that you will not tell her who you are.''

He looked broodingly at her. ''Elizabeth,'' he said quietly, ''I have never seen the child. I have known of her existence for only a week. But I love her. She is the issue of my own body. I am not going to snatch her away from you or frighten her with ideas she cannot cope with. I think I must have frightened her sufficiently when I took you from her for almost three weeks. I would not have done so if I had known of her existence.''

''Then you promise?'' she said.

''For tomorrow, yes,'' he said. ''It would be far too soon for her to know the truth. But I will not promise never to tell her. If you do not do so, then I will when the time seems right, whether that is the day after tomorrow or next year. I intend to be her father for the rest of my life.''

She opened her mouth to reply. Her father would have something to say about that. So would Manley. And Martin and John. But she sensed that there was no point in arguing with him. Not now. She was mortally afraid, though whether more for Christina or herself she did not know.

''If it is not raining,'' she said, ''I shall take Christina walking in Hyde Park tomorrow afternoon. She likes to walk along beside the Serpentine.''

He nodded.

And then she thought of how long they must have been there in that room, alone, away from the ballroom and the crowds of curious people.

''I must go back upstairs,'' she said. ''Manley will be wondering where I am.''

''Oh,'' he said, ''I imagine there are a few dozen people only too eager to let him know, Elizabeth. Come, then, I'll escort you back there." He extended an arm to her.

She crossed the room toward him and set her own arm resolutely along his. But she could not stop herself from remembering as they left the small reception room and climbed the staircase toward the ballroom the race they had had down the beach at Penhallow toward the sea, when he had allowed her to stay ahead of him until the last moment and had then swung her up into his arms and threatened to throw her into the water.

John and Martin were with Lord Poole when Christopher returned Elizabeth to the ballroom. Lord Poole was angry and fretting at the return of her first husband and the possible scandal that might arise from her having disappeared with him for all of half an hour.

Elizabeth was looking pale but quite composed, John saw with approval. Christopher was tight-lipped. He had changed. He looked as if he had seven years of hard living behind him. But then they were all changed. John himself had now experienced all the horrors and hardships of real war after playing with the glamour of it for a few years at a home posting. That summer of Elizabeth's marriage and his own rejection by Nancy Atwell seemed longer ago than seven years.

Christopher bowed distantly and moved away without a word. John touched his stepbrother's sleeve and drew him away.

Elizabeth looked at Lord Poole in some apprehension. "He wanted to talk with me," she said. "I could hardly refuse without causing something of a scene, Manley."

"This is very awkward, Elizabeth," Lord Poole said, careful not to frown in such a public place.

"Yes," she said.

"You must realize how foolish you made me look, going off like that with your former husband," he said.

"I am sorry, Manley." She set a hand on his sleeve. "He has recently returned to England. He wants to see Christina."

"That is out of the question," he said. "He no longer has any claim to either you or the child."

"He is her father," she said. "I have promised to take her to Hyde Park tomorrow afternoon for him to see her.

It will be the only time. I will persuade him that that is enough."

"And so shall I," he said, flushing. "Christina will be under my care as soon as we are married, Elizabeth. I will not have Trevelyan interfering."

"I don't think you need worry," she said. "He will be returning to Penhallow soon."

"Penhallow?" he said. "In Dorsetshire?"

"Devonshire," she said.

"Even better," he said. "It is far enough away. I wish tomorrow's meeting could be avoided, Elizabeth. I wish you had consulted me first. But there must certainly be no more."

"There will be no more," she agreed. "But she is his daughter, Manley. I thought it only fair that he should be allowed to see her just this once."

"Come and dance," he said. "We must not give anyone the impression that we have been upset by events."

"No," she said, smiling.

"Let's move on," John said to Martin. "Are you bound on staying at this ball until the bitter end?"

"Lizzie—" Martin said.

"—is engaged to Poole and needs some time alone with him," John said. "Christopher's return is a little awkward for her. She is going to have to work it out with Poole on her own. She seems to have grown her own wings since I was home last. I approve. You helped her, Martin?"

"It took a long time," Martin said. "But being at Kingston all those years and being mistress there finally gave her confidence in herself. She has done very well."

"And so have you," John said. "It must have been quite a sacrifice to stay there with her all that time, Martin."

"Nothing is a sacrifice as far as Lizzie is concerned," Martin said.

"Shall we leave?" John suggested. Since dancing so unexpectedly with Nancy, he seemed to have lost his earlier enthusiasm for eyeing all the new beauties that the Season had to offer. He felt in something of a bad mood. "Seek out other pleasures, perhaps?"

Martin raised his eyebrows, but he did not object. Soon

the two brothers were outside the house, waiting for their carriage to be brought up.

"Where is the best place to go?" John asked.

"For ladies?" Martin asked.

"Preferably not." John grinned. "I am quite out of touch with London houses. Which is the best?"

"It depends on your tastes." Martin looked at him a little warily. "Do you like a simple throw, or do you prefer something rather more titillating?"

"Like what?" John stood aside while someone else's carriage drew up and a lady was helped inside by a man who climbed in after her.

Martin shrugged. "Young girls?" he said. "Or boys? Or more than one at a time? Or a bit of roughness as an appetizer?"

"Perversions?" John looked at him with interest. "And violence? Do you know where such entertainments can be found, Martin? Do you like any of them yourself?"

"I daresay I know where they can all be found," Martin said. "Who doesn't if he keeps his ears open? I'll take you to one if you want. My own preference is for something plain and ordinary, of course."

John chuckled. "I hope not too plain or too ordinary," he said. "Take me somewhere where the girls are pretty and lively, Martin. But nothing perverted, please. I merely want a warm and pretty and shapely armful and a mattress for her back."

Martin gave an address to the coachman before climbing into the carriage after his brother.

"You are not disappointed at my choice?" John asked, grinning again. "You don't enjoy deflowering young virgins or being chained and whipped with knotted cords by naked goddesses or suchlike, do you, Martin?"

"Good Lord, no," Martin said. "I have rather more respect for the female sex. Sometimes I even feel guilty using the favors of ordinary whores. I have to keep reminding myself that they have to earn a living too. And that they might have it a lot rougher with someone else."

John lapsed into silence. But he did look at Martin curiously. He could not quite imagine Martin with a woman, and yet it seemed that his brother was accompanying him to a brothel, not just taking him there. It was not strange, perhaps, that his stepbrother should know where the better brothels were in London. But the slimier, more violent types of sexual activities that some men craved? Martin knew where they were to be found?

He turned his thoughts to himself. He had had the same Spanish mistress for most of his years in the Peninsula and had taken his leave of her a couple of months before with some regret. It was many years since he had gone whoring. He had not thought to do so again. He had thought to look about him for a wife now that he was home to stay and settle to a life of marital fidelity.

He wished he had not met Nancy again. He had not thought seriously of her for years. But seeing her tonight had filled him with dissatisfaction and the ridiculous need to prove his virility with a brothel whore. Had he still not got over her unexpected rejection, then, even after almost seven years? But it had not been merely the rejection. When he had asked her to marry him, he had also tried to touch her—the day after she had appeared to rather enjoy their first kiss. She had recoiled in horror, and her face had shown revulsion as well as horror. The actual rejection had been almost an anticlimax.

Yes, John thought ruefully, it had been enough to send a man scurrying to prove his manhood on a prostitute even years after the fact.

17

CHRISTOPHER was nervous. He had scarcely touched his breakfast and had merely pecked at his luncheon. And now he was pacing about the sitting room of the hotel suite, unable to sit still or settle to anything.

Nancy was working at her embroidery. She was almost glad that her brother was so preoccupied with his own anxieties that he had noticed nothing unusual about her. Or perhaps he had.

"You did not enjoy the ball last night, Nance?" he asked her.

"I did," she said, looking up from her work and smiling at him. "It was rather exciting to be back in such an atmosphere, and three gentlemen danced with me. All of them surprised me by remembering me and complimenting me on my continued good looks. I believe remarks like that to ladies of above five-and-twenty must be obligatory. Are they, Christopher?"

"They are the simple truth in your case, Nance," he said. "But you did not really enjoy the evening, did you? You did not want to dance with John, but I forced you."

She bent her head to her work. "It is a little embarrassing for a lady to seem to assume that a gentleman wishes to dance with her," she said.

"You rather fancied each other at one time, didn't you?" he asked. "When Elizabeth and I were betrothed?"

"Oh, not really," she said hastily. "We were thrown together by the occasion and liked each other. But there was nothing more than that."

"A pity," he said. "I always liked John." But the mention of Elizabeth had distracted him again. "Do you suppose they will really be there, Nance? Did she say they would last night just to pacify me?"

"I don't know, Christopher." Nancy looked up at him in some sympathy. "But apparently you made it clear to her that you intend to see the child before you leave London."

"What if she does not take to me?" he said, staring broodingly from one window. "She is six years old. Children of that age frequently distrust strangers. What if she actively dislikes me or is frightened of me? Would I look frightening to a child, Nance?"

"When you frown like that, perhaps," she said. "Don't worry, Christopher. Just don't expect too much. Don't expect her to sense that you are her father. Don't expect her to rush into your arms."

He drew a deep breath and let it out unsteadily. But before he could say any more there was a knock on the other door. They heard Antoine Bouchard going to answer it.

The next moment Nancy had bundled up her embroidery and dropped it onto a table and scrambled to her feet. Her heart felt as if it had leapt into her throat and was beating there at double time. John Ward, Viscount Aston, had stepped into the room.

"I hope I am not intruding," he said, addressing himself to Christopher after greeting both of them. "The trouble with staying at hotels is that visitors are upon one before one has a chance to send the message that one is from home."

"I have an appointment in an hour's time," Christopher said. "But you are welcome, John. Do have a chair."

Nancy resumed her seat when John looked at her before accepting the invitation. She considered picking up her embroidery again so that she would have something at which to direct her attention. But she was afraid that her hands would not be steady enough.

"Ah, yes, the appointment," John said. "Elizabeth is in quite a flutter about it. We have been careful to keep it from our father. He would not approve, Christopher. You must know that."

"I would like to see him try to keep me from my own daughter," Christopher said. Nancy watched his hands closing into fists at his sides.

"So you found out at last," John said. "It was inevitable, of course. I said that right from the start, when it was decided to keep it as the great family secret. Elizabeth did not have much say in that decision, by the way. Other people made her decisions for her in those days. I am happy to see that she has changed. Perhaps you should be aware of that if you did not notice it last night, Christopher. If you decide to fight her on any issue, you may find that you have a fierce opponent.''

Christopher said nothing.

''When did you come back to England?'' John asked.

''A month ago,'' Christopher said. ''I have been at Penhallow.''

''And learned of the existence of a daughter,'' John said. ''Is that what brought you to London?''

''Yes,'' Christopher said.

''Well''—John shrugged—''Elizabeth is bound and determined that this afternoon's encounter will be the only one.''

He did not know, Nancy thought. Elizabeth and Martin had kept the secret. She could understand why Elizabeth had done so. But Martin? She would have expected him to protect his stepsister by getting rid of Christopher in the obvious way. Of course, Elizabeth's reputation could suffer if the truth came out, and Nancy had no doubt that Elizabeth was the most important person in the world to Martin.

John was looking at her. Nancy resisted the impulse to clench her hands in her lap.

''I came to ask you how you enjoyed last evening's ball,'' he said to her.

''I enjoyed it very well, thank you,'' she said.

''And to ask you if you would care for a walk in the park,'' he said. ''It is a beautiful afternoon. More like June or July than May.'' His eyes were smiling, but there was a certain wariness in his expression. He was uncertain of himself, Nancy realized.

Her mind reached frantically for an excuse. But Christopher was going out and there was no way of pretending that she was otherwise engaged. There was no excuse to be made, only a bald refusal. How could she give that?

''Thank you,'' she said. ''That would be pleasant.''

His eyes told her that he understood that she meant

just the opposite. They hardened for a moment before he smiled and got to his feet.

She got up too. "I'll fetch my bonnet," she said.

He was not dressed in uniform today. He looked even more magnificent today, she thought, because today one saw the man himself and not just the splendor of a dress uniform. He was ten times more attractive than the uniform. The thought did strange things to her stomach.

She would give a fortune, she thought, if only she could think of some reason for staying in her room at the Pulteney instead of going out walking with him.

They were walking in the park, green lawns stretching to either side of them, green trees sheltering them from the noisy bustling world of London beyond, blue sky and warm sunshine overhead.

He was mad, John thought as he made labored conversation with his companion. She had made it quite clear the evening before that she did not wish to be near him, and it had never been his way to press his attentions where they were not welcome. He was mad to have invited one of the few women not to be attracted to him to walk with him. But the night before had not been a success. The girl had been pretty enough and lively enough and had taught him a few interesting new tricks. He had got his money's worth and more. But he had woken up this morning feeling that he was suffering from a hangover even though he had scarcely drunk the night before. He had felt dissatisfied and determined that he would never again yield to the temptation to go whoring. He would choose a wife, or failing that, set up a regular mistress.

He had felt resentful of Nancy. And he had felt the need to see her again, to put a definite end to something that had never ended. Though what he meant by that he did not know. He had asked her to marry him and she had said no. What could be a more definitive ending than that?

"Have you found it difficult returning to London after so long?" he asked her, changing the subject on which they had been talking drearily for several minutes. "Penhallow is rather remote, is it not?"

"Yes," she said. "I came to be with Christopher. I was afraid he would get himself into trouble."

"He was angry with Elizabeth?" he asked. "I can hardly blame him."

"He was overwhelmed with the knowledge that he has a daughter," she said.

"Was he?" He looked down at her and was struck, as he always was, by her dark, vivid beauty and her full, quite voluptuous figure. The woman could have the whole male world at her feet if she so chose. Perhaps she did not realize that. "You have been alone at Penhallow since your father died?"

"Yes," she said. "It took a long time for a letter to reach Christopher and for him to come home."

"I thought you loved me, Nancy," he said abruptly, knowing that he should leave the past alone, that it was unmannerly not to do so.

She stiffened and moved a little farther from his side, though her arm was still resting lightly on his. "That was a long time ago," she said. "We were children."

"I was twenty-three and you were twenty," he said. "Hardly children, Nancy. You were already a little past the usual age for a come-out. And a little past the usual age for marriage."

She seemed not to be able to find words with which to answer him. She shrugged her shoulders, obviously in some distress. If he were a gentleman, he would start talking about something else again.

"You encouraged me," he said. "I did not imagine that. You participated in that kiss as eagerly as I did. Indeed it was a rather improper kiss for a couple who did not after all become betrothed the next day."

"Please," she said, "I do not want to talk about this. It is over, John. It is the distant past."

"Just as it is over between Christopher and Elizabeth?" he said. "Sometimes I think there must have been some kind of curse on our two families when they tried to intermarry. Have you ever known another couple to divorce, Nancy? And on really such slight grounds? Adultery! Parliament would not have time to conduct its day-to-day business if it had to hear all such cases."

"He did not commit adultery," Nancy said. "I would believe it of any man before I would believe it of him. It was a trumped-up charge. Someone meant him mischief. Someone wanted to spoil his marriage. I wonder if whoever it was succeeded even better than he expected."

"Probably," he said. "And what happened between us, Nancy? Someone else's mischief was at work against us too?"

She turned her face sharply away and he realized in some shock that he had hit on a raw nerve.

"*Was* there someone else?" he asked.

"No." She had stopped walking and withdrawn her arm from his. "I want to go back to the Pulteney, John. Please?"

"What was it, Nancy?" he asked quietly, looking intently into her face. But her expression made him instantly contrite. There was agony there. "No, it's all right. I'll take you back. You gave me your answer a long time ago. Forgive me for being less than a gentleman."

But she was biting her lip and looking back into his eyes. "It was not you, John," she said. "It was nothing to do with you. I had an unpleasant—experience. It happened before—before I met you. I thought it did not matter. I thought—when we became friends—when you k-kissed me that it would be all right. But it was not. I c-couldn't—" She shrugged again.

He did not realize he was gripping her upper arm until he saw his hand there. His face felt cold as if all the blood had drained from it. "Someone else had—touched you?" he said.

She pulled her arm free and began to walk back the way they had come. "No!" she said. "Nothing like that. It was not—Oh, please."

They walked side by side, not touching, not talking for a few minutes. She broke the silence at last, her voice calm again.

"It was not you, John," she said. "I was very fond of you. I think I hurt you. I did not realize that. I thought you would have forgotten all about it very quickly. You are so very—oh, so very attractive. I'm sorry."

"I'm sorry too, Nancy," he said, "for upsetting you again. I thought I had forgotten about it too until I saw you last evening. If I thought of you at all, I suppose I imagined you with a husband and family."

They walked on again in silence. He had not realized they had come so far into the park.

"Do we say good-bye now when we reach the Pulteney?" he asked. "Do we try to avoid each other for the rest of the time we are both in London?"

"I suppose so," she said after a while.

"I don't want to," he said. "I want to see you again. Can we forget about the past and pretend we are new and friendly acquaintances? Will you come for a drive to Kew Gardens with me? Tomorrow perhaps?"

She directed her gaze to the ground in front of them for a while. "John," she said finally, "I cannot ever—I cannot *be* with a man. I don't want to get into a situation in which I will have to reject you again. Is it conceited of me to think that is possible?"

"We will be friends," he said. "Kew Gardens tomorrow?"

"I don't know what Christopher's plans will be," she said. "But yes. Tomorrow, John. It will be pleasant."

He smiled at her. "Take my arm," he said, offering it to her. "I will find it easier to match my step to yours."

She took it and they walked the rest of the way in silence. But it was a more comfortable silence than it had been.

One thought bothered him, though. If she had had some unpleasant encounter with a man before she met him and if that were sufficient to draw that look of horror and revulsion on the evening when he had offered her marriage; and if it had kept her from marrying anyone else ever since and had caused her to say, as she just had, that she could never be with a man—then how had she been able to participate in that kiss they had shared? It had been more than a meeting of lips. His hands had roamed over her, and he had held her body close against his. Their mouths had shared desire.

She must have been raped, he thought, that coldness in his head again making him feel almost that he would faint. It was the only cause that could draw such a violent and long-term reaction. But before she met him? He did not think so. It was something that had happened after their kiss—but before he had asked her to marry him. There had been only one day separating those two events.

She had been raped during that twenty-four hour period? But she had been staying at Kingston. The servants? His mind ran over all the likely possibilities. But there did not seem to be many, if any. The guests? There had been only a few. He thought of each of the men in turn, married as well as single. His father? Martin? Martin had been just a boy. The likelihood that one of them had done that to her was like a nightmare that he would far prefer not to face.

But it had to have happened during the night following their kiss or during the next day, before he had made her his offer and tried to touch her again.

He escorted her to the outer door of her suite at the Pulteney and smiled at her. "I shall look forward to tomorrow, Nancy," he said. "I am glad we can be friends again."

"So am I." She smiled back. "Thank you for the walk, John."

He turned away without touching her. He was fully aware that it was already too late for simple friendship between them. Seven years too late.

There were two ladies strolling beside the Serpentine, one of middle years, the other elderly. They looked like mother and daughter. There was a youngish woman, probably a nurse or perhaps a governess, watching three children who played noisily at the water's edge. A gentleman, or perhaps a businessman or a lawyer, hurried along the path as if he had only his destination in mind and did not even notice the beauty of his surroundings.

They were not going to come, Christopher thought. She had either deceived him the evening before or else had changed her mind. Perhaps Martin had persuaded her not to come. Perhaps the duke had discovered that he was in town and had forbidden her to leave the house on Grosvenor Square. They were not coming. He felt a mingling of panic and despair.

And then he saw her. Elizabeth, that was. Someone was beside her, holding her hand, but for some strange reason he could not bring himself to look. He kept his eyes on Elizabeth. She had seen him, but she had looked away again and was listening with tense, unsmiling face to the child who was skipping along at her side and prattling. He could see that with his peripheral vision, though he did not look directly.

She was wearing a light green muslin dress, not one she had had with her at Penhallow, and a wide-brimmed straw bonnet. She looked like a girl still, he thought, with her slender, shapely figure. She had come. He wondered if she had done so because he had almost threatened her or because she had wanted to. If she had said nothing to Nancy when she was leaving Penhallow, he would still not know of the child's existence. Had she spoken deliberately then? Or had she been so upset that she had not known what she was saying?

Had she wanted him to know that they had a child?

His heart felt like a heavy hammer beating in his chest.

Elizabeth looked up, startled, when they drew close to each other. "Oh, Lord Trevelyan," she said, smiling brightly at him. "Are you out for a walk too? Isn't it a lovely afternoon?"

"Hello, Elizabeth," he said. He was terrified to take his eyes from her face. The child at her side had stopped skipping.

"This is a friend of mine, sweetheart," she said in that bright and brittle voice that was so unlike her usual way of speaking. She smiled quickly down at the child. "The Earl of Trevelyan. This is Christina, my lord. My daughter."

It took almost a physical effort to move his gaze downward and across. She was looking back at him from beneath the brim of a bonnet like her mother's with wide and candid blue eyes. Her face was thin, a little pale, not very pretty. A few dark curls tumbled over her forehead from beneath the bonnet. He felt as if he had reverted suddenly to childhood. She was Nancy all over again, except that Nancy's eyes were green.

"Christina," he said. "You have a name like mine. I am Christopher."

His daughter stared at him for a few moments before looking up at her mother. "Papa was Christopher," she half whispered.

"Yes, sweetheart."

Papa! He felt as if a knife had been plunged into his heart and twisted. Elizabeth had told the child something about him and had called him papa.

And so there she was, he thought, his daughter. His own flesh and blood. Product of his own seed. She had grown inside Elizabeth's body. He had put her there. With love. He had loved his wife and she had conceived Christina.

He had been staring at her silently. She moved closer to her mother and rested one cheek against Elizabeth's leg. She still watched him with steady eyes.

What did one say to a daughter one was meeting for the first time when she was six? "I have been wanting to meet you since coming to London last week," he said. "Your mother and I used to be particular friends, Christina."

She half turned her face into her mother's skirts and regarded him from one eye.

"Whom do you look like?" he asked. "You certainly do not have your mama's coloring."

"I look like Papa," she said into Elizabeth's skirts. "I have Papa's blue eyes. Don't I, Mama?"

"Yes, sweetheart."

"May I walk with you?" he asked. "It is so summery in the park this afternoon, is it not?"

He looked up at Elizabeth. Her face had lost all color. She stared at him intently.

"We must not keep you, my lord," she said. "You must be busy."

"No." He shook his head. "Only busy hoping I would meet someone I know to share the afternoon with me. May I walk with you, Christina?"

The child nodded against her mother's leg and looked up at her.

And so they turned and walked, he and Elizabeth pale and silent, Christina between them, holding to Elizabeth's hand and stealing glances at him once in a while. It was a disaster, he thought. He had expected some huge emotional moment, and there had been nothing but awkward silences and stilted talk. He was a stranger to his daughter. She kept very close to her mother's side and left a noticeable gap between herself and him. She had not spoken a word beyond answering his questions.

A man and woman were walking toward them, their arms entwined, a small child up on one shoulder of the man, clinging to his wildly curly hair. The man wore no hat. The woman was carrying it in her free hand. All three of them were laughing and watching the swans on the Serpentine.

Christopher looked across at the tense pale face of his former wife and down at the shy face of his child. He noted again the distance between them.

"Would you like to ride up on my shoulders?" he asked his daughter. But he wished he could recall the words. She drew closer to Elizabeth and shook her head slightly. He looked ahead and tried not to feel hurt. Perhaps it was just that she felt herself too big for such a thing.

"Yes," a little voice said suddenly. "Yes, please, sir. May I, Mama?"

His eyes locked with Elizabeth's. Please, he begged her silently.

"Of course," she said, "if Lord Trevelyan is willing."

He stooped down and picked up the child and settled her on one shoulder. She was lighter than a feather. She giggled suddenly and he felt one warm little hand circle around the back of his neck and come to rest over his ear. "Don't drop me," she said.

"I'll guard you with my life, Christina," he said.

"I'm wearing new shoes," she announced.

"And very handsome ones they are too," he said. He moved to Elizabeth's other side so that he could see her. He stepped closer to her and offered his arm. She took it after a moment's hesitation.

There, he thought, though he did not speak aloud, a family. We are a family. His child was soft and warm and small. Elizabeth was graceful and beautiful.

There was a tightness and an aching in his chest. He found himself having to fight tears.

18

ELIZABETH felt like crying. He had set Christina down some time after an elderly couple had smiled and nodded at them, suggesting that they looked like a close and contented family. They were strolling away from the Serpentine, their daughter between them, holding to a hand of each. She had reached for Elizabeth's hand as soon as she had been set down on the ground, and when Christopher had stretched out a hand to her, she had looked at it, looked up at him, and taken it.

There had been so many dreams. Dreams of his hovering over her as she nursed Christina at her breast, gazing in wonder at their child; dreams of him sitting in the nursery, Christina on his lap, telling her stories; dreams of lying in his arms and being separated from him by the worming body of their child, come to wake them up in the morning. So many dreams over the years—even recently. The dreams had never stopped. But they had all faded when she had awoken. Sometimes she had known even before she woke that they were only dreams.

And now he was there, walking beside her, Christina between them. None of them spoke much. But Christina must not be feeling as uncomfortable as Elizabeth expected she might. After a few minutes she resumed the skipping she had been doing before they met Christopher and she started to hum a tune quietly to herself.

Elizabeth's eyes met Christopher's briefly. They both looked away again. Neither spoke. The need to cry was almost a pain. He was looking down at Christina, she saw, and actually smiling. A warm and tender and rather sad smile. And then he felt her gaze on him and looked up. His eyes were bright—with tears?

I love her, he had said the evening before. Without

ever having seen Christina, he had claimed to love her. Did he? Could he?

"We are going to be late home for tea," Elizabeth said to her daughter. She was aware that her voice was too bright, too different from normal. But there was nothing normal about this afternoon. "Grandpapa will be waiting for us, sweetheart. It is time to say good-bye to Lord Trevelyan."

Please accept it, she begged him silently without looking at him. *Please realize that anything else would hopelessly complicate our lives.*

"Would you prefer tea with your grandfather or ices with me, Christina?" Christopher asked.

Christina looked up at him with solemn eyes and then across at Elizabeth. "Ices, Mama?" she said. "May we?"

"Grandpapa will be disappointed," Elizabeth said.

Christina set her head to one side and considered. "He can have tea with Uncle Martin and Uncle John," she said.

Elizabeth looked accusingly at Christopher. "Thank you, my lord," she said.

And so a short while later they found themselves seated at Gunter's, eating ices, and talking. At least, Christopher was talking.

"I was a grown man before I tasted my first ice," he was telling Christina. "I grew up in a place where no one had even heard of ices. A long way from here. A place called Penhallow. The house is within a short walk of the sea. Have you ever been to the seaside, Christina?"

The child looked up at her mother and then shook her head.

"It is wonderful," he said. "From the house you walk up to a high cliff with a sheer drop to a beach of golden sand. There is a steep path down. You have to take your heart in your throat and walk down very carefully."

"Did you ever fall?" Christina asked.

"No." He shook his head. "Though sometimes I broke the rules and ran. My father would have thrashed me if he had ever known. My sister used to scold me. She looked a little like you except that her hair was always long."

Don't you dare, Elizabeth told him with her eyes. *You wouldn't dare*!

"There is nothing like running on sand," Christopher said. "It is soft and firm beneath your feet all at the same time. Your bare feet, that is. Only bare feet will do on sand. You can write in it or build castles with it. And you can walk into the sea and watch the waves break over your feet and sometimes over your breeches too. Another broken rule." He smiled.

Christina was listening as intently as she listened to stories at home. "I wish Grandpapa lived close to the sea," she said.

"Perhaps you will be able to spend some time close to it one of these days," he said. "Every boy or girl should have the chance to run along a beach at least once. You can smell the salt from the sea and almost taste it. And you can hear the roar of the water and the crying of gulls."

"I have a pony," Christina said. "I can ride him without a leading rein."

"Can you?" he said. "And you are only six years old? You are going to be an accomplished horsewoman."

"Uncle Martin won't let me ride in his curricle," the child said. "But Uncle John says I can go in his one day soon."

Christina was normally shy with strangers. But sometimes if she felt comfortable enough, she could begin to prattle. She was about to do it now, Elizabeth thought.

"You have finished your ice, sweetheart?" she asked. "We really must be going. Grandpapa will be calling out the militia."

"How would you like to ride in mine tomorrow?" Christopher asked. "You and your mama?"

Elizabeth's head shot up. "You have a curricle?" she asked. It was a foolish question when there were so many other things she might have said. A very firm no, for example.

He looked steadily back at her. "I will have, Elizabeth," he said.

He was going to purchase a curricle by the next day merely so that he could take Christina for a ride in it? Elizabeth felt suddenly afraid. And she knew that she had been fooling herself, trying to persuade herself that he would be satisfied to see their daughter once.

Papa was going to find out about it, she thought. And Manley was going to be angry and justifiably so. She should have listened to Martin and gone to Kingston straight from Devonshire. She would have been safe there. And Christina too. But she pushed the thought away. She would not run from him. Not any longer. She would face whatever had to be faced.

"You would like to drive in the park with me tomorrow?" he asked, his eyes returning to Christina.

She nodded, big-eyed.

"Then it is settled," he said briskly. "I shall escort you home to Grosvenor Square now and I shall come for you there tomorrow afternoon."

Elizabeth got to her feet and said nothing. He was issuing the larger challenge, then. He was coming to Grosvenor Square. He was telling her in so many words that he was not afraid of her father, that he was not going to hide from him. He was telling her that this meeting with their daughter was not an end to anything but perhaps only a beginning.

When they were outside Gunter's, Christina raised both hands, one to her mother and the other to the gentleman who had walked in the park with them and carried her on his shoulder just like that little boy's father had been doing for him, treated her to an ice, and given her dreams of one day running along a sandy beach and wetting the hem of her dress in the tide and building castles.

Martin paid a call on Lord Poole the same afternoon. He was not happy. Why did she have to bring suffering on herself all the time? Why must she force him to make that suffering worse before he could make it better? Could she not see that there was only one course open to her if she wanted peace in her life? And yet she was becoming entangled with Trevelyan yet again. And she was continuing with her betrothal.

Lord Poole was ready to go out when Martin arrived and appeared more cheerful than he had been the evening before. "The Regent was booed in the streets this morning," he said. "It seems that the people of London will not stand for his shabby treatment of his wife any longer. The powers that be are not going to allow her to be received anywhere during the state visits that start next week, you know. The queen has made that very clear."

"Yes, well," Martin said, "they have to support their own. Everyone knows that the Regent's life is many times more immoral than the princess's has ever been, but he is British royalty. She is only German."

"We are going to advise her to force the issue," Lord Poole said, his eyes alight with an almost fanatic gleam. "Let her appear somewhere they cannot make her stay away from—the theater or the opera, perhaps. Devil take it, Honywood, the King of Prussia is her own uncle, yet she is not to be allowed to welcome him to the country in which she is wife to the heir to the throne."

"It is not right," Martin said. "The theater idea sounds like a good one. I assume that you mean her highness to attend on a night when the Regent will have some of his guests there?"

"And then we will see for whom the crowds will cheer," Lord Poole said, nodding. "And what the foreign guests think."

"It will be a golden opportunity for your party to curry favor with the people," Martin said. "You will pay your respects to her in public, I assume?"

"By Jove, and so I will," Lord Poole said, looking as if the idea were new to him.

"With Lizzie on your arm," Martin said. "The daughter of a good Tory. It will be excellent. She will respect you for it, Poole."

Really, Martin thought a short while later as he headed in the direction of the Pulteney, Poole had made his task remarkably easy. Elizabeth would not enjoy being drawn into the rather nasty and sordid squabble between the Princess of Wales and her followers on the one hand and the Prince of Wales and the queen, his mother, on the other. She would not like having to pay her public respects to the princess. She might well find her betrothal no longer to her liking and London an uncomfortable place in which to be living.

A start had been made, anyway.

Martin turned his footsteps toward the Pulteney. He must see what he could accomplish in that direction. He asked the receptionist what suite Lord Trevelyan was occupying and went upstairs to knock on the door. A maid answered it—the same little blond maid who had reminded him of Elizabeth when he was at Penhallow but who had turned out to be nothing but a sniveling slut. He looked her over now as her eyes widened and her cheeks flushed and could not understand how he had seen any resemblance at all. Neither Trevelyan nor Lady Nancy was at home. He told the girl he would wait downstairs.

He saw Lady Nancy go up a short while later. He did not show himself. She had been out alone, had she, without even her maid as a chaperone? Well, it was no worse than he would expect of her. He remembered the time when she had wandered off alone more than once at Kingston with John, and once with him down by the river among the trees. And then she had had the effrontery to squawk about proper gentlemanly behavior.

Christopher came in eventually, very late. Martin beckoned to him and they went to sit at a table on the far side of the dining room, empty at that time of day.

"John came before I went to meet her," Christopher said, "and you after I return. She is fortunate to be so well protected."

"John came too?" Martin said. "Can you blame us for being concerned, Trevelyan? She has suffered a great deal in the past and there was that nasty shock just a month ago and an aborted wedding. Of course we are anxious to see that she does not suffer any more."

"It was decent of you not to say anything last evening, Martin," Christopher said. "I'll not forget that I owe you for that. I'll not harm Elizabeth. Or Christina. Though I don't believe Elizabeth likes having me here."

"I'm glad you came," Martin said earnestly, looking down at the table and drawing an invisible pattern on the white tablecloth with his finger. "Of course she is not happy about it, and you know that her happiness has always been important to me. But I don't believe she can be happy without you either."

Christopher did not reply.

"I don't know about all that business in the past,"

Martin said. "At the time I believed you and then I didn't. And now?" He shrugged. "But whatever the truth of the matter is, it is long in the past. And I think Lizzie feels that too, though she won't admit it even to herself. What did you think of Christina?"

"Such feelings cannot be put into words," Christopher said.

"Keep insisting on seeing her," Martin said. "And seeing her will mean seeing Lizzie too, of course. Force her hand if you must."

"Force her hand?" Christopher raised his eyebrows.

"Maybe hint to a few people that your return to England and her abduction were somehow connected," Martin said. "Let people start guessing, putting two and two together. Make it too uncomfortable for her to continue the connection with Poole. Give her only one choice of what to do with her life."

"You wish to see her publicly embarrassed?" Christopher asked.

"Of course not," Martin said, flaring. "I want to see my sister happy. And God curse me for a fool, but I want to see you happy too, Trevelyan. Don't ask me why. You have not acted in the noblest of manners during the past month."

Christopher looked at him consideringly. "I am not sure you are giving me the wisest advice," he said. "But your motive is sound. Thank you for that, Martin."

Martin shrugged and got to his feet. "She is not going to be happy with Poole," he said. "His political ideas are becoming rather radical. I do believe he is thinking of publicly espousing the cause of the Princess of Wales. That will be an embarrassment to Lizzie if it happens. Besides, he is not overfond of Christina." He held out his right hand to Christopher. "Good luck."

Christopher shook his hand. "I am taking them out again tomorrow," he said. "Christina wants to be driven in a curricle. I am calling at Grosvenor Square for them. I don't know if your stepfather will blame Elizabeth as well as me. Can you shield her from her share of his wrath?"

Martin nodded. "You can depend upon it," he said and withdrew his hand.

"Thank you," Christopher said again before Martin turned and left the hotel.

It was dangerous, Martin thought. If Trevelyan followed his advice, which he might well be planning to do anyway, there was the chance that Lizzie would ultimately take him back. She had seemed besotted with the man while her memory was gone. And he knew that she had no strong emotional attachment to Poole. But there was the chance that she would turn from Trevelyan in disgust and horror if he tried to be too forceful or if he did anything deliberately to destroy her reputation.

It was something to work on anyway, Martin decided. It was worth the risk. Lizzie was worth the risk.

Antoine Bouchard was in the earl's dressing room hanging up shirts that had just been returned from the laundry when the door crashed inward and a small figure hurtled toward him and clawed at his sleeve.

"Winnie!" he said, turning to wrap his arms about her. "Winnie, ma petite. Ah, but your 'eart is beating like an 'ammer. What is it?"

The little maid had seemed to be almost herself again since their arrival in London. She had even been out alone on errands for Lady Nancy. Antoine had accompanied her whenever he could. Duties were not arduous for either of them in London.

"What is it, ma petite?" he asked again as she whimpered and burrowed against his chest.

"Didn't you hear the knock?" she said. "I answered the door. And it was *him*, Mr. Bouchard."

"The diable 'imself?" he said. " 'Onywood? 'E did not come in?"

"He wanted Lord Trevelyan," she said. "He said he would wait downstairs. He took my clothes off with his eyes. I was so scared I couldn't even hear what he was saying to me until he said it twice."

"Ah," he said. "But you were safe, my little one. Antoine was 'ere and would 'ave 'eard if you 'ad called out. You must always remember that you are safe when Antoine is close, non?"

She looked up at him with miserable eyes. "I was too terrified even to think of you until after he had gone," she said. "I hate being like this. I used to enjoy living,

Mr. Bouchard. I used to feel that perhaps I was a little bit pretty. I used to think that some handsome fellow would want to marry me one day. I used to—oh, life is not fun any longer."

"Poor little Winnie," he said. "Antoine will take you out and about, eh? We will explore this amazing city together when we 'ave the free time, non? We go to the Tower of London and to Madame Tussaud's. And to Vauxhall to see the fireworks and maybe to dance. Do you like to dance, ma petite?"

"We dance about the maypole on the village green at Penhallow," she said. "I always liked dancing more than anything else in the world. But isn't Vauxhall too grand a place, Mr. Bouchard?"

He shrugged. "Anyone can go there," he said, "or so I 'ave 'eard. We go there one evening, Winnie, and we 'ave fun there, non? And you will be quite safe because you will be with Antoine. Antoine will not let anyone treat you with disrespect or take off your clothes with 'is eyes. Not unless 'e wants my fist between 'is eyes."

"The Crown Jewels are in the Tower," Winnie said, "and all the strange animals from all over the world. And those wax figures at Madame Tussaud's are supposed to be ever so lifelike, Mr. Bouchard. And fireworks? I have never seen fireworks. We can really go? We will be allowed?"

"We will go, ma petite," he said. "Some of the joy will come back into your life, non?"

She rested her face against his chest and breathed in deeply. "You are so kind to me, Mr. Bouchard," she said. "I don't know what I would have done without you."

"Now you go," he said, patting her back, "while Antoine finishes 'anging up these shirts. It would not look good if 'is lordship were to find you in 'ere, little one. We don't want to 'arm your name."

"No, Mr. Bouchard," she said, and her smile as she left the room was almost sunny again.

The following morning Christopher renewed his membership of White's Club and a short while later was in possession both of the knowledge that Nigel Rhodes was in town and of his address.

Mr. Rhodes was from home, Christopher was informed by a manservant after he had sent his card upstairs in the rooming house to which he had been directed.

"Then I shall wait until he returns," Christopher said, turning toward the stairs and beginning to climb them. He continued to climb even when the servant came after him, protesting that his master was expected to be gone all day and perhaps all night too.

Christopher opened the door into what appeared to be a sitting room, the protesting servant still behind him. Rhodes, his back to the door, was bending over a desk.

"Did you get rid of him?" he asked.

"No, he did not," Christopher said. "I am planning to wait until you return home, Rhodes."

The man spun around, color mounting his cheeks. "Trevelyan," he said. "I have a pressing appointment. It seemed easier to send down the message that I had left already. You will excuse me?"

"For lying?" Christopher said, looking about the room and seating himself on a sofa. "We all do it from time to time."

"I really am in a hurry," Rhodes said as his servant withdrew from the room and closed the door. "What can I do for you, Trevelyan?"

"Was I the evening's winner in the green room?" Christopher asked. "Is that where I took her from?"

"I don't know what you are talking about," Rhodes said, frowning.

"Or did I sneak her out of the theater after a private liaison?" Christopher asked.

"I have to be going," Rhodes said. "I would advise you not to start drinking so early in the day, Trevelyan."

"If I took her from the green room," Christopher said, "there would have been several other witnesses, apart from you. You will doubtless be able to refresh my memory. I cannot for the life of me remember who any of them were. I cannot even remember your being there. Or my being there, for that matter. If we slipped out together privately, I will need to have you explain how you came to see us. Were you sneaking out with someone else? Through the same door? It must have been rather crowded. But you will enlighten me, I am sure."

"I can see that you are referring to that unfortunate incident that happened years ago," Rhodes said, licking his lips. "I had forgotten about it, Trevelyan. I'm afraid I cannot remember any of the details."

"You must live either a violent or a depraved life," Christopher said, "if you have forgotten your small involvement in what seems to have been a rather brutal murder. I would have expected the fact that you saw me with the girl, the last person to be seen with her, to be etched on your memory."

"There are some things best forgotten," Rhodes said.

"Yes," Christopher said. "I can believe that. Your reason for fabricating such a story, perhaps."

"It was no fabrication," Rhodes said, his manner becoming more blustering. "I saw you, Trevelyan. I am not saying you did it. The girl was a whore. She might have had one or more customers after you before one of them or someone else killed her or caused her death. But I did see you with her."

"Where?" Christopher asked.

"At the theater."

"Where at the theater?" he persisted. "In the green room?"

"Leaving from one of the side doors," Rhodes said.

"Immediately after the performance?" Christopher asked. "Or a little later?"

"A little later, I suppose," Rhodes said. "It was all a long time ago. How am I supposed to remember things like that?"

"From a side entrance some time after the performance," Christopher said. "Presumably after the crush of carriages had taken away the members of the audience. Correct?"

Rhodes shrugged. "I suppose so."

"But I cannot understand," Christopher said, "what you were doing still there and in sight of a side door. The street whores would not have been in such a quiet place if you had stayed to engage one. They would not do a brisk business in such a place, would they? What were you doing?"

"I have to go," Rhodes said. "I am late for my appointment."

"I had better not keep you, then," Christopher said.

"Let's end this cat-and-mouse game and get on to straight questions and answers. Who paid you?"

"Paid me?" Color mounted Nigel Rhodes's neck and cheeks again.

"To say that you had seen me with the girl," Christopher said. "Who paid you?"

"This is outrageous," Rhodes said. "I must ask you to leave, Trevelyan."

"Gladly," Christopher said, "when I have had my answer. And you may be assured that I will never call again. I do not believe I have any quarrel with you, Rhodes. As you have just said, you did not accuse me of killing the girl, merely of having left the theater with her. And people can be mistaken about identities, especially late at night. Who was it who suggested that perhaps you had seen me?"

Rhodes said nothing for a while. "Perhaps you had better discuss the matter with your former brother-in-law, Trevelyan," he said at last. "Maybe he will know what you are talking about."

"Aston?" Christopher frowned.

Rhodes laughed. "Honywood," he said. "The weasel. Perhaps it was not you I saw, Trevelyan. As you just said, it was dark. I merely reported what I thought might have been so."

"For a small price," Christopher said, getting to his feet. "Or more probably a large one. Good day to you, Rhodes. Don't waste time summoning your servant to see me out. I shall find my own way."

Good God, he thought as he strode down the street a minute later, Martin!

Martin? But Martin had always been excessively fond of Elizabeth and had always gone out of his way to shield her from any unpleasantness. And Martin had always been his friend. Martin had stuck by him even when everyone else was turning away. Even after Elizabeth had left, Martin had still called on him and suggested all possible and impossible ways of winning her back. He had had tears in his eyes when he knew that Christopher was going away to stay.

Martin. There had to be some explanation, surely. But what?

Christopher hurried back toward the Pulteney. He needed to talk with Nancy. But when he arrived there and entered their sitting room, it was to find that his sister was not alone. Elizabeth was with her.

19

ELIZABETH had attended a private concert with Lord Poole the evening after she had taken her daughter to meet Christopher in the park. He told her of his plans for the coming weeks, and she tried to feel interest. It was important to him, she realized, this coming state visit and the sort of impression he would make as a politician in the awkward position of being a Whig.

They were to attend the opera when the Regent and his foreign guests were also to be there, and on the evening following that they were to be at Carlton House for a grand reception in honor of the dignitaries and for a formal presentation to the queen.

It was only when he remembered what she had been doing that afternoon that his good mood faltered. Understandably he resented the fact that she had made a second appointment to drive with Christopher in the park even though she assured him that she had done so entirely for Christina's sake.

Elizabeth felt confused and guilty by the time she arrived home. And very tired. But she was not to be allowed to go straight to bed. A footman informed her that her father wished to speak with her in the library as soon as she returned home. She sighed. She did not feel quite able to cope with an interview at almost midnight, especially after such a busy and emotional day. And being summoned to the library always meant an interview rather than a social visit. The library was where Papa always summoned servants to be dismissed or family members to be scolded.

Had he heard? she wondered. She had not expected her meeting with Christopher to remain secret for long. But she could have wished that it had kept at least until the morning.

She had guessed right. She knew that as soon as she entered the library and found her father regarding her from beneath brows of thunder. And he was seated formally behind the desk.

"What is this I have been hearing, Elizabeth?" he asked. "No one saw fit to inform me until this evening that the Earl of Trevelyan was even back in England. And yet it seems that you danced with him last evening at Lady Drummond's and even absented yourself with him from the ballroom for half an hour?"

"Yes, Papa," she said, looking steadily back at him.

"Are you quite mad, girl?" he asked. "And you took Christina to meet him this afternoon? Tell me that that information at least was false."

"He is Christina's father, Papa," she said.

He brought a fist crashing down on the desk. "He is not fit to bear the name," he said. "I went to considerable pains, Elizabeth, to sever your relations with that scoundrel. Considerable pains. And yet now you dance with him? And walk with him in the park? And allow him to claim fathership of my granddaughter?"

Elizabeth lowered her eyes. "He is coming again tomorrow, Papa," she said. "Here, to the house. He is to take Christina and me driving."

"If I am dead and in my grave," the Duke of Chicheley said. "Your maid is packing your trunks, Elizabeth, and Christina's nurse is packing hers. Martin will take the two of you to Kingston early tomorrow morning. You will remain there until I have made it clear to the Earl of Trevelyan that London is not a large enough city for both him and me."

Elizabeth raised her eyes again. "Christina and I will be staying in London, Papa," she said. "I will not run from Christopher. Besides, Manley needs me here. The next few weeks will be important for him. He must be seen among all the important dignitaries who will be here, and I should be seen at his side."

"Perhaps you should have remembered that during the past two days," he said angrily, "and not have brought shame and embarrassment on him instead, Elizabeth. You are defying me, then?"

"I am twenty-five years old, Papa," she said, "and determined to lead my own life as far as it is possible to do so. Of course I owe you obedience now as I will to Manley once we are married. But not mindless obedience, Papa. Sometimes I must be allowed to decide things for myself."

He seemed to be making a conscious effort to control his temper. "Where is he living?" he asked.

"Christopher?" she said. "He is at the Pulteney with Nancy."

"I shall send," he said, "and inform him that he is not welcome at this house or anywhere else in company with either you or Christina. You must totally ignore him if you should happen to see him anywhere."

She drew a deep breath. "Christina and I will drive with him tomorrow afternoon, Papa," she said. "And that will be the end of it."

"You are a fool, Elizabeth," he said. "What does Poole have to say about all this?"

"He knows," she said. "I have told him what I have just told you."

"You are a fool," he said again, slapping his open palm on the desk.

He did not say good night. She turned and left the room as he was lifting the brandy decanter to pour himself a drink. She was shaking a little. She had never openly defied her father before. And so when she went into her dressing room and found Martin sitting there, close to two packed trunks, she thankfully went into his arms as he got to his feet.

"Poor Lizzie," he said, patting her back soothingly. "Did he read you a dreadful scold? But he is right, you know. It is impossible for you to stay here under the circumstances."

She drew away from him. "Were you the one to tell him?" she asked.

He looked contrite. "He would have heard soon enough," he said. "Better from one of us than from a stranger, Lizzie. And I have not known what to do to make you see sense. John feels as he always did that you have to be given the chance to work things out on your own. But I can't accept that. I can't bear to see you hurt. And you are going to be hurt if you stay here."

"Perhaps," she said. "But the pain of running can be

just as fierce as the pain of standing and fighting, Martin. I proved that once before."

"You wish you had stayed, then?" he said. "You wish you had forgiven Trevelyan and carried on as if nothing had happened?"

"I could not have done that," she said. "And at that time I don't think I had the strength of character to do any fighting. But now things are different."

"Well," he said, smiling gently at her, "men sometimes see these things more clearly than women, Lizzie. I suppose that is why fathers have command of their daughters and husbands of their wives. Papa in his wisdom has decided that you must return to Kingston. For your own protection and happiness. And I'll be there with you. It will not be so bad, will it? We were happy there before, weren't we?"

She frowned at him. "Sometimes," she said, "I wonder if you have realized that I am no longer a girl. You are more protective even than Papa. Don't you see that you can no longer protect me from life? We are twenty-five, Martin. You are going to ruin your own life if you keep feeling obligated to me. And you will ruin my life too. I am not going to Kingston. I have told Papa that already. I am going to see Christopher tomorrow. And I am going to spend the next few weeks being seen in all the right places and with all the right people at Manley's side. He is to be my husband later this year."

Martin had turned pale, but he said nothing.

"I didn't mean to speak harshly," she said tenderly. She laughed. "I think that is the closest I have ever come to quarreling with you, Martin. But you must see that I have passed girlhood and I have passed that dreadful stage of my life when I leaned on you more heavily than anyone has a right to lean on a brother. I need to live my own life now. And you are free to live yours. At last."

She was touched to see misery in his eyes. "You are headed toward disaster, Lizzie," he said. "I can't bear the thought of that. It was such a relief when Papa made his decision earlier. I thought we would both be saved from unhappiness."

She smiled and took a step forward to set her arms around him and hug him. "Don't worry about me, Martin," she said. "I don't intend to get hurt, but if I do, well, then, I will pick myself up and keep on going. Life cannot be without pain."

He sighed and touched the backs of his fingers to her cheek. "Well, we tried," he said. "Papa and I both. We tried."

"Yes, you did," she said. "Thank you for caring. But don't wrap me about with care, Martin. I need to be free. As far as a woman can be free, that is."

"Good night," he said, and he kissed her cheek and left her to stare ruefully at her packed trunks.

Martin was right about one thing, she thought. She had got herself into an impossible situation. She was Manley's betrothed and it was important that for at least the next few weeks she be everything that a politician's betrothed should be. Her behavior must be exemplary. She could not keep on seeing Christopher even if she did sympathize with his need to be acquainted with their daughter.

She was so weary, she thought suddenly, sinking into the chair Martin had been sitting on when she entered her dressing room. So very weary. Almost too tired to drag herself to bed and sleep. She had been weary all day and for days before that.

She was going to call on Christopher in the morning, she decided suddenly as she climbed into bed a few minutes later. She was not going to wait until the afternoon when Christina would be with them. They needed to straighten out a few things, not the least of which was the fact that that drive was to be their last encounter.

The bed was cold and the pillow uncomfortable. It was strange she thought, turning over onto her side and reaching up a hand to touch the smooth and empty pillow beside her, that a hard-muscled arm could provide a far cozier headrest than a feather pillow.

Then, just when sleep might have been expected to come, she remembered the stab of envy and sadness she had felt in the park at sight of that family laughing at the swans on the Serpentine, the father with his little child up on his shoulder, the mother with her arm linked through his. And then suddenly—perhaps Christopher had noticed too—they became that family, or one just like it.

He had taken Christina up on his shoulder and offered his arm to her, Elizabeth.

For a few minutes, a few minutes out of their lives, they had been a family.

She remembered watching him a little later looking down at Christina, who had been humming and skipping along between then, a smile of such tenderness on his face that she had felt a deep pain.

She remembered—oh, she could not stop remembering.

It was embarrassing to find only Nancy in the suite that Christopher had taken at the Pulteney. He had gone out on some private errands, it seemed. The temptation was to leave rather than have to sit with Nancy and make conversation. But Elizabeth wanted to talk with him before the afternoon. She sat down on the chair indicated by Nancy, and they proceeded to talk about the weather and the success of Lady Drummond's ball and the excitement of having the Grand Duchess Catherine in residence at the Pulteney. Not a mention was made of Penhallow or the weeks they had spent there together.

It was a relief when the door opened abruptly and Christopher came striding inside, still dressed for the outdoors. A relief and a new ordeal.

He stopped short when he saw her. Both she and Nancy had risen to their feet.

"Elizabeth is here," Nancy said unnecessarily. "I shall leave you to talk with her privately, Christopher."

She left the room. At least, Elizabeth assumed she had left. She did not take her own eyes from Christopher. He set his hat and gloves and cane down on a chair close to the door and turned to look at her.

"Elizabeth," he said. "This is an unexpected pleasure."

There was no point in engaging in pure courtesy talk. "You have a curricle?" she asked.

He looked at her strangely. "Yes, actually," he said. "Brand new. Purchased only this morning. Were you afraid that I would be unable to give Christina her treat?"

"Your mind is set on it, then?" she asked.

He looked keenly at her. "You did not need to ask that, did you, Elizabeth?" he said.

"I wish you would change your mind," she said. "Even so, it must be the last time, Christopher. Twice is enough. She cannot mean that much to you after all. You did not even know of her existence until recently."

"Twice is enough," he repeated. "If you knew that you were to see her twice more, would you agree that that was enough, Elizabeth? For the rest of her life and yours she would be a stranger to you. Would you accept that?"

"Of course I would not," she said crossly. "I am her mother."

"Yes, you are," he agreed. "And I am her father."

"I have been with her all her life," she said. "It is a different matter entirely."

"Yes," he said. "I have not been with her because you chose to deprive me of those years. There is much to make up for. Six years. I never will be able to make up for them, Elizabeth, years in which she has thought me dead. Years when she will think I did not care once she knows that I am still alive."

That line of appeal was clearly having no effect on him. She had not really expected that it would.

"My father knows," she said, flushing. "He wanted to pack us off to Kingston without delay. He will not let you come near her, Christopher. You must know that. There will be dreadful unpleasantness if you persist."

"Then so be it," he said. "I had a note from him early this morning instructing me to wait on him when I arrive at Grosvenor Square this afternoon. I believe the advance notice is designed to have me quaking in my boots by the time I arrive."

He had always been a little in awe of her father. She could remember how very nervous he had been when he had been going to ask her father for her hand. Now he was standing in his sitting room at the Pulteney, his feet slightly apart, his eyes hard, his jaw set, and she knew that this line of appeal would not have any effect either.

"I have something of an appetite for battle, having avoided it seven years ago," he said.

"I could put powerful weapons into his hands with just a few words," she said.

"By telling him how I deceived you into living with me as my wife after I kidnapped you?" he said. "Yes, do that, Elizabeth. We will see how much of a stomach he has for public scandal yet again."

She looked at him and swallowed. That had been her trump card, though she had feared that she would not be able to use it with conviction. He must know that she would never reveal that piece of information and that she was very thankful that the only other two people who knew, Nancy and Martin, could also be trusted to keep the secret. She turned to look out of a window.

"You might as well save your breath, Elizabeth," he said quietly. He had come up behind her to stand quite close.

"Christopher," she said, staring out toward the park, "do you hate me so much that you would ruin my life all over again? I don't believe you care. And if you do, or think you do, then you must remember that you forfeited the right to care years ago."

"By running," he said. "Yes, it was a grievous fault, Elizabeth. We all make them, unfortunately. I would like to believe that there was as little malice in your grievous fault as there was in mine."

"Mine?" she said.

"I ran because I was in despair," he said. "Because I did not see how I was to clear myself of a charge that appeared so black against me. I had been lured to that woman's house and she had her bodice off and my coat down to my wrists even before shock could register on my inexperienced mind. Your arrival was timed for that exact moment, of course. When she cried and claimed that we were longtime lovers, that I had promised to marry her, that I had married you only to get enough money to keep her and our child in comfort, I knew that it was a carefully concocted plot and that I would be fortunate indeed to get myself out of it. I could only rely on your faith in me. But it did not exist."

"You were clearly guilty," she said indignantly. "If you would just admit it, Christopher, I would be far more inclined to forgive you."

"Despair caused my great sin," he said. "What caused yours, Elizabeth? Spite? Did it give you the satisfaction of getting even to keep from me the fact that we were to have a child? And the fact of Christina's existence?"

"I did not want you as the father of my child," she said. "You were not worthy."

"But I was the father," he said. "Who has played papa all these years? Your father? Martin? John has been away, hasn't he?"

"Martin has been wonderful to me," she said. "He tried so hard to make excuses for you, Christopher. He tried to stop me from hating you. And he stayed with me and Christina all the time we were at Kingston before coming back here. He is even willing to go back there with me now."

"Yes, Martin," he said. "Everyone's best friend. Have you ever been able to explain to yourself why you disliked him and even feared him before you recovered your memory?"

"Yes," she said. "It was shame. Some part of me knew that I would be ashamed of myself and would find it difficult to face him when I knew the truth. But I need not have worried. Martin never condemns. He always looks for the best in people. He is always willing to love without asking for anything in return."

"Perhaps it is Martin you should have married," he said.

"Our feelings for each other have never been like that," she said. "We have always felt for each other the love of brother and sister."

"Convenient," he said.

"You may choose to believe otherwise," she said, anger flaring. "I do not care."

"She is beautiful, Elizabeth," he said, changing the subject so abruptly that for a moment she felt bewildered. "You would not realize how much like Nancy at her age she is, except that she has those lovely blue eyes. She seems like a happy child."

"I have had a great deal of love to give her," she said. "She does not usually take to strangers."

"She was a little shy," he said. "I have no experience with children. She seemed not to be afraid of me after a while. Did she say anything about me afterward?"

Christina had said that she liked that gentleman because he did not smile at her and chuck her under the chin and call her a good girl and a pretty girl, which she knew she was not, and then turn his attention to Mama and forget all about her. She had said that she liked that gentleman better than Lord Poole, who pretended to like her but did not. She had been scolded for those final words.

"No," Elizabeth said. "Nothing." She glanced at him but could not tell from his expression if he was disappointed. But she felt guilty for the lie.

"Ah," he said.

"Christopher"—she would try her final line of appeal—"it has taken me a long, long time to get my life back in order again. I have finally done it. I have chosen a good man to marry. And I know that life with him will appeal to me. I will be busy and useful as a politician's wife."

"Will you?" he said.

"But Manley feels vulnerable," she said. "He is a Whig in a country that has gone mad for the Tories in light of the recent victory. Soon all the foreign visitors are going to be here and life will grow frantic. It is important that he be seen celebrating with everyone else. And it is important that I be seen at his side. This is not the time for scandal, and I am afraid that you being in London has already aroused gossip as will the fact that we were walking in the park together yesterday and will be driving together today. There must be no more, Christopher. Please. You must see that. Have some feeling for Manley and for Christina even if you can have none for me."

"If you are a millstone about his neck, Elizabeth," he said, "perhaps you should set him free before it is too late."

"There is no argument that will weigh anything at all with you, is there?" she said bitterly. "You do not care for anyone but yourself."

"I cannot allow him my daughter," he said. "I will not have him in a position to call himself her father or even her stepfather. I am her father, Elizabeth."

"You are despicable," she said. "Very well, then, if it is what you want, I shall fight you. Try to ruin the Season for both me and Manley. Perhaps you will succeed. But that will be your only satisfaction. During the summer months Manley and I will be marrying. And then he will be Christina's stepfather. There is nothing you can do to prevent it, Christopher."

"I think," he said quietly, "that you had better marry me, Elizabeth."

"What?" She could only look at him in shock.

"We had better put right what was put so very wrong almost seven years ago," he said. "We were married then and produced a child. We have been married during the past month. We might as well make it official again."

"We are divorced!" She almost spat the words at him.

"There was no just cause," he said. "Besides, when we were married, we both agreed that it was until death. We spoke those words to each other before a vicar and witnesses. And before God. Neither of us is dead, Elizabeth."

She had a sudden and unwelcome memory of the small chapel at Kingston and of Christopher beside her, holding her hand, looking handsome and pale and nervous. And of herself calm and happy and drinking in the moment and telling herself quite deliberately that she would remember it until her dying breath. She felt a rush of tears and turned her head sharply away toward the window again.

"I would not marry you," she said, "if you were the last man left on earth."

"And yet," he said, "you loved me just a few weeks ago. Without the memory of what happened in the past, you loved me. What if those things you thought happened actually never did, Elizabeth? There would have been no reason for the divorce, would there? You would still be my wife. And there would be no cause for you not to love me."

"But there was cause," she said.

"And there would have been no cause for keeping my child from me," he said. "I would be the one who has been terribly wronged, Elizabeth, not you."

For perhaps the first time she felt a dreadful and almost overpowering surge of doubt. She had wanted to feel it seven years before, had tried to feel it, and had failed. She had longed for his innocence too much to allow herself to hope for it.

"How clever you are with words," she said, her voice

low and bitter. "You would like to add guilt to all the other things I have suffered, Christopher. No, thank you. My emotions are not so easily devastated as they used to be."

She had not realized he was standing quite so close until his hand reached out and took her by the chin and turned her face, teary eyes and all, for his scrutiny.

"For better, for worse," he said. "We said those words too, Elizabeth. No one in the marriage service promised us a happily ever after. That was our own personal mistake. We were too young and did not understand that life would not be like that despite the fact that we were in love. The marriage service merely made us promise that we would live through and work through all the difficulties life and marriage would bring us—together. We failed the very first test quite miserably. Both of us."

She felt humiliation when one tear dripped onto his hand and he dried her cheek with his thumb.

"You are far more dangerous than you used to be," she said. "You have developed a persuasive tongue. I don't want to be hurt again, Christopher. I don't want all this. I want peace and contentment. I want Manley. Please leave me alone. And leave Christina alone. Your presence in her life can only confuse her."

"Marry me," he said. "I want us to be a family."

"You merely want her because she is yours," she said. "A piece of property you have come home to claim, like Penhallow. And because through her you can get even with me for allowing Papa to bring divorce proceedings against you. Let us go, Christopher. Accept reality."

"You can think about it," he said. "I'll not press for an immediate answer, Elizabeth."

He touched the pad of his thumb to her lips and his eyes watched what he was doing. She thought for one moment that he was going to kiss her and longed for the touch of his lips. And almost panicked at the thought. But he released her and took a step back.

"This afternoon will not be the last time you will wish to see Christina, then?" she said.

"No."

She looked down at her hands for a while, but there was nothing else to be said. He was not to be moved. She crossed the room, picked up her bonnet from a small table, and found that he was already at the door to hold it open for her. She half ran down the stairs, tying the strings of her bonnet as she went, but even if dignity had allowed her to run as fast as her legs would carry her, she would not have been able to outstrip her realization that she wished he had kissed her, put his arms about her, forced the issue as he had when he had taken her from outside St. George's.

She might have said yes. It was a shameful admission to have to make even in the privacy of her own thoughts. Perhaps especially there. He exerted a very powerful magic over her. Even more powerful than when she had first known him. He had been an inexperienced boy then. He was a man now.

Inexperienced. Had he been? And a boy? Even though he had been twenty-four years old? And yet at the time he had convinced her that he was a tough man of the world. The very naive girl she had been had believed him. Yet she could look back now and realize both his inexperience and her own naïveté.

And that in itself was a frightening admission. If it was true, was it likely that he would have taken a mistress during his years at Oxford, fathered a child, moved the family to London, and planned a coldhearted marriage with a rich heiress so that his mistress and child could live in comfort? Could he have ruthlessly stripped a man of his fortune while at Oxford and shown no remorse when that man committed suicide? Could he have beaten a prostitute until she fell and killed herself?

Her father's carriage was waiting outside the Pulteney. Elizabeth climbed into it gratefully and sank back against the cushions. She was feeling so very tired despite the fact that she had slept surprisingly well the night before. Weary right through her bones. And unwilling to think. She must not begin to have doubts now. Had he not proved his ruthlessness again just recently? Had he not kidnapped her and taken full advantage of the fall that had robbed her of her memory and might as easily have robbed her of life?

No, she must not begin to doubt. She hated him. She hated him because he had brought turmoil into her life again. And emotion. And bitter regret for all that might have been. She hated him.

20

JOHN arrived promptly at the Pulteney to take Nancy to Kew Gardens. He had felt exhilarated during the morning to find that the weather was as lovely as it had been the day before and that there were no distant clouds to threaten the afternoon.

He was feeling as excited as a boy, he found to his own amusement. He had thought himself well past the age of feeling aroused by romance or any other enthusiasm for women beyond the purely sexual. But there was more than just the physical in his enthusiasm for Nancy.

She was waiting for him—alone. He was quite happy that Christopher was not there too. He did not like to interfere in family affairs, yet it was obvious that Christopher's return to England was causing some commotion at home and especially in Elizabeth's emotions. Even Christina was not immune. When he had wandered into the nursery that morning, as he had done most mornings since his return, she had told him about the gentleman who had put her up on his shoulders the afternoon before and was to take her for a drive in his curricle that afternoon and who had eyes as blue as hers and who liked her, not just Mama.

If it were to come to a contest between Christopher and Poole, John thought, then he would secretly cheer for the former. And perhaps not so secretly either if Elizabeth asked his opinion. But he would not interfere unbidden. So he was relieved to find that he did not have to say anything to Christopher.

"Nancy," he said as she came across the room toward him, all ready to leave, "how lovely you look." He was not merely flattering her. She was all in primrose yellow from her bonnet to her slippers. And as fashionable as any lady he had seen recently.

"Thank you." She looked at him rather uncertainly and he smiled. They were to be friends, were they not? Then he would cultivate her friendship and forget about all else. If it were possible to do so.

They talked all the way to Kew. He told her about Portugal and Spain and about crossing the Pyrenees into France. She told him about Penhallow and its wild and lovely scenery and about her friends and activities there. By the time he lifted her down from his curricle and they began to stroll in the gardens toward one of the pagodas, she was relaxed and smiling. She looked almost like the Nancy he had fallen in love with, only more serene, more mature. Several times more lovely.

"I am glad you came to London again," he said. "Are you?"

"Yes," she said. "No matter how lovely one place is or how attached one is to it, it is always good to see other places and meet other people. London is an exciting place to be. Especially at the moment."

"Especially because London is celebrating and preparing to celebrate even more?" he asked. "Or especially because I am here?"

He spoke lightly and he laughed, but her smile faded. "I meant because of the celebrations," she said.

His little joke had spoiled his mood. He felt suddenly depressed, and for the first time a silence fell between them. He set a hand over the primrose gloved one on his arm.

"I want to see you again, Nancy," he said. "And again and again. Are you to be at the Clemens' ball tomorrow?"

"We have accepted our invitation," she said.

"Good." He removed his hand. "Will you save two waltzes for me? The first and the last? And will you come to the opera as my guest next week? It is to be a grand occasion. Prinny is to be there with as many of the foreign guests as can be persuaded to go. Doubtless the Haymarket will be bursting at the seams. Will you come?"

She hesitated. "I don't know," she said.

"We will be members of a party of eight," he said.

"Will anyone from your f-family be there too?" she asked.

"With us?" It struck him that she did not want to find herself in a party that included Elizabeth and Poole. "Absolutely not. Will you come?"

"Very well, then," she said. "If we are still in town. I think we will be."

"And the waltzes too?" he asked.

"Yes," she said. "Thank you."

He was back to boyhood yet again, he thought. He felt rather like shouting for joy. Or like clasping her about the waist and twirling her around. He glanced about them. There were other people in sight. He grinned just as Nancy looked up at him and raised her eyebrows.

"I was hoping there was no one in sight," he said. "I wanted to pick you up and twirl you about. Maybe even try to steal a kiss. Be thankful that there are other people here."

There was naked terror on her face as she snatched her hand from his arm, hesitated, and then continued walking along the path almost at a run. John caught up to her but did not attempt to touch her or even talk to her. There was a wrought-iron seat a little back from the path ahead, surrounded by rhododendron bushes on three sides.

"Come and sit down, Nancy," he said to her quietly. "We will be in full view of others. And even if we were not, I would not harm you. I promise that on my honor as a gentleman and as an officer of His Majesty's cavalry."

If they did not sit down, their path would take them within the next minute or two into a group of people approaching. Nancy hesitated again and then turned without a word to sit close to one side of the seat. John sat at the other side.

"I'm sorry," she said. "I know you were merely joking. Forgive me. It is what comes of living a restricted life for several years."

"No," he said. "That is not what it comes from, Nancy."

She looked straight ahead and they waited until the group approaching along the path had passed after nodding and exchanging greetings with them.

"It happened between the time when I kissed you one evening and the time when I asked you to marry me the next," John said. "Am I right?"

"No," she said. But it was a quick reflex answer and lacked conviction.

"Someone hurt you during that time," he said, "and frightened you. Try as I will to avoid the horror of it, I can think of only one thing that would have frightened you for seven years and made you live the life of a hermit spinster. God, I hope I am wrong. Were you raped, Nancy?"

"No!" she said vehemently, still staring ahead, her body rigid.

"Oh, God!" he said, wishing he had not met her again, wishing he did not have to know. "Who did it to you? It was someone at Kingston. One of the guests?"

"It was no one," she said. "Nothing happened. I want to go back home, John. The air has turned chilly."

"No," he said. "The air is as warm as it was when we left. It is you who have turned chilly. You don't have to suffer it quite alone, Nancy. Not any longer. Is that what you have done all this time? You have told no one?"

He watched her bite on the inside of her lip and try to keep control of herself.

"Do you think telling anyone would have brought me any comfort?" she said eventually. "I was the one who was violated. It was my body it happened to. No one else's. There could be no comfort from anyone else."

"There might have been punishment," he said. "Justice."

"I had been violated," she said. "No amount of vengeance could have changed that. I don't want to be talking about this, John. I have learned to live with it. I have learned to put the memories behind me. I have learned that it was something done to me, against my will, that I was in no way to blame, and that it has not changed me in any essential way or made me less of a person. I have learned to like myself again. I would rather leave it all in the past, where it belongs."

"And yet," he said, "you cannot bear to be touched? At least, not in any way that suggests however remotely the intimacy of a man and a woman."

"No," she said, "I cannot. It is one thing that can make me panic. I have learned to live with that too. Some people are terrified of thunderstorms or snakes or fast vehicles. I am terrified of men. One learns to live with one's terrors."

"And so," he said, "this thing that happened to you snatched you away from me and has kept us apart ever since and will keep us apart for the rest of our lives."

She turned her head to look at him then. "I thought we were to be friends," she said. "That is what we agreed to."

"Yes." He sighed. "Is that what you really want, Nancy? Can you be satisfied with that?"

"It is not possible, is it?" she said sadly. "We had better not meet again, John. I'll stay away from that ball tomorrow, and you will find someone else to escort to the opera next week."

"I want to kiss you," he said. "Here and now. I want to prove to you that a kiss can be pleasant, that it does not always lead to the sort of nightmare you have been carrying around with you for so long. But there is something else more important, and when you have told me, neither of us will be in the mood for kissing. I want to know who it was, Nancy."

"No," she said.

"I must know," he said. "He deprived you of freedom and me of a bride. Was it a member of my family?"

"No," she said, her voice an agony.

"My father?" He held his breath.

"No!" The shock in her eyes brought him the relief of knowing that she spoke the truth.

"Martin?" He held his breath again.

"No." She leapt to her feet.

He got up too and possessed himself of her hands, which he held very tightly. "Look at me, Nancy," he said, unconsciously using the voice that had commanded men for many years past. She obeyed him. "Was it Martin who raped you?"

"He was only eighteen," she said. "Always smiling and charming. I thought of him as a boy even though he was only two years younger than I. It did not occur to me to take someone else or a chaperone with me when he asked me to go walking down by the river with him. And when he tried to kiss me, I laughed and was embarrassed. I was furious with him when he started to get rough with me. But it did not occur to me at first to be frightened."

John could feel the blood draining from his head. He drew her back down onto the seat, keeping his hold of her hands.

"And then he had me facedown on the ground," she said, "and tied my hands behind me with something. It was only then, when he lifted my clothes and I could not stop him, that I started to get frightened. I was very naive. He beat me at first. I thought that would be all, but then he got on top of me and tried something else. It hurt terribly and then he grew more angry. Why am I telling you this?" She tried to pull her hands free. "I don't want to be telling you this."

"Tell me." It was still his officer's voice.

"He turned me over onto my back," she said. "My hands were beneath me and still tied. And then he came onto me and did what he had been trying to do the other way, but this time he succeeded." She pulled a hand away and set the back of it, shaking, over her mouth. "It was horrible, horrible. I could not stop vomiting afterward and he was laughing and teasing me and being charming and acting as if we had just done something that both of us had found pleasurable. Something of no great significance."

John pushed very firmly from his mind the fact that it was Martin she was talking about. He could not think of that now. He set his hands on her shoulders, molding them, massaging them, trying to let his strength flow into her.

"And just a short while later," he said, "I was trying to kiss you and asking you to marry me."

"Yes." She looked at him from eyes that had seen years of nightmares. "I had been so wanting it and hoping for it. I loved you so very much."

"It is pointless for me to say that you should have told me, isn't it?" he said. "I could have brought you no comfort. Me least of all."

"It is long in the past," she said. "It is best left there."

He cupped a hand very gently to her cheek. She did not jerk back. "I have never stopped loving you," he said. "I realized that as soon as I saw you again. I am going to woo you, Nancy. I am going to teach you that lovemaking can be beautiful and very pleasurable. No, don't protest. I'll take a year doing it, or two or three if necessary. We have all the time in the world—the rest of two lifetimes. I am going to see to it that there are no terrors to shadow your life. That is a promise."

She set her hand over his and held it to her cheek. "I want you to be happy," she said, "with someone who is capable of happiness."

He smiled at her. "Then we are agreed," he said. "We both have the same goal in mind." He got to his feet and drew her to hers. "Shall we stroll back to the curricle?"

She took his arm and they walked in silence for a while.

"John," she said at last, "will you promise not to say anything or do anything? It was all a long time ago and I don't want unpleasantness between our families any more than I did then when Christopher and Elizabeth were so happy. I think there is the smallest chance that they may be happy again, though I do not doubt that you will not wish for it. I want them to have that chance. I think they love each other when all else is stripped away except their basic feelings for each other."

"You do me an injustice," he said. "I was quite comfortable with Christopher as a brother-in-law and thought the divorce a grand piece of nonsense. I'll do nothing to jeopardize their chance of a reconciliation, Nancy."

"Promise?"

"I promise," he said. But he had not promised that he would not kill Martin or at the very least castrate him.

"Thank you," Nancy said.

John remembered suddenly Martin's knowledge of the London brothels that catered to perverted sexual tastes. A knowledge he had found surprising and considered out of character at the time.

Christopher had spoken the truth to Elizabeth. He was very ready for a fight with the Duke of Chicheley, having avoided it seven years before. He had not been unhappy early that morning to receive the duke's terse note. He had arranged to pick up Elizabeth and his daughter from Grosvenor Square in the hope of provoking such a confrontation. He was not intending to sneak around London, seeing them behind the duke's back.

The duke received him in the library, a room of heavy splendor. He sat behind a huge desk, a cane propped against his chair. He did not invite his guest to sit down. Christopher pursed his lips and wondered how long it would take his former father-in-law to realize that he was no longer easily cowed.

"Trevelyan?" the duke said stiffly. "I did not think to see you again."

"Sir?" Christopher inclined his head.

"And I cannot pretend that it is a pleasure," the duke said.

Christopher raised his eyebrows.

"That you would take up residence in London at all is impertinence enough," the duke said. "That you would communicate with my daughter and my granddaughter shows an appalling lack of decency and principle. I demand an explanation."

"It it very simple and I would have thought obvious," Christopher said. "Christina is my daughter. It would seem indecent and unprincipled to me not to want to see her and get to know her."

"My granddaughter," the duke said, "is well cared for, Trevelyan, and will be for the rest of her life. However, I did not summon you here to argue with you. I wish to make one thing perfectly plain. You are not welcome in this house, and you are to keep away from my daughter and granddaughter. Do I make myself clear?"

"Abundantly so," Christopher said. "Your house I will stay away from, sir. I am inside it now only because you have invited me here. My daughter and yours I will see as often as it can be arranged. This afternoon, for example, we will be driving in Hyde Park."

"I forbid it," the duke said.

"I believe King Canute said something similar to the incoming tide," Christopher said. "But his feet got wet nonetheless. May I ask why you feel it necessary to say this to me? Is it not enough to say it to Elizabeth? If she refuses to see me, there is not much I can do about it, is there?"

"My daughter," the duke said, "is easily intimidated

and needs a great deal of protection by the men who care for her. I care for her.''

''I see,'' Christopher said. ''But you have not been able to intimidate her enough to get her to agree not to see me. I was foolish seven years ago. Or perhaps just young. I was quite sure that I would never be able to persuade anyone to believe that my wife was the only woman I had ever known, that I had never had either a mistress or a whore. How was I to prove my innocence when my wife caught me in the arms of a half-naked woman? It seemed impossible to me. So I did the one thing that made me seem undoubtedly guilty. I ran away.''

''And showed how much you cared for your wife by staying away for years until there was a title and property and a fortune to come back to,'' the duke said, his voice vicious with sarcasm.

''Yes,'' Christopher said. ''When one discovers, after one's passage home has been purchased and one's bags packed, that one has been divorced, one can very quickly change one's plans. I stayed in Canada. But I am back now, sir, and I find that the past is not a closed book after all. I have a daughter I did not know about until very recently.''

''She has lived very well without you all these years,'' the duke said.

''As Elizabeth told me,'' Christopher said, ''she has had a great deal of love to give the child. I do not doubt the truth of what she says. But a child needs a father too, preferably a real father rather than a stepfather. I have asked Elizabeth to marry me.''

The duke was speechless for a moment. ''You have *what*?'' he said eventually. ''This is preposterous, Trevelyan. My daughter is betrothed. She would have been married if some scoundrel had not ruined her wedding day by kidnapping her and then proving too inept to demand his ransom.''

''I heard of it,'' Christopher said. ''I bless the man. He saved my wife from becoming a bigamist.''

The Duke of Chicheley looked at him keenly. ''Maybe I should have your whereabouts on the day of the wedding investigated,'' he said.

''If I had kidnapped her,'' Christopher said, ''I would

not have lost her on the road to some kindly philanthropist, you may be certain. I want Elizabeth to marry me. I want us to be a family again."

The duke's hand was opening and closing on the desktop. "I shall do everything in my power to prevent such a disaster," he said. "You found out once before that it is not wise to cross me, Trevelyan."

"I think it would have been the wisest thing I could have done," Christopher said. "You did not oppose our marriage, sir. I believe you thought the heir to an earldom was a good enough catch for Elizabeth, especially when I was her personal choice. I believe you would have remained pleased with me if you had not so readily accepted the lies that were told about me. And then pride got in the way. You could not bear to think that you had so misjudged your daughter's husband. And so it must be arranged that I no longer be her husband. And now, of course, pride will get in the way of your admitting that perhaps you acted hastily. Or maybe quite unjustly."

"Get out of my house," the duke said. "And stay away from my daughter if you know what is good for you, Trevelyan."

"Perhaps by the time I marry her," Christopher said, "you will have no choice but to admit that you were wrong. Good day, sir."

He turned and left the room and sent a servant upstairs to inform Lady Elizabeth that he was waiting below. She came down almost immediately, Christina holding her hand, shy again, half hiding against her skirt, eyeing him warily. He smiled at her and winked and watched her face disappear entirely. His heart leaped with joy at the sight of her, dainty in pink today.

Elizabeth was unsmiling and straight backed. He wondered, shifting his gaze to her, why she was defying her father to come out with him. She had the perfect excuse not to do so. His heart leaped no less at the sight of her, dressed in a darker shade of pink.

He wondered why he had asked her to marry him and realized even as he asked that the idea was not new to him, that he had been planning it for days. Was it just because of their daughter and his unwillingness that any other man have the right to call himself her father? That was a very large part of his reason. There was no denying that. He wanted her with a fierce paternal longing he would not have suspected himself capable of.

But was it his only reason? Would he want to marry Elizabeth even if Christina did not exist? It was a foolish question. There was nothing future about her being his wife. She was his wife. "For better, for worse," he had said to her in the chapel at Kingston. "Until death do us part."

She reached the bottom of the stairs and looked at him. "Hello, Elizabeth," he said and transferred his gaze to Christina, who was looking at him with wary eyes. "Hello, Christina. We have the most fashionable curricle in all London to ride in or so I was assured this morning. And a pair of grays that can only be described as prime goers. Everyone we pass on the streets and in the park is going to turn a shade of green with envy. People are going to turn and stare, but we will not stop to tell them that it is rude to do so. Not unless you insist, that is."

Christina hid her smile against her mother's skirt.

When they were outside, he handed Elizabeth up to the high seat of the curricle and turned to his daughter. "You have a choice, Christina," he said. "Either you can ride between your mama and me like a proper lady, or you can sit between my knees like a famous whip and help guide the horses. Which is it to be?"

But it was too early in the outing and she was separated from her mother by several feet. "I want to sit by Mama," she whispered.

He clasped her about her tiny waist and lifted her up to Elizabeth's waiting arms. She was snuggled close against her mother when he climbed into his own seat. He smiled and hid his disappointment.

But the excitement of riding in an open carriage so far above the ground soon overcame shyness. And the fear of falling. Christina was soon gripping his sleeve as well as her mother's and exclaiming about everything she could see. As they turned into the park, she leaned toward Elizabeth.

"Can I sit there?" she whispered, pointing to his lap.

"Lord Trevelyan needs to concentrate," Elizabeth said.

"She may sit here," Christopher said. "I will need some help now that we will be among more traffic." He lifted his daughter to sit between his legs, holding her steady with his thighs, letting her small hands clutch the ribbons above his.

She giggled with delight. "Look at me!" she said, and she tipped her head sideways and back to look up at him with sparkling eyes and flushed cheeks—Nancy as she had used to look when they had played on the beach.

He almost despised himself for the happiness of the next half hour. It was late in the afternoon of a beautiful spring day during the Season, and they were in the place where the whole fashionable world congregated daily to see and to be seen, though the excuse was fresh air and exercise. The vast majority of people who drove or rode or strolled there that afternoon would know that Elizabeth was once his wife and that Christina was his daughter. Those who did not know would do so before they left the park.

He smiled and talked with Christina, nodded to acquaintances, exchanged pleasantries with some, and felt full to bursting with triumph and happiness. Only one thing marred his joy. Elizabeth sat rigidly and silently at his side. After half an hour he drove to a quieter part of the park. Christina had climbed onto his lap and relinquished her hold on the ribbons.

"I am going to tell Uncle John that I am a famous whip," she said, looking up into Christopher's face.

"Not Uncle Martin and Grandpapa?" Elizabeth asked.

"Them too," Christina said. "Uncle John rides a horse to war. I love horses."

"Then you would enjoy the horse shows at Astley's Amphitheater," Christopher said. He heard Elizabeth beside him draw breath.

"Uncle John is going to take me there one day," Christina said. "Lord Poole won't take me. He is too busy."

"He would if he had time, sweetheart," Elizabeth said. "He is an extremely busy and important man."

"How about tomorrow?" Christopher asked. "Shall I take you and Mama there tomorrow? And then when Uncle John takes you, you will be able to tell him what is coming next."

Elizabeth was silent.

"Tomorrow?" Christina was staring at him saucer-eyed. "Aren't you busy?"

"I have all the time in the world for you, Christina," he said.

"Do you like me?" She sounded surprised. "Not just Mama? Uncle John likes me."

"I like you very much indeed," he said. "Quite as much as I like your mama."

"Oh," she said, and she sounded pleased. "I am not going to tell Uncle John that I am going to Astley's Amphitheater tomorrow. Then when he takes me, I can surprise him by knowing all about it." She giggled.

"In three days' time," he said, "there is going to be a grand show in London. The Prince Regent has invited important guests from all over Europe to come and visit him and celebrate the victory that Uncle John helped win. They are going to be arriving all together from Dover. The streets are going to be packed with cheering people out to greet them. Shall we be among them?"

"Ye-e-es," Christina said. "Grandpapa said I could not go. He said it would be unseemly. May we, Mama? Oh, please!" She bounced on his lap in an agony of suspense.

Elizabeth looked coolly at him. "Why not?" she said. "It will be a day to be remembered in history. You should be there, Christina."

His daughter relaxed against him, comfortable and happy and no longer even a little shy with him. She began to tell him about the puppies in the stables at Kingstone, and prattled all the way home. Elizabeth tried to hush her when they were back in the busy street traffic, but he set a hand on her wrist and shook his head.

"Don't stop her," he said. "I want to hear all she has to tell me. Everything that has happened in her life."

Elizabeth turned her head sharply away.

When they returned to Grosvenor Square, he lifted Christina to the ground first and she darted into the house, intent on finding someone interested in the fact that she had become a famous whip. He lifted Elizabeth down, holding her deliberately close to his own body. A selfish indulgence, he thought when he saw the unhappiness on her face.

"She is delightful," he said. "You surely cannot want

to deprive me of her any longer, Elizabeth. I don't believe you do. Do you?''

She looked directly at him but did not answer.

''Are you going to the Clemens' ball tomorrow evening?'' he asked.

She nodded. ''With Manley,'' she said. ''Please, Christopher, be content with the afternoons. Stay away from me there.''

''I want the supper dance,'' he said. ''Save it for me?''

She shook her head. ''You do not understand, do you?'' she said. ''He is going to be my husband.''

''The supper dance,'' he said. ''You see? I ask for only one.''

''And you will not take no for an answer, will you?'' she said.

He shook his head and wondered if what he was doing amounted to harassment. Undoubtedly it did. And yet she did not have to endure it. A firm no would suffice. She could draw on her not inconsiderable arsenal of male protectors to warn him off and even do more than warn. He was being persistent, but he was not using force.

''The supper dance, then,'' she said and turned and fled up the shallow steps to the doorway, almost colliding with Martin as she did so. She did not stop to talk to him but hurried on by.

21

MARTIN was in a buoyant mood. Or perhaps that was not quite an accurate description of his feelings since he knew that he was going to cause Elizabeth pain and humiliation. And he had never ever wanted to cause her pain. Quite the opposite. He wanted to bring peace and contentment into her life. But she had grown stubborn and she must be made to see that there was only one road to happiness. And only one person to walk that road with her.

His mood was at least partly buoyant because he had finally worked out a definite plan. From the moment of his return to London he had rejected the simple and seemingly attractive plan of divulging his knowledge of the kidnapping. Both his father and Poole would have reacted with fury, and undoubtedly the betrothal would have come to an end. But Martin was not convinced that such an outcome would send Elizabeth back to Kingston. She had developed an alarming strength and independence of character in the past few years.

Something far more drastic was needed.

And finally—finally!—he had it all worked out. He knew how he would get Elizabeth to flee, never to return, and he knew how he would nip in the bud her renewed attraction to Trevelyan.

Hence his buoyant mood.

He had been at a front window awaiting their return from the drive in the park. He walked unhurriedly down the stairs when he saw the curricle approach. The damn fool had bought a new curricle merely because Christina had wanted to ride in one. And he must have wormed his way into her affections too. The brat was sitting on his lap.

Christina ran past him in the hall. He smiled at her.

"So," he said, "what do you have to tell Uncle Martin about your drive?"

But she ran on past him. "I am going to tell Uncle John," she called over her shoulder.

Martin compressed his lips. His hands often itched to give the child a good spanking to teach her better manners. But Lizzie would not like it. She doted on Christina. He strolled outside onto the steps and almost collided with Elizabeth, who ran on past, not looking any too happy. Martin shrugged and raised his eyebrows to Christopher.

"She is proving difficult to please?" he asked. "Have patience with her, Trevelyan. She has had Christina all to herself for six years. She is finding it difficult to share. Fond uncles are not such a threat, you see."

Christopher nodded curtly and looked at him keenly. He was in a bad mood, Martin thought. Things were not going well.

"I hope Lizzie has not refused to let you see Christina again," Martin said. "I'll have a word with her. She is a little hysterical these days. But I pride myself on thinking that I usually have a calming influence on her. And she should be made to see reason on this. You are understandably fond of your daughter."

"Yes," Christopher said, "I am. But you know all, Martin. Why is it you are willing to help me when you have it in your power to do just the opposite?"

Martin shrugged and smiled. "You know me," he said. "Always more heart than head. And I can't help liking you, Trevelyan, and feeling rather uneasy over the fact that I believed all those things about you once you had gone away. I should have investigated the charges more closely, I suppose, before passing judgment. But it is too late now, isn't it?"

"Yes," Christopher said. "Too late. And I daresay whoever hated me so much was careful enough not to leave any trail anyway."

Martin shook his head. "That is the part I have most difficulty with," he said. "Who would have hated you that much? Anyway, I want to make amends if I can. You want Lizzie back, don't you?"

Christopher's eyes narrowed, but he said nothing.

"I can see it," Martin said, "even if you do not want

to admit it. But there is something about Lizzie, Trevelyan, that I know perhaps better than you. She likes to have her hand forced. If she has to make decisions for herself, she is likely to be stubborn. If she is forced, she will follow her heart. I think that was proved at Penhallow, wasn't it?"

"At Penhallow," Christopher said, "she had lost her memory."

"Of course," Martin said. "But would she have accepted just any man who had said he was her husband at that time? I think not. I think her heart remembered even if her brain did not."

Christopher said nothing.

"Kidnapping was the best thing for her," Martin said. "I never thought this idea of marrying Poole was right for her."

"No," Christopher said, "I don't suppose you did. You think I should kidnap her again, Martin?"

Martin considered. "I think not," he said. "She would probably not stand for it again. You have to stay firm over Christina, I think. You have to convince her that you will never let your daughter go."

Christopher raised his eyebrows. "Even to the extent of kidnapping her, perhaps?"

Martin thought again. "That is a little extreme, I must admit," he said. "I had not thought of it. But it might just work, by Jove. Elizabeth would follow in a vast hurry if you had Christina. But of course." He flashed a boyish grin. "It is a foolish idea, isn't it? Crazy. We'll think of something else."

"Perhaps not so crazy," Christopher said, swinging himself back up into the high seat of his curricle. "Thank you, Martin. You are a true friend."

Martin laughed nervously. "You are not seriously considering it, are you?" he asked. "We will have to talk further. I'll have to talk you out of it. I will have guilt pangs tonight for even considering it as a joke."

Christopher touched his hat. "Don't lose any sleep over it," he said, turning his horses' heads and pulling out into the square.

Martin watched him go. Trevelyan thought himself so much the man of the world now that he had spent years in America and had made himself a successful businessman there. He was the veriest babe when it came to being manipulated.

Trevelyan was not going to succeed with Lizzie again, Martin thought, gazing after the departing curricle with hatred naked in his eyes. She was his now and always would be. He would see to that, and she would eventually know that only with him could she be happy. As they always had been happy before Trevelyan came into her life seven years before.

Christina was wildly excited. Elizabeth had not seen her daughter more animated. Everything at the horse show had to be gasped over and exclaimed upon—ponies prancing in a circle; horses jumping through hoops and over barrels; ladies standing on the backs of trotting horses and holding their arms out to the sides. There was a seemingly endless stream of entertainment to be wondered at.

Most of the child's comments and exclamations were directed at Christopher. Perhaps it was that she herself could not show outward enthusiasm, Elizabeth thought, though she loved seeing her daughter so happy. Before the show was half over, Christina was on Christopher's lap, the better to see what was happening, though her view had been quite unobstructed from her seat.

"I like that gentleman, Mama," she had said when they were getting ready for the afternoon's outing. Christopher was never "Lord Trevelyan." He was always "that gentleman."

"Do you, sweetheart?" Elizabeth had asked, tying the ribbons of her daughter's bonnet and looking into her face to note again how much like her father she was.

"He likes me," Christina had said simply and happily. Elizabeth had felt like crying.

There had been none of the shyness of the previous day when Christopher's carriage had come for them and he had handed them inside.

"I didn't tell Uncle John," Christina had announced, her voice excited. "But I wanted to. I nearly burst."

"Did you?" he had said, looking amused. Christopher always lost his habitual harsh expression when he was looking at or talking with Christina. "That must have been painful. I'm glad you didn't."

Elizabeth had remained silent during most of the journey and after their arrival at Astley's Amphitheater, despite the fact that she had never been there before and found it all very fascinating. Or would have done, perhaps, if she had not had so much weighing on her mind. She was tired again but pushed the thought from her mind as if by doing so she could also push away her awareness of why she was so often tired these days. She had known for a while but had not admitted her knowledge until the night before. She had been trying hard to think of a reasonable explanation for the very obvious symptoms.

She longed for someone in whom to confide. But she had no women relatives and no woman friend close enough for such a confidence. Martin had always been her closest friend and instinct had led her to him the evening before. He had been getting ready to go out, late as the hour was, and had looked rather startled when his valet had admitted her to his dressing room.

"Where can you be going at this hour?" she had asked.

"To a friend's." He had turned to smile at her. "He needs some advice on love, which I am not at all qualified to give, of course. Mostly he needs a sympathetic ear, poor fellow."

"Ah." She had smiled back. Martin was an expert at that. She had felt guilty for having been just a little impatient with his protectiveness lately. He was always so selfless in his concern for others, especially her.

"Are you in need of one, Lizzie?" he had asked. "A sympathetic ear, that is?" He nodded to his valet and the man left the room.

But looking into his face, the smiling, kindly face of her adopted twin, she had been unable to blurt the words she was longing to say and had come to say—*I am pregnant.* For perhaps the first time, not counting the time when she had lost her memory, she had hesitated to talk to him as freely as she would talk to the other half of herself.

"It is Trevelyan, Lizzie?" he had asked gently, setting an arm about her shoulders and drawing her to sit beside him on a small sofa. "He is causing turmoil in your life again? I have always liked him, as you know, and still do, but I cannot help feeling somewhat uneasy.''

''Uneasy?''

''He really has taken to Christina, hasn't he?'' he had said. ''I spoke to him briefly after you returned from the park this afternoon. He seems almost obsessed with her.''

''I suppose it is natural,'' she had said. ''I think I was wrong to agree to have her existence kept from him, Martin. I blame myself. I should have insisted on doing what I knew to be right. He really loves her, I think.''

''I just hope,'' he had said, ''that he does not—'' But he shook his head and got to his feet. ''Nothing. I had better be going or Blakeney will think I have forgotten him.''

''That he does not what?'' Elizabeth had asked.

Martin had laughed. ''No, he would not,'' he had said. ''Sometimes one gets stupidly fanciful at close to midnight. He would not try to take her for himself for six years to make up for the six she has been with you. That is a nonsensical idea. Trevelyan is quite incapable of kidnapping, isn't he?'' He had winced then and turned away from her. ''Forget I said that, Lizzie. Is everything going well with Poole?''

Of course she would forget what he had said. It really was nonsense. Christopher did not want Christina alone. He wanted both of them. She opened her mouth to tell Martin that Christopher had asked her to marry him, but shut it again. Something had happened. She could not seem to share her deepest self with him any longer. Perhaps she had taken the final step to growing up, she thought a little sadly.

''Well enough,'' she had said.

''It is with him you really belong, you know, Lizzie,'' Martin had said, looking at her again, his head to one side. ''He can keep the turmoil from your life. And you can be very important to him, especially during the next few weeks.''

Yes, she could, Elizabeth thought, returning her attention to Astley's and the horse show going on in front of her. Christina was screaming at her to watch the lady turning a hoop over her head and jumping through it at each revolution, while standing on a moving horse. Christopher was laughing.

Yes, she could. And must. She owed Manley that. She owed him a few weeks even though she could not now marry him, of course. But it would be cruel to break off the engagement now and leave him to face the gossip and the humiliation just at a time when his respectability should be obvious to the public eye.

Yes. Elizabeth sighed. Circumstances were going to force her to play the hypocrite for a while longer. Poor Manley. He did not deserve such shabby treatment. She felt very guilty.

"Ahhh!" Christina's comment on the show's finale mingled regret and contentment. "But we just got here."

"Two hours ago." Her father chuckled. "How about ices? Would it be terribly wicked to have them twice in one week, I wonder?"

Christina turned to look solemnly at him. She shook her head. "No," she said.

"No ices?" His eyes widened.

Christina giggled. "Not wicked, silly," she said.

He turned to look at Elizabeth, his eyes still laughing, and her heart turned over. Stupidly. Ah, foolishly.

Would she marry him, then? she asked herself. He wanted her to. She could marry no one else, and Christina needed a father. So would this new child. Why not their natural father? She could live at Penhallow for the rest of her life. Her children could grow up there. The thought was treacherously sweet. But could she ever forgive him? Or trust him again? How long did one withhold forgiveness before doing so became mere stubbornness? How much did one harm only oneself if one was unable to trust?

But he had wrecked their marriage. He had married her only for her dowry. More recently he had taken away her freedom and had thought nothing of seducing her when even her freedom of mind was gone. How could she trust him with what remained of her life and with her children's lives?

Children! She had his child in her.

"Are you all right?" He was looking searchingly at her after lifting Christina into his carriage and turning to hand her in.

She nodded. "I am just hoping that she will not get sick from too many ices," she said.

"I think there is more chance of you and me getting fat," he said. "We could just watch her eat, I suppose, but that would involve an almost superhuman self-denial, wouldn't it?"

"More than almost," she said. "Thank you, Christopher. You have made her very happy this afternoon."

She would have to go back to Kingston, she supposed. The thought was depressing. She loved Kingston, but it was her childhood home. The adult in her wanted her own home now. And of course Martin would come there with her. She loved Martin dearly and was ever grateful for the time he had spent with her during those years when she had desperately needed him. But Martin too was the companion of her childhood. She was an adult now. She needed—oh, she needed a mate, a husband.

"I'll burst not telling Uncle John," Christina was saying in a voice that was at the level of a shriek. "But I won't tell. It will be such fun when he brings me back here and I can tell him what the horses and the people are going to do."

As soon as Christopher had sat down in the carriage next to Elizabeth, Christina had crossed from the seat opposite and climbed onto his lap, seemingly without conscious thought, as if it were the most natural thing in the world to do.

As if she were out for an afternoon's treat with her mama and papa.

Winnie was excited to be going to Vauxhall. It was an evening entertainment and people from all classes of society went there to dance and eat and stroll along the many walks and beneath the swaying lanterns in the trees. Often there were fireworks. To Winnie it sounded as if it must be one of the seven wonders of the world.

She and Antoine had seen London by day during their time off. They had exclaimed with astonishment over the wax figures at Madame Tussaud's and found the courage to climb to the Whispering Gallery in St. Paul's and marveled at all the statues in Westminster Abbey. They had wandered among the stalls of a street market, and Antoine had bought a length of bright red ribbon for Winnie's hair. Winnie had felt some of the terror and tension of those last weeks at Penhallow begin to drain from her.

There was a special thrill to knowing that they were going to Vauxhall, she and Antoine. She was as excited as Lady Nancy and Lord Trevelyan must be feeling to be going to a ball at Lord Clemens'. They had given her and Antoine the night off since they had been invited out to dinner before the ball and never worried about having assistance when they returned home late.

A whole evening free to spend at Vauxhall!

"Ah, ma petite," Antoine said, looking at her appreciatively when they were ready to leave, " 'ow pretty you look. You wear the red ribbon."

She had threaded it through her hair, not sure that it was the right thing to wear with her best blue dress. But it was beautiful satin ribbon. She could not bear not to wear it.

"Mr. Bouchard?" she said anxiously. "It will be all right for us to go to Vauxhall? I mean us being servants and all that?"

"Everyone will look at you and think you are a duchess," he said. "And once they 'ave looked at you, Winnie, they will not even see Antoine."

Winnie giggled. Sometimes she surprised herself when she did so. She had not thought that she would ever laugh again.

She was enormously happy when they arrived at Vauxhall, because no one turned them away at the gate and no one looked askance at them when they were inside. And the gardens were magical. The trees and the lanterns made a fairyland of them and the music wafting from the pavilion made one forget about the ordinary world beyond. The wealthier people seated in the boxes were eating and drinking, but Winnie was not hungry. There was too much splendor to be devoured and drunk in from her surroundings for physical hunger to intrude.

"Oh, Mr. Bouchard," she said, clinging to his arm lest they be separated in the crowds that milled before the pavilion and boxes, "isn't this the most wonderful place in the world? Isn't it?"

"I think it is, little one," he said, patting her hand.

They did not want to sit or eat or dance. They strolled the paths instead, their arms linked, not saying much. There was too much to see.

And yet despite herself Winnie found her exuberance slipping from her as the evening wore on. She forced herself to smile and to feel the wonder of it all. It would be a terrible sin to feel dissatisfied. She was not sure about the people in the boxes and on the dance floor. Maybe they were at Vauxhall merely to enjoy themselves. But that was not true of the people who strolled the walks. They were almost invariably couples and almost all unmistakably lovers. There was a way couples had of walking, their shoulders touching, sometimes even with their arms about each other's waists, talking quietly together, their eyes tangled up with each other, oblivious of their surroundings or other people that proclaimed them lovers.

Winnie, walking with her arm linked through Antoine's, wearing her best dress and her red satin ribbon, knew that she was on the outside looking in. And that it would always be that way.

Antoine touched her fingers. "What is it, ma petite?" he asked.

She smiled quickly up at him and shook her head. But there was no point in saying "Nothing" as she had been about to do. Antoine had grown very sensitive to her moods. She felt a tickle in the back of her throat and hoped she was not about to cry.

"I am being very ungrateful to you and the kind chance that brought me here," she said. "I am feeling sad, Mr. Bouchard. Isn't that silly?"

"Non," he said. "You wish you really were a duchess, Winnie, and sitting in one of the grand boxes?"

"Oh, no," she said. "I don't want to be a duchess or a grand lady, Mr. Bouchard. I just wish—I just wish I could be like other people."

"And you cannot?" he asked her. "Because of what 'appened to you? You are as clean and as pure as a newborn lamb, ma chère. But Antoine cannot quite understand, eh? 'E is just a stupid man."

She shook her head. "No, you are not," she said. "But sometimes I wake up and think of the old dream of having a husband and a little home and maybe a few children and living happily ever after. And then I remember. And everything seems spoiled, Mr. Bouchard. The whole world seems spoiled."

"It is not impossible, ma petite," he said gently. "The dream."

"Yes, it is." She spoke passionately. "Even if someone was willing to have me, I cannot bear to be touched, Mr. Bouchard. I am afraid that every man is going to be like him. I know it isn't true, but I keep thinking it."

"But you let me touch you, Winnie," he said.

"That's different." She looked earnestly into his eyes. "You are my friend and you are wonderful. I would trust you with my life, Mr. Bouchard. You fancied me, didn't you, before—I know you did. But you never showed disgust after you knew. And you never tried to take advantage of me, neither, even though I was a whore." She began to sob and hid her face against his arm, ashamed both of her tears and of what a man had made her into against her will.

"Mon Dieu!" Antoine said. "Is that what you think you are, my little Winnie? Non, non, non, that is the great foolishness. An 'ore sells 'er body for money. You 'ave never done that."

"But he gave me money," she wailed.

Antoine set an arm about her shoulders and drew her off the public path on which they had come to a halt and a little way down a darker, narrower path.

"What you need, Winnie," he said, "is another man to love you and make you feel good again. You 'ave always been good, my little one, but you think you are bad. And you are afraid. You must meet someone else, someone good, and try to like 'im and trust 'im."

"You are the only good man I know, Mr. Bouchard," she said. "I like you and trust you."

Antoine held her shoulders with firm hands. "I am not right for you, Winnie," he said. "Antoine is not right for you. 'E cannot settle in England. 'E feel the craving for Canada again and freedom. For that little farm where everyone speak French and worship in the Catholic church and 'ave big, big families."

Winnie sniffed and drew a handkerchief from the

pocket of her dress. "You have been so kind to me, Mr. Bouchard," she said. "I don't want you to think that I am trying to trap you. You deserve far better than what I have become. But please, because it is Vauxhall and I am wearing my best dress and my new ribbon—"

She stopped and set her forehead against his chest.

"Yes, ma petite," he said, his fingers light against the back of her neck. "Antoine show you that you are pretty and desirable because you are Winnie and not just because of the pretty dress and ribbon. And you tell Antoine if you are frightened and 'e will stop."

She lifted her face and he set his lips to hers, lightly, closed, and slid his arms about her to draw her against him. After a few seconds she could feel her lips tremble out of control. She had sought comfort in his arms before, but this was different. The mere touching of their mouths indicated that this was sexual contact between them. He parted his lips slightly so that he could control her trembling.

And she remembered. She remembered being bent forward over the tree branch and her skirt and petticoat being flung over her head and her legs forced apart. She remembered the stabbing of pain and humiliation and violation. The loss of her world. The loss of everything that had made life worth living.

"Ma petite, ma petite." Antoine was holding her hands in a warm clasp, and she realized she must have panicked. "You do not 'ave to fight Antoine. 'E will not force anything from you, you see. Come. We go back where there are people and you will feel safe again."

She stared at him blankly. "He didn't kiss me," she said. "He just did that other thing. I don't think there can be anything uglier in this world."

He cupped her face with gentle hands. "Ah, you are right, my little one," he said. "Rape is an ugly, ugly thing. But love can be beautiful, Winnie. I 'ope that one day there will be a man who will teach you that. You should 'ave that 'ome and those children."

"Kiss me again," she whispered. "Please? I won't fight you again."

He kissed her, holding her face with light hands, moving his lips warmly and gently over hers, up to her eyelids, down to her chin. She was gripping the lapels of his coat when he lifted his head. Winnie smiled at him.

"When you first came to the house with Lord Trevelyan," she said, "I used to look at you and I used to try to imagine you doing that."

"Ah," he said, smiling back. "Was it as good as in the imagination, eh?"

"Yes," she said. "No. It was better. It made me feel good down to my toes."

"We go back to the main path now, non?" he said. "Antoine is a man, you know, and you are a beautiful woman, ma petite, and this path is too lonely."

Her eyes widened. "You want me, Mr. Bouchard?" she said. "That was not just kindness?"

"Sacré coeur!" Antoine said.

She set a trembling hand against his cheek, which was still smooth from the careful shave he had given himself before coming out. "It would be beautiful with you, Mr. Bouchard," she said. "I know it would be beautiful. You would make me forget the ugliness, and when I remembered I would remember only that it can be beautiful."

"Winnie, ma chère," he said, "I can't 'urt you. I 'ave nothing to offer you. No future. I cannot live as an English servant even if I 'ave the best master in the world. I will be leaving before the last ship sails before winter. I will not come back."

"I don't want to keep you here," she said. "I don't want to burden you. I want one good memory. Just one, Mr. Bouchard. If you want me. Not if you don't. Not just out of kindness. But if you want me. I don't want to be afraid all my life. I don't want to think life is ugly for the rest of my days. I want to remember my wonderful friend and how he made life beautiful again."

She could hear him inhaling as he held her to him. She shut her eyes very tightly, not at all sure whether she hoped for acceptance or rejection. Either prospect held terror for her.

"Not 'ere, Winnie," he said. "Not on the cold, 'ard ground for your beautiful loving. I would want to put you under me, and you would need a soft mattress at your back.''

Winnie could feel her cheeks grow hot. ''Then back in my room or yours,'' she said.

''No, my little one,'' he said. ''We might get caught and it would look all wrong. It would look like something dirty. We find an 'otel, oui?''

It was suddenly all startlingly real. She had not really expected that he would agree. Had she? But then she had not planned to ask him until a moment before she had spoken.

''Yes, Mr. Bouchard,'' she said.

They missed the fireworks after all. At the time they were lighting up the sky over Vauxhall and delighting dozens of revelers, Winnie and Antoine were lying, relaxed and sleepy, in a cheap, shabby inn room that was nevertheless surprisingly clean and comfortable. Winnie was smiling against the broad chest of her lover.

''I didn't 'urt you, Winnie?'' One hand was lightly massaging her scalp through her hair. Her precious ribbon had been laid carefully along the top of a chest of drawers.

''It was lovely,'' she said. ''You know it was lovely. I'm sorry I cried at first.''

His hand continued its lullaby. Winnie sighed with deep contentment but held herself back from sleep a few moments longer. She wanted to enjoy the feeling of beauty he had left behind with a slight soreness when he had withdrawn from her body after loving her. And she had something to say.

''Mr. Bouchard,'' she whispered against his chest, ''I want to tell you something. It is just to say thank you. A free gift, not a snare. I love you. I think you must be the most wonderful man in the world, and if you wanted it I would have all those children for you and I would learn French too and I would turn Catholic, even though my mum says the Pope is the Antichrist. I would leave England forever if you wanted me to. But when it comes time for you to go, I won't cry over you or try to persuade you to stay or to take me with you. I'll smile and wish you a safe voyage and a happy life. I will. Because I love you.''

"Ma petite. Ma chère," he said, kissing her temple. And then against her ear, "Mon amour."

Winnie could not understand French, but she slid into a happy sleep anyway. She had given a gift and had expected nothing in return.

22

CHRISTOPHER recognized Winston Rawlings as soon as he spotted him in the Clemens ballroom. They had been at Oxford together. But seeing him now sparked a memory. Of course! Rawlings had been present on that ghastly night when Edgar Morrison had lost at cards and then gone home and blown his brains out. Christopher had been trying to remember who had been there and had been unable to do so until he set eyes on Rawlings.

Nancy was talking with a group of acquaintances. Christopher was glad for her sake that they had made some in London. Young Lord Priestley had reserved the opening set with her. Christopher strolled across the room.

"Rawlings?" he said. "I thought it was you. How are you?"

"How d'ye do, Trevelyan," Winston Rawlings said. "I had heard you were back in England. But then, who has not heard that?"

"For some reason I have been thinking a great deal in the past few days about our Oxford years," Christopher said. "It seems quite coincidental to see you this evening. They seem a long time ago, don't they?"

"Gad, yes. Don't they, though?" Rawlings said. "A lifetime ago. They were good years."

"One incident in particular has been rolling around in my head," Christopher said. "That time when Parkins stripped Morrison of everything at cards and the poor fellow shot himself the same night. Ghastly, wasn't it?"

Rawlings grimaced. "Someone should have put a stop to it," he said. "One of us should have. But Morrison was always such a conceited bastard that we were rather delighted to watch his humiliation."

"You were the one who took him home eventually," Christopher said.

"Yes." Rawlings shook his head ruefully. "When it was too late. He took the only way out. He had a destitute mother and a few sisters to face the next day."

"You are planning to be in London for a while?" Christopher asked.

Rawlings grimaced again. "Lord, yes," he said. "M'wife always likes to see the Season to its bitter end. This year especially. If she could be in two or three places at the same time, Trevelyan, she would be."

"Good to see you again," Christopher said. Perhaps if he felt before the end of the spring that he had a strong enough case, he would arrange a meeting between Elizabeth and Winston Rawlings. Rawlings could vouch for the fact that at least one of those charges had been false. In fact, whoever had trumped up the charges had not been very clever about them. This one in particular was very easily disproved by anyone who cared to investigate for himself. But of course Christopher, the only one who would really have wanted to investigate, had already left the country when the charge was made.

Martin? Was it Martin? Christopher wondered yet again. He still found it difficult to believe what Nigel Rhodes had told him. And yet there was Martin's conversation with him outside the Grosvenor Square house the previous afternoon. Martin had been trying to nudge him into kidnapping Christina. The charm and the friendliness and the desire to help, all of which Christopher had always taken at their face value, had suddenly seemed very false to his newly cautious and suspicious mind.

"Gad," Winston Rawlings was saying. "I had not thought of poor Morrison for years. The last time I spoke of him was with your brother-in-law years ago. Your former brother-in-law, that is. Though Honywood was not even quite that, was he? He is Chicheley's stepson?"

All of Christopher's senses quickened. "You told Martin about Morrison?" he asked.

"Can't think how the subject came up," Rawlings said. He thought for a moment and then shook his head. "I know he was very interested in you, Trevelyan. A touch of hero worship, if you ask me. He was just a boy at the time. But things had already gone sour for you. I would have expected that you would have fallen from your pedestal. But Honywood has always been a friendly fellow. I doubt he bears any grudges. He wanted to know all about your life at Oxford. Women and all that." He chuckled. "I had to tell him the shameful fact that there were none as far as I knew. You were quite unlike the rest of us."

Christopher could feel his heart beating in his throat. Would Elizabeth believe Rawlings if he could be persuaded to repeat that piece of information to her? Christopher's mistress and child were supposed to have come from his Oxford days.

"So you told him about that incident with Morrison," Christopher said.

Winston Rawlings shrugged expressively. "I just can't remember how it came about," he said. "It's not a memory I am proud of or enjoy recounting. He was very sympathetic, though. Agreed that none of us were to blame for the way it turned out. I think he was looking for things that turned to your favor, Trevelyan. I went to Ireland just a few days after talking with Honywood, I remember. Government appointment for five years, you know. Met my wife there. The dreariest five years of my life."

Probably the only person who might have contradicted the story as it was told to Elizabeth, then, had the story become public, was conveniently far away in Ireland.

No, Christopher thought, Martin had not been a master conspirator. But he had been clever enough. Quite clever enough. He would doubtless have got away with it for a lifetime if Christopher had not returned to England.

"Here comes the music," Rawlings said, wincing. "I had better find my way to my wife's side without delay, Trevelyan, or I'll not hear the end of it for a week. Good to talk to you."

Christopher drew a deep breath. Elizabeth had just entered the ballroom with Lord Poole. John and Martin would doubtless be there soon. Martin had wrecked his marriage. Quite deliberately and quite viciously. He was a smiling, charming demon.

But why? What could his motive have been? There

could be only one answer, of course. He was Elizabeth's stepbrother. He had always been very close to her. And yet despite the fact that there was no blood relationship, his feelings for her had always seemed purely filial. Obviously they were not. Obviously they were a lover's feelings, but for reasons of his own Martin had always been unwilling to come into the open with them. Or perhaps he had and Elizabeth had rejected him. Obviously no other man was to be allowed to lay permanent claim either to Elizabeth's heart or to her person.

Martin was in the ballroom and smiling as he watched Elizabeth dance with Lord Poole. To Christopher, the scales fallen from his eyes, he looked like the devil incarnate.

Nancy was enjoying herself. She was aware, from early in the first set, of John, standing with a group of gentlemen, talking with them and watching her at the same time. She felt exhilarated by his presence. *I have never stopped loving you,* he had said immediately after she had told him everything. *I am going to woo you, Nancy.*

She had known something then. Oh, she had known it forever, but she had realized it again as a powerful present truth. She had never stopped loving him either. And she wanted to be wooed by him more than she had ever wanted anything in her life. He was going to see that there were no more terrors to shadow her life, he had promised her.

The fifth set was a waltz and finally, after what had seemed an eternity, he was coming to claim his set. He was in his scarlet regimentals, and Nancy despised the thrill of girlish pleasure she felt in the fact that Miss Gustafston next to her was looking at him with open admiration and at her with envy.

"At last," he said, setting one hand at her waist and taking her hand with the other. He smiled. "In a way I have been dreading tonight. I have feared that perhaps you would regret telling me what you told me at Kew. I thought perhaps you would be tense and uncommunicative."

"And I thought that perhaps you would have developed a disgust of me after all," she said. "I thought perhaps you would be stiff and coldly polite."

"Nancy!" he said softly, holding her eyes with his.

"Oh," she said in a rush. "It is all right? It is all right that I told you?"

She saw him swallow. "If there is a secluded corner anywhere in this building or its garden," he said, "will you come into it with me, Nancy, and let me kiss you? Or am I rushing you? I will wait for a year to kiss you if I must."

She shook her head. "I would rather not wait," she said. "But, John, I cannot come to you untouched."

"Heavens, Nancy," he said, "I cannot come to you untouched either. Does it matter? Should there be a difference just because you are a woman and I am a man? Where are we likely to find that corner? Indoors or outdoors, do you suppose?"

They found it in a small rose arbor after they had danced out onto the stone balcony outside the ballroom and descended the steps to the lantern-lit garden. The arbor was not lit. Nancy felt breathless when they stopped walking and he turned her to face him.

"I used to dream about you," John said, "when I first went to Portugal. Every night until I trained myself not to do so. I pretended that the Portuguese and Spanish women were just as lovely and just as desirable as you."

He took her hands in his as he spoke, holding them loosely at their sides but in such a way that they had to stand close. She felt the stiffness of his coat against the tips of her breasts, felt the heat of his thighs almost brushing hers. She waited for the expected panic and prepared to fight it. It did not come.

"There is no other woman as lovely as you," he said. "And only you can satisfy my soul."

"Oh, John," she said, closing her eyes. His words were like a soothing ointment, easing away the wounds and the pain of years. But she could not explain the feeling to him.

He drew her arms about his waist and held them there so that she was forced to take another half step forward until her breasts were resting unmistakably against his chest and her thighs against his. There was no panic, she found, waiting for it again. He was John.

"I'll worship your body all my life, Nancy," he said, "and nourish your soul with my love."

Her arms stayed where they were when he removed his own from them and set them lightly on either side of her waist.

"Kiss me," he said.

She looked up into his face, startled. She could see it only dimly in the darkness.

"Kiss me, Nancy," he said.

She hesitated before standing on tiptoe and setting her lips against his. He did not move.

"There," he said when she went back down on her heels and looked warily into his eyes, which looked very dark in the shadows of the arbor. "The first hurdle is over and you have survived it."

"But that is not as we kissed before," she said.

He smiled and lowered his mouth to hers again. And so she rediscovered with a shock of recognition the fact that a kiss between lovers involved mouths more than lips, and tongues and even teeth. And warm breath and murmured words. And seeking and caressing hands.

"My love." His breath was warm, arousing, against her ear.

"John."

"Enough," he said finally, holding her close but still against him. "There is a limit to my control, you know, and I am approaching it."

Nancy could feel his heart thumping against his chest. "But I was not afraid," she said in some wonder.

"Because I have been touching you with love," he said. "Love that comes from deep inside me, Nancy, and not just from my lips or my hands. On our wedding night you will find that you are not afraid of the greatest intimacy of all. We will join our bodies and our whole selves too."

"Our wedding night," she whispered, and dreams were reborn as she rested her face against his neckcloth.

"Where shall we marry?" he asked. "Penhallow or here? Not Kingston, I think. And when? This summer after I have sold out of the army? Or sooner? How many children do you want? Will you like being a duchess one day, my love, and mother to a future duke?''

Nancy laughed—and found for several moments that she could not stop laughing, softly, but with amusement and happiness bubbling out of her. It was wonderful healing laughter.

''It is time to return to the ballroom,'' he said. ''I shall call on you tomorrow afternoon if I can wait that long and we will make definite and rational plans. Happy?'' He kissed the top of her head.

She nodded. ''Do I take it that an offer has been made and accepted?''

He chuckled. ''It seems to me that that was what this conversation was all about,'' he said.

''John,'' she said softly. She wondered as she smiled up into his eyes if there could be any happier moment in life.

Lord Poole stood watching Elizabeth dance the supper waltz with Christopher, and made a conscious effort not to scowl. He was quite thankful when Martin came to stand by him. The necessity of making conversation would distract his mind. He wished heartily that he had not got somehow trapped into this betrothal. Especially to a woman who had been involved in scandal once in her life. He might have known that she would be nothing but trouble to him even if her father was a duke and her fortune enormous.

''One would think,'' he said to Martin, nodding in Christopher's direction, ''that he would have the decency to leave town now that he has satisfied himself by seeing his daughter.''

Martin smiled apologetically. ''I'm not sure matters are as simple as that,'' he said.

Lord Poole forgot not to frown. ''What the devil is that supposed to mean?'' he asked.

''I thought it was just Christina too,'' Martin said. ''Maybe it is. Probably it is. There must be some decency in him after all, mustn't there? I used to like him. I still do in a way.''

''Honywood,'' Lord Poole said irritably, ''if you would just stop this constantly trying to make excuses for everyone and get to the point, I would appreciate it. What are you saying? That he has his eye on Elizabeth again? I have been having the same thought."

"She was his wife once," Martin said. "And then, of course . . ." He shrugged and sighed.

"And then of course what?" Lord Poole looked at him keenly.

"No," Martin said. "It is really not my place to interfere. Anyway, I have promised faithfully not to breathe a word to anyone. Besides, you know I would never say or do anything knowingly to hurt Lizzie or to show her in a bad light."

Lord Poole's nostrils flared. "And so you would keep some secret, which is obviously devilish incriminating, from her future husband," he said, "just because of a misplaced promise. What is between them, Honywood?"

Martin bit his lips. "I have a great deal of liking and respect for you, Poole," he said. "I was delighted when Lizzie told me she was to marry you. I have hoped that after all everything else would blow over and you and she could live happily ever after. But I am afraid that much as I love her I can't avoid seeing that Lizzie is sometimes headstrong and not always straight in her dealings with others. It is a trait that pains me and that I hate to have to admit to others. But you are her fiancé."

"Yes, Goddamn it," Lord Poole said. "I am. Out with it, Honywood."

"Not here," Martin said, his face troubled. "Maybe not at all. I'll have to think about it, Poole, and call on you tomorrow. I am not sure if I can reconcile it with my conscience to break a confidence. But then I am not sure I can live with myself if I have to watch you deliberately deceived. I'll call tomorrow."

Lord Poole looked anything but satisfied. But he did become suddenly aware of his surroundings again and smoothed out his frown.

"The devil!" he said. "All Europe will be here the day after tomorrow and the sky is about to fall on my head. Your precious sister had better keep away from Trevelyan from this night on if she knows what is good for her, Honywood. I shall tell her so myself later, and you may tell her from me too. I'll not stand being made a laughingstock."

"No," Martin said. "Even I can see that. It would be grossly unfair. We will have to see that it does not happen, Poole. Perhaps we can make some plan tomorrow."

Lord Poole nodded curtly and went in search of a drink.

23

THEY waltzed in silence for five whole minutes. She was supple in his arms and moved lightly on her feet. The apricot color of her gown suited the honey blond of her hair and gave her a delicate femininity, Christopher thought.

"Did Christina get sick from the ices?" he asked, breaking the silence between them at last.

"No." She looked up into his eyes. "But she was terribly excited, Christopher, and does not know how she will live through until the day after tomorrow. Is it known exactly when the foreign heads of state will be arriving from Dover and by what route they will enter London? I would hate to see her disappointed when her heart is so set on seeing them."

"Educated guesses can be made," he said. "And everyone will converge on St. James's Palace eventually."

"You have been very kind to her, Christopher," she said. "I must thank you."

"She is my daughter," he said.

"She likes you," she said, "because you like her. Not because you take her out and give her treats, but because you like her. I am afraid that children are frequently only nuisances to the adults in their lives. And children can sense that."

"Especially when those adults are only uncles or grandfathers or prospective stepfathers," he said. "She needs the father who begot her, Elizabeth. How could she ever be a nuisance to me?"

"I don't want to talk about this," she said.

"We are going to have to tell her soon," he said. "I hope we can tell her together. I hope I will not have to do it alone."

She drew breath, but she closed her mouth again and

shook her head. An ambiguous gesture, Christopher thought. They danced the rest of the waltz in silence.

"I had better join Manley for supper," she said when the music came to an end. Her eyes were directed at his waistcoat.

"Have social conventions changed in the last seven years, then?" he asked. "It used to be that the supper dance entitled a man to lead his partner in to supper?"

"Do you not think there is enough gossip about us now?" she asked him. "And enough speculation? Must we make it worse by sitting together and conversing at supper while my betrothed sits with other people?"

"Frankly," he said, "I do not care what other people say, Elizabeth. I asked for the supper dance for a purpose. We will not go into the dining room, then, where other people can watch us and put their own interpretation on every change in our expressions as we talk together. Are you hungry?"

"No," she said.

He took her by the arm and let everyone else move past them from the ballroom. Even the members of the orchestra abandoned their instruments and disappeared in search of their own supper.

Elizabeth closed her eyes. "There will be a great deal of gossip about this," she said.

"You care too much about what other people say," he said.

Her eyes snapped open. "Yes, I care," she said, "because other, innocent people are involved. Manley is involved and Christina too indirectly. What sort of a future can she expect if her mother puts herself beyond the pale?"

He drew her out onto the balcony, deserted now. The air felt cool and delicious after the stuffy perfumed warmth of the ballroom.

"Have you thought about my offer?" he asked her. "Are you going to marry me?"

"No, of course not," she said. "I am going to marry Manley." But her voice faltered and her eyes slipped from his. She was standing with her back to the stone balustrade. "Or better still, I will marry no one. I will release him from the scandal that is beginning to brew around us and go home to Kingston."

"With the faithful Martin," he said.

"You hate him, don't you?" she said. "Because he is faithful, Christopher? Because he shows up your own infidelity in contrast? No, not with Martin. I will not allow him to sacrifice any more of his life to my care. I don't need a man to lean on. Not any longer. I can stand on my own feet."

"You will not be allowed to," he said. "You will find that Martin will not take no for an answer."

Her chin jutted. "What is that supposed to mean?" she asked.

But he looked at her broodingly and shook his head. It was too soon to reveal half-formed suspicions. She was more likely to believe in her beloved stepbrother than pay credence to the little proof he could offer her of Martin's perfidy. He himself would still be an adulterer in her eyes and a man who had married her so that he would be able to support his mistress and bastard child in comfort.

"Martin's feelings for me are those of a brother," she said. "I suppose someone like you would find it hard to believe that there is nothing improper in our relationship even though there is no blood bond between us."

"And yet," he said, "I can remember a time, Elizabeth, when you fled from him in a panic because you thought he was making improper advances toward you."

"That is unfair," she said. "I had lost my memory at that time."

"Does Martin like Christina?" he asked.

There was a small hesitation. "Yes, of course," she said. "It is just more difficult for men to be patient with children. And he has little experience."

"I have even less," he said. "I love her, Elizabeth. I want her at Penhallow."

"No," she said.

"With you," he said. "And I want her to have her proper name. It is Atwell, not Ward. And so is yours."

"I did not want to keep your name," she said, her voice trembling, "or Christina to have it. I wanted to forget you."

"And yet," he said, "after she was born you saw me in her every time you looked at her, didn't you? It was unfortunate for you that she did not look like you. Perhaps Martin would have liked her better if she had. And your father."

She frowned. "Papa arranged it all," she said. "The divorce and the shedding of your name. He has treated Christina as if she is his own daughter."

"But she is not," he said. "She is mine. Lady Christina Atwell. And if it seems to you that I am bitter, Elizabeth, then you are right. 'What God hath joined together, let no man put asunder.' Your father is not my favorite person, I'm afraid."

"Why did you not take that woman with you when you went away?" she asked. "Was it easier to abandon her? And the child?"

"I did not even know her, Elizabeth," he said. "Good Lord, I don't even know her name. She was supposed to be one of the Johnsons from the village at Penhallow, according to the messenger who came to fetch me to her. A poor woman fallen on hard times and not knowing where to turn."

"Lucy Fenwick," she said, her voice angry. "You were certainly giving wonderful comfort to a poor destitute woman, Christopher. I want to go back inside. It is chilly out here."

"It must have been very dreadful for you," he said quietly, "as a bride of three months to see your husband in the arms of a half naked woman as you did. A bride who was already with child. I used to blame you more than anyone for the way things turned out. In fact I have always blamed you for not having faith in me, for not knowing instinctively that I was incapable of such behavior. But my own pain made me too harsh, perhaps."

"Oh, Christopher"—her voice was even more angry—"you have such a golden tongue. You used not to have. You used not to talk very much at all. But don't be cruel. Don't make me doubt now when really I know there cannot be any doubt. Don't have me believe that I have wasted all these years and allowed Christina to be without a father when there was no need. Don't do that to me."

"Have they been wasted years?" he asked. "Have they been empty years without me, Elizabeth?"

"No," she said. Her eyes were bright with what appeared to be unshed tears. "I have not spent seven years pining for you. You are not worth it."

"But I would be if I were innocent, wouldn't I?" he said.

"Don't," she said. "Don't do this to me, Christopher. If you have any feelings left for me, don't do this. Let me go and find Manley."

"You are afraid to believe me, aren't you?" he said. "Believing me would reveal to you too much of wrong advice and hasty conclusions and broken vows and empty years."

"I wish I had insisted on going in to supper," she said, her voice shaking.

"You believed in me a few weeks ago at Penhallow," he said.

"I had lost my memory," she said.

"You saw me as I am," he said.

"No." She took a step away from the balustrade. "I saw you as you pretended to be. I saw a man who does not exist. I am going to the supper room."

But he moved sideways as she stepped forward, and she came right against his chest, her hands coming up protectively to rest against it.

" 'I'll never stop loving you. Don't expect it of me.' Do you remember saying those words, Elizabeth?" he asked her.

She closed her eyes tightly and grimaced. "I spoke them to a man who does not exist," she said.

His mouth was open when he brought it down over hers. Her lips trembled out of control and parted. She moaned and her hands slid up his chest and came to rest half on his shoulders and half on his neck.

If there was ever a time when he had hated her, he knew then, it was long in the past. He had fallen in love with Christina during the past few days because she was his daughter. And Elizabeth's. Because she was theirs. And because he loved Elizabeth. Always had. And always would.

"Do I exist now?" he asked her, lifting his head after a long and deep kiss. "Or am I still a man who is not really here?"

She looked back at him from miserable eyes.

"Those weeks at Penhallow could be repeated for the

rest of a lifetime," he said. "Christina could grow up there, Elizabeth. Perhaps there could be more children. Perhaps there could be noise and laughter in the nursery there again. And muddy feet in the hall. And sand on the carpets. We could make up for the missing years."

He could see that she was biting the inside of her upper lip. He touched his fingertips to her cheek.

"Keep thinking about it," he said. "I'll be asking you again. And again and again. I'll not be slamming any doors in your face."

"I want to go and find Manley," she said. "I want people to see us together before the dancing resumes."

He nodded. "You want me to escort you to the supper room?"

"No," she said, "I'll go alone."

He nodded again as she hurried past him and into the ballroom. He stood against the balustrade, leaning his hands on it and looking down into the lantern-lit garden. Lucy Fenwick, he thought. But how after seven years did one trace a woman one knew only by that name? And that name might be as false as the name Johnson had been.

But somehow she had to be traced. Elizabeth might marry him, Christopher thought. He could sense that she was wavering, that one part of her wanted to say yes. Part of her still loved him. It had been there in her kiss. But they would never be happy together unless she could be convinced beyond all doubt that he had married her for love and for no other reason and that he had had no adulterous relationship with any woman while they had still been legally married.

Lucy Fenwick would always be a dark shadow between them unless she were found and persuaded to tell the truth. The truth was clear to Christopher. But it had to be equally clear to Elizabeth.

Could he remember the address to which he had been summoned? he wondered. It should be etched indelibly on his memory. He frowned in thought.

Nancy looked at her image in the looking glass, pleased with the way her new pale blue muslin dress complemented her dark coloring. She should have kept the muslin for the afternoon, of course, but he had said that perhaps he would not be able to wait for the afternoon to come. She would probably be feeling quite wilted by the time he did arrive.

"That looks good, Winnie," she said, turning her head from side to side and viewing critically what her maid had done to her hair. Then her eyes focused on Winnie. "Did you and Mr. Bouchard go to Vauxhall after all last evening?"

"Yes, mum," Winnie said, blushing.

Nancy looked more critically. "Well," she said, "I need not ask if you had a wonderful time. You are looking remarkably pleased with yourself."

"Yes, mum," Winnie said.

Nancy had been a little worried about her maid for a while. She had lost her spirits lately. Nancy had even remarked upon it before they left Penhallow, but Winnie had insisted that there was nothing wrong. Nancy had not wished to pry further, but she had suspected that perhaps Christopher's valet was the problem. Certainly he was a strange man and doubtless attractive to a girl like Winnie. His French accent alone was attractive. Nancy had hoped that he was not in the process of breaking the girl's heart, but it was not her place to interfere unless a complaint was made. Winnie had cheered up considerably since they came to London. This morning she positively glowed.

"Did you watch the fireworks?" Nancy asked. "They must make be a wonderful sight."

"No, mum." Winnie made a great to-do about setting the brush and comb back down on the dressing table. "We left early."

"Oh," Nancy said, sympathy in her voice, "what a shame, Winnie. Were you very disappointed?"

"No, mum." The glow was back in Winnie's cheeks.

Nancy smiled. "I'll not ask why," she said. "Is he courting you then, Winnie? Am I about to lose the best maid I have ever had?"

"Oh, no, mum," Winnie said earnestly. "He is going to go back to his home in Canada, mum. He has just been very kind to me. Wonderfully kind."

"Kind?" Nancy turned on the stool to look at her maid. "Kind to lead you on, Winnie, just to abandon you when he returns to Canada? I should call that taking advantage of a girl.''

''Oh, no, mum,'' Winnie said passionately. ''That is not true. Mr. Bouchard is the kindest and most wonderful man in all the world, he is. I'll not let anyone say one word against him, not even you, mum. If it was not for Mr. Bouchard I would have surely died, I would. I would have wanted to die. He made me believe that I was not a bad girl, mum. He says I am as white as snow. He has made me feel clean again.''

''Winnie.'' Nancy was sitting very still. ''What are you saying?''

The passion went out of Winnie suddenly. She paled and stared back at Nancy. ''Nothing, mum,'' she said. ''Someone is knocking at the outer door. Shall I answer it?''

''No,'' Nancy said. ''Mr. Bouchard or my brother will get it. Winnie, what happened to make you want to die? Why did you feel bad and dirty?''

''Nothing, mum,'' Winnie said, staring. ''I didn't.''

Nancy could remember bathing twice a day for what must have been weeks, scrubbing herself until her skin was red, never feeling clean. She could remember lying on her bed at Penhallow for days on end, staring listlessly at the canopy over her head, wishing she could die. She remembered feeling that she must be to blame. She had gone with him without even thinking of taking a chaperone with her. She must be a bad and wicked woman.

''Winnie,'' she said, ''who did it to you?'' But she knew. Oh, dear God, she knew. And if only she had spoken up seven years ago, perhaps she could have prevented him from being able to do it to anyone else. How many other women had he made to suffer?

''Nobody, mum.'' Winnie looked frightened. ''He didn't do nothing, mum.''

''Who didn't?'' Nancy asked. ''Mr. Honywood?''

Winnie started to cry. ''I didn't ask for it, mum,'' she said. ''I didn't want to go with him. He made me. You got to believe me, mum.''

Nancy rose to her feet and surprised her maid by gathering her into her arms and hugging her tight. ''I don't blame you, Winnie,'' she said. ''Not for a moment, my poor girl. He is a wicked and an evil man and I am going to try to see to it that no other girl is made to suffer at his hands. Mr. Bouchard is right, Winnie, bless his heart. You are as white as snow. You must believe that you were not in any way to blame. You must. Oh, don't let it ruin your life."

Winnie was sniveling. "I thought you would dismiss me for sure if you knew, mum," she said. "But ooh, it was horrible, mum. He beat me and then he did *that.*"

Nancy released her. "I won't need you until later this afternoon," she said. "Go for a walk in the park, Winnie. Or go and look in the shops. Go and do something cheerful. Perhaps Mr. Bouchard will be free to go with you. Dry your eyes and put it all behind you. Don't let such a monster be responsible for scarring you permanently."

"Oh, no, he won't, mum," Winnie said. "Mr. Bouchard made me feel pretty again and good again."

Perhaps it would be as well not even to try to find out how he had done so, Nancy thought, or why the two of them had missed the fireworks at Vauxhall when they had been what Winnie had most been looking forward to. But however he had done it or for whatever reason he had taken Winnie away early from Vauxhall, Nancy blessed his good heart. Perhaps Winnie would not have to suffer for as long as she had done.

The thought brought memories of the night before and the realization that men's voices were coming from the sitting room and that one of them must belong to John. She turned to look in the mirror again to make sure that no crease had suddenly appeared in her dress and no strand of hair had worked loose from her chignon. She hurried through into the sitting room.

John had found himself quite incapable of waiting until the afternoon. Although he and Nancy had agreed to a betrothal the night before, he was longing to see her again, to make more definite arrangements, to make everything official. He arrived at the Pulteney when it was still morning, a quite ungenteel time at which to pay a social call. He grinned to himself as he climbed the stairs to the suite Nancy shared with her brother.

Nancy was not in the sitting room when Trevelyan's man admitted him. Christopher was there alone.

"John?" he said, looking somewhat surprised. "I was just on my way out. I'm glad I did not miss you. Or is it Nancy you are calling on?"

"Perceptive of you." John chuckled. "Actually I should talk with you first, though. One might as well do things properly if they are worth doing, after all. She doesn't need your consent, Christopher, but I would like to have it nonetheless."

Christopher's eyebrows rose. "Good Lord," he said, "do you mean that you have come here to offer for Nancy?"

"She doesn't give anything away, does she?" John said. "She is expecting me, though later in the day, perhaps. I could not wait. Actually, though, I must confess, the offer has already been made."

"Well," Christopher said, "you have taken me totally by surprise. Though I do not know why that should be except that Nancy has seemed so confirmed in the single state. And the last time I thought the two of you fancied each other, nothing came of it."

It was obvious, John thought, that Nancy's brother did not even suspect the truth. She had kept the secret very well guarded.

"I am nothing if not persistent," John said. "Can I hope for your blessing, Christopher? I rather fancy having you as a brother again, you see."

Christopher smiled and came toward him, right hand outstretched. "I could not be more pleased if I tried," he said. "I'll even give away the bride. I suppose I should go and bring her in."

But before Christopher could do more than turn toward the door that led to Nancy's dressing room, it opened and she stepped into the room. And John could see, with a rush of relief and tenderness, that she had indeed been expecting him this early and that she had taken as much pains with her appearance as he had with his.

Her eyes found his and held them. Her cheeks were flushed and her eyes bright. But even as she looked and he began to smile at her, her expression changed and he saw anxiety and panic in her face. She came rushing across the room to him, her eyes on his, completely ignoring Christopher, and hurried straight into his arms.

"John," she said, burying her face among the careful

folds of his neckcloth. "Oh, John, it has happened again and it is all my fault."

John, his arms coming protectively about her, met Christopher's eyes over the top of her head. Both men raised their eyebrows.

24

CHRISTOPHER was inclined to slip from the room. He had already been delayed from the outing he intended for that morning. But he stayed where he was when he saw how distraught his sister was.

John closed his eyes briefly and hugged her tight. He seemed to understand what she was talking about despite his raised eyebrows when she had first spoken.

"What has happened?" he asked.

She struggled out of his arms and seemed to notice her brother's presence for the first time. "He h-hurt my maid a fews weeks ago," she said. "He beat her and ravished her."

"Martin?" John said.

Christopher could feel himself turning cold.

Nancy nodded. "And it is all my fault," she said. "I could have prevented it and perhaps other attacks I do not even know of if I had had the courage to speak out sooner. I have been very selfish."

"No," John said. "You cannot blame yourself for someone else's evil."

"Martin raped Winnie?" Christopher asked. "And beat her? Why in heaven's name did she not speak up at the time, Nance? I would have horsewhipped him. I'll still do it." His hands clenched into fists at his sides. Though he might well do more than take a horsewhip to Martin Honywood's hide.

"It is not easy to report such a thing, Christopher," Nancy said gravely. "It is almost impossible to tell another person about such shame and degradation and guilt."

"Guilt?" Christopher looked at her blankly.

"When you have been raped," she said, "you feel guilty, as if somehow you must have been asking for it."

He felt as if the blood were draining from his head. Nancy leaving Kingston Park quite inexplicably when his wedding was only one week in the future and when she had seemed to be enjoying herself and perhaps even falling in love with John. And Nancy staying at Penhallow ever since and refusing to consider marriage despite her beauty and vitality.

"It sounds as if you are talking from personal experience," he said. He could scarcely get the words past his lips.

"I am."

He was looking at her as if down a long tunnel. John, he noticed, had an arm about her shoulders.

"It was Martin," John said. "A beating and rape. The day before Nancy left Kingston. I did not know of it myself until two days ago. If I had, I would have killed Martin."

"Why have you not done so during the past two days?" Christopher asked. He was surprised at the calmness of his voice. His eyes were on the pale face of his sister.

"Because I wanted no trouble," Nancy said. "I wanted it all left in the past. Although I have always understandably hated Martin, I have also thought that perhaps he was overwrought to be losing Elizabeth, who had been almost like a twin to him all his life. I have considered the fact that he was only eighteen and had not learned how to control his impulses. I have never excused him in my mind, but I have always assumed that it was something he did once only in his life—to me."

Christopher turned away and sat down rather heavily on a chair. He rested his elbows on his knees and buried his face in his hands.

"I have begun to see in the last few days," he said, "that he is a demon straight from hell. But this is worse than anything else I have yet uncovered about him."

John drew Nancy down onto a sofa. He kept an arm about her shoulders. "Uncovered?" he said. "What do you mean?"

Christopher looked up at him with weary eyes. "Elizabeth and I," he said, "Nancy, you—he has ruined all our lives. Coldly, methodically, and ruthlessly. And he has remained smiling and charming the whole time."

John and Nancy were looking intently at him.

"The dancer who was beaten and died," he said. "Nigel Rhodes has admitted to me that he was paid to report that he saw me leave the theater with her. Paid by Martin. She was beaten, poor girl, before she died. Having heard what I just have, I would have to say that it has rather the stamp of Martin on it, doesn't it?"

John's head was down. "I have been inclined to think as Nancy did," he said, "that Martin gave in to a boyish impulse, looking for love himself or an approximation of love because Elizabeth had found it with you."

"And Winston Rawlings," Christopher said, "who was present with me and a few others at that notorious card party in Oxford when Morrison was stripped of his fortune, can testify to two truths. The first is that I was a mere spectator of the game, guilty as I felt afterward for not doing something to stop it since Morrison was so drunk that he did not know what he was doing. The second is that Martin wormed the whole story out of Rawlings seven years ago, a few days before Rawlings was to leave to take up a government appointment in Ireland."

"Oh, Christopher," Nancy said.

John's head was still down. "Christ!" he said. "And I merely laughed and told my father and Martin and Elizabeth that it was all nonsense. I did not do anything positive to disprove either charge. Did Martin count on that? Did he know us that well? And did we know him that little? It is appalling."

"But why would he do it?" Nancy asked. "How can anyone be so diabolical? It was so obvious that you and Elizabeth loved each other deeply, Christopher."

"Because he had an obsession with her," Christopher said. "*Has* an obsession. No one else can have her if he cannot. Did he ever try to have her for himself, John?"

"My father would surely not have allowed it," John said, looking up at last. "Though I never heard of any such thing happening. Poor Elizabeth. But, yes, Christopher is right. It is an obsession Martin has for her. A sick obsession."

"I was on my way out this morning," Christopher said, "to try to find out if I can what involvement Martin had with getting that woman to send for me and arranging matters that Elizabeth walked into the house a few minutes after me and drew all the wrong conclusions.

She had Martin with her, of course. He was almost as upset as she."

"Christopher," Nancy said, "it happened seven years ago."

"I know," he said. "I have remembered the address, but I have no hope that the woman will still be there. I just hope that somehow I can track her down."

"Maybe we will just pry the information out of Martin instead," John said through his teeth. "I learned a thing or two about torture in Spain from looking at the bodies of some of its victims."

"I'll try my way first," Christopher said.

"That was the one charge I did not even scorn at the time," John said. "All I did argue in your defense was that I was sure you must have ended the affair before your marriage. I did not believe you had been unfaithful to Elizabeth. I certainly ridiculed the idea that you had married her only so that you could support that doxy and her child. But it never occurred to me to probe into the woman's story. I blame myself now."

"Don't," Christopher said. "I might have checked it too. I ran instead. I think Martin did know us all rather well, didn't he? Did he plot for the divorce too, do you suppose? Divorce is so very rare, especially with the husband cited as the partner at fault."

"Perhaps the devil helped his own," John said, "using my father's pride. I'll come with you, Christopher."

"Oh, yes, do, please," Nancy said. "Thank you, John."

Christopher looked at them both. "You had other business this morning," he said. "I wouldn't want to spoil that."

John took Nancy's hand in his and kissed it before drawing her to her feet. "It will wait," he said, smiling at her rather wanly. "This seems the wrong moment, doesn't it, Nancy?"

"Yes," she said.

Christopher got to his feet. "We had better go, then," he said. "Is Winnie going to be all right, Nance? Does she need a physician?"

"I believe she already has one," she said. "Antoine Bouchard has been very good to her, Christopher."

"Ah, yes," he said, "the romance. Or the apparent

romance.'' He crossed the room and kissed her cheek. ''Nance, I am so sorry that you had to go through that all alone. Somehow I am going to avenge what happened to you. And what was done to Elizabeth's life.

''You look after Elizabeth,'' John said grimly. ''I'll settle the score for Nancy.''

John kissed her briefly on the lips before the two men left the room.

Lucy Fenwick was not living in the rooming house where Christopher had once been summoned to her. Neither he nor John had expected to find her there. It was a neighborhood, they found, where tenants came and went with fair frequency. None of the other occupants of the house whom they talked with and none of the closest neighbors remembered her.

But there were a couple of tenants from home. One of them returned while the two gentlemen were still interviewing neighbors. And that one did remember Mrs. Fenwick, or claimed to do so. Not a whore, she was not. Oh, no. Kept very much to herself, she did. Put on airs. Inherited money, she did, from an old aunt and went to America. As far as the informant could remember, anyway. It was a long time ago.

The returned tenant was gratified by the close attention the two gentlemen paid her story. She was disappointed when they continued with questions she could not answer. Had Mrs. Fenwick entertained any visitors? Was there any particular gentleman who visited her regularly? The tenant could not recall.

Christopher and John turned away eventually. It seemed obvious that they would obtain no really important information from this particular woman. And if it was true that Lucy Fenwick had gone to America, her passage there doubtless paid by Martin, then it seemed that the trail had come to an end. Not that it had been anything of a trail to start with.

''If I were you, sir,'' the informative neighbor said, ''I'd talk to the landlord. 'E's been 'ere forever and a day, 'e 'as.''

John nodded. The landlord had been next on their list of people to call on for possible information. It was encouraging to think that a man who had been at the job "forever and a day" must have been there seven years ago.

The landlord, unshaven and unwashed and scratching at flea bites through the frayed fabric of his clothing, did not look to be a reliable witness to anything. His eyes were glazed from the effects of gin consumed already that morning. But he remembered Lucy Fenwick.

"A cut above your ordinary tenant, guv," he told Christopher. "Could talk genteel. Went to America, she did after all the 'ow-d'ye-do."

"The how do you do?" Christopher raised his eyebrows and looked interested.

"Called to testify in a divorce case, she were, guv," the landlord said, pausing for the ecstasy of a good scratch. "Some nobs. Then off to America she goes as fast as you please. Money came from 'er old aunt or grandmother or someone, she said, guv. But those of us with some'at upstairs"—he leered and tapped his right temple—"knows different."

"Indeed?" Christopher said. "The money came from another source, you think?"

The landlord nodded and yawned loudly. "Come from the same source wot started paying the rent when it got in arrears despite 'er genteel airs, guv," the man said. "Bet a pint of good gin on it, I would. Not that it were my business, of course."

"Of course not," Christopher agreed, exchanging a glance with John. "And who was it who paid the rent, may I ask?"

The landlord scratched and pursed his lips in thought. His eyes darted once to Christopher and once to John.

"You like good gin, do you?" John asked, drawing a coin from his pocket and bouncing it tantalizingly on his palm. "You must allow us to help you refill your almost empty bottle, sir. Was it a gentleman?"

"Not exactly, guv," the landlord said, rubbing a dirty hand over the bristles on his chin and trying not to watch the bouncing coin. "A businessman, 'e were. Let me see now. Perkins, were it? Prewett? Powell? Powers? That's it." He stopped and thought for a moment. "That's it, guvs. Powers were 'is name. Like to think 'e was a nob, but 'e weren't one no more nor I am for all 'is fancy coats and fobs and canes."

Mr. Powers, businessman. It was very little to go on, Christopher and John agreed when they were making their way back to more familiar areas of London. But the landlord had known no more.

Christopher was depressed. "It is far too little to go on," he said. "We do not know the man's first name or what type of businessman he is or was. We do not know that he is still alive or still in London. Maybe he was sent to Africa or China. We do not even know that it was not a false name. Maybe it was Martin himself.

"Men like our shrewd landlord," John said, "can recognize a true nob, as he calls our kind, through any disguise. And he can recognize equally a fake nob. Lucy's rent payer was a fake nob. Of that we can be sure. He was not Martin."

Christopher sighed. "So we know we are not looking for a member of the *ton,*" he said. "That narrows the field considerably."

John laughed. "Let's not give up yet," he said. "What we will do is pay a call on my man of business and pose the problem to him. Perhaps by some miracle he knows Powers. If he does not, maybe he has means of tracking him down. I believe we are going to have to exercise some patience. Remember that we will not reach a total dead end. If all else fails, there is still the Spanish torture." It did not sound as if he was totally joking.

John's man of business did not know a Powers in business in London. Neither did his partner nor any member of their staff. But he quite cheerfully undertook the task of finding him.

"If he is in London, colonel," he told John briskly, "I shall find him within a day or two." He bowed to Christopher. "You may depend upon it, my lord."

They had to be content to leave it at that.

Lord Poole was pacing his rooms in nervous excitement. He looked pleased to see Martin.

"Well," he said, "everything is set for two evenings hence. The Princess of Wales has been persuaded that it will be in her best interests to appear at the opera while her husband and all his guests are there. Thus she will show them that she holds herself aloof not from choice but because she has been unjustly ordered to do so."

"I applaud such a bold move," Martin said. "And will you come out openly in support of her royal highness, Poole?"

"I shall pay my respects to her publicly in her box," Lord Poole said, "taking Elizabeth with me. And then during the reception and presentation at Carlton House the following evening we will see how I am received. I am willing to gamble on the belief that the various visitors will applaud my move and that many of the other guests will look upon me with renewed respect."

"Yes," Martin said, "if only Lizzie can be counted upon to behave herself. But I do admire your courage, Poole. You must be looking forward to the coming days."

Some of Lord Poole's excitement had waned. He frowned. "You think she will not?" he asked. "What were you hinting last night, Honywood? I am beginning to wish that I had never set eyes on your stepsister."

"She is not entirely to blame," Martin said. "Indeed I do believe she is in no way to blame. But then I am partial. I am very fond of Lizzie."

"The point, please," Lord Poole said sharply. "To blame for what?"

"Yes, I suppose she is to blame," Martin said, slumping into the nearest chair and staring gloomily at the carpet. "I cannot continue to shield her, especially when her actions are about to affect someone who is totally innocent. Yourself, I mean."

Lord Poole merely stared at him, one hand clenching and unclenching at his side.

"That kidnapping," Martin said. "I was persuaded against my better judgment to tell a lie. But I must tell the truth now. Trevelyan was the kidnapper. He took Lizzie to Penhallow, where apparently she fell into his arms. She might still be there if I had not found her and jolted her conscience. You, Christina, her father, decency—all had been forgotten in her lust for Trevelyan."

"The lost memory story?" Lord Poole asked, his voice tense.

Martin shrugged. "False, I'm afraid," he said. "And yet now I think she wants you, Poole, and intends to have you. Trevelyan wants to take her off back to Devonshire, you see, but Lizzie likes the social life of London that you can offer. So all must be covered up."

"The bitch!" Lord Poole said from between his teeth. "I'll kill her."

"And swing for it?" Martin said. "I could cry for her, Poole. But I have to think first of you since you are the innocent victim in all this."

"The betrothal must be ended," Lord Poole said. "Quickly and quietly. I shall call on Chicheley. I shall advise that she be returned to Kingston Park without delay. The whore is fortunate not to be exposed for what she is."

Martin sighed and rested his face in his hands. "I should be rejoicing that you are prepared to let her off so lightly, Poole," he said. "But I have to be fair about all this. Fair to you. You were to be my brother-in-law after all, or almost so. Have you considered carefully? If the real reason for the ending of your betrothal is not known, there will be rumor and gossip, almost all of it directed against you since you will appear to be the one jilted. You will be the laughingstock."

Lord Poole crossed to the window and stared out. "What do you suggest, then?" he asked.

"Oh, God," Martin said, "how can I say this? Oh, poor Lizzie. Perhaps it was not all her fault, after all. He was her captor, wasn't he? Who knows that he did not force her—at first anyway? But no, I must stay firm. After all this is over, I'll go to Kingston with her and help her see her error and live it down. You have to repudiate her publicly, Poole."

Lord Poole frowned out of the window.

"The more publicly the better," Martin said. "At the opera, perhaps. Or better, at Carlton House. Let the truth be known there. Let people understand why you are putting her aside. You will earn a great deal of sympathy from the ladies and respect from the men. You will show that you are a man of firm principle and not to be trifled with. When the Whigs come to power, I imagine that they will look to you for leadership."

"And she would deserve it too, the slut," Lord Poole muttered.

Martin sighed.

"I'll let the rumor of where she really was during those weeks circulate," Lord Poole said. "And when it comes time to be presented to the queen, I shall refuse to escort her up to the throne. It will be the moment when all eyes will be upon her. And all tongues will have been wagging for an hour or more before it. It will work, by Jove. It will be as good as stripping her naked and whipping her. She will never be able to hold up her head in public again."

"Oh, God," Martin said, his voice shaking, "perhaps we should just persuade my stepfather to send her home after all, Poole."

Lord Poole turned to look at him, a spark of contempt in his eyes. "You are too good-natured for your own good, Honywood," he said. "Especially where your precious stepsister is concerned. No, we will do it this way. She must be punished."

Martin looked unhappily at him. "Yes," he said, "I'm afraid she must. Very well, then, Poole, I'll make sure that Trevelyan does not show his face at Carlton House. Ah, poor Lizzie."

He left soon afterward. He would call on Trevelyan before the day was out, he thought. All his plans must be laid. A few more days and it would all be over. Lizzie would be his forever.

But he could not put from his mind what Poole had said about stripping her naked and whipping her. Martin had wanted to kill him for that. He gritted his teeth now in fury. He had had to listen to Poole call her a slut and a whore and plan a punishment that would hurt and humiliate more than the stripping and whipping. And he himself had been forced to put the plan in Poole's head, Martin thought, turning his hatred for Lord Poole against himself. He had had no choice. She had left him no choice.

Ah, Lizzie.

His hands opened and closed at his sides as he walked. He must see Trevelyan first, but he knew where he must go after that. He could not wait for the nighttime, and there was no need to do so. Those girls worked day and night when there were customers to pay for them. He could not decide whether he more wanted to have the whip in his own hand and watch the red marks slash across the delicate back of the whore he would hire or to place it in her hand and strip off his own clothes and lie spread-eagled on the bed on his stomach so that he could suffer the painful ecstasy of punishment for what he was being forced to do to Lizzie.

He would make it up to her, he swore to himself, his back prickling in eager anticipation of the needle-sharp pain he would be paying handsomely to feel later. He would spend the rest of his life making it up to her.

25

ON June 6 the Tsar of Russia and the King of Prussia crossed the English Channel from Boulogne on board H.M.S. *Impregnable,* accompanied by numerous other heads of state, statesmen, and generals. Prince Metternich, Chancellor of the Austrian Empire, was there as were the famous Hetman Platoff of the Don Cossacks, Field Marshal von Blücher, and Prince Hardenberg, Chancellor of Prussia.

They arrived in Dover in the evening and set out for London the following morning. In London itself an excited populace had been gathering in the streets since dawn. All the streets between London Bridge and St. James's Palace were lined with a multitude of people on foot and with carriages and carts. Not a window of any building along the route was not crowded with heads.

Christopher, with Elizabeth and Christina, did not venture out until mid-morning and consequently found that it was impossible to take a carriage anywhere near the expected route of the procession.

"Anyway," Christopher said, taking his daughter firmly by the hand as they walked, "who wants to watch such an exciting event from a carriage window?"

Christina was wildly excited. She skipped along the pavement between Christopher and Elizabeth, holding to a hand of each, asking if the King of Prussia would be wearing his crown and if Marshal von Blücher would be waving his sword over his head.

The crowd became denser as they approached the street along which the landaus would pass on their way to St. James's Palace. Christopher lifted Christina to his shoulder so that she would have a better view and so that he would not lose her in the crowd, and he drew

Elizabeth's arm through his free one and held it against his side.

"We can only hope that they will not be late arriving," he said to her.

"When they have to come all the way from Dover," she said, "it is impossible to predict the exact time of their arrival. I hope they will not be too long."

"Mama," Christina sang out from her high perch, "when will they be here?"

It was a question that was often repeated during the next hour and a half. But the expected procession did not come. Occasionally there were stirrings of excitement among the crowd and even once or twice the beginnings of cheering. But always they were false alarms. Perhaps the sea had been too rough for them to make the crossing the day before, some people began to murmur, though word had arrived in the capital that the *Impregnable* had come safely to Dover with its precious cargo. Perhaps there had been some delay at Dover. Perhaps they were to stay there for the day to be feted. After all half the army was down there to greet them.

"When are they going to be here?" The tone of Christina's voice had become plaintive.

And then Elizabeth sagged against Christopher's side and when he looked quickly down at her, it was to find her with chalk-white face and half-closed eyes. He set Christina down on the ground in a hurry and wrapped both arms about her mother.

"Elizabeth?" he said. Christina was clinging to her skirt and gazing up.

"Oh," Elizabeth said, drawing a deep breath, "how foolish of me. It is what comes of standing so long in one place and in such a crowd. I am so sorry."

But Christopher had turned to move back out of the crowds.

"The lydy 'as fainted, poor lamb," a buxom woman declared shrilly and a path formed for them to withdraw.

"I'll be all right," Elizabeth said. "I feel very foolish."

"I think," Christopher said, keeping one arm firmly about her waist and looking down apologetically at their daughter, "that the delay might go on all day, Christina.

Shall we give up? These visitors are going to be in London for a few weeks. We will have another chance to see them, when we can be more sure of the time they will appear.''

Christina looked woebegone. ''Yes, sir,'' she said. ''That will be all right.''

He rubbed two knuckles across her chin. ''I'll take you and your mama back to the Pulteney with me,'' he said, ''and we will have tea and cakes even though it is scarcely past midday. Will that be good?''

She brightened somewhat.

''You don't need to hold me up, Christopher,'' Elizabeth said. ''It was just a momentary wave of faintness. I am quite well now.''

So they resumed their former positions, one on each side of Christina, holding her hands. This time she was not skipping. As they approached the Pulteney along Piccadilly, a plain landau drew up outside the hotel, and even as they watched, waiters rushed out to form a line across the pavement and a tall young man stepped out of the landau, smiling. He looked up to a first-floor window and waved.

''Good Lord,'' Christopher said, ''that is the Grand Duchess Catherine in the window. He must be her brother.''

''The Tsar?'' Elizabeth said.

''The Tsar of Russia?'' Christina shrieked. ''That is him, Mama?''

''I think it must be, sweetheart,'' Elizabeth said as the young man turned and seemed to include them in his smile and his wave before hurrying between the lines of waiters into the hotel. ''But what is he doing here, Christopher?''

''Escaping, I do believe,'' Christopher said. ''He must have heard about the unruly mob and entered London by a different route. And he is calling upon his sister before proceeding to St. James's.''

Christina was jumping up and down on the spot. ''We have seen him,'' she said. ''We are the only ones except that gentleman down the street. All those people are waiting and we are the ones who have seen him. And he smiled at me. Mama, he smiled at me.''

''Yes, sweetheart.'' Elizabeth was laughing. ''So he

did. How fortunate that we decided to leave when we did and that Lord Trevelyan brought us here.''

''We are going inside the same building as the Tsar of Russia?'' Christina asked, awed.

''We are indeed,'' Christopher said as they turned into the doorway between the stone pillars on either side.

The Tsar had gone upstairs already to greet his sister. But all was fuss and frenzy downstairs. Christopher found his way barred by the manager, who appeared not even to recognize him for the moment.

''Trevelyan,'' Christopher said.

''Ah, yes, of course, my lord.'' The manager bowed deeply to him. ''And the ladies, my lord? The Tsar of Russia has just arrived here, my lord, as you may be aware.''

''The ladies are my wife and daughter,'' Christopher said.

The manager doubtless knew enough about the British aristocracy to know that the Earl of Trevelyan did not currently have a wife or daughter, but his mind was severely preoccupied. He bowed again, murmured ''Of course, my lord,'' once more, bowed to Elizabeth and to Christina, and let them pass. Soon they were in Christopher's sitting room, standing at the windows, watching swarms of people converge on the Pulteney. Somehow word had spread already that the guest most eagerly awaited had arrived at the Pulteney.

''Within a few minutes,'' Christopher said, ''the hotel is going to be like a fortress under siege. I think we came home just in time.''

Only by sending Antoine downstairs did Christopher succeed in having tea and cakes brought up to his sitting room within a half hour. Even so the refreshments were unnecessary to raise Christina's spirits. She was far more interested in darting to the windows to watch the cheering crowds than in eating cakes. One deafening roar followed by sustained and frantic cheering must have heralded the appearance of the Tsar on the balcony, Christopher explained to the child. But it would not be wise to go outside to see. They might never get back inside again.

Christina did not want to go outside. She was very

happy to be inside the same building as the Tsar of Russia. She was puffed up with importance. Christina giggled suddenly as she returned from the window and resumed her seat. She set one hand over her mouth and her eyes danced at Christopher. "Do you remember what you said?" she asked.

He raised his eyebrows. "Said? When?"

"Downstairs," she said, "to that man." She raised her shoulders and wrinkled her nose. "You said Mama and I were your wife and your daughter. That was funny." She giggled into her hand again.

"And so I did," he said quietly.

Elizabeth, watching him, suddenly alert, felt her heart leap and begin to thump uncomfortably.

"Your papa died?" he asked. "In Canada?"

Christina nodded, her giggles fading.

No, Elizabeth begged him with her eyes, *not yet, Christopher. I am not ready yet.* But he was not looking at her.

"What if he did not die?" Christopher asked. "What if your mama thought he died and told you that he did but he was alive and came home to you?"

Christina's head tipped to one side as she looked back at him. "My papa died," she said. "There was a fire and he died rescuing a little girl. But she was safe."

Elizabeth closed her eyes as Christopher finally looked across at her. She had wanted Christina to think of her father as a hero. It seemed a foolish and embarrassing lie now.

"So was he safe," he said. "He disappeared into the smoke, but he did not die."

Christina's eyes widened as she digested the meaning of the words. "You knew Papa?" she asked. "You were there?"

"Yes, I was there, Christina," he said. His voice was very gentle. Every word cut like a knife into Elizabeth's heart. "I was in Canada and then I came home. I came to see your mama, who used to be my wife. I did not know until a very short while ago that there was a little daughter called Christina. I wanted to meet her as soon as I knew. And I found that she has dark hair and blue eyes, like me, and that her name is Christina, like mine."

Christina was watching him with open mouth. Then she got hastily to her feet, rushed to Elizabeth, scrambled onto her lap, and hid her face against her mother's bosom. Christopher's eyes, Elizabeth noticed, were suspiciously bright. Her heart felt as if it would tear in two.

"Lord Trevelyan is your papa, sweetheart," she said.

"No!" Christina wailed. "Papa is dead."

Elizabeth found that her gaze was on Christopher, whose face was as chalky white as her own had felt earlier when she had almost fainted.

"He did not die after all, sweetheart," she said. "And he has come home."

Christina was sobbing. She cried noisily for a minute or two, while Elizabeth rocked her in her arms and Christopher sat as if turned to stone.

"Why did you say he was dead?" The voice was shaky and accusing.

"I thought he was," Elizabeth said, hating herself for the lie. But how could the whole truth be explained to a six-year-old child?

"Why didn't you *say*?" Christina raised her head at last and looked up with red and hostile eyes. "You said he was Lord Trevelyan."

"We thought you should get to know him and like him first, sweetheart," Elizabeth said weakly, "before we told you that he is your papa."

"And why didn't he come to Grandpapa's if he is my papa?" Christina asked. "Why did he come here?"

"We were not expecting him, Christina," she said. "We thought he was dead. I was about to marry Lord Poole."

"I *hate* Lord Poole," Christina said vehemently.

Elizabeth did not reprove her as she normally would. There was a silence that neither she nor Christopher seemed willing to break. The cheering outside seemed very loud again.

Christina turned her accusing stare suddenly on Christopher. "Why did you go away and leave me?" she asked him. "All the other boys and girls I know have papas. You didn't like me, did you? You hate me, don't you?"

He turned paler if that were possible. "Sweetheart,"

Elizabeth said before he could answer, "Lord Trev—Papa did not know about you. He did not know he had a little girl. He would have liked you if he had known. He would have come home sooner."

"I love you," Christopher said, his voice low and not quite steady. "Since I have known about you and met you, Christina, you have been the light of my life."

"Oh, I have not!" she said fiercely. "I am not the light of anyone's life except Mama's. I am a nuisance. Nobody loves me except Mama." She hesitated, forced by honesty not to give in entirely to self-pity. "And I think Uncle John."

He came across the room then and stooped down on his haunches beside Elizabeth's chair. "I love you, Christina," he said. "You are my little girl and Mama's. My own little girl." He reached out his hands to her but made no attempt to touch her. He looked at her pleadingly.

Elizabeth was biting her upper lip so hard that she tasted blood. She should never have listened to them. Oh, she should have listened to her own heart and conscience. She should have written to him even if she had not known where to send the letter. She could have written to his father or to Nancy. They would have sent it on to him. She should have let him know about Christina. But she could not blame them either, her father and Martin. It was she who was to blame. She was Christina's mother and had been his wife.

Christina sat staring at him, her lower lip protruding in a pout. Then she reached out one finger, poked it against his chest, and withdrew it again. "You'll go back to Canada again," she said.

"No." He shook his head. "I'm always going to be your papa, Christina. I want to take you down to Penhallow some time. I want you to see the beach and paddle in the water."

"But you won't build me a castle in the sand," Christina said.

"The biggest one there ever was," he said. "I promise."

Elizabeth sat very still. It was a wicked thing she had done. Purely spiteful and wicked. No matter what he had done to her, she had had no right to retaliate as she had. She had returned evil for evil.

And then Christina reached out with both hands and touched his shoulders and she leaned forward tentatively until his hands came to rest at her waist and he lifted her from Elizabeth's lap and into his arms. He stood up, hugging her to him. She set her arms about his neck and her cheek against his.

"I'd rather have you for a papa than Lord Poole," she whispered against his ear. But Elizabeth heard every word.

"Would you?" he said.

"Yes," Christina said. "Because you are my real papa and you like me. Don't you?"

"I love you, sweetheart," he said, and he turned away with her and walked across to the window. Elizabeth knew that he did so because he was crying and did not want her to see. She stayed where she was.

"I am going to tell Uncle John that I have a papa," Christina said. She lifted her head and looked into his face. "He will be surprised, won't he?"

"Yes, sweetheart," he said. "And pleased, I think."

She took one arm from about his neck and rubbed her palm over his cheek. "Don't cry, Papa," she said. "Silly. Why are you crying?"

He laughed shakily. "Because I have my little girl in my arms," he said, "and I am happy."

"Silly," she said, withdrawing the other arm and doing the like for his other cheek. "That is silly, Papa. You cry when you hurt yourself."

But there were more tears to come. He continued to laugh as he put a large handkerchief into her hand and she continued to wipe at his cheeks. Elizabeth lowered her head and brushed surreptitiously at her own eyes.

Her hands had just been tied, she thought. Her choices were being narrowed to none at all. And she was not sure whether she was sorry or not. There was only one thing she was sure of. She felt lonely and left out. She wished it were possible to get to her feet, cross to the window, and set her arms about both of them so that they could all rejoice together at being a family reunited.

But it was not possible. Seven years could not be so easily erased and forgotten about. Forgiveness could not be given when it was not asked for and when there was not even remorse.

Oh, but she longed to forgive.

And to be forgiven.

The door opened suddenly without even the warning of a knock and Nancy and John walked in, laughing and looking very pleased with themselves.

Nancy and John had been out too to watch the arrivals. More fortunate than Christopher and Elizabeth, they had seen Field Marshal von Blücher's arrival at the Horse Guards and been part of the enthusiastic reception that had prompted the crowds to bear him off along the Mall to Carlton House. But they had left then, more concerned with themselves and their wedding plans than for historic events that were turning the citizens of London delirious with excitement.

They had to push their way through the crowds outside the Pulteney and then had to convince a porter that they had a legitimate reason for being there. They were both laughing when Nancy finally opened the door into the sitting room. Christopher was in the room with Christina in his arms. Elizabeth was there too.

"Oh," John said, "a party. Is it you everyone is cheering for, then, Christina?"

"No!" She giggled happily and waved a large white handkerchief from her hand. "The Tsar of Russia is here. We saw him. He smiled at me."

"Ah," John said, "so you are famous after all."

"I have a papa," Christina said.

John pursed his lips and glanced from Christopher to Elizabeth.

"My real one," Christina said. "He didn't die after all, Uncle John, and he has come back from Canada to see me. He loves me and he is going to stay. And he is going to build me the biggest castle in the sand there ever was. Aren't you, Papa?" she concluded triumphantly.

"And bigger even than that, sweetheart," Christopher said, smiling at her.

It was the first time Nancy had seen her niece. She stood very still and gazed at the child. Oh, how very like Christopher she was. And how happy he looked. As happy as he had looked at Kingston when—But no. She and John had agreed that morning that they would not spoil the day with talk or even thoughts about any of those matters.

"Are you surprised, Uncle John?" Christina asked.

"If you had a feather in your hand instead of a very large handkerchief," he said, "you could knock me down with it. It's the best surprise of the day. Better even than mine."

"What is yours?" she asked.

"Oh," he said, "I had better not even mention it after hearing yours. You will think it a very sorry surprise."

"Uncle John!" Christina protested.

"Very well, then," John said, turning and setting his arm about Nancy's shoulders. "Two surprises actually, scamp. This is your Aunt Nancy. I don't think you have met her before, have you? She is your papa's sister. And if she were not, she would soon be your aunt anyway—your only aunt, right? Aunt Nancy is going to be my wife."

Nancy watched the curiosity in Christina's face. She dared not look at Elizabeth. But Elizabeth got swiftly to her feet and came across the room.

"I am so glad," she said. "I always wondered why it did not happen before. You seemed fond of each other. I am so glad that you have found each other again."

She hugged and kissed John, then turned, hesitated, and hugged Nancy too. "I am glad," she said. "And I am sorry about that other, Nancy. I know that love of a brother is a very powerful force."

Nancy hugged her in return.

"I would send for champagne," Christopher said, "but I believe all the servants at this hotel have been paralyzed with awe over the arrival of the Tsar. How about some almost cold tea and some almost fresh cakes?"

John turned and grinned at Nancy. "I suppose we will always remember why we drank cold tea and ate almost fresh cakes in celebration of the announcement of our betrothal, won't we?" he said. "It will be something to tell our grandchildren about, my love."

"Lord Poole is not going to be my new papa," Christina said happily, hugging Christopher's neck, "because my real papa has come home."

26

JOHN escorted Elizabeth and Christina home from the Pulteney Hotel. He carried his niece upstairs to the nursery, Elizabeth walking beside them.

"Why I am carrying a six-year-old girl I do not know," he said, "unless it is that she had a more wonderful surprise to tell of than I. It really knocked me off my feet."

Christina chuckled. "What I don't know," she said, "is why Papa could not come home with us instead of staying in that place."

"He wants to be near the Tsar," John said. "Besides, he has to look after Aunt Nancy until she marries me. It would not do for her to stay in a hotel alone, you know. Ladies do not do such things."

"She could have come here too," she said.

"Not until we are married," he said firmly. "Shall we keep your surprise a secret for a while—just between you, your mama, and me?"

"Why?" she asked.

"Because secrets are fun, that's why, scamp," he said, setting her down inside the nursery and smiling cheerfully at her nurse. "We will wait for the very best time to tell it—a time we are all three agreed upon. Good idea?"

"Good idea," she said, turning her back on her nurse and wrinkling her nose at him and her mother. "It's a wonderful secret."

"Why did you suggest that she keep it a secret?" Elizabeth asked John when they had left the nursery.

"They will take all her joy away," he said, setting an arm loosely about her shoulders. "They will not think it such a wonderful secret. Papa and Martin, I mean."

"Martin will." She frowned. "No, maybe not. He

thinks that my best chance of happiness lies with Manley. He will not like this complication."

"And what do you think?" John asked.

She hesitated. They were walking slowly downstairs. "I need to talk with someone," she said. "I need it so desperately. May I burden you, John? You probably have a thousand other things to rush off to."

"Not a single one," he said. "Come along to my dressing room, Elizabeth, and unburden your mind. This feels rather good actually. I have not had many chances to play big brother, have I?"

"No," she said, waiting for him to open the door and preceding him inside. "I have always loved you dearly, John. You were the greatest hero in my life when I was a girl. But there was always Martin to confide in."

"And there isn't any longer?" he asked quietly, closing the door firmly behind them.

"Yes, there is." She turned to look at him unhappily. "I don't know what it is, John. Well, I do know. Something happened. But it was something to do with me, not him, and it does not seem fair to have reacted the way I have. I can't—Well, I can't seem to think of him as the other half of myself as I always used to do. I hate myself for it. He has always been so good to me. You would not believe the patience he has had with me since the divorce, John. And the way he gave up all his own chances for pleasure just to be at my side."

"Yes," he said, "perhaps I would believe it. What happened to change things?"

"Nothing really." She shrugged. "He thinks I should settle for peace and contentment with Manley. It is wise advice. Even better than that, he wants me to go back to Kingston, where I can avoid all this confusion and all the gossip that Christopher's arrival in town has caused. He is even willing to come with me. He is so very selfless, John. How can I confide to him all the turmoil in my life? He has the answers already, and I am not sure that that is what I need. I think I need someone to help me find the answers myself."

"You want my ears but not my tongue," he said. "Talk on then. They are yours."

She looked at him apologetically. "I didn't mean quite that," she said. "And I shouldn't be burdening you at all, should I? This is a wonderful day for you. You love Nancy, don't you? I could see it in your eyes when you looked at her. And it was in her eyes too. I was so glad. I will let my hero brother go only to a woman who loves him, you see."

He smiled at her.

"What happened the last time you were together?" she asked. "You were in love then too, weren't you? But she ran away. Did you frighten her?"

His smiled faded and he shook his head. "Something happened," he said. "I don't want to talk about it. Tell me about yourself, Elizabeth. You want to marry Christopher again, don't you? And he has asked you. What is the problem?"

She turned away from him, playing absently with a brush on the dressing table. "I'm going to have another child," she said.

She heard him suck in his breath. "Then Poole had damned well better move the wedding date forward," he said through his teeth. "I'll not have my sister—"

'It isn't Manley's," she said. "It's Christopher's."

There was silence behind her. "He has been here only a week or so," John said at last.

"He arrived in London from America at the end of April," she said. "The day before my wedding. He kidnapped me and took me to Penhallow. The fall from the carriage and the loss of memory really happened. He told me I was his wife and I lived as his wife for a few weeks until after Martin found me."

John said nothing.

She turned to look at him. "I loved him," she said. "Until I remembered, until Martin showed me Christina's portrait and I remembered everything, I loved him, John. More than I loved him when we were first married. I was timid then and homesick and a little afraid of him. At Penhallow life was paradise."

"All right." John swallowed. "I have provided the ears, Elizabeth. What do you want to do about all this?"

"I cannot now marry Manley," she said. "That is certain. But I cannot break off our betrothal either. Not now. It is the worst possible time. He does not deserve to be scorned as a jilted man. I had decided that I would continue the betrothal for a month or two and then break it off as quietly as possible before going home to Kingston."

"With Martin," he said.

"No." She frowned. "I cannot allow him to give up his life for me any longer. I would feel too much guilt. No, I have to shape my own life, live it myself. Martin means well, but I think sometimes that he tries to overprotect me. Is that very unfair?"

"No," he said. "What happened to change your feelings about him, Elizabeth? His arrival at Penhallow to break up your idyll?"

"Perhaps that was it," she said. "I did not know him, you see, and I disliked him and feared him from the first moment. And then when I went walking outside with him and he touched me as he has always done it felt as if—oh, John, this sounds terrible—as if he were making indecent advances to me. He gave me the shudders. Poor Martin. I feel so guilty. But I can't seem to get back to the old relationship."

"Perhaps you shouldn't, then," he said. "As you say, Elizabeth, perhaps you need to become entirely your own person. You have done very well growing toward that ideal in the past few years."

"Have I?" she said. "Yes, I think you are right."

"You said that you had decided what to do," John said. "But now you are not so sure?"

"Christina has found her father again," she said. "She has always had Papa and Martin and you when you have been home. I did not really realize until today how much she has missed not having a father. And one who cares. Manley has never cared for her. I was selfish even to think of marrying him, wasn't I? Christopher cares, John. He cried when she finally let him pick her up in his arms today after we had told her the truth. It was just before you came back to the Pulteney. I thought my heart was tearing in two."

John nodded.

"Our unborn child is going to need a father too," she said.

He nodded again.

Elizabeth drew a deep breath. "I have always thought that the whole fault in our breakup and divorce was his," she said. "I have always thought that I was entirely blameless. I know now that in reality my own actions were quite as bad and quite as cruel as his. We are equally guilty. I kept all knowledge of Christina from him. I believe now that he would have fought for me and for our marriage if he had known. He would have asked forgiveness and been granted it long ago. It was a terrible thing I did, John. I don't know if I can do it again. This child is one he can know from the beginning—if I allow it."

"And will you?" John asked after a short pause.

"He has never asked forgiveness," she said, staring down at the backs of her hands and spreading her fingers. "Or admitted his guilt. That is all I ask, John. Is it too much? I find I can no longer feel the moral outrage that I used to think would make me hate him for the rest of my life. All I want is the truth told with some sign of remorse. I don't think I can accept anything else."

"Can't you?" he said. "Christopher has always said he is innocent, Elizabeth. Have you ever wondered if he is telling the truth? I am inclined to think that he is."

She looked up at him with agonized eyes. "Don't say that," she said. "Oh, please, John. It is what I longed to believe years ago, but now I could not bear it. It would mean that everything was my fault, that our marriage collapsed and ended in such ugliness because of my lack of trust. It would mean that I have kept him and Christina apart for no reason whatsoever. I would not be able to live with my guilt."

"Perhaps in time you can be convinced both of his innocence and of your diminished guilt, Elizabeth," John said. "You have really made your new decision, haven't you?"

"Have I?" she asked. "Yes, I suppose I have. We have a daughter who needs both of us and are to have another child who will need us too. He wants to marry me again for Christina's sake and will be even more determined when he knows that I am with child again."

"And?" John prompted.

She looked at him with luminous eyes. "Yes, that too, of course," she said. "I love him. I have never for one moment stopped loving him. Not even when I hated him most."

John crossed the room to her, set his hands on her shoulders, and kissed her cheek. "I know," he said. "I have always known. Let me say to you what I said to Christina a little while ago. Let's keep this our secret for now, shall we? And before you can ask why, I'll tell you. Because secrets are fun."

"You are afraid that Papa will explode and Martin try to change my mind?" she asked.

"Something like that," he said. "This is something you have decided for yourself, Elizabeth. I have not influenced your decision. At least I have tried not to do so even though you must suspect that I approve of it. Listening to Papa and especially to Martin can only confuse you again."

"You don't like Martin, do you?" she asked, looking into his eyes.

"Never mind my feelings for Martin," he said. "You are the important one at the moment, Elizabeth. You have made a decision. Act upon it. And until you do, keep it a secret."

She smiled slowly at him. "Thank you, big brother," she said, "for lending me your ears and your heart but for respecting me enough not to try to manipulate and control me. Would things have turned out differently if I had looked to you for advice seven years ago instead of to Papa and Martin?"

"We can never know," he said. "But that is the past, Elizabeth. It is the present that counts and what we can make of the future."

"For both you and me," she said. "I am glad you found Nancy again, John."

"That makes two of us, then," he said. "Tell me. When Martin came to Penhallow, was Nancy there too?"

"Yes, of course," she said. "She was there the whole time."

John gritted his teeth.

"Don't be angry with her," she said. "She went along with Christopher's lie, but she was kind to me. And I know how fond one can be of a brother."

He smiled and hugged her tightly.

Nancy had gone shopping with one of her newfound acquaintances. The Tsar and the Grand Duchess had also gone out together in a carriage a short while earlier amid enthusiastic cheers from the ever-present mob. The Tsar, for reasons of his own, seemed to have decided to stay at the Pulteney instead of moving into the state apartments prepared for him at St. James's.

There were still crowds outside, though, Christopher saw, gazing idly through the window. He and John were to call on John's man of business again during the afternoon, and he was finding it hard to settle to anything while he waited. But he became alert suddenly. Elizabeth was descending from a carriage outside the doors of the hotel. She would have a hard time getting past the porter. He hurried from the room and down the staircase, his heart leaping with pleased anticipation.

She did not have Christina with her, he noticed as soon as he reached the outer doors and assured the porter that she was not a hired assassin awaiting the Tsar's return. Part of him was disappointed; he wanted to hear his daughter calling him "Papa" again. He wanted to feel her child's arms tight about his neck. Part of him was happy; he would have Elizabeth alone for a short while even if she had come to argue with him, to beg him to leave her and Christina alone. She was looking pale and none too happy.

"How is Christina?" he asked when he had ushered her into his sitting room.

"Well," she said, removing her bonnet and dropping it onto a table inside the door. She crossed immediately to the window and stood with her back to him. "Do you still want to marry me, Christopher?"

He held his breath. "Yes," he said.

"Very well, then," she said. "You can start to make the necessary arrangements for the summer. By then I will be free of my betrothal to Manley."

She spoke in a matter-of-fact voice, as if she were talking about some ordinary business dealing. She was talking about their wedding!

"You are ready to betroth yourself to me now," he said, "but to continue with your old betrothal too for a while? Isn't that almost like bigamy?"

"No," she said, "of course not. Sooner or later I am going to be treating Manley shabbily. We are betrothed. Half the *ton* were at our wedding, which you put an end to. For the next few weeks there are going to be daily and nightly celebrations for our foreign guests. It would be cruel to humiliate him now. It will be cruel anyway. I do not feel proud of myself."

"Why are you going to marry me rather than him, then?" he asked. "Is it just because of Christina?"

"Partly," she said. "Half for Christina."

And half for herself? he wondered. She was standing straight-backed at the window, staring out.

"And half for Christina's brother or sister," she said so quietly that for a moment he thought he might have imagined the words. But he knew he had not.

He gazed at her rigid back and felt as if a giant fist had just buried itself in his stomach. "You are with child again?" he asked.

"Yes," she said.

His chest was sore, and his eyes were burning as they had done the afternoon before when Christina had put her arms about his neck and her soft cheek against his. He wanted to cry. They were going to have a child! His eyes moved down Elizabeth's body from behind. His child was inside her now. She was going to grow large with it. And then there would be a tiny baby. Their son or daughter. Their second child.

"Elizabeth," he said. He had not intended to whisper.

"It will be workable," she said. "I know you love Christina. I believe you will love this new child too. Penhallow will be a good place for them to grow up. And I will need somewhere other than London to live for a while at least. It will be only fair to Manley for me to stay away from here. Devonshire is far enough. I shall try to be a good wife. I shall try to attend to your needs."

"You should have told me sooner," he said. "I would not have kept you standing for an hour and a half yesterday, Elizabeth, jostled by the crowds."

She turned to look at him. Her face was hard and set. "One thing, Christopher," she said. "I will not tolerate mistresses and whores. If there are any in the future—even one—I will take our children and leave you."

"There have been a few women since our divorce," he said. "There were none either during our marriage or before, Elizabeth. There have been none since I returned to England—none except you, of course. There will be no others for as long as we both live. I have always believed that marriage vows were meant to be kept."

She flushed and looked away from his eyes. "I know you will want to see something of Christina," she said. "I thought perhaps once a week until I can decently put an end to my betrothal. Out of respect for Manley, Christopher, please do not ask for more. Once the summer comes and we are married, she will be with you every day."

"I'll get a special license today," he said. "We will marry tomorrow."

She looked back at him, startled. "Tomorrow?" she said. "Are you mad?"

"You are with child by me," he said. "I will not risk dying before the summer and having my son or daughter born a bastard."

Her cheeks flushed a dull red.

"What are these engagements that are so important to Poole's pride?" he asked. "List them."

"There are too many to name," she said. "Let me see. There is the opera tonight. Manley is very excited about that. I am not quite sure why. And then tomorrow night, of course, there is the reception at Carlton House and the presentation to the queen. And dinners and balls and routs by the dozen for the next several weeks."

"Tomorrow night is the occasion that will be most important to him," he said. "You may go to that with him, Elizabeth, even though you will be marrying me in the morning. The day after tomorrow you will break the news to him in any manner you think best."

She laughed. "You expect me to marry you in the morning and go to Carlton House with Manley in the evening?" he asked.

"I expect you to marry me in the morning," he said. "I will permit you to go to Carlton House in the evening. You do not have to go. You are the one concerned about Poole's pride, not me."

She stared at him. "Very well," she said at last. "It is to be only a marriage of convenience anyway, isn't it? It should not matter that it will be a very strange wedding day."

"No," he said. "I suppose not. I'll stay away from Carlton House myself."

He wanted to cross the room to her. He wanted to gather her into his arms and kiss away the set, business-like look on her face. He wanted to feel the wonder of her body pressed to his, his child inside that body. He wanted to tell her with kisses and words that for him it would be anything but a marriage of convenience. He stayed where he was and clasped his hands behind him.

"Well, then," she said, "that is all settled. Where is it to be, Christopher? The wedding, I mean. May I bring Christina? And John? I am not going to tell anyone else at the moment."

"Not Martin?" he asked.

"No," she said. "Not Martin. Will you bring Nancy?"

"Yes," he said. "Have John bring you here with Christina by ten o'clock. We'll go to the church together."

"Very well," she said.

This was a wedding they were planning, he thought. Their own wedding. Yet they were standing twenty feet apart, both of them unsmiling and unemotional. They talked as if it were an outing to Kew they were planning. No, not even anything that exciting.

"I'll see you tomorrow morning, then," she said, taking a step toward him—and toward her bonnet and the door.

"I'll escort you to your carriage," he said.

They were a pair of polite strangers.

"Oh," she said when she reached the table and her bonnet. She lowered her head for a moment and then opened her reticule and reached inside. She drew out a small cloth clasp purse and held it out toward him without looking at him.

He took it and opened it. Her gold wedding ring was inside. He touched it with one finger.

"I want the same one," she said in a tight voice.

"Yes," he said. "It will be the same marriage really, won't it? With a seven-year interruption."

"Do you know what tomorrow is?" she asked him, closing her reticule carefully.

"Yes," he said. "Our seventh wedding anniversary. Why did you bring the ring if you intended not to marry me until the summer?"

She raised her eyes to his. "I take it with me everywhere," she said. "Except to Penhallow. When you picked up my trunk to go there, you left my reticule behind. I never did ask you there why I had no wedding ring, did I? I did not even notice that I had none. Or perhaps I did not want to notice."

It was good there between us, he wanted to say. And her eyes held his as if she waited for him to say it. *Our child was conceived there. In love. It was good.* But she lowered her eyes before he could form the words and the moment passed.

"I'll take you downstairs," he said, "and see you safely past the mob to your carriage."

"Thank you," she said.

They were polite strangers again.

Christopher ascended the stairs again a few minutes later with his head down. For some reason she had decided not to tell Martin. That was a relief, at least. His mind flashed back to the visit Martin had paid him two days before.

Martin had been his usual smiling, charming self. He had been rather upset to find, he had said, that Elizabeth was adamant in her plan to marry Poole, even though she did not love him, merely because she did not want to embarrass him. He knew, as any man of any feeling would, that she loved Trevelyan and wanted to marry him. And ought to marry him if only for their daughter's sake.

The more he thought about it, Martin had said in obvious distress, the more he was convinced that that mad scheme they had talked about as something of a joke was after all a good idea. Dear Lizzie was just longing to be forced to follow her heart. She should be forced. And what better way was there to do it than to take Christina and make off to Penhallow with her? It would not be kidnapping, after all, would it? Trevelyan was the child's father.

Christopher had pursed his lips and considered carefully and looked dubious. He did not want to do anything that would cause Elizabeth unnecessary anxiety.

But of course, Martin explained, he would leave a note for her so that she would know that Christina was safe. Had he not kept Elizabeth safe when he kidnapped her? Apart from the bump on the head, of course. But really that had been her fault, poor dear, impulsive Lizzie.

It might work, Christopher had agreed finally, frowning and looking anything but confident.

But of course it would work, Martin had said. They would plan it for the night of the Carlton House reception. He would bring Christina to the Pulteney, where Trevelyan would be waiting, all ready to leave. Lizzie would be gone almost all night. She probably would not look in on the nursery even when she returned. The nurse would be heavily drugged. By the time Lizzie read the note and checked the nursery to see that it was true, Trevelyan would be well on his way to Penhallow with his daughter. Lizzie of course would follow without delay, and she and Trevelyan would fall into each other's arms as soon as they were reunited.

"It might work too," Christopher had said, frowning with anxiety. "I'll do it, Martin. I have lost her for sure if I don't, haven't I?"

"It seems so," Martin had said, smiling in sympathy. "I've always liked you, Trevelyan, and I no longer believe those stupid stories I was foolish enough to believe after you went to Canada. She belongs with you. She should marry you again."

The two men had shaken hands heartily while Christopher had looked at the smiling Martin and wondered if he would ever have the satisfaction of smashing the smile and the face to smithereens. He fervently hoped so.

Looking back on that visit now, Christopher could begin to see how he might more easily put his own plan into effect. Elizabeth would be his wife by tomorrow. In fact he would make a new plan, one that should be quite easy to carry out.

If only she kept to what she had said and did not tell Martin about the wedding.

27

IT seemed to Christopher as he and John approached the offices of John's man of business later that afternoon that they had set the man an impossible task.

"I rather wish now that I had decided upon the Spanish torture first," John said. "It might have been quicker and would certainly have given me more satisfaction. When I look at Martin's good-natured smile now, I cannot believe that all my life I have not seen the devil behind it."

"There is a certain kidnapping scheme I have devised with Martin's help," Christopher said. "Involving Christina this time. I should tell you about it so that you will know what is happening if he tries to involve you in it. He might. But I need you to be involved on my side."

He told John Martin's plan and his own twists on that plan.

"Well," John said, "I just hope Nancy does not have her heart set on going to Carlton House tomorrow evening. I don't suppose she will when she knows that Martin will be getting his comeuppance instead, will she?"

Mr. Roberts stepped out of his inner office beaming and rubbing his hands together when the two gentlemen arrived on his premises. He was pleased to report that Powers had been found with a great deal of difficulty only that morning.

"Simon Powers is not exactly what would be described as a respectable solicitor," Mr. Roberts said. "He conducts shady dealings, if you were to ask me, my lord." He nodded sagely in Christopher's direction.

Neither did Mr. Simon Powers have his office in a respectable neighborhood. In fact, John remarked as the two men approached it half an hour later, he appeared to do business in the midst of moneylenders.

A shabby, hollow-eyed clerk was writing in a ledger in the outer room of Mr. Powers's office and informed the gentlemen that Mr. Powers was out on business and not likely to be back for the rest of the day. Christopher opened the door into the inner room, despite the feeble protests of the clerk, but it was indisputably empty.

He looked helplessly at John and back to the clerk. "We will be back tomorrow to consult with Mr. Powers," he said. "Tomorrow afternoon."

"Inform him we are potentially lucrative clients," John said, withdrawing a coin from his pocket and tossing it to the clerk.

"It was probably more than Powers pays him in a quarter," he said to Christopher as they left the office with some reluctance. "The poor devil looks somewhat cadaverous, wouldn't you agree?"

Christopher sighed. "Although I have been persuading myself that it would not happen," he said, "I have been hoping that it could all be settled today—the proof discovered, Martin confronted, Elizabeth informed. I have been hoping that tomorrow could be a happy day. Now we will not even be able to talk with Powers before the wedding."

"Perhaps it is as well," John said. "She has agreed to it, Christopher. She is going to be very upset when she learns the truth about Martin, you know, and realizes the years of suffering he brought on the two of you. The knowledge would not put her in the best mood for a wedding."

"You are probably right," Christopher said.

He had come home from America, he thought, determined to discover the truth and to do so as slowly and patiently as necessary. Yet now that he was close, perhaps within a day of uncovering the whole truth, he found that patience was deserting him. He wanted to know now or even sooner.

"Yes," he said, "I'm sure you are right, John."

The opera house at the Haymarket was quite as crowded as John had predicted it would be. Every row and every box were crammed with people, everyone dressed in such splendor and glittering with such extravagant displays of jewels that it was difficult to imagine how they all hoped to outdo themselves the very next evening at Carlton House.

When the Regent arrived with his foreign visitors, everyone rose and sang the national anthem and cheered for minutes on end.

Only one box was empty and very conspicuously so. There were those afterward who swore to the fact that the Regent glanced at it nervously all through the first act of the opera and only when it was over seemed to breathe a sigh of relief and bask in the reflected glory his guests brought him.

But he relaxed too soon. Just as the second act was about to begin, there was a general stir and the empty box was suddenly empty no longer. With a loud rustling the Princess of Wales appeared, looking grotesque in a spangled gown, bright yellow curls, and heavy rouge that could be detected even in the farthest corner of the theater.

All eyes swiveled from the apparition to the Regent, who was sitting rigid and pale in his own box. And then the Tsar of Russia got to his feet and bowed to the princess, the other monarchs followed his lead, and the Regent, left with no choice, rose and bowed to his estranged wife. Only then did the strange silence of the opera house erupt into loud and sustained cheers. The Regent covered his confusion and his fury by smiling and bowing and acknowledging the cheers as his due.

The second act of the opera was further delayed when some members of the audience, three prominent Whig gentlemen with their ladies, saw fit to take their personal greetings to the princess's box. Amid further applause, she bowed graciously to them, they withdrew, and the main business of the evening could be proceeded with.

Elizabeth was angry. She had always known that Manley was a Whig and that his sympathies lay with the Princess of Wales. She had always respected his opinions even when she disagreed with them. She did not entirely disagree about the princess, though she considered the woman vulgar and unworthy of being the future queen of England. But then the Regent was no better.

What angered her was that she had been forced, without her permission, in full view of the Regent himself and all his foreign guests and of the *ton*, to appear to be giving her public and unqualified support to the princess. Lord Poole had taken her into the princess's box, and she had been forced to curtsy deeply and receive the woman's smile and the audience's applause. She could have avoided doing so only if she had made a rather public issue of it. She would not do that. This evening and tomorrow evening were to be devoted to bolstering Manley's pride.

But what he had forced her into was unfair. She was more than angry. She was furious. And she had to sit smiling by his side for the rest of the evening. They were late leaving the theater because the crowd waiting outside mobbed the Princess of Wales's carriage, cheering for her with loud ecstasy, and would not let it pass for a long while. And then the Tsar and the King of Prussia and all the others had to have their turn.

"It was a wonderful evening," Lord Poole said, turning to Elizabeth with a look of satisfaction when they were finally inside his carriage. "Do you see how everyone adores her, Elizabeth? The Regent is going to be forced to give her her rightful place at court, and then you may be sure she will remember who helped her to achieve it. And if the Tories continue to support the Regent, they will soon be dragged down with him, victory or no victory." He took her hand. "You were magnificent."

She drew her hand away. "What you did was deplorable," she said. "You should have asked me first, Manley, if I wished to enter her box. I would certainly have said no."

His eyes blazed instantly. "You would have said no, madam?" he said. "I would remind you that you are my betrothed and will be my wife soon."

"I still have a mind and opinions of my own," she said. "I found that display quite undignified."

"I will decide what is to be in your mind and what your opinions are to be, Elizabeth," he said. "And I will decide what is dignified."

She could turn their disagreement into a full-scale quarrel, she thought. She could break off the betrothal that very evening. It was a tempting thought. He would even be glad to see the back of her. But his anger appeared to have disappeared as quickly as it had flared.

"Forgive me," he said, taking her hand again. "I forget sometimes that you are a strong-minded woman, Elizabeth, and that I respect you for it. I am sorry that you did not share my feeling of triumph this evening." He smiled at her.

She had to meet him halfway. She owed him that. "I am glad you found it so satisfactory," she said. "And I applaud your courage in making such a public gesture, Manley."

He appeared relieved. "I am looking forward to tomorrow evening," he said. "All the fashionable world will be there. It will be a night for reputations to be made. We will see how many people remember what I did tonight—what we did. You will see that we are not despised for it, Elizabeth, but rather admired."

"I am sure you are right," she said.

"And it will be a night for reputations to be broken," he said, smiling directly at her. His eyes glittered suddenly with the reflected light of a passing street lamp. "I pity anyone foolish enough to set a foot wrong tomorrow evening."

"Surely no one would be that careless or that unfortunate," she said, allowing him to raise her hand to his lips as they arrived at her father's house.

She rather regretted, as he handed her down from the carriage and she hurried inside the house, that she had been unable to carry their quarrel to its completion. It would have been an easy way out. Now she would have to face the more difficult task of telling him that their betrothal was at an end without a quarrel to help her along. But it would have to be done after tomorrow night. Tomorrow night was to be devoted to making him feel and look respectable.

And tomorrow, she thought, with a sick lurching of the stomach, was to be her wedding day.

John was falsely hearty; Nancy was smiling constantly and stiffly; Christopher was looking morose; Elizabeth was pale and expressionless; Christina was loudly excited. It was a strange wedding party.

They could take his carriage to the church, John offered rather too loudly, rubbing his hands together and smiling jovially at everyone around him. Nancy smiled determinedly back. It had been brought out anyway and his horses needed more exercise than they had got coming from Grosvenor Square.

"Is everyone ready?" he asked.

Christopher and Elizabeth rose silently to their feet. Christina was bounding up and down close to the door.

"Yes, of course," Nancy said. "We must not be late."

"You are well?" Christopher asked Elizabeth as they left his suite. Her arm was resting formally and stiffly along his.

"Yes, quite well, thank you," she said.

Christina was jumping down the stairs with both feet together, her aunt and uncle flanking her.

She did not look in the best of health, Christopher thought, glancing down at his bride. She was pale and unsmiling, obviously less than delighted to be on her way to marry him. But she looked very lovely nevertheless in a pale green muslin dress with slippers and bonnet of a darker shade. She was more lovely than she had been the first time she was his bride. And more desirable.

They sat side by side in the carriage, Christina between them. Nancy and John carried on a bright conversation about the weather. It was amazing how much could be said on the topic when silence was the alternative.

Christina was stroking Christopher's leg and gazing shyly up at him. "You are going to be my proper papa," she said. "I am going to be Christina Atwell instead of Christina Ward. Mama told me."

"*Lady* Christina Atwell," he said, his expression softening as he looked down at her. "And Mama is going to be Lady Elizabeth Atwell, Countess of Trevelyan. Rather grand, isn't it?"

Christina nodded and he reached out to rub two knuckles across her nose.

He did not look pleased to be getting married again, Elizabeth thought. He had not once smiled at her, and his face looked cold and harsh—until he had started to talk with Christina, that was. She must always remember why he was marrying her again. She must never allow herself to become vulnerable by hoping that perhaps there was more to it than love for his children.

But he looked so very handsome, she thought, swallowing. He was wearing a green form-fitting coat, surely a creation of Weston, and a paler green silk waistcoat with buff-colored pantaloons and shining Hessians. He wore crisp white lace at the throat and wrists, as if he were attending an evening entertainment. At least, she thought, he had dressed for a wedding. He had shown her that much courtesy.

Not that his manner was discourteous either. Just cold and distant. She wished she did not love him. It would be easy to marry him again if it were just for the children's sake. It would be easier to forget that there were huge barriers between them.

"Well," John said with hearty lack of necessity when the carriage stopped outside a modest church far from the fashionable center of town, "here we are."

"Yes," Nancy said brightly and foolishly. "And so we are. Will you hold my hand inside the church, Christina? We will stay close to Mama and Papa, but they will have business to conduct with the rector."

Christina nodded. "Mama is going to marry Papa," she said.

Christopher had been very relived to find that their daughter had not thought to ask why they were not already married. The questions would doubtless come later, when she was a little older, but by that time perhaps they would have had a long enough and stable enough relationship that they could answer truthfully without doing her any serious emotional damage.

"Well," he said, lifting Elizabeth to the pavement after the others had already descended and keeping his hands at her waist for a few moments, "this is where I entered at a gallop on your last wedding day."

He did not know why he said those words. He certainly had not planned them or even thought them before he said them. For a moment there was a ghost of a smile on her face, but then it disappeared to leave her pale and serious again and to leave him wondering if he had imagined it. He hoped not.

The church was dark and cold inside and empty. It was very different from the light coziness of the chapel at Kingston where they had married the first time seven years ago to the day. And vastly different from the splendor of St. George's, where she was to have married Manley less than two months before in the presence of half the *ton*.

This was where they were to marry. By the time they emerged into daylight again, they would be man and wife once more. The reality of it hit her. She turned to look up at him. It was a beautiful church in which to marry. And all she really needed or wanted was him there with her and her brother and his sister and their daughter.

She closed her mind to all the barriers there were to their happiness. She tried to see him as she had seen him when her memory was gone and found that after all it was not so difficult. Not now on her wedding day anyway. She loved him. It was as simple as that. Not simple at all, of course. Love never was. But simple enough for a wedding day if one held one's thoughts blank and allowed feeling to dominate.

He would have liked to offer her more, he thought. More than an obscure and not particularly lovely church with only their child and two adults as witnesses and guests and well-wishers. And a strange rector to perform the ceremony. And yet for himself he could not imagine anything that he might find more moving. He had Elizabeth there and their daughter and their unborn child, and by the time they left the church they would be a family again, bound by the ties of church and state and honor. He could not possibly wish for more. He loved her. And soon—perhaps even that very day or the next—he would be able to lay his innocence of those seven-year charges at her feet and there would be no barriers left to their happiness.

She might grow to love him again, he thought. She had loved him when she married him the first time. She had loved him at Penhallow.

And then the rector, garbed in his clerical robes, was bowing before them. And it was all beginning: the rector's words and admonitions, their vows to each other, the gold ring on her finger, the sudden—was it really to be this quick and this simple, then?—pronouncement that they were man and wife. He had eyes only for her face, she for his hands. They listened to each other, and both heard their daughter whispering behind them and being hushed by Nancy.

Christopher kissed his new wife, very briefly, on the

lips and a certain spell was broken. The rector was offering his congratulations; John was hugging Elizabeth; Nancy was weeping in Christopher's arms; Christina was clinging to Elizabeth's skirt. And then John was pumping Christopher's hand and slapping him on the shoulder; Nancy was weeping in Elizabeth's arms; Christina was clutching Christopher's leg.

Elizabeth and Christopher bent down at the same moment to pick her up. They looked into each other's eyes and each picked her up with one arm. She wrapped her arms about their necks.

"Am I Christina Atwell now?" she asked.

"Lady Christina Atwell," Christopher said.

"Yes, sweetheart," Elizabeth said.

"I like it better than my old name," Christina said. "I am Lady Christina Atwell, Uncle John."

"And so you are," he said. "Am I to bow to you, scamp?"

"No, silly," she said, giggling.

They all went back to the Pulteney. It felt strange. They seemed not to have been gone long. And yet everything had changed. Elizabeth looked down at the ring she had refused to look at for several years, though she had carried it around with her always in her reticule. She was Elizabeth Atwell again. She had stopped thinking of herself by that name a long time ago. She was the Countess of Trevelyan.

She looked at Christopher, who was sending his man, the strange Mr. Bouchard, downstairs for wine and cakes. He was her husband. She wondered briefly what her father would say when he knew and what Martin would say. She felt guilty particularly about not saying anything to Martin. He would be upset to know that John had been at her wedding but not he. She pushed the thought from her mind. Tomorrow she would explain to Manley, and then she would be free to tell her father and her stepbrother the truth.

In the meanwhile it was her wedding day, and her seventh wedding anniversary. She looked at her husband again. He had sat down, and Christina had climbed onto his lap.

"You will be coming home with us, Papa?" she asked, gazing up at him hopefully. "You won't be staying in this place any longer now that you have married Mama and are my real *real* Papa? Aunt Nancy can come too."

"Not today, sweetheart," he said. "Perhaps tomorrow or the next day. Today we will enjoy ourselves by keeping it all a secret, will we?"

"I can't tell?" she asked.

"It will be much more fun if you can tell after keeping it a secret for a whole day or maybe two, won't it?" he said. "Think how surprised everyone will be."

She smiled a little wistfully. "I wanted you to come home with Mama and me," she said.

"I tell you what." He cupped her chin with one hand. "Mama has to go to Carlton House this evening to meet the queen. It was arranged some time ago. I'll not be going and neither will Aunt Nancy. How would you like a real adventure and come to stay with us here tonight?"

He had not said anything yet to Elizabeth, though Nancy knew all about it already and had willingly given up the chance to be part of the Carlton House reception. She would not want to go anyway, she had said in all honesty, if neither Christopher nor John was going to be there.

"Just me?" Christina said. "Not Mama?" She turned to look at Elizabeth with shining eyes. "May I, Mama?"

Elizabeth was looking tense and bewildered. "I tell you what," Christopher said. "I'll talk it over with Mama before she takes you home. I'll see if I can persuade her to say yes."

Conversation became labored again after the refreshments arrived, though both John and Nancy worked very hard to prevent silences and to make it appear that a wedding celebration was indeed in progress. John proposed several toasts. But finally he got resolutely to his feet.

"Nancy," he said, "you look as if you could do with a walk in the park. A long walk. Even a very long walk. And Christina certainly looks as if she can do with the exercise and perhaps even an ice at the end of it all since by that time all the cakes will have been walked off. Put on your bonnets, both of you. I'll be the envy of every other man with a lady for each arm. Elizabeth, I'll deliver Christina safely to her nursery in Grosvenor Square some time this afternoon before escorting Nancy back here. I'll send a servant upstairs when we arrive, Christopher."

By the time he had finished this speech Nancy had her bonnet on and tied and was helping Christina with hers.

"You are not coming, Mama and Papa?" Christina asked.

"Gracious no," John said. "Then there would be only three ladies for two gentlemen. I would not like the odds at all, scamp. Ready?"

"We will be very delighted to have you walk with us, Christina," Nancy said, holding out her hand.

Christina took it, turned to wave the other hand to her parents, and disappeared through the door her uncle was holding open for them. A moment later the door closed and left silence in the room behind it.

Both its occupants drew a deep and slow breath.

28

SHE turned to him resolutely. Anything was better than the awkward silence.

"What did you mean by asking Christina to spend the night here with you and Nancy?" she asked.

"I meant just that," he said. "This is a special day for her too, Elizabeth, and it is true that you will not be home this evening. You could see that she liked the idea. We will set up a truckle bed in Nancy's room for her."

"She belongs at home," she said firmly.

"Precisely," he said. "Home is where her parents are, is it not?"

"I meant Grosvenor Square," she said. "She belongs there."

"I am her father, Elizabeth," he said, "and your husband. I want her here with me tonight."

"Ah." She looked at him angrily. "So you are going to use your authority over me without any delay, are you? I am to discover immediately that you mean to be obeyed?"

He looked at her and said nothing.

"You are going to take my children from me, aren't you?" she said. She could feel panic knotting in her stomach. What had she done? "I'll not allow it, Christopher. I'll fight you."

"It takes two to quarrel," he said. "All I am asking, Elizabeth—or demanding, if you like—is one evening with my daughter. After tomorrow we will be free to announce our marriage quietly to your family and leave for Penhallow. You will be living there with me and our children. We will have equal access to them. There will be no competition."

She had wanted a quarrel, something on which to focus the tension that pulsed between them. But he spoke quietly and reasonably.

"I hope you understand," she said, "that this is to be a marriage of convenience."

"Meaning that it is to be without sex?" he said. "Do you seriously believe that we can live together for the rest of our lives and abstain, Elizabeth?"

She had given him an ultimatum. There were to be no more mistresses or whores in his life. She had also told him that she would try to satisfy all his needs. She waited for him to remind her of those two details, both of which made nonsense of her claim now that she expected a sexless marriage.

And did she? She looked at him and wished that he had not dressed so carefully for their wedding. He looked overwhelmingly attractive. But then he always did, whatever he wore—or did not wear. She had an unbidden image of the beauty of his naked body with which she had grown familiar at Penhallow.

"We have married because of the children," she said.

"Both of whom exist because we had sex together," he said.

There was no answer to that. She looked down at her hands. John had left them alone, taking Nancy and Christina with him and making it clear they would all be gone a long time and would not return without warning.

Christopher stood looking at her, at her pale and fragile beauty. He crossed the room to her and cupped one hand lightly about her cheek, stroking his thumb across it. She did not look up, but she dropped her arms to her sides. She did not pull away. He slid his hand down the side of her neck, across her shoulder, beneath the light muslin fabric of her dress. Her skin was soft and warm, like silk.

She was his wife. They had married in an obscure London church just a couple of hours before. Their signatures were side by side in a register there. His wedding ring was on her finger. He let the wonder and the reality of it envelop him.

"Come," he said to her, and he set a hand at the small of her back and guided her into his bedchamber. He closed the door behind them and locked it.

She heard the key turning in the lock. She looked at

the bed. It was neatly turned down, perhaps for the night, or perhaps just for this occasion—the consummation of their second marriage. She felt a surge of tension to her breasts and a weakness between her thighs. What had she done? She had married her husband, the man she loved, that was what.

He came up behind her, stood against her as his arms came beneath hers to fondle her lightly through her clothing. His hands moved slowly over and around her breasts, pressed into her waist, almost meeting about it, moved over the shapeliness of her hips. They spread over her still-flat abdomen and one moved down until his palm was against the sensitive mound of her femininity and his fingers curled into the heat between her legs.

She set her head back against his shoulder and closed her eyes. Desire for him was beginning to throb in her. She waited for him to turn her and kiss her. She longed to feel the touch of his mouth. She wanted it—she needed it—to take away her loneliness and her doubts. She tried to remember that he was a man she could not love, but she could not marshal her thoughts sufficiently. She needed the reassurance of his mouth.

He would not kiss her. He could not. A kiss was the most intimate of sexual touches despite the fact that in the marriage act he was about to perform he would deeply penetrate her body. Perhaps it was because a kiss was much more than sexual. It was total intimacy, emotional as well as physical. She did not love him, or if she did, she did not want to love him. She wanted this to be a marriage just for the sake of the children, even though it was clear that she was going to submit to granting him his conjugal rights.

She was doing more than submitting. She wanted him. He could feel the heat and tensions of her body. He could see the taut peaks of her breasts through the thin muslin of her dress. It was a physical need only, though. She did not want to want him. He would not kiss her.

But he turned her and unclothed her with deft, experienced hands, his eyes, half closed, devouring her beauty. It seemed an age. Penhallow seemed a lifetime ago. His body was throbbing and on fire for her. He drew her naked body against him, slid his hands down her sides, cupped her buttocks, nestled her against the center of his pain and desire. Her head was thrown back, her eyes closed.

She ached for him, throbbed for him, was ready to explode for him. She resolutely closed her mind to all the reasons she had for fighting her feelings. This was her wedding day and her wedding bed. She settled her back against a cool sheet and a firm mattress as he laid her down on it. Her husband was going to make love to her and she to him. That was all that mattered. She watched him with half-closed eyes as he undressed.

She was wet. She could feel that and hear it as soon as his fingers touched and teased and probed. But she had learned at Penhallow that wetness was not embarrassing but an erotic accompaniment to passion. When he mounted her, he would slide inside without pain to her or impediment to himself. She closed her eyes and spread her arms and legs wide, setting her hands palm down on the mattress.

Come to me, she begged him silently, though she did not open her eyes. *Love me. Kiss me. Please kiss me.*

It was a posture of passive surrender. But he wanted her too fiercely to feel more than a momentary stab of sadness. It would be all right. Once he could explain everything to her, she would come to him with love, not just with desire and wifely submission.

He loved her. He wanted to tell her so as he lowered his body onto hers, her silky, shapely warmth beneath him. He wanted to say the words into her open mouth as he entered her body. He wanted their eyes open and their mouths wide and their tongues at play while he worked in her. But he must not ask too much. He had her physical consent. That must be enough for now.

He positioned himself between her spread thighs and pushed upward into the heat and the wetness of her. He could feel and hear her draw a slow breath and found himself doing the same. He buried his face in her hair and felt her cheek against his ear. He began to move with slow rhythm, listening to the suck and pull of their coupling, knowing that he could not prolong it for nearly as long as he would wish. Her knees were hugging his waist. One of her hands was in his hair, the other spread on his back.

Her eyes were very tightly closed. She was biting her

lower lip. Every muscle in her body was clenched, every particle of her being focused at the point of his deepest and repeated penetration. There was soreness there and resistance and the knowledge of glory to come—but glory not easily won.

She recognized the workings of his body, knew the familiar riding rhythm and the subtle changes that took them upward from one stage of passion to another. Her body knew that soon the relentless thrusting would slow and deepen still further, that there would be a slight pause between thrust and withdrawal and that that pause would set the whirlpool slowly but irreversibly in motion until sensation spread outward from that central point and whirled beyond her control and hurled her into glory.

He had learned her body during those brief weeks at Penhallow. He knew that there came a time after the sheer pleasure of the early stages of the act when her body would stop riding with his rhythm and prepare itself in intense stillness for climax. He had learned how to bring on that climax with slow deep strokes. He had learned that by knowing her body and its rhythms and satisfying its needs he could also satisfy his own. He had learned to anticipate the moment of her climax, and the expectation of it inevitably brought on his own. Peace and joy came from releasing into the relaxed center of her shuddering ecstasy.

And so they came together, tension shattering into momentary oblivion, their sighs of satisfaction, unheard by either, spoken together.

She was lying on her side, her head on his arm, her face against his chest, breathing in the familiar and quite distinctive scent of him. They must have been sleeping, she thought. At least, she seemed to have lost track of time after he had withdrawn from her body and moved to her side. But they had rolled into their usual positions for sleep—usual during their brief first marriage and usual during their even briefer liaison at Penhallow—which were familiar and comfortable. She could very easily slip back into sleep.

She tried to lay claim to reality. Somewhere out there, beyond the window, Christina was walking in the parks with John and Nancy. She could hear the ever-present crowds outside the hotel. They were already gathering, she guessed, to watch the Tsar and his sister leave for the dinner at Carlton House later. Word had it that the Regent was sending his state coach for them. Somewhere out there Manley was about the day's business, as were Martin and her father. Somewhere in here, in her womb, her new child—hers and Christopher's—was growing to birth.

Perhaps he was sorry, she thought. Perhaps if she asked him, he would tell her how bitterly over the years he had regretted his former way of life. And she would be able to tell him how equally bitterly she regretted the cruel punishment she had meted out. Perhaps they would be able to look deeply into each other's eyes as they had always looked at Penhallow.

"Christopher," she whispered, drawing her head back to look into his face. It was without expression. She could see no deeper into his eyes than the blue color. He must have been awake and still and silent for a while.

"Yes?" he said.

"You have consummated the marriage," she said. "You must be satisfied that I am yours again and that you now have more authority over our children than I have. I cannot now refuse to allow Christina to come here this evening, can I?"

She waited to see hurt in his eyes or anger. She hoped to see hurt so that she could rush on into saying what she had planned to say in the first place. His expression did not change.

"Do you want to?" he asked. "Stop her from coming here, I mean?"

She shook her head. "She belongs to you as much as to me," she said. "I think you love her as much as I do." It was a strange thought, but true. She knew it was true.

They looked into each other's eyes, though neither could see beyond the barriers.

"So," she said, "you mean me to be your wife in every sense of the word, Christopher? We are to struggle on with an imperfect marriage?"

"I think we have both grown up enough this time, Elizabeth," he said, "to know that there is no such thing as a perfect marriage. Yes, we are to struggle on. Perhaps it will become easier. Tomorrow, perhaps, I will have something to tell you that will make some difference. But it will never be easy. No marriage ever could be."

"What will you have to tell me?" She tried to see what was behind his eyes.

He shook his head. "Tomorrow," he said.

She wondered when he would get out of bed or when she should. Perhaps John and Nancy would be back soon. She should be home soon to begin the hours of preparation for the evening's entertainment—she felt a deep repugnance at the thought of it. Her wedding day was at an end. She closed her eyes and turned her face in to his shoulder. It had been a strange and imperfect wedding day. But she did not want it to end. She wanted to stay with him. Forever and ever she wanted to stay. She would send a message to Manley, she thought. But she could not be so cruel. She could not jilt him on this of all days.

"I should be going," she said.

"Yes."

But they lay quietly in each other's arms until he lifted her upper leg over his hip, nestled her into position, and mounted her again. It was a sex position they had never used before. It felt good—comfortable, cozy, warmly intimate. She closed her eyes and worked with him, slowly, almost lazily, without passion. It was wonderful. Warm and wonderful marital intimacy. She was very aware, as she had not been the first time, of their child in her womb.

When it was over, they held each other, not disengaging. Neither slept though they did not talk at all.

And then it was time to get up and to dress—in silence. And to feel relief that John and Nancy returned soon after to fill the silence. Relief and embarrassment at Nancy's blushes and John's affectionate grin.

John escorted her home. Her husband did not even kiss her when she left, though John kissed Nancy.

The wedding day was over. There was a reception and a presentation to the queen to prepare for.

An hour later Christopher and John were on their way to keep their appointment with Powers. Christopher tried to pretend that the whole of his future happiness might not rest on what Powers had to say—if he was in his office this time.

But he was. It seemed that his clerk had convinced him that they were two wealthy and fashionable gentlemen intending to use his services. He had left instructions that they were to be shown in to his inner sanctum as soon as they arrived, and he rose importantly to greet them, a large and greasy-looking man with glistening bald head and a gold tooth that gleamed when he smiled.

"Colonel Lord Aston and the Earl of Trevelyan?" he repeated after John had presented them. "Have a seat, do, my lords. How may I be of service to you?" His eyes darted from one to the other. Their names seemed to mean nothing to him.

"We need information about a past client of yours," Christopher said.

"Ah, my lord." Mr. Powers held up a ringed hand, palm out. "I am sure you understand that all business I conduct is entirely confidential."

"We are prepared to pay a sizable fee," John said.

Mr. Powers looked shrewdly at him. "Well, I tell you what, my lord," he said. "You tell me what the problem is and what you need to know, and I will decide what I can tell you without violating a client's trust. Is that agreeable?"

"You paid the rent on the rooms occupied by a Mrs. Lucy Fenwick," Christopher said, "for several months seven years ago. You also arranged passage for her and her daughter to America." He was guessing on the latter point. He kept his eyes steadily on Mr. Powers, but the man was experienced enough at his job to show nothing but a polite interest.

"Seven years ago, my lord," he said, shaking his head slowly. "It is a long time. I conduct such business for many clients. It is impossible to recall such trivial and routine matters from so long ago."

"I believe this must have been a memorable piece of business," Christopher said. "The lady was involved in a divorce case. She was the other woman, so to speak."

"Dear me," Mr. Powers said. "I did hear of that divorce, my lord. The Duke of Chicheley's daughter was the aggrieved wife, I believe? I had nothing whatever to do with that case, though. I would be sure to remember that."

"There are those who can identify you as the man who paid the rent," Christopher said.

Mr. Powers shrugged.

"I wonder how much your client paid you," John said. "I wonder what double that figure would amount to. Not to a sum that would be beyond the means of Lord Trevelyan and myself, I would wager, Mr. Powers."

"I wish I could help you, my lord," Mr. Powers said. "As a businessman of course I am interested in making money. But I have nothing I am able to tell you."

It was as he had feared, Christopher thought. The man was guilty as sin. But fear was stronger in him than greed. Fear of Martin, perhaps? Fear of Chicheley if the truth came out and his part in it? Fear of scandal and the loss of his living?

"Name your price," John said quietly. "Lord Trevelyan and I will undertake not to divulge the source of our information."

"On the contrary," Christopher said, "I believe it is in the interest of all honest citizens who are in search of an equally honest man of business to know that in coming to you, sir, they would be dealing with a man who helps underage clients conduct shady dealings."

For the first time Mr. Powers's calm was shaken. "I did not know he was underage, my lord," he said. "I swear it. He looked older."

"And paid well," Christopher said. "And so you paid the rent and the sizable salary of a woman you doubtless believed to be the doxy of a minor."

"I did not, my lord," Mr. Powers said, running one finger beneath the neck of his cravat. "He assured me that she was a destitute relative for whose well-being he felt responsible."

"I suppose," Christopher said, "that we can allow the public to judge the truth of your story for themselves. It is possible, I suppose, that an eighteen-year-old boy would be so affected with concern for a destitute relative that he would pay both her and you a small fortune for her upkeep and then pay her passage to America. People might believe it is true—unless his stepbrother saw fit to deny the existence of such a relative, of course." He indicated John.

"I acted in good faith, my lord," Mr. Powers said.

"People can sometimes be generous in their judgment of others," Christopher said, "when presented with the facts. Perhaps they will be generous with you, sir. Perhaps your business will not be affected."

Mr. Powers turned one of the rings imbedded on his fingers. He licked his lips. "If I can have your word as gentlemen, my lords," he said, "that the source of your information will never be known to more than the two of you, perhaps I can see fit to whisper a name to you. Perhaps for five hundred guineas? I cannot violate a sacred trust for less." He looked at John.

Christopher got to his feet and set ten guineas on the table before laying his hand flat on top of them. "Ten rather than five hundred," he said. "Handsome payment for the use of fifteen minutes of your time, I believe, sir. The name, if you please?"

"I cannot—" Mr. Powers began.

"The name?"

Mr. Powers's eyes darted from one to the other of them and down to the guineas visible beneath Christopher's hand. "Mr. Martin Honywood," he said, "as you knew all along, my lord."

Christopher raised his hand. "As I knew all along," he said. "Thank you for your time and information, Mr. Powers. John?"

They were standing on the pavement outside the office one minute later.

"Devil take it!" John said. "I was quite prepared to hand over the five hundred guineas and think we had got off lightly. Is this how you conducted business in Canada?"

"One learns something of human nature and economy," Christopher said. "For ten more guineas he will give us something in writing if it becomes necessary—and think that he has got off lightly."

"It is beyond doubt now, isn't it?," John said. "Martin is a consummate villain. Will you kill him or will I? I beg for the first chance." His usual light humor had completely deserted him. Christopher guessed that the grim man before him was the lieutenant-colonel his men knew during battle.

"We will deal with him tonight," Christopher said. "You are still ready to follow my plan?"

"Now more than ever," John said. "Especially since the only possible danger will be to the two of us. Christina will be safe with Nancy at the Pulteney."

"And Elizabeth will not be frightened when she finds her gone," Christopher said. "I got her to agree to allow Christina to spend the night with Nancy and me. Provided Christina can keep secrets, Martin should be none the wiser."

"Good," John said grimly as they got into their waiting carriage. "We can decide later who is to kill him, Christopher. Or perhaps we can devise a way to do it together."

"I just want to see him stripped of his smile and his charm," Christopher said. "I want to see Elizabeth finally free of his clutches. And I want to see him squirm. Oh, yes, I want to see that too."

29

MARTIN's plans were all proceeding far more smoothly than he had anticipated. Both Trevelyan and Poole were jumping like puppets on a string. And now Christina, the one link in the chain he had worried most about, was proving surprisingly docile. As soon as he had suggested to her that she might enjoy a night at the Pulteney with her new acquaintances there, she had run to pack a small bag. He had not even needed the arsenal of persuasions with which he had come prepared. She had seemed not to notice as they left the nursery that her nurse was already nodding in her chair, the cup of tea Martin had brought her empty on a table beside her.

When they reached Christopher's suite at the Pulteney, Martin knocked on the door and waited. Christina was bouncing at his side as if she were expecting the greatest adventure of her life. Perhaps that was what she was about to get, Martin thought, though not in the way she expected.

Lady Nancy's maid opened the door—the little slut he had had at Penhallow. Her eyes widened. Christina darted past her into the sitting room and Martin could hear her excited child's voice.

"Here I am!" she shrieked. "I am going to stay all night. Where shall I put my bag? Has the Tsar left yet? I want to see him getting into the coach. There is ever such a big crowd outside. Uncle Martin could hardly get past."

Trevelyan's voice answered her, pitched low.

By the time Martin entered the sitting room, Christopher was there alone, looking tense and excited. "I have sent Christina into the other room," he said, gesturing with one hand. "She is with Nancy. I have ordered the carriage for half an hour's time. By then the crowds outside should have dispersed. Elizabeth did not see you or suspect anything, Martin?''

''No,'' Martin said, allowing himself to look agitated and unhappy. ''But devil take it, Trevelyan, I had a hard time going through with it. She is going to be distraught. Promise me that you will take care of Christina on the way to Devonshire? I will never forgive myself if anything happens to her.''

''She is my daughter,'' Christopher said. ''I will guard her with my life. You are sure Elizabeth will follow, Martin? You think I will be able to win her back this way?''

Martin nodded slowly. ''She will be angry and tearful,'' he said. ''But she will see that you did it out of love, Trevelyan. She will melt. I know Lizzie. Do you have the note ready?''

Christopher reached into an inner pocket and drew out a folded piece of paper. ''It was the most difficult letter of my life to write,'' he said. ''I wanted to pour out all my feelings, but I forced myself to keep it terse. Time enough for the feelings later.'' He smiled, but the expression was more grimace than smile.

Martin took the note and patted Christopher reassuringly on the shoulder. ''It will all work out, you will see,'' he said. ''A few more days and you will be able to start living happily ever after. I'll speak up in your defense as I have always done. But Lizzie will not need my words, only the urgings of her own heart.''

Christopher stretched out his right hand. ''Well,'' he said, ''it is a gamble, Martin. We both know that. It may not work. But at least I'll always know that you did your best to make things turn out well.''

Martin clasped his hand firmly. He almost laughed. If only Trevelyan knew the ambiguity of his own words, he thought. ''I'll not keep you,'' he said. ''You must have last-minute preparations to make. Good luck!''

''Thank you, Martin,'' Christopher said.

Martin checked Elizabeth's room as soon as he returned to Grosvenor Square. She had left for Carlton House already. So had John. Christina's nurse was snoring in her chair in the nursery. A fairly light blow to the side of her head ensured that she would not wake up for a while longer. The duke, fortunately, was not going to Carlton House, having declared that it would be too great a circus for his tastes. Martin quickly read the note Christopher had given him and smiled with satisfaction.

The Duke of Chicheley was in his private sitting room, his feet resting on a stool, a book open on his lap when Martin burst in on him after only the merest courtesy of a knock.

"Good God, Papa," he said, "thank heaven you are here. What are we going to do? He has made off with Christina, the scoundrel, and left her nurse half dead from a blow to the head. It might not have been discovered until morning if I had not gone into Lizzie's dressing room to see if she had left yet and found this note propped on the washstand. Lord!" Martin clutched his head with both hands. "It is all my fault. I thought the lie would be for the best. I should have known that only the truth will ever do."

"Silence!" the duke ordered, setting his book down beside him. "Stop the babbling, Martin, and explain yourself like a man."

"I'm sorry." Martin drew a few steadying breaths. "It was Trevelyan who kidnapped Lizzie from Hanover Square, Papa. He took her to Penhallow and kept her there and ravished her. When I brought her back to London I persuaded her to tell a different story, God help me. I thought she would be ruined and her chances of marrying Poole lost if the truth were known. I warned Trevelyan not to try to follow her to London, but he found out about Christina and came here in defiance of me. I have kept my mouth shut since, thinking that no harm could come to Lizzie in such a public setting. And once she was married, I thought, she would be safe from Trevelyan at last."

The duke had set his feet on the floor and was gripping the arms of his chair.

"But Christina was not safe," Martin said. "She has gone, Papa. I ran up to the nursery after finding the note in Lizzie's dressing room and before running down here." He handed the note to the duke and stood silently while it was being read.

"He cannot live without his daughter," the duke said, still staring down at the note. "He is taking her to Penhallow. If Elizabeth wants to see her again, then she must go there too. I'll see him swing for this."

Martin swallowed. "He is probably doing it out of a mistaken sense of love, Papa," he said.

"Silence!" the duke thundered again. "Enough of your excuses for everyone, Martin. It is time you grew up and learned some of the harsher realities of human nature. The man is a villain. The note has appeared since Elizabeth left for Carlton House. That cannot be long ago. He can't have gone far with her. I'll have him overtaken almost before he is clear of London. Pull the bell rope. What are you waiting for, you fool?"

"You are going to send men after them?" Martin said. "I think that's a good idea, Papa. We can have Christina back in her nursery before Lizzie even knows she is gone. I'll go too. There must be someone to bring the poor little child home."

"Yes, go," the duke said. "I'll have my men bring Trevelyan back here and then he will be sorry that he was born. I'll watch him swing, Martin. You may be too soft for the sight, but I am not."

Six of the duke's stoutest servants, in addition to Macklin, accompanied Martin half an hour later on his pursuit of Christopher's carriage along the road west.

Once it had left the confines of the city, the carriage proceeded at a pace only a little faster than a snail might take. Antoine was at the ribbons. Christopher, seated alone inside, wondered how far he would travel before turning back. But he did not think he could have guessed wrongly about what Martin's next move would be. Pursuit surely could not be far behind. He had not seen John since leaving the Pulteney, but he trusted that a good cavalryman would be able to keep out of sight beside the road without losing the carriage. How could anyone lose such a slow-moving carriage even if he tried?

Christopher was not given long to think. He did not hear the horses come galloping up behind the carriage, but the suddenly increased speed of the vehicle alerted him to the fact that they were being pursued at last. And then, just as the sounds of pursuit became audible even above the noise of his own horses and the carriage wheels, there was a single shot.

Christ! Christopher reached for the pistol in its holster against the side of the carriage. He had counted on there being no gunfire since Martin and the other pursuers would believe that Christina was in the carriage with him. He could hear Antoine swearing vociferously from the box and was relieved to know that at least he had not been killed. The carriage drew to a halt and one of the doors was thrown open.

"Out!" a harsh voice said—it was not Martin's. "Leave the child inside. Throw any weapons you have to the ground. There are eight of us. We all have guns pointed at the doorway."

Christopher tossed out the pistol and drew a deep breath. This was the unknown moment. Would they gun him down once there seemed no danger of hitting Christina too? He jumped down into the roadway.

"Put your hands above your head, Trevelyan," Martin said. "I have already taught your coachman a lesson for not stopping as soon as he was ordered to do so."

Antoine was still swearing in French. He was holding his left arm, but it did not seem to be immobile. Christopher guessed that it had only been grazed.

"What is this all about?" Christopher asked, looking politely about him.

"It is about the kidnapping of a child," Martin said. "The Duke of Chicheley's granddaughter and my stepsister's daughter."

"And mine," Christopher said, raising his eyebrows.

Martin pointed his gun at him like an accusing finger. "No longer yours, Trevelyan," he said. "My stepsister divorced you well over six years ago. You will answer for this crime in a court of law. These men will take you back to London to face the duke. I shall take Christina back to her mother."

Christopher frowned in incomprehension. "You are under the impression that my daughter is in the carriage?" he asked. "What a strange time of day it would be to take a child for a drive. I would imagine that she is fast asleep in her bed at the Pulteney."

"At the Pulteney?" It was Martin's turn to frown. Then he nodded sharply at one of the servants. "Check the inside of the carriage, Macklin. Stand aside, Trevelyan."

Christopher stood obligingly aside. Macklin looked and shook his head. "Empty, sir," he said.

Christopher raised his eyebrows again.

"Ah," Martin said. "So you thought to outwit us, Trevelyan? We will fetch her from the Pulteney. It is as much kidnapping to keep her there as to take her in your carriage to Penhallow, as your cowardly note to my stepsister indicated was your intention."

"My daughter will stay where she is," Christopher said. "She is there at my invitation and under my protection. And with my wife's full knowledge and consent."

Martin sneered. "That will be for a magistrate to decide," he said. "This is the end, Trevelyan. You have gone too far this time." His eyes sparked noticeably even in the darkness. "And that will be the last time you will refer to my stepsister as your wife if you know what is good for you."

"The Countess of Trevelyan is my wife," Christopher said. "She became both this morning, Martin, when she married me. John witnessed the marriage."

"Seize him!" Martin told the gawking servants. "Enough of this. I have to go rescue my niece."

"I did indeed," John's voice said from the darkness beyond the carriage and the circle of men. "So you see, Martin and anyone else here present who is interested, Lord Trevelyan has every right to have his daughter at the Pulteney or even in this carriage on the way to Penhallow, with or without his wife's consent. In actual fact, he has that consent."

Martin whirled about and stared at John, who was sitting casually on his horse, smiling.

"Put the guns away," John told his father's servants. "This scene looks like a well-contrived farce and would be vastly entertaining to anyone else who happened along. There has been an embarrassing misunderstanding obviously. Lord Trevelyan is out for a leisurely drive just as I am out for a ride. Lady Christina Atwell is safe with her aunt at the Pulteney and will not be disturbed tonight. You may all return to Grosvenor Square."

A few of the servants looked somewhat dubious, but the word of Viscount Aston meant almost as much to them as that of the Duke of Chicheley and certainly more than Martin's. Soon all seven of them were trotting back in the direction of London.

"I see," Martin said, "that you have been making a pretty fool of my stepfather and me, Trevelyan. He left a note in Lizzie's room, John, to say that he was taking Christina. Naturally enough, since no one saw fit to inform either of us of the wedding this morning, we assumed that it was kidnapping that was taking place. Papa was frantic, as you might imagine. I offered to come after Trevelyan. Why was I at least not informed of the wedding? Lizzie must have known that I would be delighted."

"Martin," John said, his smile gone, "it will not do. Not any longer."

"I would not have tried to stop her," Martin said. "She knows that I did not support Papa's idea of divorce in the first place."

"It will not do," John said a little more firmly. "Not any longer, Martin."

Martin looked at him uncertainly.

"You hired the woman who claimed to be my mistress and mother of my child," Christopher said, "and sent her safely off to America as soon as the divorce was accomplished. You paid Rhodes to say that he had seen me with that poor whore who died. You spread the quite erroneous story that I was the one who stripped Morrison of his fortune at a card game—after the one witness in London had left for Ireland. You deliberately and ruthlessly broke up my marriage, Martin."

"How preposterous!" Martin said. He turned to John. "You see what he is like?"

"We have proof in all three cases," John said. "You beat and raped Nancy at Kingston Park, Martin. You made her life a living hell and ruined my chances of happiness with her."

"If she says that, she lies," Martin said, flaring. "She was as eager as I was. More eager. I was only a boy. I did not know how to fend off her advances."

"And you beat and raped my sister's maid at Penhallow a few weeks ago," Christopher said.

"A maid," Martin said with some contempt. "A slut who begged and panted for it. She got what she asked for."

"As I 'ope you will, m'sieur," the forgotten Antoine said from the box of the coach.

"And now you have been scheming," Christopher said, "to make sure that Elizabeth and I never get back together again. Doubtless you have some plan to make sure that she does not marry Poole either."

"You are a villain, Martin," John said, his voice quite dispassionate. "You deserve to die."

Martin laughed rather nervously. "Can I be blamed for wanting to protect my sister from hurt and a lifetime of misery?" he asked. "You lust after her, Trevelyan, as does Poole and as do a thousand other men, just because she has been blessed with beauty. You don't love her. No one loves her. Only me. I have loved her all my life and will love her until my dying day. You went off to Canada as soon as there was a little trouble. You went off to Spain to fight and perhaps to die, John. You had your own life to live when Lizzie was suffering. Who stayed with her and loved her back to strength? I stayed. I did."

"She would not have been suffering if you had not broken her heart," Christopher said. "She was a new and young bride, Martin, very much in love with her bridegroom. Until your satanic plot ruined it all."

"Why?" John asked. "That is what I cannot understand, Martin. If you loved her, why not win her for yourself? Would she not have you in that way? Could she see you only as a brother?"

Martin's voice was shaking when he answered. "Only someone with a filthy mind would even suggest that I try to defile Lizzie," he said. "My love for her is pure. The love of a brother for a sister. But I would expect you to suggest that there is more. Living among soldiers has coarsened you, John."

"What you have for her is an obsession!" Christopher said.

Martin whirled to face him, dismounted quickly from his horse, and stepped close so that his face was almost against Christopher's. "What I feel for her is love!" he said fiercely. "An emotion you would not understand, Trevelyan. You would not be able to love and keep your love pure and in restraint, would you? I love her. I loved her as a child and a young boy. I loved her as a lover briefly until my mother died when we were sixteen and told me the truth." He stopped abruptly.

"The truth?" John prompted.

Martin was crying. Christopher watched in mingled fascination and embarrassment and disgust as his face contorted and tears coursed their way down his cheeks. "No one knew but her," he said between sobs. "Why did she have to burden me with it on her deathbed? I hate her for doing so. I'll hate her to all eternity. Even he did not know. Chicheley is my father. My mother was his doxy when they were both still married to other people. He is my father, damn him to hell."

There was silence for a few moments except for the sounds of his racking sobs.

"Lizzie is my sister," Martin said after a while. "We have the same father." He tried to laugh. "That is why we look alike. The old lecher was lying with my mother and his lawful wife both. I could no longer think of being Lizzie's lover after my mother had told me, you see. I have loved her in purity ever since. No one can love as I have loved. I have sacrificed everything for her. No one else can say that. I am the only one who will be willing to stay with her until death and give up everything else that might make life pleasurable in order to protect her and keep her safe from harm."

"And if there is no harm to protect her from," Christopher said quietly into the silence that followed Martin's impassioned words, "then harm must be created. Tonight she was to be made frantic for Christina's safety in order that she would turn against me and toward you. Your mind is sick, Martin."

"In order to stay pure for Elizabeth," John said, "you have to work off your fury against your mother by beating other women, Martin, and your sexual frustrations by raping. And your guilt? Do you feel guilt?"

Martin turned to glare at him. John had also dismounted and was standing quietly beside his horse. "There are whip marks on my back," Martin said viciously. "I have suffered too. I constantly suffer. What would you do, John, if you were to find suddenly that the woman you love was your sister? What if Lady Nancy Atwell were your sister? But even then you would not understand. You have not been with Lady Nancy every moment since the cradle. You don't know what real love is."

"God!" John said. "You are a pathetic worm, Martin.

And the worst part of it is that I feel sorry for you. I wish I had run my sword through you before you said a word tonight, or I wish I had thrashed you within an inch of your life. I owe Nancy one or the other. But now I cannot find the energy to do either."

"I'll be calling at Grosvenor Square tomorrow," Christopher said. "Elizabeth and I have our marriage to announce. Perhaps your father will not even be displeased once he knows the truth about our first marriage. If I were you, Martin, I would tell him the full truth before being forced to it. I should kill you and will perhaps always regret that I did not, but I find myself too much of a civilized being to do so. Since your father decided the fate of my marriage, perhaps it is fitting that he decide your fate too."

"Perhaps you would be well advised to throw yourself on Papa's mercy," John said. "God in heaven!" He stared at Martin before swinging back up into his saddle. "You are my brother. We share common blood. Are you coming, Christopher?"

"Yes," Christopher said but his eyes were still on Martin. "Stay away from my wife from this moment on. If you come near her or try to communicate with her or influence her in any way, I will kill you. That is a promise. Do you understand?"

Martin did not answer. But Christopher was appalled to see two more tears trickled down his brother-in-law's cheeks.

Christopher strode over to the spare horse John had brought with him, eager suddenly to be gone from there, to be away from the oppressive atmosphere of the dark stretch of road where he had listened to such a dark story.

"Antoine," he called, swinging himself up into the saddle, "you can drive the carriage back to the Pulteney. Let's go, John."

They rode side by side in silence for a while.

"What are we doing?" John asked at last, his voice subdued. "Why are we riding back home and leaving that villain alive and unmarked back there? Good God, Christopher, we did not even throw one punch at him between us."

"He is sick," Christopher said. "I am not making excuses for him. There are no excuses for his behavior.

But by the time he had finished his story there was not enough raw fury left in either of us to enable us to mete out punishment."

But he could no longer focus his mind on what they had just left behind them. Something else was weighing on it. "It can't be very late, can it?" he said. "Is dinner over at Carlton House yet, do you suppose? How much time before the presentations to the queen begin? They will go on for hours probably. Elizabeth is there with Poole, John. I let my wife go there with another man. On our wedding day. Have I quite taken leave of my senses?"

"Probably," John said. "It seems to be the order of the day."

"I'm going there," Christopher said resolutely. "I accepted my invitation before I knew that all this would keep me from going. I want to see her. I want to know that she is safe. Is it selfish of me to want to go when I promised to give her this one last evening with Poole?"

"Utterly selfish," John said. "If I were in your shoes, I would not be able to resist going."

"You wouldn't?"

"No way on this earth," John said.

"Can that horse of yours gallop?" Christopher asked. "If not, I shall have to leave you behind. I have a very tonnish affair to get ready for—all within the hour."

Martin cursed and punched one fist sideways against a panel of the carriage. Not satisfied, he turned and kicked the paneling and swished his riding whip viciously against it. Only then did he become aware of the silent witness of his impotent rage and humiliation.

"You!" he said through his teeth, pointing upward to the box of the carriage. "You dared to speak insolently to me a few minutes ago? You dare to sit there now, watching me? You need a lesson in manners, you French bastard." He swished his whip viciously at Antoine.

Antoine jumped down from the box, and by the time he landed in the roadway in front of Martin, there was a knife in his right hand. The whip leaped out at him again.

"Your brothers 'ave pity on you, m'sieur," Antoine said, "because you cry the real tears like a baby, non? And so they leave you alive to 'urt people who are weaker than yourself, mostly women, oui? I am glad they 'ave the pity. They leave you to Antoine."

Martin eyed the knife. "You are a savage from the wilderness," he said contemptuously. "Trevelyan should be shot for bringing you to a civilized country."

"Sacré coeur!" Antoine said. "In the wilderness, m'sieur, we do not savage 'elpless and innocent women. We kill those who do."

Martin laughed. "In England," he said, "murderers hang by the neck until they choke to death if they are not fortunate enough to break their necks on the drop. And there are about to be witnesses to your crime. Get this carriage turned around and on its way back to London and I may consider not bringing charges of assault against you."

Antoine grinned as a carriage approached, traveling in the direction of London. Its coachman drew it to a stop a short distance away and yelled at the two men to clear the road. A lady's head appeared out of one of the windows. She called to her coachman to ask what was the cause of the delay. She sounded rather fearful, as if she suspected that the scene ahead of her was a highwayman in action.

"Ah, but, m'sieur," Antoine said, taking a step closer to Martin, "I am pleased to 'ave the witnesses. I would not 'ave either my master or the colonel blamed for what Antoine Bouchard 'as done. I do this, not for all your evils known and unknown, but for one particular evil. You die for Winnie, Monsieur 'Onywood."

The knife went in skillfully beneath Martin's ribs, angled upward until the point penetrated his heart, and was withdrawn again. The other coachman was still yelling out in annoyance and the lady was still making fearful inquiries as Martin looked at Antoine, surprise on his face, and a trickle of blood flowed black in the darkness of the night from one corner of his mouth, and he fell forward, dead, on his face.

Antoine held up the knife with its darkened blade until the other coachman's tone changed and he babbled with fear. Then the knife disappeared and Antoine vaulted back up to his seat on the box, turned the carriage with some difficulty in the roadway, and made off back in the direction of London.

He had maybe a few hours, he reckoned. Maybe until morning. Maybe.

30

ELIZABETH and Lord Poole dined with acquaintances and arrived early at Carlton House as most of the other guests seemed to be doing. There was a general fear of being late though everyone knew very well that the state dinner would run at least an hour later than planned and that far more time than expected would then elapse before the queen was seated in the throne room and ready to nod graciously to her subjects as their names were announced and they filed respectfully past her throne.

They were at least an hour and a half early, Elizabeth estimated, looking about her in awe at the entrance hall, which appeared massive with its open screen of Ionic columns on every side and its high coffered ceiling. One felt dwarfed, overwhelmed. One felt like a subject approaching one's monarch.

They were gradually ushered, along with everyone else, through an octagonal room and two anterooms into the antechamber to the throne room. It was already crowded with gorgeously clad men and women. She had felt overdressed until she arrived, Elizabeth thought. She normally did not wear satin, but it seemed that no other fabric would do for a presentation to the queen. And she certainly did not like the fashion of wearing high plumes in her hair. But tonight she wore them as did all the other ladies present.

The antechamber was a large and splendid apartment. But then she had heard that it had once been the throne room itself until the Regent had decided that an even larger and more imposing room was needed for the purpose. The walls, and even the large mirrors in each wall, were draped with gold-trimmed light blue velvet hangings. A magnificent chandelier hung from the center of the gilded ceiling. Large portraits of members of the royal family were mounted in gilded frames on the walls.

She was nervous, Elizabeth realized in some surprise. Her heart was beating uncomfortably and she felt breathless. How foolish of her! Yet seven years had passed since her first presentation to the queen at her come-out. She could remember the terror of that occasion. She turned to Lord Poole for reassurance.

But he was not at her side. He was talking with a Whig friend of his, a man whom Elizabeth disliked for no reason that she could ever articulate. It was very warm in the room, she thought as Lord Poole returned to her and they began to mingle with the crowds. He was not in a good mood. He had been rather cold and remote all evening. She smiled at him, determined that for this evening at least there should be no rumor of an estrangement between them. Tomorrow she would find a way of telling him the truth in private. She hated the thought of the embarrassment and perhaps even pain she would cause him.

The wait was quite as long as Elizabeth had guessed it would be, and it seemed twice as long as that. The room grew hotter and hotter—she had heard that heat was a characteristic of all the Regent's residences. The scarcity of chairs forced the vast majority of those in the room to remain standing. No refreshments were served.

And surely, Elizabeth thought as time went on, she and Manley were becoming more and more the focus of attention. Surely she must be imagining it, she thought at first. How foolish and conceited of her to believe that so many members of the beau monde were looking at her and talking about her. And if they were, then they were really looking at Manley and remarking on his behavior of the evening before. She guessed there would be some who would admire him and others who would censure him.

But it was not her imagination. And it was not Manley who was taking their attention. When he was called away for a few minutes by another acquaintance and she stayed where she was, attention did not drift with him but stayed on her.

Of course she was imagining things! She looked deliberately to one side, to a large group of elderly people.

Several of them let their eyes move casually away from her as if they had merely been engaged in a visual survey of the room's inhabitants. When she looked the other way, the same thing happened except that one dowager continued to look directly at her with haughty disapproval.

Manley could not have been gone from her side for longer than a minute at the most. But suddenly she felt very alone and very exposed to view. She smiled at a lady of her acquaintance who was standing with a group close by and took one step closer. She had a remark on her lips ready to deliver. But the lady turned her back and addressed the group herself. Because she had not seen Elizabeth or realized her intention of joining the group? Or because she had intended the genteel snub?

Elizabeth began to feel hotter.

When Manley rejoined her, his manner was colder and stiffer than before. He stood farther back from her than he had before. He was tight-lipped.

"What is it?" she asked him.

"Nothing." His voice was icy, abrupt.

"Nothing?" She frowned. "Manley—"

"This is neither the time nor the place to discuss it," he said. "My God, everyone knows. We are the center of attention. May you rot in hell for this, Elizabeth."

"What—?" She felt as if she had stepped into some nightmare. Had news of her wedding leaked out? And was Manley now the laughingstock? *Oh, please, God, no,* she prayed silently. *Please don't let him be hurt and humiliated in this way.*

Her question could not be completed. At long last and yet quite suddenly the great doors into the throne room were thrown back and a buzz of heightened excitement in the antechamber faded to a hush. The state dinner was over, the Regent and all his illustrious guests were beyond the doorway, and the queen was seated formally on the throne ready to receive the homage of her subjects. The people waiting in the antechamber began to take their prearranged places.

Christina was fast asleep in Nancy's room despite her excited claim when she arrived that she was going to stay awake all night. Nancy was sitting quietly reading in the sitting room. At least, she had a book open on her lap. In fact she was thinking and dreaming. Christopher had told her everything while he was getting ready hurriedly to go to Carlton House.

Her thoughts were interrupted by the sound of a knock on the door. Her heart leaped as Winnie opened the door and she recognized the voice of the man who was outside. A moment later she was in John's arms and they were hugging each other wordlessly. Winnie had disappeared.

"My love," John was saying. "I am so sorry. Forgive me. I could not kill him for you. Evil and pathetic as he was, Nancy, he was a man and my brother. At least that is how I saw him at the time. I could not kill the man who committed such ugliness against you."

She lifted her face to kiss him. "I am so glad you did not," she said. "Leave him to your father and his own conscience, John. Christopher thinks perhaps he will go away, leave the country. It will perhaps be the best solution."

"I could not kill him," he said. "I have killed dozens of men, Nancy, without a qualm of conscience."

"Killing in battle is not like killing your brother in cold blood," she said. "Oh, John, he is your half brother. Christopher told me."

He hugged her to him again until she led him to a sofa, where they sat, his arm about her, her head on his shoulder, and enjoyed peace and quietness and long minutes of comfortable silence.

"It's over," she said at last. "The past is over and there are only the present and the future to be concerned with. I feel lightheaded, John, as if a great burden had been lifted from my shoulders."

"I thought I had failed you," he said.

She smiled and touched his lips with the fingers of one hand. "I love you so much," she said. "You cannot imagine what a happy ending this is for me, John."

He tightened his arm about her and kissed her.

Winnie had not been able to eavesdrop on the conversation between her mistress and Christopher. And she had not been able to bring herself to ask Nancy. She longed to know what had happened. She had sagged with relief when Antoine had finally come back almost an hour after Christopher.

Now her curiosity could not be quelled any longer. After letting John in, she knocked timidly on the door of the little room next to Christopher's dressing room, where Antoine slept. The door opened immediately. He was dressed for the outdoors. There was a bundle on the bed behind him. Winnie knew immediately.

"You are leaving," she said, her voice a whisper.

"Yes, ma chère," he said. There was a look in his eyes that she had not seen there before, but it softened as he gazed at her. "The time 'as come. There is a ship sailing on tonight's tide. I found that out this morning. It is time for me to go."

"You found out in case you needed to leave in a hurry tonight," Winnie said, looking earnestly at him. "And you do need to. Did you kill him?"

Antoine cupped one hand about her cheek. "You must not worry about 'im any longer, ma petite," he said. " 'E will not 'arm you anymore."

"You killed him," she said. "I am glad it was you and not one of them. I wanted it to be you. Yes, you must leave. They will hang you if they catch you, Mr. Bouchard. You must hurry." Her manner was very calm and matter-of-fact.

He cupped his other hand about her other cheek. "Remember," he said, "that you are white and clean and innocent as a little lamb, Winnie. Remember that, mon amour."

"Yes," she said, lifting a hand to set over one of his. "You have made me clean again, Mr. Bouchard. And you have killed him and put yourself in grave danger because of me. And I know what those words mean. I asked lady Nancy. They mean 'my love.' "

Antoine kissed her lightly on the forehead and turned to pick up his bundle.

"Are they just words like the other ones you use?" Winnie asked. "I can smile at you and say good-bye as I promised. I can let you go and set you free. But if by any chance you mean those words, Mr. Bouchard, I can be ready to go with you in five minutes."

"Winnie." He turned back to her. "You do not know what it is like to live in a foreign country, not even knowing the language. You do not know of the 'ardships of living in my country. All would be strange to you, my little one, and you would soon be 'omesick, non?"

"*You* would not be strange," she said. "And you are all the home I will ever long for, Mr. Bouchard. Now and for the rest of my life even if I do not see you again after tonight. I will be homesick here in England. Just say the word—yes or no. But quickly. You need to be gone."

"Yes, mon amour," he said. "I need to be gone. Two people saw me plunge the knife into 'is black 'eart. And saw the carriage—the Earl of Trevelyan's carriage. Come then, ma petite, if you will marry a murderer. Antoine will spend 'is life loving and protecting you from 'arm."

"And I'll spend mine making you comfortable," Winnie said, smiling radiantly and turning to race from the room.

"Five minutes, ma petite," Antoine said urgently. "No longer."

"Four minutes," she said. "Three, Mr. Bouchard."

Four minutes later they were hurrying down the stairs of the Pulteney, Antoine with two cloth bundles thrown over one shoulder. They were well over an hour ahead of pursuit.

Christopher was looked at askance for arriving so late at Carlton House. The liveried servant who led the way toward the throne room showed him all the contemptuous courtesy that many servants were so expert at.

And yet, Christopher discovered when he had finally been abandoned to his own devices in the doorway of the antechamber to the throne room, the presentations to the queen had barely begun. The doors into the inner sanctum were open, and people were beginning to file through, but the antechamber itself still swarmed with people.

And Elizabeth was still there, he saw, hanging back so that she would not see him. He should not have come, he thought immediately. She would be annoyed to see him there. She would think that he did not trust her. But he had wanted to see her more than anything in the world. And there had been almost a compulsive need to see her, as if even now she was not safe from all harm.

She was with Poole close to the door into the throne room. But she was looking pale and bewildered. And he was looking stiff and furious. Alarm bells sounded in Christopher's mind. Something was wrong. She had not after all been able to resist telling him the truth. Or more likely he had discovered it for himself somehow. They were not about to have a public row, were they?

And then someone touched his sleeve. He nodded politely at Lord Hardinge, husband of one of Nancy's newly formed friends. But the man had not approached him merely to greet him.

"A word with you, Trevelyan," he said, and they stepped back, just beyond the doorway into the antechamber.

Christopher raised his eyebrows.

"I saw you arrive," Lord Hardinge said. "You may wish to turn tail and make your way back the way you came, old chap. The cat is out of the bag."

Poor Elizabeth, Christopher thought. Her efforts to save Poole from public humiliation were about to explode in her face. Someone had heard wedding bells.

"Someone—I have no idea who—has circulated the rumor that you were the masked rider who kidnapped Lady Elizabeth from her wedding to Poole a while ago," Lord Hardinge said. "And that the two of you spent a few weeks, er, cohabiting. I don't know if there is any truth in the story, old chap, but there does not need to be in a situation like this. And Landsdowne has just been idiot enough to whisper the story in Poole's ear. A nasty situation, Trevelyan. I would make off with all haste if I were you."

Christ! It was far worse than he had thought from that one glance he had had of them. And somehow, Christopher thought as he nodded a curt thanks to Lord Hardinge and turned to stride into the antechamber rather than away from it, Martin was responsible for this. What better way to stop Elizabeth from marrying Poole and to ensure that she would want to leave London behind her for a long time to come?

Elizabeth and Lord Poole had reached the open doorway by the time Christopher had elbowed his way toward them. A gorgeously uniformed court official had turned toward them for their names so that he could lead them forward to the throne and present them to the queen. But Lord Poole stopped to face her, and he spoke to her in an appallingly distinct voice. It carried at least halfway across the antechamber.

"No," he said, "I cannot do this. I cannot have my name linked with a fornicator. I cannot bow to my queen with this woman by my side."

Elizabeth, Christopher saw, somehow as if time had been suspended and was moving at only a fraction of its normal speed, raised her chin. She was facing the appalling ordeal of having to turn back into the room and walk through it and past more than half the beau monde, most of whom had heard what Poole had said, and all of whom must have heard the gossip that Hardinge had just repeated.

Christopher stepped forward, ahead of Lord Poole. Now it was all clear to him. Yes, Martin was responsible. Of course he was. But Poole had been his dupe just like so many other people and had set the story in motion himself so that he could publicly dissociate himself from Elizabeth and perhaps gain some points for courage and moral rectitude. Christopher bowed and reached out his arm for Elizabeth's.

"My lady?" he said in a voice quite as distinct as Lord Poole's had just been. He looked at the uniformed court official. "The Earl and Countess of Trevelyan," he said. "Married just this morning."

He did not look back. But he could imagine that it was Poole and not Elizabeth who now had to make his way back red-faced through the antechamber.

Elizabeth walked silently at Christopher's side, her arm resting on his. They walked the length of the throne room, past the red velvet draperies and gilded pillars on either side, beneath the stuccoed and painted ceiling with its elaborate candelabrum. They walked past the Regent and his dinner guests, past those who had already been presented to Her Majesty, and approached the throne beneath its canopy at the far end of the room.

The queen inclined her head graciously to them as she had to those who had gone before when the court official had murmured their names. Christopher bowed deeply and Elizabeth curtsied low. And then the official leaned forward and murmured again.

''Newly marritt?'' the queen said with her heavy German accent. ''Vhen vere you marritt?''

''This morning, your majesty,'' Christopher said.

''This morning. Ach!'' The stiff little queen smiled benevolently at them. ''I vish you much happiness and many children.''

''Thank you, your majesty,'' they murmured together and were ushered to one side to make way for the next arrivals.

Christopher, for the benefit of those gathered in the throne room, and for his own satisfaction too, raised his wife's hand to his lips and kissed it.

31

FOR several minutes John had been trying to persuade himself to leave the Pulteney.

"Tell me to go away," he said, kissing Nancy and preventing her from telling him any such thing. "It's late and you have no chaperone."

"Go away," she said, kissing the side of his jaw.

He sighed and got resolutely to his feet just as a loud knocking sounded on the outer door. He drew Nancy to her feet and kissed her again as they waited for Winnie or Antoine to answer the summons. But there was another knock and no sign of either of the two servants. John answered the door himself.

He came back into the sitting room a couple of minutes later, when Nancy was feeling rather alarmed at the prolonged sound of quiet voices.

"It is Martin," he said. His face, she noticed, had lost all its color. "He has been murdered."

Nancy stood very still.

"There were witnesses," John said. "He was stabbed by a small man, who was driving your brother's carriage. Antoine is not here, Nancy. Did he go with Christopher?"

"No," she said. She knew that the men who had come were just outside the door, probably within earshot.

"Do you have any idea where he might have gone?" John's eyes looked intently into hers.

She shook her head.

"It seems that your maid has gone too," John said. "I have told these men that both servants came up from Penhallow with you and Christopher and will almost certainly be headed back there. Would you agree?"

"Yes,' she said. "They would have nowhere else to go. That is where they will be running, no doubt, hoping that no one will pursue them that far. Murder—it is a dreadful crime."

"Yes," John said, "it is."

He talked quietly outside the door for another few minutes before rejoining Nancy in the sitting room. He looked rather like a ghost, she thought.

"I forgot about Antoine," he said. "I forgot that he had as good a reason as either Christopher or I to kill Martin but none of the reasons to stay his hand. He stabbed him with a knife, Nancy, in full view of two witnesses."

"At least," she said with an attempt at calmness, "neither you nor Christopher can be a suspect."

"He will be fleeing the country," John said. "I hope there is a suitable ship ready to sail."

"Yes," Nancy said. "Will they pursue him to Devonshire first before they start thinking of ships?"

"Unless they discover more of his identity," he said. "Your maid seems to have gone with him."

"She worships him," Nancy said.

They had been standing calmly at almost opposite sides of the room.

"Martin is dead," John said, passing a hand over his eyes. "Oh, God. Why do I feel like crying? I have looked on battlefields where thousands have lain dead. And many of them good men."

"He was your brother," Nancy said quietly, hurrying toward him and putting her arms about him.

"I am going to have to go and tell my father," he said. "Perhaps the news has not reached Grosvenor Square yet. Oh, God, and Elizabeth. I am going to have to tell her too."

"Yes," Nancy said, setting her face against his neckcloth and closing her eyes briefly. "Go to them, John. I must stay here with Christina."

He kissed her swiftly and fiercely. "I am sorry I did not have the courage to do for you what Antoine did for his Winnie," he said.

Nancy smiled. "Martin was your brother," she said. "I am glad you did not kill your brother even for me, John."

But she was glad, she thought, staring at the closed door after he had left the suite, that Martin was dead.

God help her, she was glad. She prayed silently that Antoine would escape safely to Canada and live happily ever after with Winnie.

Nancy spread her hands over her face and wept.

Elizabeth settled into one corner of the carriage while Christopher sat in the other. She had behaved mindlessly during what had remained of the evening after the presentation to the queen. She had resolutely refused to think or to try to have a private word with Christopher. She had smiled and received with cool graciousness the congratulations of those who had been turning on her in the antechamber to the throne room just a short while earlier. Manley had disappeared.

There was silence until the carriage began to move.

"He did it quite deliberately, didn't he?" she said quietly. "Somehow he found out the truth and decided to punish me. It would have been very effective punishment. The humiliation would doubtless have driven me from society for a very long time. I did not realize that he was capable of thinking up such a clever and heartless scheme."

"He had help," Christopher said.

She looked across at him. "Help?" she said. "From whom?"

He was gazing straight ahead. "From Martin," he said.

She looked at him in incomprehension. "Martin?" she said. "How foolish. If Martin had had any idea of what Manley knew and planned, he would have gone out of his way to protect me. He would have whisked me off back to Kingston. Martin always protects me. Rather too much, perhaps."

His silence was disturbing. She could tell that he was trying to bring himself to speak but could not do so.

"What do you mean," she asked in annoyance, "by saying that Martin helped Manley?"

"It would have got you back to Kingston, wouldn't it?" he said. "If you were not married to me, that is. But before this evening no one knew about that except John and Nancy. And you and I, of course. Poole's public denunciation would have got you back to Kingston for a very long time. Perhaps for the rest of your life. Martin would have had you to himself again. He would have had a lifetime in which to comfort you. He is expert at doing that, isn't he?''

''What are you suggesting?'' She could feel anger rising.

''That he is obsessed with you,'' he said. ''That he must have you to himself. That he will go to any lengths—*any* lengths—to make sure that you belong to him and to no one else.''

''That is a vicious and cruel thing to say,'' she said, her eyes blazing at him. ''You are jealous of him, Christopher, because he has always been good to me and always kind and faithful. You hate him because he is only my stepbrother while you were my husband, yet he has shown you what selfless love and fidelity are.''

''Elizabeth.'' He closed his eyes. His voice sounded weary. ''I know you have always loved him. I know the two of you have always been close. And yes, I know that in many ways he has always been good to you. Will you listen to what I have to say? There is quite a lot of it and you will want to shout me down from the beginning. Will you listen? I might add that John can vouch for the truth of everything I am about to say.''

''John?'' She looked at him, puzzled.

''Yes.'' He nodded. ''Will you hear what I have to say?''

''Say it,'' she said, lifting her chin. ''But if you are going to try to turn me against Martin, then you might as well save your breath. You can only succeed in making me despise you more.''

''Lucy Fenwick,'' he said, ''the woman who—''

''I remember who Lucy Fenwick is,'' she said, her voice icy.

Christopher drew a deep breath. ''Martin paid her rent,'' he said, ''and gave her other large sums of money. He paid her passage to America, and the child's, after our divorce. He led me into a trap when he had me summoned to her house with the message that she was a Johnson from Penhallow and in trouble. And he brought you fast on my heels.''

She knew instantly that he spoke the truth. There was no reason in the world why he would say what he had just said if he could not prove it and if John could not corroborate his words. He was telling the truth. Perhaps that was why she was so furious.

"It is a lie!" she said, her voice shaking. "A filthy lie, Christopher. Set me down. I'll walk home."

"Hear me out," he said. "There is a great deal more."

She turned her head away sharply and gazed at the dark paneling of the carriage while he talked.

"That gambling incident in Oxford and the unfortunate suicide that followed it really happened," he said. "I was there while poor Morrison was stripped of his fortune. And I am ashamed that like the other spectators I did nothing to try to put an end to the game even though it was obvious that he was too foxed to know what he was doing. But I was not a player in that game, Elizabeth. Martin found out about the incident from someone else who had been there—from someone who was conveniently leaving England to take up a post in Ireland."

He paused as if expecting her to say something but she continued to stare at the paneling as if to see through to the other side.

"The man who identified me as the one that left the theater with the unfortunate girl who was later found beaten and dead," Christopher said, "has recently admitted that Martin paid him to say so."

Elizabeth set the side of her head against the paneling and closed her eyes.

"Divorce for simple adultery is rarely granted against a husband," he said. "There usually have to be other aggravating circumstances. Brutalizing a whore and causing her death is not good husbandly behavior, is it? Neither is gambling for outrageously high stakes and driving an opponent to take his own life. And we had to be separated forever, Elizabeth, however many reckless charges it took. You had to be broken completely so that you could be nursed back to health and happiness at Kingston by a devoted brother."

She said nothing.

"I know you are listening," he said, "and I know you are understanding what has happened, Elizabeth, and believing me. I know you are beginning to suffer. Forgive me. I must tell you everything."

"There is more?" Her voice seemed disembodied. It

sounded very normal. She listened to her words as if someone else had spoken them.

"Before our marriage," he said, "while we were at Kingston Park, Nancy went home to Penhallow instead of staying for our wedding. I was annoyed with her."

"Yes," she whispered.

"She went home," he said, "because Martin had beaten and raped her."

Elizabeth made a sound deep in her throat. She could not have spoken or cried or opened her eyes to save her life.

"I must confine myself mainly to facts," he said, "but I will add that his motive was probably anger, frustration, and bitterness over the fact that he was about to lose you to me."

She moaned. "Is that all now?" she asked. There was pleading in her voice. "That must be all. Oh, please, that must be all."

"I don't think Martin could have wanted you to return recently to London and society," he said. "It must have been your idea, Elizabeth."

She opened her eyes at last. "He did not want me hurt again," she said. "He thought I would be happier at Kingston."

"You have seen this evening how he intended to ensure both that you did not marry Poole and that you left London again," he said. "He had plans to make sure that you would not turn to me either, Elizabeth."

Yes, she thought wearily, there would have been plans. Of course there would. He would have turned her against Christopher again.

"When I asked Christina to spend the night at the Pulteney," he said, "when I insisted upon it, I did it for a reason. I was not playing the part of autocratic husband."

"He did not mean to harm Christina." She looked at him, pleading in her eyes. "He would not do that, Christopher. Oh, please, he would not harm a child."

"He wanted me to kidnap her," he said. "He argued that if I did so and took her to Penhallow, you would follow me and realize that you belonged there with me."

"I would have hated you forever," she whispered.

"Yes," he said, "I know. That is what he intended. I

went along with his scheme, Elizabeth. Oh, don't worry. Christina has been with Nancy at the Pulteney all evening. She was fast asleep when I left for Carlton House. Martin brought her to the hotel, took my kidnapping note back to you, presumably showed it to your father without delay, and came riding after my carriage with a large escort of your father's stoutest servants. I had Antoine with me, and John came riding out of the shadows before it was all over."

"So," she said and was surprised again at how steady her voice sounded, "when I arrived back at Grosvenor Square distraught over what Manley had done to me at Carlton House, I was to be greeted with the news that you had kidnapped Christina and would have escaped with her if Martin had not caught up to you in time. Yes, I would have been on my way to Kingston again tomorrow, wouldn't I? And this time I would have stayed for the rest of my life."

"Yes," he said.

The carriage had stopped, presumably in Grosvenor Square, but neither of them made any move to open the door.

"What did you do to him?" Elizabeth asked. "Presumably you and John both confronted him. John has as strong a grievance against him as you, doesn't he? He loves Nancy and loved her seven years ago. Did you kill him?"

"No." He sat looking at her steadily. "I thought I would, Elizabeth, and I believe that John thought he would too. Perhaps we both anticipated an argument over which of us should have the privilege of doing it. But we did nothing when it came to the point. I don't know if he will come back to face your father or if he will run away and never appear in any of our lives again. But I am afraid that his obsession with you will not allow him to stay away. I am afraid that I might eventually be forced to kill him."

"Obsession," she said. "He is my stepbrother. He was my playmate, my comrade, my confidant. How can he have been obsessed? How can I have been so close to him and yet not have seen so much of what he is?"

"Elizabeth." She could hear him inhaling and could

see from a glance at his face that he had not finished even now.

"Tell me," she said.

"He told us that he was the only living person to know," he said. "Before she died his mother told him that your father is his father too. He is not your step-brother, Elizabeth, but your half-brother. His budding feelings for you suddenly became incestuous."

She spread her hands over her face. "Martin," she whispered.

She did not know how long they sat in silence. Eventually he touched one of her hands very lightly.

"Come back to the Pulteney with me tonight," he said. "There is no reason now for you not to do so, Elizabeth. And Christina is there. I don't want you staying here tonight. And I think perhaps you need company."

Yes, she needed company. She needed arms about her and a shoulder to lay her head on. She was so very, very tired. Even her pregnancy could not account for such total weariness. She would need to think. A whole lifetime of feelings and impressions would need to be adjusted. And there was guilt to be faced. A heavy burden of overwhelming guilt. But not tonight. She could not think or feel guilt tonight. She would not.

But before she could nod to Christopher so that he might call directions to the coachman, there was a sharp knock on the door and it opened to reveal John, looking pale and tight-lipped.

"There you are," he said. "Both of you. Good. Elizabeth." He reached inside to take her by the upper arms and lift her to the ground and hold her to him. "Listen to me. There is no easy way of saying this. Martin has been killed. By Christopher's Canadian valet, it seems. Has Christopher told you anything?"

Christopher jumped down onto the cobbles and drew Elizabeth away from John, wrapping his own arms tightly about her. "Everything except the reason why Antoine would want to kill him," he said.

So there is more, Elizabeth thought. More and endlessly more.

"Martin is dead?" she said. She was being hurried into the house, Christopher's arm tight about her shoulders. She was glad he was dead. She was glad. She had never been more glad of anything in her life. If she had had to face him, knowing what she now knew, she would have killed him herself. She wished he were still alive so that she could kill him herself.

He was her brother, her half-brother. The fact that they looked alike was no accident. He was her brother. *Had been* her brother. He was dead. Martin was dead.

Someone was crying hysterically. Someone else was picking her up and carrying her in strong arms through the hall and up the staircase to the drawing room, where her father was sitting, ashen-faced. And then she was in his arms and he was patting her back and Christopher was hovering over her and John was standing behind their father.

She realized who it was who had become hysterical.

Martin was dead.

32

It was a long and tedious journey home. It was not at all what Christopher had expected. He had expected a cloud to lift as soon as they left London behind them. He had expected that they would drive off into the happily ever after, the three of them. There were no further obstacles to their happiness. And yet they were not happy.

Christina rode with them most of the time instead of in the baggage coach behind with her nurse, Elizabeth's maid, and Christopher's newly hired valet. She was their salvation, perhaps, her eager chatter and her endless questions about Penhallow masking the silence that would otherwise have hung heavy between her parents. As often as not she sat on her father's lap, gazing up at him with trusting eyes as she listened to stories of the paradise where they were going to live—she and her mama and papa and her new brother or sister when the baby arrived. She was excited at the prospect of a new baby in the family. She always transferred to Elizabeth's lap when she felt sleepy. A mother's breast made a more secure pillow, it seemed, than a father's arms.

They spent two nights on the road. He and Elizabeth shared a room and a bed, Christina being in an adjoining room with her nurse on both occasions. They even made love both nights, slowly and silently, their bodies joining to give and receive pleasure, their mouths remaining apart.

They were man and wife again. They were on their way home to a place where they belonged and where they had once loved. They were taking with them their daughter, whom they both loved to distraction. And they both awaited, with equal eagerness and impatience, the arrival of their new child. The barriers were all down. There was nothing left for them to do but live out what remained of their lives in peace and happiness.

Yet they were not happy.

Elizabeth would, of course, have to be given time to recover from the dreadfully upsetting events of the past week. Learning the truth about Martin and having to cope with the knowledge of his murder all on the same night had almost driven her from her mind. The week since, in particular the funeral, had imposed an enormous strain on her.

Everything had worked out well for him, Christopher thought. The Duke of Chicheley, broken by Martin's death and by the story of his villainy that John had told, had accepted the remarriage of his daughter. He had even begged Christopher's pardon. He appeared to approve of the betrothal of Nancy and John. He had been so visibly shaken by Martin's death that Christopher wondered if he knew the truth after all—if he knew that he had lost a son. It was the one piece of information that John had withheld.

It was impossible to talk of things having gone well for Elizabeth. It was true that she had been finally freed from all the plotting that had caused her such misery through the years. And it was true that she could now face her new marriage with the knowledge that her husband had not been so cynically unfaithful to her during their first marriage.

But she had lost a brother whom she had loved for as long as she could remember. Despite what she now knew about him, there would always be those memories.

Neither Christopher nor John had wanted her to go up to Martin's room that first night. His body had been brought home and laid out on his bed. But she had insisted on going. Christopher had accompanied her there and had been horrified and even angry at first when she had stopped standing silently beside the bed looking down at the still body and had leaned over Martin, taken his cold hand in hers, and gone down on her knees, pressed her face against his hand, and collapsed in a storm of weeping.

The weeping had stopped after a few minutes, but she had stayed where she was for a long time. And Christopher's anger had dissipated. He had understood. She had loved Martin—as a sister loves a brother. That could not change just because of what she had so recently learned about him. And one of the things she had just learned was that Martin was indeed her brother. It was something she had learned too late.

And so she had kept an almost constant vigil beside his bed until the day of the funeral. And she wore the deepest mourning for the brother who had destroyed her marriage and would have destroyed her too if things had not turned against him at the end.

"He loved me," she told Christopher when they stood together at his graveside, the last to leave. "It was a sick and a twisted love. An obsession as you called it. But a sort of love nevertheless. I can't hate him. Forgive me, but I can't. I wish I had had a chance to tell him that I forgave him."

There had been no word at all about Antoine or Winnie, though discreet inquiries had revealed that a ship of the Northwest fur trading company had indeed sailed for Canada very early on the morning following the murder. They would be on that ship, Christopher was sure.

Nancy had stayed in London, moving from the Pulteney to stay with her friend, Lady Hardinge. Her betrothal was to be publicly announced despite the fact that John was officially in mourning. They were planning to marry at Penhallow in August.

Penhallow! Christopher hoped that it would bring Elizabeth and him peace. He hoped that they would be able to love there as deeply as they had loved during those weeks when her memory had been gone.

He hoped so. His wife and his children had become the focus of all his dreams. He watched Elizabeth as she held Christina asleep in her arms and gazed out the carriage window with eyes that looked large and sad and not quite focused on the passing scenery.

Christina was past the age of needing regular afternoon naps. But she was sleeping this afternoon. A day and a half at Penhallow seemed to have exhausted her. It was the sea air, Christopher said. There was no more effective sleeping potion in the world. It was all the activity, Elizabeth thought.

On the morning after their arrival Christopher had

taken their daughter for a walk up the side of the valley opposite the house. The slope was steep enough, he had said, that it had one puffing on the way up and shrieking with delight as one ran down again trying to make one's legs keep up with the momentum of one's body. Elizabeth had heard Christina's shrieks and Christopher's laughter as she gathered flowers from the kitchen garden. They had climbed the hill four times in all.

And then in the afternoon they had all walked up the hill behind the house and across the headland to the cliffs and down the cliff path to the beach. They had walked at a sedate pace because Mama was carrying the fourth member of their family, Christopher had explained to Christina, and he could not yet help her with it. On the beach the long-promised sand castle had been built. If it was not the most splendid one ever to have been constructed, it was not for want of trying. They had spent all of three hours on it. At least Christopher and Christina had. She herself had lain down for a rest and had even drifted off to sleep after Christopher had spread his cloak on the sand for her and insisted that half the family could build while the other half rested.

He had grinned at her. In fact, he had done a lot of smiling in the past day and a half, mostly at Christina, but occasionally at her. He seemed happy to be home and happy that they were with him. And yet there was a wariness in his eyes. And she did not blame him. How did he know that he could trust her when she had been so untrustworthy almost from the beginning of their acquaintance?

They had all played games in the house during the evening until Christina's bedtime. This morning they had ridden along the valley, the three of them, at first away from the sea, into denser, quieter forest, into quietness and beauty, and then toward the sea, turning back only when they reached the marshy sand of the estuary. While Elizabeth walked back to the house from the stables, Christopher was dragged off for one more run down the opposite hill that apparently had developed into three.

And so Christina was asleep, exhausted by sea air and vigorous exercise and happiness. Christopher had disappeared about some business. Elizabeth had escaped to the beach.

She stood with her back against the large boulder before the lovers' cave, feeling the salty breeze against her face, knowing that there was enough heat in the sun's rays to bronze her face if she was not careful. She closed her eyes and felt warmth and did not want to be careful.

She had stood just here as her memory came back to her. As the idyll of the weeks preceding its return slipped away from her. As she gave up the consuming love and passion she had felt for Christopher during those weeks.

All was well that ended well, she thought. She was back again. She was married to him again. They had Christina here with them. Their new child was growing in her womb. She loved Christopher. She thought he probably loved her though he had not said so recently.

It was a happily ever after she was living in. Except that there was an emptiness. Her eyes strayed to the shapeless mound that had been a splendid castle the day before until the tide had come and ravaged it during the night. And her eyes strayed farther, to the foot of the cliff path.

He was coming, walking unhurriedly toward her across the sand. She felt a welling of love for him and a sinking of sadness. If only seven years could be erased.

She was exactly where he had expected to see her. Somehow he had known she would be there, not only on the beach but against the boulder, close to their cave. He felt a surging of hope, seeing her there. She had come to the place where they had loved and been happy.

She was pale. She appeared to have lost weight. And yet she was beautiful. She was his wife, his love. And she was unhappy and distant. She was watching him.

He came to stand beside her, one shoulder propped against the rock. His eyes were on hers, though he said nothing. And she found that she could not look away from him.

"The only thing I was guilty of," he said after a few moments of silence, "was cowardice, Elizabeth. I ran instead of staying to force you to listen to me, to force you to come back to me. I ran instead of staying to find out the truth. I was not guilty of any of those other things. I was never unfaithful to you even in my thoughts. I loved you totally. I told the truth when I said I came to you a virgin. Can you not forgive me for the one thing I did wrong? Will it always stand between us?''

He did not understand. Could he not understand? He thought that he was the one at fault. *Oh, Christopher. My love.*

He watched tears well into her eyes and hover there, ready to spill over. She did not look away from him though he knew from the way she swallowed that she could not answer him immediately. If she said no, then all would be over for them. No, not quite that drastic. But they could never be quite happy unless she could forgive him. And for that one fault he could rely only on her forgiveness. He had no excuse to offer beyond youth and inexperience and foolishness.

''Can *you* forgive *me*?'' she said at last, her voice high-pitched, at the edge of tears. ''I am the one at fault, Christopher. It has all been my fault. All of it. I believed everyone but you. I said I loved you, I married you, I made all sorts of vows that were to last until eternity. Yet after three months I lost faith in you and destroyed everything. I can't forgive myself. How can I expect you to forgive me?''

She blinked her eyes and one tear spilled down each cheek. He reached out a thumb to cover one and bent his head to lick the other one away. She was looking at him, her head turned sideways when he drew back his head. He could feel hope bubbling up inside him.

''You must not blame yourself,'' he said. ''None of us saw through his schemes, Elizabeth. I thought him the only friend I had left even as I sailed away to Canada. Your father was convinced enough to take the almost unprecedented step of bringing divorce proceedings against me. Martin was your brother, your dearest friend. How could you have seen the truth?''

''You should have been my dearest friend,'' she said. ''You were my dearest love, but I was very young and very foolish. I was a little afraid of you. And so I let myself believe that you could have done those things. If I had made you my friend, nothing could possibly have come between us. I would have known!''

''Neither of us could help our youth,'' he said. ''We were not given time to become really close friends, Elizabeth. We were too busy with our love and our fears and uncertainties to have done more than begin the process of developing a lifelong friendship. It would have come with time. Our love would have seen to that. But time was taken away from us deliberately and ruthlessly. What happened was neither your fault nor mine."

He was going to forgive her? He was even going to insist that there was nothing to forgive? She looked at his face through her tears and wondered that she could ever have been afraid of him. It was a beloved face, a kindly and understanding face.

"I kept Christina from you," she said, "and all knowledge of her. You told me yourself not so long ago that you did not know if you could ever forgive me for that."

That fiend whom she still mourned was responsible for all that had happened. Could she not see it? Or must she blame herself for not being the only one to see through his deceptions? Was there no way he could reassure her? It seemed that perhaps there was only one way.

"Elizabeth." He took her right into his arms, drawing her away from the rock, so that she leaned against him and not it. "If you need forgiveness, it is yours. And everything is forgotten as of this moment. Is that clear? Everything is washed clean just as that poor castle has been by the tide. Perhaps—just perhaps—if our love had never been tested it would have become a humdrum thing in time. It will never be that now, will it? We both know how very near we were to losing each other forever. And we have both learned that married people do not live happily ever after once the wedding ceremony is over. We know that we must work at our marriage every hour and every day for the rest of our lives. It has been a lesson worth learning, hasn't it?"

"*Do* you love me?" she asked him, lifting her face to his. "I know that you have committed yourself to this marriage, Christopher. I know that the children—"

He kissed her. She clung to him, tasting his answer in his mouth.

"The children were my excuse," he said. "Oh, I suppose I would have married you if only for their sakes, Elizabeth. Yes, I suppose I would. I ache with love for them, you know, even though I will not even see this little mite for another how many months? But I don't ache for other people's children. I don't recall even feeling a mild affection for anyone else's. I ache for these because they are ours. Because we created them together. Because they are a visible product of our love. I never was very good at words, was I? That was part of the trouble with our first marriage. Always force me to put into words what I sometimes take for granted you know. Will you? Promise me?''

''Say it.'' Her arms had slipped up about his neck. The magic was coming back. She was feeling as she had felt on this beach with him on other occasions. But perhaps it was better now because there was all the richness of memory to link them together, memories of love and joy, memories of pain—oh, too much pain. The magic was returning. And she could see from his eyes, his blue, blue eyes, that it was coming back for him too. They were smiling into hers.

''I love you,'' he said. ''From the first moment I set eyes on you, Elizabeth. And every moment since. I have never stopped loving you. I never will.''

''Oh.'' She sighed with satisfaction. And she lifted her face, smiling, at the unfamiliar sensation of his nose rubbing against hers. ''Christopher, me too. At the back of the pain and the hatred and the—oh, the foolish, foolish stupidity. I kept it very quiet and very deep and very secret from all but the inner depth of my heart. I even felt ashamed of it. But I always thought of you. Every night before I slept. I never once missed, even the night before I was to marry Manley. Especially that night. I thought of you and prayed for you and loved you. I used to imagine your arms about me. That is how I got myself to sleep.''

Her face was eager, open, happy. He wanted to shout for joy. And why not? If a man could not shout out with joy on a wide open beach on his own property when the wife he had thought lost to him for life has been restored to him and along with her a daughter and another child in the making and the prospect of a life lived happily ever after—although he would have to work for that ending for the rest of his life. If a man could not shout out with joy under such circumstances, then he might as well be mute all his life.

He had been smiling at her, quietly, contentedly. She was taken completely by surprise when he lifted her suddenly by the waist, twirled her about and about, and shouted out with a sound that was not quite a bellow and not quite a yodel but a strange mixture of both and neither. Elizabeth found herself giggling helplessly.

And then they were standing on the beach again, several yards away from the great boulder, and they were smiling at each other again with smiles that threatened to break into laughter or into some other exuberance at any moment.

He was wonderful, she thought. And miraculously everything was going to be all right. He was her husband and her friend and her love. And she was going to make sure that it stayed that way. For the rest of their lives. No matter what.

She was beautiful, he thought. And happy. All the shadows had gone from inside her and he could see only love for himself and hope for their future in her eyes. It was a future he would live moment by moment, holding each of those moments in his hand as if it were a fragile blossom soon to wither. Not one of those moments was to be wasted. He would make each one precious to her and therefore to himself until he drew his dying breath.

And even then.

"Christina will want you to rebuild her sand castle," she said.

"Of course." He rested his forehead against hers. "That is what sand castles are for—to build and to rebuild when they fall down. Like marriages."

"Yes. Oh, yes." She turned her head so that their mouths met. And then she drew it back again and looked up to the top of the cliff.

"The whole world might be lined up there to watch us at any moment," he said.

"Oh dear," she said, "that would not do at all, would it? What do you suggest?"

They smiled into each other's eyes again like a pair of conspirators.

"We will get awfully sandy," he said.

"But there is plenty of water back at the house," she said.

"Yes, of course," he said. "How sensible."

But they risked the world's eyes and the world's censure anyway by kissing deeply for several minutes before withdrawing to the sandy privacy of the lovers' cave.

Historical Note

The events happening in England from April to June of 1814 as described in this book are accurate with a couple of exceptions. London went almost wild with excitement over news of Wellington's invasion of France from Spain and the allied entry into Paris from the north, both of which facts forced Napoleon Bonaparte to surrender and to abdicate as Emperor of France. Most of the allied rulers and head statesmen went to England in June, at the invitation of the Prince of Wales, the Regent, in order to celebrate the victory. At the same time the Regent was very unpopular with the British while his estranged wife, the Princess of Wales, was correspondingly popular.

One inaccuracy in the book concerns chronology. In reality the Carlton House dinner, reception, and presentation to the queen took place during the evening of the day following the arrival of the visitors in London. The visit to the opera and the embarrassing arrival of the Princess of Wales before the second act began happened later in the visit. For the sake of my plot I have moved back the Carlton House evening one day and moved up the opera visit.

The other inaccuracy concerns Pulteney's Hotel in London. I believe, though I am not certain, that the Grand Duchess Catherine rented the whole of the hotel for her stay and that of her brother, the Tsar of Russia. However, my hero is an earl and his sister is the daughter of an earl. They are important enough that I squeezed them into a suite at the hotel, though they do have rather poor service after the unexpected arrival of the Tsar.

ONYX (0451)

FLAMING PASSION

☐ **SO BRIGHT A FLAME by Robin LeAnne Wiete.** A beautiful woman journalist and a dashing playboy were playing a game of deception with one another. But there was no masking their deepening love. . . .
(402812—$4.99)

☐ **NO GREATER LOVE by Katherine Kingsley.** Beautiful young Georgia Wells is plunged into a vortex of desire when the handsome Nicholas Daventry returns to Ravenwalk to reclaim his legacy. (403029—$4.99)

☐ **HEARTS OF FIRE by Anita Mills.** Their flaming passion lit their perilous path of love. Fiery-haired Gilliane de Lacey's love for Richard of Rivaux ignited in her a burning need, but Richard was honor-bound to wed another. Yet nothing—not royal wrath or dangerous conflict—could stop Gilliane and Richard from risking all for love, giving all to desire.
(401352—$4.99)

☐ **THE EDGE OF LIGHT by Joan Wolf.** Two headstrong lovers vow to fight to change the world rather than forfeit their passion—in the magnificent tale of Alfred the Great and the woman he could not help but love.
(402863—$5.99)

☐ **NEW ORLEANS by Sara Orwig.** Chantal was the daughter of the most powerful family in Louisiana and lived like a princess on a vast plantation. Now in a city of pride and passion, she must choose between a man who offered her everything she had ever wanted and a man who led her to ecstacy beyond her wildest dreams. (403738—$4.99)

Prices slightly higher in Canada.

Buy them at your local bookstore or use this convenient coupon for ordering.

NEW AMERICAN LIBRARY
P.O. Box 999 – Dept. #17109
Bergenfield, New Jersey 07621

Please send me the books I have checked above.
I am enclosing $_______________ (please add $2.00 to cover postage and handling). Send check or money order (no cash or C.O.D.'s) or charge by Mastercard or VISA (with a $15.00 minimum). Prices and numbers are subject to change without notice.

Card #_______________________________ Exp. Date ____________
Signature____
Name____
Address____
City _______________ State _____________ Zip Code ___________

For faster service when ordering by credit card call **1-800-253-6476**

Allow a minimum of 4-6 weeks for delivery. This offer is subject to change without notice.

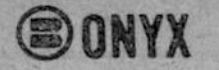 (0451)

SUPERB TALES OF ROMANCE AND HISTORY

☐ **THE ROAD TO AVALON by Joan Wolf.** Shimmering with pageantry, intrigue and all the magic of Camelot, here is the epic story of Arthur—the conqueror, the once and future king who vanquished the Saxons and loved but one woman, the beautiful Morgan of Avalon. (401387—$4.50)

☐ **BORN OF THE SUN by Joan Wolf.** This compelling saga about a beautiful Celtic princess who gives her heart to a Saxon prince explodes with the passions of love and war. "Triumphant ... majestic ... a grand adventure!"—Booklist (402252—$5.50)

☐ **THE EDGE OF LIGHT by Joan Wolf.** Two headstrong lovers vow to fight to change the world rather than forfeit their passion—in the magnificent tale of Alfred the Great and the woman he could not help but love. (402863—$5.99)

☐ **WHEN MORNING COMES by Robin Wiete.** This is the story of a beautiful young widow, alone with her small child on the American frontier, seeking a white man who lived among the Shawnee to heal the child. They meet in a wilderness ravaged by violence, only to discover that they are not strangers but lovers ... "Tense and tender, sweeping and intimate ... a poignant love story."—Karen Harper (403363—$4.99)

☐ **WILD RAPTURE by Cassie Edwards.** The untamed frontier, set aflame by a passionate and fiery forbidden love as a Chippewa man and woman from Minnesota stake their undying love against the forces of hate. "A shining talent!"—*Romantic Times* (403304—$4.99)

Prices slightly higher in Canada

Buy them at your local bookstore or use this convenient coupon for ordering.

NEW AMERICAN LIBRARY
P.O. Box 999 – Dept. #17109
Bergenfield, New Jersey 07621

Please send me the books I have checked above.
I am enclosing $__________ (please add $2.00 to cover postage and handling). Send check or money order (no cash or C.O.D.'s) or charge by Mastercard or VISA (with a $15.00 minimum). Prices and numbers are subject to change without notice.

Card #__________ Exp. Date __________
Signature__________
Name__________
Address__________
City __________ State __________ Zip Code __________

For faster service when ordering by credit card call **1-800-253-6476**
Allow a minimum of 4-6 weeks for delivery. This offer is subject to change without notice.

SIGNET ONYX (0451)

SWEEPING ROMANCE by Catherine Coulter

☐ **EARTH SONG.** Spirited Philippa de Beauchamp fled her ancestral manor rather than wed the old and odious lord that her domineering father had picked for her. But she found peril of a different kind when she fell into the hands of a rogue lord, handsome, cynical Dienwald de Fortenberry. . . . (402065—$4.99)

☐ **FIRE SONG.** Marriage had made Graelam the master of Kassia's body but now a rising fire-hot need demanded more than submission. He must claim her complete surrender with the dark ecstasy of love. . . . (402383—$4.99)

☐ **SECRET SONG.** Stunning Daria de Fortesque was the prize in a struggle between two ruthless earls, one wanting her for barter, the other for pleasure. But there was another man who wanted Daria, too, for an entirely different reason. . . . (402340—$4.95)

☐ **CHANDRA.** Lovely golden-haired Chandra, raised to handle weapons as well as any man, was prepared to defend herself against anything . . . until the sweet touch of Jerval de Veron sent the scarlet fires of love raging through her blood. . . . (158814—$4.99)

☐ **DEVIL'S EMBRACE.** The seething city of Genoa seemed a world away from the great 18th-century estate where Cassandra was raised. But here she met Anthony, and became addicted to a feverish ecstasy that would guide their hearts forever. . . . (141989—$4.99)

☐ **DEVIL'S DAUGHTER.** Arabella had never imagined that Kamal, the savage sultan who dared make her a harem slave, would look so like a blond Nordic god. She had never dreamed that his savage love could make her passion's slave. . . . (158636—$4.99)

Prices slightly higher in Canada

Buy them at your local bookstore or use this convenient coupon for ordering.

NEW AMERICAN LIBRARY
P.O. Box 999 – Dept. #17109
Bergenfield, New Jersey 07621

Please send me the books I have checked above.
I am enclosing $______________ (please add $2.00 to cover postage and handling). Send check or money order (no cash or C.O.D.'s) or charge by Mastercard or VISA (with a $15.00 minimum). Prices and numbers are subject to change without notice.

Card #______________________________ Exp. Date ______________
Signature____
Name____
Address____
City __________________ State ______________ Zip Code ___________

For faster service when ordering by credit card call **1-800-253-6476**

Allow a minimum of 4-6 weeks for delivery. This offer is subject to change without notice.

"A winner . . . absorbing reading right up until the end!—*Publishers Weekly*

"An utterly absorbing, powerful tale of a love that was once doomed and yet blooms again amidst the intrigue and ordeal of war."—*Romantic Times*

BEYOND THE SUNRISE

Mary Balogh

When Jean Morisette, the daughter of a French count, and Robert Blake, the illegitimate son of an English lord, first meet, they both know that they can never share a life together. However, when they meet again, they are much older and wiser in the ways of the world. For both have been cast into a sea of intrigue and a storm of violence as England and France fight a ruthless war. Now, not even the lies they are forced to tell each other in their roles as spies can extinguish their desire for one another . . . as this proud and bewitching beauty and this handsome and dauntless officer come together in a passion that flares in the shadow of danger—and a love that conquers the forces of hate. . . .

Buy it at your local bookstore or use this convenient coupon for ordering.

NEW AMERICAN LIBRARY
P.O. Box 999 – Dept. #17109
Bergenfield, New Jersey 07621

Please send me ________ copies of BEYOND THE SUNRISE 0-451-40342-8 $4.99 ($5.99 in Canada) plus $2.00 postage and handling per order.

I enclose ☐ check ☐ money order (no C.O.D.'s or cash)

Name____

Address______________________________________

City ____________________ State ______________ Zip Code ______________

Allow a minimum of 4-6 weeks for delivery.
This offer, prices and numbers are subject to change without notice.

Coming from Onyx